Praise for *Stone Butch Blues*

"Reading this book changed my life. The narrator of *Stone Butch Blues* both walks achingly alone and tells the sweet story of connecting to a society in which agency becomes possible. Feinberg's Jess witnesses the vast criminality of homophobia, the tenderness and the wildness of love, and the tiny, massive vitalities of friendship, work, and political community. Everyone needs to know *Stone Butch Blues* and pass it around. It's history out loud."

—Eileen Myles, author of *Cool for You*

"In a world of polarities, where all we're taught is black and white, *Stone Butch Blues* added to what we know is really a rainbow. How we choose to live in our bodies and our hearts is much more than a Dick-and-Jane reality. This book opened our eyes to a transgendered hue now recognized among our many colors."

—Jewelle Gomez, author of *Don't Explain*

"*Stone Butch Blues* is a unique take on the universal theme of self-love and identity...written with a compelling passion that has its very own sound."

—Emanuel Xavier, author of *Americano* and *Christ-Like*

"*Stone Butch Blues* is a masterpiece of U.S. fiction and should be required reading in high school and college classes across the country. This novel takes its place not only within a long tradition of queer narratives of alienation and opposition, but, in form and content, it also hearkens back to radical proletarian U.S. literature from the 1930s. By weaving the story of Jess Goldberg, a working-class gender warrior, through the narratives of 1960s and '70s social movements, Feinberg insistently reminds us that our individual struggles are always part of a larger fabric of resistance. *Stone Butch Blues* will be read for years to come!"

—Judith Halberstam, author of *Female Masculinity*

"*Stone Butch Blues* is a must-read for butches, femmes, and those who care about them."

—Lesléa Newman, author of *The Little Butch Book*

"*Stone Butch Blues* is the queer great American novel—it will be read, loved, studied, and denounced for a long, long time."
—Holly Hughes performance artist and author of *Clit Notes: A Sapphic Sampler*

"*Stone Butch Blues* is wrenching, compelling, provocative. Feinberg examines the straitjacket of the gender binary and the price it exacts."
—Zsa Zsa Gershick, author of *Gay Old Girls*

"In this revolutionary novel, Feinberg explodes the myth of the binary gender system and the feminist notion that butchness is apolitical. The scenes of early queer society are brought to vivacious life—I laughed, I cried, and felt right at home."
—Chrystos, author of *Fire Power* and *Fugitive Colors*

"Leslie Feinberg is one of the coolest hot people around, and *Stone Butch Blues* is both extraordinary and required reading if you want to know what being queer is really about in the U.S."
—Felice Picano, author of *Onyx* and *The Book of Lies*

"Leslie Feinberg has written a poignant, multilayered story involving class, race, religion, politics, and gender that touches the hearts and souls of anyone that has lived outside the purported norms imposed by mainstream society."
—Michael M. Hernandez, transgender writer/activist

"*Stone Butch Blues* has probably touched your life even if you haven't read it yet. It's a movement classic, one of those books that spilled right out of its binding and into the world, changing the landscape irrevocably."
—Alison Bechdel, creator of "Dykes to Watch Out For"

"*Stone Butch Blues* is a powerful novel written by a founder of the contemporary transgender movement. It is also an important historical text documenting the profound shift in how we all came to think about gender at the end of the last century."
—Susan Stryker, executive director, GLBT Historical Society

STONE BUTCH
BLUES

STONE BUTCH BLUES

A NOVEL

LESLIE FEINBERG

All characters in this book are fictitious. Any resemblance to real individuals—either living or dead—is strictly coincidental.

Manufactured in the United States of America.

This trade paperback is published by Alyson Publications,
P.O. Box 4371, Los Angeles, California 90078-4371.

First published by Firebrand Books: 1993
First Alyson Books edition: November 2003

04 05 06 07 a 10 9 8 7 6 5 4 3 2

ISBN 1-55583-853-7
(Previously published with ISBN 1-56341-030-3 by Firebrand Books.)

Library of Congress Cataloging-in-Publication Data
Feinberg, Leslie, 1949–
Stone butch blues : a novel / Leslie Feinberg.—1st Alyson Books ed.
1. Coming out (Sexual orientation)—Fiction.
2. Transsexuals—Fiction. 3. Lesbians—Fiction. I. Title.
PS3556.E427S76 2004
813'.54—dc22 2003062838

Credits
Cover photography by Marilyn Humphries.
Cover design by Matt Sams.

Dedicated to the memory
of trans warrior Sylvia Rivera:
Long live the spirit of Stonewall!

A Decade Later: Thanks

To each reader who has taken the time and caring to convey to me the impact of *Stone Butch Blues* on your heart and mind and viewpoint, I extend my heartfelt gratitude. You have widened my world of human interaction.

To the crew at Alyson Publications, and particularly editor in chief Angela Brown, thank you for the work each of you put into this beautiful new edition of *Stone Butch Blues* and for being a pleasure to work with. My appreciation goes out to my literary agent, Laurie Liss, and the staff at Sterling Lord Literistic for your labor and for your support.

Much belated but very earnest thanks to dear friend Beverly Hiestand. Dissatisfied with my original manuscript at the eleventh hour when the novel was almost due at the publisher's, I tore up the ending and set out to create a new character: Ruth. I traveled to Buffalo to cull from Bev memories about the tiny rural community of Vine Valley where she was raised. We took a trip there to meet and talk with people whose lives are rooted in the vineyards. As a result, I was able to write Ruth, not as an idea birthed in the womb of creativity, but from the immersion pool of memory, the dark and rich organic soil, the bouquet of concord grape, the basin lake that mirrors a changing sky, and the hardscrabble lives of Vine Valley.

I also want to thank Beverly and Linda Shamrock—as friends and as hardworking registered nurses—from the bottom of my defibrillated heart. When I was in the grip of grave illness, abruptly left without a primary care doctor, you both created an emergency trans health network of care, patient advocacy, and partner support in Buffalo. Your tireless efforts helped me live to see this novel take on new life.

An adult lifetime of thanks to teamster Milt Neidenberg—Duffy to my Jess. When I was a child in Buffalo, if I was lucky enough to find a penny, I made my way into the nearby woods, summer hot or winter cold, to place the precious copper coin on the train tracks. Moments later, the massive engine would hurtle past. I can't recall ever finding the flattened penny after the train passed over it, flipping it into the dense weeds that grew up in and around the rails. The great thrill was that the engineer who drove this powerful locomotive along the tracks would blow the steam whistle for me, waving as he passed. Milt, you are that engineer for me. Thank you for taking me aboard for the ride of a lifetime.

And to my beloved warrior Minnie Bruce Pratt: Thank you for teaching me that happiness is not overrated. We came into each other's lives just as I was putting the last tinkering touches on this manuscript. The dirt from your garden is still smudged on my blues. Oh, my love, haven't we written a chapter together since!

CHAPTER 1

Dear Theresa,

I'm lying on my bed tonight missing you, my eyes all swollen, hot tears running down my face. There's a fierce summer lightning storm raging outside.

Tonight I walked down streets looking for you in every woman's face, as I have each night of this lonely exile. I'm afraid I'll never see your laughing, teasing eyes again.

I had coffee in Greenwich Village earlier with a woman. A mutual friend fixed us up, sure we'd have a lot in common since we're both "into politics." Well, we sat in a coffee shop and she talked about Democratic politics and seminars and photography and problems with her co-op and how she's so opposed to rent control. Small wonder—Daddy is a real estate developer.

I was looking at her while she was talking, thinking to myself that I'm a stranger in this woman's eyes. She's looking at me but she doesn't see me. Then she finally said how she hates this society for what it's done to "women like me" who hate themselves so much they have to look and act like men. I felt myself getting flushed and my face twitched a little and I started telling her, all cool and calm, about how women like me existed since the dawn of time, before there was oppression, and how those societies respected them, and she got her very interested expression on—and besides it was time to leave.

So we walked by a corner where these cops were laying into a homeless man and I stopped and mouthed off to the cops and they started coming at me with their clubs raised and she tugged my belt to pull me back. I just looked at her, and suddenly I felt things well up in me I thought I had buried. I stood there remembering you like I didn't see cops about to hit me, like I was falling back into another world, a place I wanted to go again.

And suddenly my heart hurt so bad and I realized how long it's been since my heart felt—anything.

I need to go home to you tonight Theresa. I can't. So I'm writing you this letter.

I remember years ago, the day I started working at the cannery in Buffalo and you had already been there a few months, and how your eyes caught mine and played with me before you set me free. I was supposed to be following the foreman to fill out some forms but I was so busy wondering what color your hair was under that white paper net and how it would look and feel in my fingers, down loose and free. And I remember how you laughed gently when the foreman came back and said, "You comin' or not?"

All of us he-shes were mad as hell when we heard you got fired because you wouldn't let the Superintendent touch your breasts. I still unloaded on the docks for another couple of days, but I was kind of mopey. It just wasn't the same after your light went out.

I couldn't believe it the night I went to that new club on the West Side. There you were, leaning up against the bar, your jeans too tight for words and your hair, your hair all loose and free.

And I remember that look in your eyes again. You didn't just know me, you liked what you saw. And this time, ooh woman, we were on our own turf. I could move the way you wanted me too, and I was glad I'd gotten all dressed up.

Our own turf.... "Would you dance with me?"

You didn't say yes or no, just teased me with your eyes, straightened my tie, smoothed my collar, and took me by the hand. You had my heart before you moved against me like you did. Tammy was singing "Stand By Your Man," and we were changing all the he's *to* she's *inside our heads to make it fit right. After you moved that way, you had more than my heart.*

You made me ache and you liked that. So did I.

The older butches warned me: if you wanted to keep your marriage, don't go to the bars. But I've always been a one-woman butch. Besides, this was our community, the only one we belonged to, so we went every weekend.

There were two kinds of fights in the bars. Most weekends had one kind or the other, some weekends both. There were the fist fights between the butch women—full of booze, shame, jealous insecurity. Sometimes the fights were awful and spread like a web to trap everyone in the bar, like the night Heddy lost her eye when she got hit upside the head with a bar stool.

I was real proud that in all those years I never hit another butch woman. See, I loved them too, and I understood their pain and their shame because I was so much like them. I loved the lines etched in their faces and hands and the curves of their work-weary shoulders. Sometimes I looked in the mirror and wondered what I would look like when I was their age. Now I know!

In their own way, they loved me too. They protected me because they knew I wasn't a "Saturday-night butch." The weekend butches were scared of me because I was a stone he-she. If only they had known how powerless I really felt inside! But the older butches, they knew the whole road that lay ahead of me and they wished I didn't have to go down it because it hurt so much.

When I came into the bar in drag, kind of hunched over, they told me, "Be proud of what you are," and then they adjusted my tie sort of like you did. I was like them, they knew I didn't have a choice. So I never fought them with my fists. We clapped each other on the back in the bars and watched each other's backs at the factory.

But then there were the times our real enemies came in the front door: drunken gangs of sailors, Klan-type thugs, sociopaths and cops. You always knew when they walked in because someone thought to pull the plug on the jukebox. No matter how many times it happened, we all still went "Aw. . ." when the music stopped and then realized it was time to get down to business.

When the bigots came in it was time to fight, and fight we did. Fought hard—femme and butch, women and men together.

If the music stopped and it was the cops at the door, someone plugged the music back in and we switched dance partners. Us in our suits and ties paired off with our drag queen sisters in their dresses and pumps. Hard to remember that it was illegal then for two women or two men to sway to music together. When the music ended, the butches bowed, our femme partners curtsied, and we returned to our seats, our lovers, and our drinks to await our fates.

That's when I remember your hand on my belt, up under my suit jacket. That's where your hand stayed the whole time the cops were there. "Take it easy, honey. Stay with me baby, cool off," you'd be cooing in my ear like a special lover's song sung to warriors who need to pick and choose their battles in order to survive.

We learned fast that the cops always pulled the police van right up to the bar door and left snarling dogs inside so we couldn't get out. We were trapped alright.

Remember the night you stayed home with me when I was so sick? That was the night—you remember. The cops picked out the most stone butch of them all to destroy with humiliation, a woman everyone said "wore a raincoat in the shower." We heard they stripped her, slow, in front of everyone in the bar, and laughed at her trying to cover up her nakedness. Later she went mad, they said. Later she hung herself.

What would I have done if I had been there that night?

I'm remembering the busts in the bars in Canada. Packed in the police vans, all the Saturday-night butches giggled and tried to fluff up their hair and switch clothing so they could get thrown in the tank with the femme women—said it would be like "dyin' and goin' to heaven." The law said we had to be wearing three pieces of women's clothing.

We never switched clothing. Neither did our drag queen sisters. We knew, and so did you, what was coming. We needed our sleeves rolled up, our hair slicked back, in order to live through it. Our hands were cuffed tight behind our backs. Yours were cuffed in front. You loosened my tie, unbuttoned my collar, and touched my face. I saw the pain and fear for me in your face, and I whispered it would be alright. We knew it wouldn't be.

I never told you what they did to us down there—queens in one tank, stone butches in the next—but you knew. One at a time they would drag our brothers out of the cells, slapping and punching them, locking the bars behind them fast in case we lost control and tried to stop them, as if we could. They'd handcuff a brother's wrists to his ankles or chain him, face against the bars. They made us watch. Sometimes we'd catch the eyes of the terrorized victim, or the soon-to-be, caught in the vise of torture, and we'd say gently, "I'm with you honey, look at me, it's OK, we'll take you home."

We never cried in front of the cops. We knew we were next.

The next time the cell door opens it will be me they drag out and chain spread-eagle to the bars.

Did I survive? I guess I did. But only because I knew I might get home to you.

They let us out last, one at a time, on Monday morning. No charges. Too late to call in sick to work, no money, hitch-hiking, crossing the border on foot, rumpled clothes, bloody, needing a shower, hurt, scared.

I knew you'd be home if I could get there.

You ran a bath for me with sweet-smelling bubbles. You laid out a fresh pair of white BVD's and a T-shirt for me and left me alone to wash off the first layer of shame.

I remember, it was always the same. I would put on the briefs, and then I'd just get the T-shirt over my head and you would find some reason to come into the bathroom, to get something or put something away. In a glance you would memorize the wounds on my body like a road map—the gashes, bruises, cigarette burns.

Later, in bed, you held me gently, caressing me everywhere, the tenderest touches reserved for the places I was hurt, knowing each and every sore place—inside and out. You didn't flirt with me right away, knowing I wasn't confident enough to feel sexy. But slowly you coaxed my pride back out again by showing me how much you wanted me. You knew it would take you weeks again to melt the stone.

Lately I've read these stories by women who are so angry with stone lovers, even mocking their passion when they finally give way to trust, to being touched. And I'm wondering: did it hurt you the times I couldn't let you touch me? I hope it didn't. You never showed it if it did. I think you knew it wasn't you I was keeping myself safe from. You treated my stone self as a wound that needed loving healing. Thank you. No one's ever done that since. If you were here tonight. . .well, it's hypothetical, isn't it?

I never said these things to you.

Tonight I remember the time I got busted alone, on strange turf. You're probably wincing already, but I have to say this to you. It was the night we drove ninety miles to a bar to meet friends who never showed up. When the police raided the club we were "alone," and the cop with gold bars on his uniform came right over to me and told me to stand up. No wonder, I was the only he-she in the place that night.

He put his hands all over me, pulled up the band of my Jockeys and told his men to cuff me—I didn't have three pieces of women's clothing on. I wanted to fight right then and there because I knew the chance would be lost in a moment. But I also knew that everyone would be beaten that night if I fought back, so I just stood there. I saw they had pinned your arms behind your back and cuffed your hands. One cop had his arm across your throat. I remember the look in your eyes. It hurts me even now.

They cuffed my hands so tight behind my back I almost cried out. Then the cop unzipped his pants real slow, with a smirk on his face, and ordered me down on my knees. First I thought to myself, I can't! *Then I said out loud to myself and to you and to him,* "I won't!" *I never told you this before, but something changed inside of me at that moment. I learned the difference between what I can't do and what I refuse to do.*

I paid the price for that lesson. Do I have to tell you every detail? Of course not.

When I got out of the tank the next morning you were there. You bailed me out. No charges, they just kept your money. You had waited all night long in that police station. Only I know how hard it was for you to withstand their leers, their taunts, their threats. I knew you cringed with every sound you strained to hear from back in the cells. You prayed you wouldn't hear me scream. I didn't.

I remember when we got outside to the parking lot you stopped and put your hands lightly on my shoulders and avoided my eyes. You gently rubbed the bloody places on my shirt and said, "I'll never get these stains out."

Damn anyone who thinks that means you were relegated in life to worrying about my ring-around-the-collar.

I knew exactly what you meant. It was such an oddly sweet way of saying, or not saying, what you were feeling. Sort of the way I shut down emotionally when I feel scared and hurt and helpless and say funny little things that seem so out of context.

You drove us home with my head in your lap all the way, stroking my face. You ran the bath. Set out my fresh underwear. Put me to bed. Caressed me carefully. Held me gently.

Later that night I woke up and found myself alone in bed. You were drinking at the kitchen table, head in your hands. You were crying. I took you firmly in my arms and held you, and you struggled and hit my chest with your fists because the enemy wasn't there to fight. Moments later you recalled the bruises on my chest and cried even harder, sobbing, "It's my fault, I couldn't stop them."

I've always wanted to tell you this. In that one moment I knew you really did understand how I felt in life. Choking on anger, feeling so powerless, unable to protect myself or those I loved most, yet fighting back again and again, unwilling to give up. I didn't have the words to tell you this then. I just said, "It'll be OK, it'll be alright." And then we smiled ironically at what I'd said, and I took you back to our bed and made the best love to you I could, considering the shape I was in. You knew not to try to touch me that night. You just ran your fingers through my hair and cried and cried.

When did we get separated in life, sweet warrior woman? We thought we'd won the war of liberation when we embraced the word gay. *Then suddenly there were professors and doctors and lawyers coming out of the woodwork telling us that meetings should be run with* Robert's Rules of Order. *(Who died and left Robert god?)*

They drove us out, made us feel ashamed of how we looked. They said we were male chauvinist pigs, the enemy. It was women's hearts they broke. We were not hard to send away, we went quietly.

The plants closed. Something we never could have imagined.

That's when I began passing as a man. Strange to be exiled from your own sex to borders that will never be home.

You were banished too, to another land with your own sex, and yet forcibly apart from the women you loved as much as you tried to love yourself.

For more than twenty years I have lived on this lonely shore, wondering what became of you. Did you wash off your Saturday night makeup in shame? Did you burn in anger when women said, "If I wanted a man I'd be with a real one?"

Are you turning tricks today? Are you waiting tables or learning Word Perfect 5.1?

Are you in a lesbian bar looking out of the corner of your eye for the butchest woman in the room? Do the women there talk about Democratic politics and seminars and co-ops? Are you with women who only bleed monthly on their cycles?

Or are you married in another blue-collar town, lying with an unemployed auto worker who is much more like me than they are, listening for the even breathing of your sleeping children? Do you bind his emotional wounds the way you tried to heal mine?

Do you ever think of me in the cool night?

I've been writing this letter to you for hours. My ribs hurt bad from a recent beating. You know.

I never could have survived this long if I'd never known your love. Yet still I ache with missing you and need you so.

Only you could melt this stone. Are you ever coming back?

The storm has passed now. There is a pink glow of light on the horizon outside my window. I am remembering the nights I fucked you deep and slow until the sky was just this color.

I can't think about you anymore, the pain is swallowing me up. I have to put your memory away, like a precious sepia photograph. There are still so many things I want to tell you, to share with you.

Since I can't mail you this letter, I'll send it to a place where they keep women's memories safe. Maybe someday, passing through this big city, you will stop and read it. Maybe you won't.

Good night, my love.

CHAPTER 2

I didn't want to be different. I longed to be everything grownups wanted, so they would love me. I followed all their rules, tried my best to please. But there was something about me that made them knit their eyebrows and frown. No one ever offered a name for what was wrong with me. That's what made me afraid it was really bad. I only came to recognize its melody through this constant refrain: "Is that a boy or a girl?"

I was one more bad card life had dealt my parents. They were already bitterly disappointed people. My father had grown up determined he wasn't going to be stuck in a factory like his old man; my mother had no intention of being trapped in a marriage.

When they met, they dreamed they were going on an exciting adventure together. When they awoke, my father was working in a factory and my mother had become a housewife. When my mother discovered she was pregnant with me, she told my dad she didn't want to be tied down with a kid. My father insisted she'd be happy once she had the baby. Nature would see to that.

My mother had me to prove him wrong.

My parents were enraged that life had cheated them. They were furious that marriage blocked their last opportunity to escape. Then I came along and I was different.

Now they were furious with me. I could hear it in the way they retold the story of my birth.

Rain and wind had lashed the desert while my mother was in labor. That's why she gave birth to me at home. The storm was too violent to be forded. My father was at work, and we had no phone. My mother said she wept so loudly in fear when she realized I was on the way that the Dineh grandmother from across the hall knocked on the door to see what was wrong, and then, realizing my birth was imminent, brought three more women to help.

The Dineh women sang as I was born. That's what my mother told me. They washed me, fanned smoke across my tiny body, and offered me to my mother.

"Put the baby over there," she told them, pointing to a bassinet near the sink. *Put the baby over there.* The words chilled the Indian women. My mother could see that. The story was retold many times as I was growing up, as though the frost that bearded those words could be melted by repeating them in a humorous, ironic way.

Days after I was born the grandmother knocked on our door again, this time because my cries alarmed her. She found me in the bassinet, unwashed. My mother admitted she was afraid to touch me, except to pin on a diaper or stick a bottle in my mouth. The next day the grandmother sent over her daughter, who agreed to keep me during the day while her children were at school, if that was alright. It was and it wasn't. My mother was relieved, I'm sure, although at the same time it was an indictment of her. But she let me go.

And so I grew in two worlds, immersed in the music of two languages. One world was Wheaties and Milton Berle. The other was fry bread and sage. One was cold, but it was mine; the other was warm, but it wasn't.

My parents finally stopped letting me travel across the hall when I was four. They came to pick me up before dinner one night. A number of the women had cooked a big meal and brought all the children together for the feast. They asked my parents if I could stay. My father grew alarmed when he heard one of the women say something to me in a language he didn't understand, and I answered her with words he'd never heard before. He said later he couldn't stand by and watch his own flesh and blood be kidnapped by Indians.

I've only heard bits and pieces about that evening, so I don't know everything that went on. I wish I did. But this part I've heard over and over again: one of the women told my parents I was going to walk a difficult path in life. The exact wording changed in the retelling. Sometimes my mother would pretend to be a fortuneteller, close her eyes, cover her forehead with her fingertips, and say, "I see a difficult life for this child." Other times my father would bellow like the Wizard of Oz, "This child will walk a hard road!"

In any case, my parents yanked me out of there. Before they left, though, the grandmother gave my mother a ring and said it would help to protect me in life. The ring frightened my parents, but they figured all that turquoise and silver must be worth something, so they took it.

That night there was another terrible desert storm, my parents told me, terrifying in its power. The thunder crashed and the lightning illuminated everything.

"Jess Goldberg?" the teacher asked.

"Present," I answered.

The teacher narrowed her eyes at me. "What kind of name is that? Is it short for Jessica?"

I shook my head. "No, ma'am."

"Jess," she repeated. "That's not a girl's name." I dropped my head. Kids around me covered their mouths with their hands to stifle their giggles.

Miss Sanders glared at them until they fell silent. "Is that a Jewish name?" she asked. I nodded, hoping that she was finished. She was not.

"Class, Jess is from the Jewish persuasion. Jess, tell the class where you're from."

I squirmed in my seat. "The desert."

"What? Speak up, Jess."

"I'm from the desert." I could see the kids mugging and rolling their eyes at each other.

"What desert? What state?" She pushed her glasses higher up on her nose.

I froze with fear. I didn't know. "The desert," I shrugged.

Miss Sanders grew visibly impatient. "What made your family decide to come to Buffalo?"

How should I know? Did she think parents told six-year-old kids why they made huge decisions that would impact on their lives? "We drove," I said. Miss Sanders shook her head. I hadn't made a very good first impression.

Sirens screamed. It was the Wednesday morning air raid drill. We crouched down under our desks and covered our heads with our arms. We were warned to treat The Bomb like strangers: don't make eye contact. If you can't see The Bomb, it can't see you.

There was no bomb—this was only practice for the real thing. But I was saved by the siren.

I was sorry we'd moved from the warmth of the desert to this cold, cold city. Nothing could have prepared me for getting out of bed on a winter morning in an unheated apartment in Buffalo. Even warming our clothes in the oven before we put them on didn't help much. After all, we still had to take our pajamas off first. Outside the cold was so fierce that the wind carved up my nose and sliced into my brain. Tears froze in my eyes.

My sister Rachel was still a toddler. I just remember a round snowsuit swaddled with scarves and mittens and hat. No kid, just clothes.

Even when I was bundled up in the dead of winter, with only a couple of inches of my face peeking out from my snowsuit hood and scarf, adults would stop me and ask, "Are you a boy or a girl?" I'd drop my eyes in shame, never questioning their right to ask.

During the summer there wasn't much to do in the projects, but there was plenty of time to do it.

The projects, former Army barracks, now housed the military-contracted aircraft workers and their families. All our fathers went to work in the same plant; all our mothers stayed home.

Old Man Martin was retired. He sat in a lawn chair on his porch listening to the McCarthy hearings on his radio. It was turned up so loud you could hear it all the way down the block. "Gotta watch out," he'd tell me as I passed his house, "communists could be anywhere. Anywhere." I'd nod solemnly and run off to play.

But Old Man Martin and I shared something in common. The radio was my best friend, too. "The Jack Benny Show" and "Fibber McGee and Molly" made me laugh, even when I didn't know what was so funny. "The Shadow" and "The Whistler" chilled me.

Perhaps outside these projects working families already had televisions, but not us. The streets of the project weren't even paved—just gravel and giant Lincoln Logs to mark the parking. Very few new things came down our road. Ponies pulled the carts of the ice man and the knife sharpener. On Saturday they brought the ponies without the carts and sold rides for a penny. A penny also bought a chunk from the ice man—chipped off with his ice pick. The ice was dense and slick and sparkled like a cold diamond that might never melt.

When a television set first appeared in the projects, it was in the living room of the McKensies. All the children in the neighborhood begged our parents to let us go watch "Captain Midnight" on the McKensies' new television. But most of us were not allowed in their home. Although it was 1955, the neighborhood still had some invisible war zones from a fierce strike that had been settled in 1949, the year I was born. "Mac" McKensie had been a scab. Just the word itself was enough to make me shy away from their house. You could still see traces of that word on the front of their coal bin, even though it had been painted over in a slightly different shade of green.

Years later, fathers still argued about the strike over kitchen tables and backyard barbecue grills. I overheard descriptions of such bloody strike battles, I thought WWII had been fought at the plant. At night when we'd drive my father to his shift, I used to crouch down on the back seat of the car and peek past the plant gates out over the now quiet fields of combat.

There were also gangs in the project, and the kids whose parents had scabbed during the strike made up a small but feared pack. "Hey pansy! Are you a boy or a girl?" There was no way to avoid them in the small planet of the projects. Their sing-song taunts stayed with me long after I'd passed by.

The world judged me harshly and so I moved, or was pushed, toward solitude.

The highway sliced between our projects and a huge field. It was against the rules to cross that road. There wasn't much traffic on it. You'd have to stand in the middle of a lane for a long time in order to get hit. But I wasn't supposed to cross that road. I did though, and no one seemed to notice.

I parted the long brown grass that bordered the road. Once I passed through it I was in my own world.

On the way to the pond I stopped to visit the puppies and dogs in the outside kennels connected to the back of the ASPCA building. The dogs barked and stood on their hind legs as I approached the fence. "Shhh!" I warned them. I knew no one was supposed to be back here.

A spaniel pushed his nose through the chain-link fence. I rubbed his head. I looked around for the terrier I loved. He had only come to the fence once to greet me, sniffing cautiously. Usually, no matter how I coaxed, he'd lay with his head on his paws, looking at me with mournful eyes. I wished I could take him home. I hoped he went to a kid who loved him.

"Are you a boy or a girl?" I asked the mongrel.

"Ruff, ruff!"

I didn't see the ASPCA man until it was too late. "Hey, kid. What you doing there?"

Caught. "Nothing," I said. "I wasn't doing anything bad. I was just talking to the dogs."

He smiled a little. "Don't put your fingers inside the fence, son. Some of 'em bite."

I felt the tips of my ears grow hot. I nodded. "I was looking for that little one with the black ears. Did a nice family take him?"

The man frowned for a moment. "Yes," he said quietly. "He's real happy now."

I hurried out to the pond to catch polywogs in a jar. I leaned on my elbow and looked up close at the little frogs that climbed up on the sun-baked rocks.

"Caw, caw!" A huge black crow circled above me in the air and landed on a rock nearby. We looked at each other in silence.

"Crow, are you a boy or a girl?"

"Caw, caw!"

I laughed and rolled over on my back. The sky was crayon blue. I pretended I was lying on the white cotton clouds. The earth was damp against my back. The sun was hot, the breeze was cool. I felt happy. Nature held me close and seemed to find no fault with me.

On my way back from the fields I passed the Scabbie gang. They had found an unlocked truck parked on an incline. One of the older boys disengaged the emergency brake and made two of the younger boys from my side of the projects run under the truck as it rolled.

"Jessy, Jessy!" they taunted as they rushed toward me.

"Brian says you're a girl, but I think you're a sissy boy," one of them said.

I didn't speak.

"Well, what are you?" he mocked me.

I flapped my arms, "Caw, caw!" I laughed.

One of the boys knocked the jar filled with polywogs from my hand and it smashed on the gravel. I kicked and bit them but they held me and tied my hands behind my back with a piece of clothesline.

"Let's see how you tinkle," one of the boys said as he knocked me down and two of the others struggled to pull off my pants and my underpants. I was filled with horror. I couldn't make them stop. The shame of being half-naked before them—the important half—took all the steam out of me.

They pushed and carried me to old Mrs. Jefferson's house and locked me in the coal bin. It was dark in the bin. The coal was sharp and cut like knives. It hurt too much to lie still, but the more I moved the worse I made the wounds. I was afraid I'd never get out.

It took hours before I heard Mrs. Jefferson in the kitchen. I don't know what she thought when she heard all the thumping and kicking in her coal bin. But when she opened the little trap door on the coal bin and I squirmed out onto her kitchen floor, she looked scared enough to fall down dead. There I stood, covered with coal soot and blood, tied up and half-naked in her kitchen. She mumbled curses under her breath as she untied me and sent me home wrapped in a towel. I had to walk a block and knock on my parents' door before I found refuge.

They were really angry when they saw me. I never understood why. My father spanked me over and over again until my mother restrained his arm with a whisper and her hand.

A week later I caught up with one of the boys from the Scabbie gang. He made the mistake of wandering alone too near our house. I made a muscle and told him to feel it. Then I punched him in the nose. He ran away crying; I felt great, for the first time in days.

My mother called me into our house for dinner. "Who was that boy you were playing with?" I shrugged.

"You were showing him your muscle?"

I froze, wondering how much she had seen.

She smiled. "Sometimes it's better to let boys think they're stronger," she told me. I figured she was just plain crazy if she really believed that.

The phone rang. "I'll get it," my father called out. It was the parent of the kid whose nose I bloodied; I could tell by the way my father glowered at me as he listened.

"I was so ashamed," my mother told my father. He glared at me in the rearview mirror. All I could see were his thick black eyebrows. My mother had been informed that I could no longer attend temple unless I wore a dress, something I fought tooth and nail. At the moment I was wearing a Roy Rogers outfit—without my guns. It was hard enough being the only Jewish family in the projects without being in trouble at the temple. We had to drive a long time to go to the nearest synagogue. My father prayed downstairs. My mother and sister and I had to watch from the balcony, like at the movies.

It seemed like there weren't many Jews in the world. There were some on the radio, but none in my school. Jews weren't allowed on the playground. That's what the older kids told me, and they enforced it.

We were nearing home. My mother shook her head. "Why can't she be like Rachel?"

Rachel looked at me sheepishly. I shrugged. Rachel's dream was a felt skirt with an appliqué poodle and rhinestone-studded plastic shoes.

My father pulled our car to a stop in front of our house. "You go straight to your room, young lady. And stay there." I was bad. I was going to be punished. My head ached with fear. I wished I could find a way to be good. Shame suffocated me.

It was almost sundown. I heard my parents call Rachel to join them in their bedroom to light the Shabbas candles. I knew the shades were drawn. A month before, we'd heard laughter and shouting outside the living room windows while my father was lighting the candles. We raced to the windows and peered out into the dusk. Two teenagers pulled down their pants and mooned us. "Kikes!" they shouted. My father didn't chase them away; he closed the drapes. After that, we started praying in their bedroom with the shades pulled down.

Everyone in my family knew about shame.

Soon afterward my Roy Rogers outfit disappeared from the dirty clothes hamper. My father bought me an Annie Oakley outfit instead.

"No!" I shouted, "I don't want to. I don't want to wear it. I'll feel stupid!"

My father yanked me by the arm. "Young lady, I spent $4.90 for this Annie Oakley outfit and you're going to wear it."

I tried to shake off his hand, but it was clamped painfully on my upper arm. Tears dripped down my cheeks. "I want a Davy Crockett hat."

My father tightened his grip. "I said no."

"But why?" I cried. "Everybody has one except me. Why not?"

His answer was inexplicable. "Because you're a girl."

"I'm sick of people asking me if she's a boy or a girl," I overheard my mother complain to my father. "Everywhere I take her, people ask me."

I was ten years old. I was no longer a little kid and I didn't have a sliver of cuteness to hide behind. The world's patience with me was fraying, and it panicked me.

When I was really small I thought I'd do anything to change whatever was wrong with me. Now I didn't want to change, I just wanted people to stop being mad at me all the time.

One day my parents took my sister and me shopping downtown. As we drove down Allen Street I noticed a grownup whose sex I couldn't figure out.

"Mom, is that a he-she?" I asked out loud.

My parents exchanged amused glances and burst out laughing. My father stared at me in the rearview mirror. "Where did you hear that word?"

I shrugged, not sure I'd ever really heard the word before it had escaped from my mouth.

"What's a he-she?" my sister demanded to know. I was interested in the answer too.

"It's a weirdo," my father laughed. "Like a beatnik."

Rachel and I nodded without understanding.

Suddenly a wave of foreboding swept over me. I felt nauseous and dizzy. But whatever it was that triggered the fear, it was too scary to think about. The feeling ebbed as quickly as it had swelled.

I gently pushed open the door to my parents' bedroom and looked around. I knew they were both at work, but entering their bedroom was forbidden. So I peeked around the room first, just to make sure.

I went directly to my father's closet door. His blue suit was there. That meant he must be wearing the grey one today. A blue suit and a grey suit—that's all any man needed, my father always said. His ties hung neatly on a rack.

It took even more nerve to open my father's dresser drawer. His white shirts were folded and starched stiff as a board. Each one was wrapped around with tissue paper and banded like a gift. The moment I tore off the paper band, I knew I was in trouble. I had no hiding places for garbage that my mother wouldn't find right away. And I realized my father probably knew the precise number of shirts he owned. Even though all of them were white, he probably could tell exactly which one was missing.

But it was too late. Too late. I stripped down to my cotton panties and T-shirt and slid on his shirt. It was so starched my eleven-year-old fingers could hardly get the collar buttoned. I pulled down a tie from the rack. For years I had watched my father deftly twist and flop his ties in a complicated series of moves, but I couldn't figure out the puzzle. I tied it in a clumsy knot. I climbed up on a footstool to lift the suit from the hangar. Its weight surprised me. It fell in a heap. I put on the suit coat and looked in the mirror. A sound came from my throat, sort of a gasp. I liked the little girl looking back at me.

Something was still missing: the ring. I opened my mother's jewelry box. The ring was huge. The silver and turquoise formed a dancing figure. I couldn't tell if the figure was a woman or a man. The ring no longer fit across three of my fingers; now it fit snugly on two.

I stared in the big mirror over my mother's dresser, trying to see far in the future when the clothing would fit, to catch a glimpse of the woman I would become.

I didn't look like any of the girls or women I'd seen in the Sears catalog. The catalog arrived as the seasons changed. I'd be the first in the house to go through it, page by page. All the girls and women looked pretty much the same, so did all the boys and men. I couldn't find myself among the girls. I had never seen any adult woman who looked like I thought I would when I grew up. There were no women on television like the small woman reflected in this mirror, none on the streets. I knew. I was always searching.

For a moment in that mirror I saw the woman I was growing up to be staring back at me. She looked scared and sad. I wondered if I was brave enough to grow up and be her.

I never heard the bedroom door open. By the time I saw my parents it was already too late. Each of them thought they were supposed to pick up my sister at the orthodontist. So they all got home unexpectedly early.

My parents' expressions froze. I was so frightened my face felt numb.

Storm clouds were gathering on my horizon.

My parents didn't talk about finding me in their bedroom in my father's clothes. I prayed I was off the hook.

But one day shortly afterward, my mother and father unexpectedly took me for a ride. They said they were bringing me to the hospital for a blood test. We rode up in an elevator to the floor where the test was supposed to be done. Two huge men in white uniforms took me off the elevator. My parents stayed on. Then the men turned and locked the gate, barring the elevator. I reached for my parents, but they wouldn't even look at me as the elevator door closed.

Terror sat on my chest like an elephant. I could hardly breathe.

A nurse explained the rules of my stay: I must get up in the morning and stay out on the ward all day. I must wear a dress, sit with my knees crossed, be polite, and smile when I was spoken to. I nodded as though I understood. I was still in shock.

I was the only kid on the ward. They put me in a room with two women. One was a very old woman who they kept tied to the bed. She keened and called out names of people who weren't there. The other woman was younger. "I'm Paula," she said, extending her hand. "Nice to meetcha." Her wrists were bandaged. She explained to me that her parents forbid her to ever see her boyfriend again because he was Negro. She slit her wrists in grief, and so they put her in this place.

We played ping-pong together for the rest of the day. Paula taught me the words to "Are You Lonesome Tonight?" She laughed and applauded as I dropped my voice low like Elvis'. "Make trivets and moccasins," Paula advised me. "Make lots of 'em. The more the better. They like that." I didn't know what a trivet was.

That night I had trouble sleeping. I heard men whispering and laughing as they came into my room. I wrapped the sheets tightly around my body and lay very still in silence. I heard the sound of a zipper opening. The smell of urine filled my nostrils. More laughter, and then the sounds of footsteps getting further and further away. My sheets were soaked. I was afraid I might be blamed and punished. Who had done this to me, and why? I'd ask Paula in the morning.

Nurses and orderlies came into our room when the light was still gray behind the barred windows. "Rise and shine," they shouted.

The old woman began calling out names.

Paula fought the orderlies, bit their hands. They cursed her, strapped her down, and wheeled her out of the room.

One nurse approached my bed. I could still smell the faint scent of urine on the sheets even after they'd dried. Would she take me away if she smelled it too? She studied her clipboard. "Goldberg, Jess." It frightened me to hear her say my name. "I don't have a signature on this one," she told the orderlies. They all left the room.

"Goldberg, Jess," the old woman shouted over and over again.

After lunch I snuck back into my room to get my yo-yo. Paula was sitting on her bed, staring at her slippers. She looked at me and cocked her head. She extended her hand to me. "I'm Paula," she said. "Nice to meetcha."

A nurse came into the room. "You," she said, pointing at me. I followed her back to the nurse's station. She held out two paper cups. Beautiful colored pills rolled around in one, the other was filled with water. I stared at both cups.

"Take them," the nurse ordered. "Don't give me a hard time." I already sensed that giving the staff a hard time might mean never getting out of there, so I took the pills. Soon after I swallowed them the floor began to tilt as I walked. They made me feel like I was moving through glue.

Every day I turned out more trivets and moccasins. I began to care about a woman who talked to ghosts I couldn't see.

And I discovered Norton's anthology of poetry in the patients' library—it changed my life. I read the poems over and over again before I began to grasp their meanings. It wasn't just that the words were musical notes my eyes could sing. It was the discovery that women and men, long dead, had left me messages about their feelings, emotions I could compare to my own. I had finally found others who were as lonely as I was. In an odd way, that knowledge comforted me.

Three weeks after I'd been brought to this ward, a nurse took me to an office. A man with a beard sat behind a big desk smoking his pipe. He told me he was my doctor. He said I seemed to be making progress, that being young was difficult, that I was going through an awkward stage.

"Do you know why you're here?" he asked me.

I had learned a lot in three weeks. I realized that the world could do more than just judge me, it wielded tremendous power over me. I didn't care anymore if my parents didn't love me. I had accepted that fact in the three weeks I'd survived alone in this hospital. But now I didn't care. I hated them. And I didn't trust them. I didn't trust anyone. My mind was focused on escape. I wanted to get out of this place and run away from home.

I told the doctor I was afraid of the grownup male patients on the ward. I said I was sure my parents were disappointed in me, but I wanted to make them happy and proud of me. I told him I didn't know what I was doing wrong, but if I could just go home, I'd do whatever he thought I should. I didn't mean it, but I said it. He nodded, but he seemed more interested in keeping his pipe lit than in me.

Two days later, my parents appeared on the ward and took me home. We didn't speak about what had happened. I concentrated on running away, waiting for the right moment. I had to agree to see the shrink once a week. I hoped I wouldn't have to see him for long, but the appointments continued for several years.

I remember the exact day the shrink dropped the bombshell: he and my parents had agreed charm school would help me a lot. The date is etched in my mind. November 23, 1963. I walked out of his office in a daze. The humiliation of charm school seemed more than I could bear. I might have killed myself if I could have figured out a painless route.

Everyone else seemed to be walking around equally as stunned. When I got home my parents had the television turned up loud and an announcer reported that the president had been shot in Dallas. It was the first time I'd ever seen my father cry. The whole world was out of control. I closed my bedroom door and fell asleep in order to escape.

I didn't think I could survive the spotlight of charm school illuminating my shameful differences. But somehow I got through it. My face burned with humiliation and anger each time I had to pivot on the runway in front of the whole class, over and over again.

Charm school finally taught me once and for all that I wasn't pretty, wasn't feminine, and would never be graceful. The motto of the school was *Every girl who enters leaves a lady.* I was the exception.

Just when it seemed like it couldn't get worse I noticed my breasts were growing. Menstruation didn't bother me. Unless I bled all over myself it was a private thing between me and my body. But breasts! Boys hung out of car windows and yelled vulgar things at me. Mr. Singer at the pharmacy stared at my breasts as he rang up my candy purchases. I quit the volleyball and track teams because I hated how my breasts hurt when I jumped or ran. I liked how my body was before puberty. Somehow I thought it would never change, not like this!

Whatever the world thought was wrong with me, I finally began to agree they were right. Guilt burned like vomit in my throat. The only time it receded is when I went back to The Land Where They Don't Mind. That's how I remembered the desert.

A Dineh woman came to me one night in a dream. She used to come to me almost every night, but not since I had been in the psychiatric ward several years earlier. She held me on her lap and told me to find my ancestors and be proud of who I was. She told me to remember the ring.

When I woke up it was still dark outside. I curled up on the foot of my bed and listened to the rain storm outside my window. Lightning bolts lit up the night sky. I waited until my parents got dressed before I snuck in their bedroom and took the ring. During the day at school I hid in a bathroom stall and looked at it, wondering about its power.

When would it protect me? I figured it was like the Captain Midnight Decoder Ring—you had to figure out how it worked.

That night at dinner my mother laughed at me. "You were talking Martian in your sleep again last night when we went to bed."

I slammed my fork down. "It's not Martian."

"Young lady," my father shouted, "you can go to your room."

As I walked through the high school corridor a group of girls squealed as I passed, "Is it animal, mineral, or vegetable?" I didn't fit any of their categories.

I had a new secret, something so terrible I knew I could never tell anyone. I discovered it about myself during the Saturday matinee at the Colvin Theater. One afternoon I stayed in the bathroom at the theater for a long time. I wasn't ready to go home yet. When I came out the adult movie was showing. I snuck in and watched. I melted as Sophia Loren moved her body against her leading man. Her hand cupped the back of his neck as they kissed, her long red nails trailed against his skin. I shivered with pleasure.

Every Saturday after that I hid in the bathroom so I could sneak out and watch the adult movies. A new hunger gnawed at me. It frightened me, but I knew better than to confide in a single soul.

I was drowning in my own loneliness.

One day my high school English teacher, Mrs. Noble, gave us a homework assignment: bring in eight lines of our favorite poem and read them in front of the class. Some of the kids moaned and groaned that they didn't have a favorite poem and it sounded "bor-ring." But I panicked. If I read a poem I loved, it would leave me vulnerable and exposed. And yet, to read eight lines I didn't care about felt like self-betrayal.

When it was my turn to read the next day, I brought my math book with me up to the front of the room. At the beginning of the semester I'd made a cover for the textbook out of a brown grocery bag and copied a poem by Poe across the inside flap.

I cleared my throat and looked at Mrs. Noble. She smiled and nodded at me. I read the first eight lines:

From childhood's hour I have not been
As others were—I have not seen
As others saw—I could not bring
My passions from a common spring.
From the same source I have not taken
My sorrow; I could not awaken
My heart to joy at the same tone;
And all I lov'd, I lov'd alone.

I tried to read the words in a flat sing-song tone without feeling, so none of the kids would understand what his poem meant to me, but their eyes were already glazed with boredom. I dropped my gaze and walked back to my seat. Mrs. Noble squeezed my arm as I passed, and when I looked up I saw she had tears in her eyes. The way she looked at me made me want to cry, too. It was as though she could really see me, and there was no criticism of me in her eyes.

The whole world was in motion, but you'd never have known it from my life. The only way I heard about the Civil Rights movement was from the copies of *LIFE* magazine that came to our house. Every week I was the first one in the family to read the newest issue.

The image burned into my mind was one of two water fountains labeled *Colored* and *White.* Other photos let me see brave people—dark-skinned and light—try to change that. I read their picket signs. I saw them bloodied at lunch counters, facing down steely-faced troops in Birmingham. I saw their clothes ripped from their bodies by fire hoses and police dogs. I wondered if I could ever be that brave.

I saw a picture from Washington, D.C. of more people than I ever could have imagined coming together in one place. Martin Luther King told them about his dream. I wished I could be part of it.

I studied my parents' faces as they calmly read the same magazines. They never said a word about it. The world was turning upside down and they quietly leafed through the pages as though they were skimming a Sears catalog.

"I wish I could go down South on a Freedom Ride," I said out loud one night at dinner. I watched my parents exchange a complex series of looks across the table. They continued to eat in silence.

My father put down his fork. "That has nothing to do with us," he firmly closed the subject.

My mother looked back and forth from his face to mine. I could tell she wanted to avoid the impending explosion at any cost. She smiled. "You know what I can't figure out?"

We all turned to look at her. "You know that song by Peter, Paul, and Mary? *The answer, my friend, is blowing in the wind?"* I nodded, eager to hear her question.

"I don't understand what good blowing in the wind would do." Both my parents collapsed in guffaws.

When I was fifteen years old I got an after-school job. That changed everything. I had to convince the shrink it would be good for me before my parents would give me permission. I convinced him.

I worked setting type by hand in a print shop. I had told Barbara, one of my only friends in homeroom class, that if I didn't get a job I'd just die, and her older sister got this one for me by lying and swearing I was sixteen.

Nobody at work cared if I wore jeans and T-shirts. They paid me a stack of cash at the end of each week, and my coworkers were nice to me. It wasn't that they didn't notice I was different, they just didn't seem to care as much as the high school kids did. After school I hurriedly changed out of my skirt and raced to work. My coworkers asked me how my day was and they told me about how it was when they were in high school. A kid could forget sometimes that adults were ever teenagers unless they remind you.

One day a printer from another floor asked Eddie, my foreman, "Who's the butch?" Eddie just laughed, and they walked off talking. The two women who worked on either side of me glanced over to see if I was hurt. I was more confused than anything.

That night, on dinner break, my friend Gloria ate her meal next to me. Out of the blue she told me about her brother—how he's a pansy and wears women's dresses but she loves him anyway and how she hates to see the way people treat him cause after all it's not his fault he's that way. She told me she even went with him once to a bar where he hung out with his friends and all these mannish women were coming on to her. She shuddered when she said that.

I wondered why she was telling me this. "What place was that?" I asked her.

"What?" She looked sorry she had opened up the subject.

"Where's the place where those people are?"

Gloria sighed.

"Please," I asked her. My voice was trembling.

She looked around before she spoke. "It's in Niagara Falls," she dropped her voice. "Why do you want to know?"

I shrugged. "What's the name of it?" I tried to sound real casual.

Gloria sighed deeply. "Tifka's." That's all she said.

CHAPTER 3

It was almost a year before I got up the nerve to call telephone information for the address of Tifka's. Finally I stood on the street in front of the bar, scared to death. I wondered what made me think this was the place I could fit. And what if I didn't?

I wore my blue-and-red striped shirt, a navy blue jacket to hide my breasts, black pressed chinos, and black Keds high-tops, because I had no dress shoes.

When I stepped inside, it was just a bar. Through the haze of smoke I saw faces glance over and look me up and down. There was no turning back, and I didn't want to. For the first time I might have found my people. I just didn't know how to penetrate this society.

I bellied up to the bar and ordered a Genny.

"How old are you?" the bartender asked.

"Old enough," I countered and put my money down. A round of smirks rolled around the bar. I sipped the beer and tried to act cool. An older drag queen studied me carefully. I picked up my beer and walked toward the smoke-filled backroom.

What I saw there released tears I'd held back for years: strong, burly women, wearing ties and suit coats. Their hair was slicked back in perfect DA's. They were the handsomest women I'd ever seen. Some of them were wrapped in slow motion dances with women in tight dresses and high heels who touched them tenderly. Just watching made me ache with need.

This was everything I could have hoped for in life.

"You ever been in a bar like this before?" the drag queen asked me.

"Lots of times," I answered quickly. She smiled.

Then I wanted to ask her something so badly I forgot to keep up my lie. "Can I really buy a woman a drink or ask her to dance?"

"Sure, honey," she said, "but only the femmes." She laughed and told me her name was Mona.

I focused on a woman sitting at a table alone. God, she was beautiful. I wanted to dance with her. The Four Tops were singing, *Baby, I need your loving*. I wasn't sure I knew how to slow dance, but I made a beeline for her before I lost my nerve.

"Would you dance with me?" I asked.

Mona and the bouncer picked me up and practically carried me into the front bar and set me on a stool. Mona put her hand on my shoulder and looked me dead in the eyes. "Kid, there's a few things I should tell you. It's my fault. I told you it was OK to ask a woman to dance. But the first thing you should know is—don't ask Butch Al's woman!"

I was making a mental note of this when Butch Al's shadow fell across me. The bouncer stood between us and the drag queens shooed her into the backroom. It happened in a flash, but a glimpse of this woman had floored me. Butch Al was a glance at power, a memory I was afraid to hang onto and afraid to let go of.

I sat trembling at the bar long after the momentary excitement had died down for everyone else. I felt exiled to the front of the bar, more lonely than before I came in, because now I knew what I wasn't a part of.

A red light flashed over the bar. Mona grabbed my hand and dragged me through the backroom into the women's bathroom. She flipped the toilet seat down and told me to climb up on it. She closed the stall door part way and said to stay there and be quiet. The cops were here. So there I crouched. For a long time. It wasn't until I frightened a femme half to death when she opened the stall door that I discovered the police had left long ago with their payoff from the owner. No one remembered that the kid was hidden in the bathroom.

As I emerged from the john, everyone in the backroom had a good laugh at my expense. I retreated to the front bar again and nursed a beer.

Later I felt a hand on my arm. Here was that beautiful woman I had asked to dance. This was Butch Al's femme.

"C'mon honey, come sit with us," she offered.

"No, I'm OK out here," I said as bravely as I could. But she put her arm around me gently and guided me off the bar stool.

"C'mon, join us. It's OK. Al won't hurt you," she reassured me. "Her bark is worse than her bite." I doubted that. Especially when Butch Al stood up as I approached their table.

She was a big woman. I don't know how tall she really was. I was only a kid. But she towered over me in height and stature.

I immediately loved the strength in her face. The way her jaw set. The anger in her eyes. The way she carried her body. Her body both emerged from her sports coat and was hidden. Curves and creases. Broad back, wide neck. Large breasts bound tight. Folds of white shirt and tie and jacket. Hips concealed.

She looked me up and down. I widened my stance. She took that in. Her mouth refused to smile, but it seemed her eyes did. She extended a beefy hand. I took it. The solidness of her handshake caught me by surprise. She strengthened her grip, I responded in kind. I was relieved I wasn't wearing a ring. Her clasp tightened, so did mine. Finally she smiled.

"There's hope for you," she said. I flushed at how I gratefully I embraced her words.

I guess you could explain away that handshake by calling it bravado. But it meant more than that to me then, and it still does. It's not just a way of measuring strength. A handshake like that is a challenge. It seeks out power through incremental encouragement. At the point of maximum strength, once equity is established, then you have really met.

I had really met Butch Al. I was so excited. And scared. I needn't have been: no one was ever kinder to me. She was gruff with me alright. But she peppered it with scruffing my hair, hugging my shoulders, and giving my face something more than a pat and less than a slap. It felt good. I liked the affection in her voice when she called me *kid,* which she did frequently. She took me under her wing and taught me all the things she thought were most important for a baby butch like me to know before embarking on such a dangerous and painful journey. In her own way, she was very patient about it.

In those days the bars in the Tenderloin district were gay by percentage. Tifka's was about 25 percent gay. That meant we had a quarter of the tables and dance floor. The other three-quarters were always pushing against our space. She taught me how we held our territory.

I learned to fear the cops as a mortal enemy and to hate the pimps who controlled the lives of so many of the women we loved. And I learned to laugh. That summer, Friday and Saturday nights were full of laughter and mostly gentle teasing.

The drag queens would sit on my lap and we'd pose for Polaroid pictures. We didn't find out till much later that the guy who took them for us was an undercover cop. I could look at the old bulldaggers and see my own future. And I learned what I wanted from another woman by watching Butch Al and her lover Jacqueline.

They let me hang with the two of them all summer long. I had told my parents I was working double shifts on Friday and Saturday nights, "to save up for college," and was staying overnight with a friend from school who lived near my job. They chose to believe my alibi. All week long I counted the hours till Friday night when I could punch out of work early and head for Niagara Falls.

After the bar closed we'd walk down the street, pretty tipsy, one of us on each of Jacqueline's arms. She'd throw her head up to the heavens and say, "Thank you God for these two good-looking butches." Al and I would lean forward and wink at each other and we'd all laugh for the sheer joy of being who we were, and being it together.

They let me sleep over weekends on their soft old couch. Jacqueline cooked eggs at 4:00 A.M. while Al taught me. It was always the same lesson: toughen up. Al never said exactly what was coming. It was never spelled out. But I got the feeling it was awful. I knew she was worried about my surviving it. I wondered if I was ready. Al's message was: *You're not!*

That was not encouraging. But I knew it was the urgency Al felt to prepare me for such a difficult life that gave her lessons a sharp edge. She never meant to cut me. She nurtured my butch strength the best way she knew how. And, she reminded me frequently, no one had ever done that when she was a baby butch, and she had survived. That was strangely reassuring. I had Butch Al for a mentor.

Al and Jackie groomed me. Literally. Jacqueline gave me haircuts in their kitchen. They took me to get my first sports coat and tie at the secondhand stores. Al combed the racks, pulling out sports coats, one after another. I tried on each one. Jackie would tilt her head, then shake it. Finally, Jackie smoothed my lapels and nodded in approval. Al gave a low whistle of appreciation. I had died and gone to butch heaven!

Then came the tie. Al picked it out for me. A narrow black silk tie. "You can't go wrong with a black tie," she informed me solemnly. And, of course, she was right.

It was fun alright. But the issue of sex was pressing on me from within and without, and Al knew it. One night at the kitchen table Al pulled out a cardboard box and handed it over to me to open. Inside was a rubber dildo. I was shocked.

"You know what that is?" she asked me.

"Sure," I said.

"You know what to do with it?"

"Sure," I lied.

Jacqueline rattled the dishes. "Al, for Christsakes. Give the kid a break, will you?"

"A butch has gotta know these things," Al insisted.

Jackie threw down her dishtowel and left the kitchen in exasperation.

This was to be our butch "father to son" talk. Al talked, I listened. "Do you understand?" she pressed.

"Sure," I said, "sure."

Al was satisfied she had imparted enough information by the time Jackie returned to the kitchen.

"One more thing, kid," Al added, "don't be like those bulldaggers who put this on and strut their stuff. Use a little decorum, you know what I mean?"

"Sure," I said. I didn't.

Al left the room to take a shower before bed. Jacqueline dried the dishes long enough that the blush drained from my face and my temples stopped pounding. She sat down on a kitchen chair next to me. "Did you understand what Al was telling you, honey?"

"Sure," I said, and vowed to never say that again.

"Is there anything you don't understand?"

"Well," I started slowly, "it sounds like it takes a little practice, but I get the general idea. I mean that noon and midnight stuff sounds, well, like you got to practice it to get it right."

Jacqueline looked confused. Then she laughed till tears streamed down her cheeks. "Honey," she'd start, but she was laughing too hard to continue. "Honey. You can't learn to fuck from reading *Popular Mechanics.* That isn't what makes a butch a good lover."

This was exactly what I needed to know! "Well, what does make a butch a good lover?" I asked, trying to sound like the answer didn't mean all that much to me.

Her face softened. "That's kinda hard to explain. I guess being a good lover means respecting a femme. It means listening to her body. And even if the sex gets a little rough, or whatever, that it's what she wants too, and inside you're still coming from a gentle place. Does that make sense?"

It did not. It was less information than I wanted. It turned out, however, to be the information I needed. It just took thinking about it for the rest of my life.

Jacqueline took the rubber cock from my hands. Had I been holding it all this time? She placed it carefully on my thigh. My body temperature rose. She began to touch it gently, like it was something really beautiful.

"You know, you could make a woman feel real good with this thing. Maybe better than she ever felt in her life." She stopped stroking the dildo. "Or you could really hurt her, and remind her of all the ways she's ever been hurt in her life. You got to think about that every time you strap this on. Then you'll be a good lover."

I waited, hoping there was more. There was not. Jackie got up and puttered around the kitchen. I went to bed. I tried to memorize every word that had been said to me before I fell asleep.

When Monique began to flirt with me, everyone at the bar was watching. Monique scared me to death. Jacqueline once said that Monique used sex like a weapon. Did Monique really want me? The butches said it was true, so it must be. Somehow everyone knew at once that I would lose my butch virginity with Monique.

On Friday night the butches punched my shoulders, clapped me on the back, adjusted my tie, and sent me over to her table. As Monique and I left together I noticed none of the other femmes were encouraging me. Why wouldn't Jacqueline look at me? She just tapped her long painted nails on that whiskey glass and stared at it like it was the only thing in the room. Did she sense the impending tragedy before I did?

The next evening I came to the bar late, hoping that Monique and her crowd would not be there waiting. They were. I slunk over to our table and sat down. No one knew exactly what had or had not happened the night before. But everyone knew something was very wrong.

I sat drowning in my own shame, remembering our date. I was scared by the time I had gotten to Monique's house. It occurred to me that I didn't really know what sex was. When and how did it begin? What was I supposed to do? And Monique frightened the hell out of me. All of a sudden I'd changed my mind. I didn't want to go through with it. I chattered nervously. Monique smirked. As I moved from couch to chair, she followed. "Whatsa matter?" she mocked me. "Don't you like me, honey? Whatsa matter, huh?" I made small talk until Monique finally stood up in exasperation. "Get the hell out of here!" She sounded disgusted with me. I mumbled relieved excuses and ran from her house.

But back at the bar, I couldn't escape the consequences. I sat at a table across from Monique and rubbed my forehead with my hands, as though I could wipe away the memory. I wondered how long this evening could possibly last. A long time. A very long time.

Monique whispered something to a butch sitting near her. The butch crossed the room and approached our table. "Hey," she called to me. I didn't look up. "Hey, femme, you wanna dance with a real butch?"

I twisted in my seat. Al whispered something to this butch I couldn't hear.

"Oh, I'm sorry Al, I didn't know she was your femme."

Al stood up and hit the butch before any of us knew what had happened. Then Al looked at me expectantly. "Well?" she said. She was holding up the butch who was doubled over. Al wanted me to hit the woman, to defend my honor. I couldn't think of anyone in the room I would want to hit, except maybe myself. I had no honor to defend.

The butches nearest Monique stood, ready to cross the room. Al and the other butches in our crowd lined up in front of the table to defend me. Jacqueline put her hand on my thigh to reassure me that I didn't have to fight. She needn't have. Mona came up behind me and put her hands on my shoulders. The femmes were closing ranks with me, too. I sat with my face in my hands, shaking my head, wanting it all to stop. But it wouldn't.

Monique's crowd finally backed down. But none of us could leave the bar until they did, otherwise we'd get jumped. It was going to be a *long* night.

Al was furious with me. "You gonna let that bulldagger talk to you that way?" She thumped the table for emphasis.

"Shut up, Al," Jacqueline snapped. It surprised me enough that I raised my face to look at her. She was glowering at Al. "Just leave the kid alone, will ya please?"

Al stopped yelling at me, but she turned her back to me to watch the couples dancing. Her body language said she was still pretty disgusted with me. Jacqueline just kept tapping her nails on her whiskey glass like the evening before. It took me a long time to learn femme Morse code.

After a while the bar crowd started thinning out. Yvette came in. Jacqueline watched her with obvious concern.

"What's the matter?" I asked, roused from my self-pity.

Jackie studied my face. "You tell me," she said.

I looked at Yvette. Like Jacqueline, she had worked the streets since she had been a teenager. Al made Jackie stop turning tricks. Al could support them both on the money she earned at her union job in the auto plant.

Yvette didn't have a butch who worked in the factories. Yvette didn't have anyone but the other working girls.

"She looks like she had a hard night," I offered.

Jacqueline nodded. "Those are mean streets. We get real hurt out there."

I marveled at the intimacy suggested in this information. Then she seemed to change the subject. "What do you think she wants right now?" Jacqueline asked me.

"To be left alone," I said, thinking of my own need.

She smiled. "Yeah, she wants to be left alone. She doesn't want one more person in this goddamn world to ask anything from her tonight. But she sure could use some comfort, you know what I mean?" Maybe I did. "She might really like it if a butch like you went over and just asked her to dance, you know? Not hit on her."

I thought maybe I could do that. Anything to take the sting out of my own shame.

Jacqueline pulled my sleeve. "Do it gently, understand?"

I nodded and walked slowly across the room to Yvette. She held her head in her hands. I cleared my throat. She looked at me wearily and sipped from her drink. "What do you want?" she asked me.

"Ah, I thought, would you dance with me?"

She shook her head. "Maybe later, baby. OK?"

Maybe it was the way I just stood there. There was no going back across the room in front of Monique's group or mine without having danced. I hadn't thought of that. Had Jackie? Or maybe Jacqueline's eyes connected with Yvette's from across the room. But finally Yvette said, "Yeah, why not," and stood up to dance with me.

I waited for her in the middle of the dance floor. Roy Orbison's voice was smooth and dreamy. I stood still, with her hand in mine until she relaxed and moved toward me. After we'd danced for a few moments, Yvette told me, "It's OK to breathe, you know." We laughed real hard, together.

Then I felt her body move closer and we kind of melted together. I discovered all the sweet surprises a femme can give a butch: her hand on the back of my neck, open on my shoulder, or balled up like a fist. The feel of her belly and thighs against mine. Her lips almost touching my ear.

The music stopped and she started to pull away. I held her hand gently. "Please?" I asked.

"Honey," she laughed, "you just said the magic word."

We danced a few slow songs in a row. Our bodies swung effortlessly in the circle of dance. The slightest shift in the pressure of my hand on her back changed the motion of her body. I never ground my thigh into her pelvis. I knew she had been wounded there. Even as a young butch that was the place I protected myself. I felt her pain, she knew mine. I felt her desire, she aroused mine.

Finally the music stopped and I let her go. I kissed her on the cheek and thanked her. I crossed the dance floor to my table. I was forever changed.

Jacqueline patted my thigh and flashed me a sweet smile. The other femmes—male and female—looked at me differently. As the world beat the stuffing out of us, they tried in every way to protect and nurture our tenderness. My capacity for tenderness was what they'd seen.

The other butches had to recognize me as sexual now, a competitor. Even Al looked at me differently.

As painful as this whole ritual had been, it was nothing less than a rite of passage. I didn't feel cocky. It taught me that humility was exactly the correct emotion when seeking to unleash the power of a woman's passion.

Strong to my enemies, tender to those I loved and respected. That's what I wanted to be. Soon I would have to put these qualities to the test. But for the moment, I was happy.

The next Friday night at the bar was boisterous. We all laughed and danced. Out of the corner of my eye I looked for Yvette. Jacqueline must have known it because she explained to me that Yvette's pimp wouldn't let her have a steady butch. My stomach tightened in rage. I still kept an eye out for her. After all, a pimp can't know everything that's going on, right?

When the red light flashed over the bar, I took myself to the women's bathroom and assumed my post on the toilet. A long time passed. I heard thumping and several shouts. Then it was quiet.

I peeked outside the bathroom. All the stone butches and drag queens were lined up facing the wall, hands cuffed behind their backs. Several of the femmes who the cops knew were prostitutes were getting roughed up and separated from the rest. I knew by now it would take at least a blow job to get them out of jail tonight.

A cop spotted me and grabbed me by the collar. He handcuffed me and threw me across the room. I looked for Al but they had already started taking people to the police vans outside.

Jacqueline rushed up to me. "Take care of each other," she said. "Be careful, honey," she added. I nodded. My wrists were painfully pinned behind my back. I was scared. I would try to be very careful. I hoped Al and I could take care of each other.

By the time they had nabbed me, the butch van was full. I rode in the police wagon with Mona and the other drag queens. I was glad. Mona kissed my cheek and told me not to be afraid. She said I'd be alright. If that was true though, I wondered why all the drag queens looked as scared as I felt.

At the precinct I saw Yvette and Monique, already arrested on a street sweep. Yvette flashed me a smile for courage, I gave her a wink. A cop shoved me from behind into the belly of the precinct. I was headed for the bulls' tank. They were taking Al out of the cell as they were bringing me in. I called her name. She didn't seem to hear me.

The cops locked me up. At least now my wrists were free from the handcuffs. I smoked a cigarette. What was going to happen? Through a grated window I saw some Saturday-night butches getting booked. They had taken Butch Al in the opposite direction.

The drag queens were in the large cell next to ours. Mona and I smiled at each other. At that moment three cops ordered her out of the cell. Her body pulled back slightly. She had tears in her eyes. Then she walked forward with them, rather than be dragged out.

I waited. What was happening?

About an hour later the cops brought Mona back. My heart broke when I saw her. Two cops were dragging her; she could barely stand. Her hair was wet and stuck to her face. Her makeup was smeared. There was blood running down the back of her seamless stockings. They threw her into the cell next to mine. She stayed where she fell. I could hardly breathe. I spoke to her in a whisper. "Honey, you want a cigarette? Want to smoke? C'mere, over here by me."

She looked dazed, unwilling to move. Finally she slid over to the bars beside me. I lit a cigarette and handed it to her. As she smoked, I slid my arm through the bars and touched her hair gently, then rested my hand on her shoulder. I spoke to her quietly. She didn't seem to hear me for a long time. Finally, she leaned her forehead against the bars and I put both my arms around her.

"It changes you," she said. "What they do to you in here, the shit you take every day on the streets—it changes you, you know?" I listened. She smiled. "I can't remember if I was ever as sweet as you are when I was your age." Her smile faded. "I don't want to see you change. I don't want to see you after you've hardened up."

I sort of understood. But I was really worried about Al and I didn't know what was going to happen to me. This sounded like a philosophical discussion. I didn't know if I was going to live to an age where experience would change me. I just wanted to live through tonight. I wanted to know where Al was.

The cops told Mona she'd been bailed out. "I must look a mess," she said.

"You look beautiful," I told her, and I meant it. I looked at her face for a last moment, wondering if the men she gave herself to loved her as much as I did.

"You really are a sweet butch," Mona said before she left. That felt good.

The cops dragged Al in just after Mona left. She was in pretty bad shape. Her shirt was partly open and her pants zipper was down. Her binder was gone, leaving her large breasts free. Her hair was wet. There was blood running from her mouth and nose. She looked dazed, like Mona.

The cops pushed her into the cell. Then they approached me. I backed up until I was up against the bars. They stopped and smiled. One cop rubbed his crotch. The other put his hands under my armpits and lifted me up, a couple inches off the floor, and slammed me against the bars. He pressed his thumbs deep into my breasts and jammed his knee between my legs.

"You should be this tall soon, tall enough your feet would reach the ground. That's when we'll take care of you like we did your pussy friend Allison," he taunted me. Then they left.

Allison.

I grabbed my pack of cigarettes and Zippo lighter and slid over to where Al was slumped on the floor. I was shaking. "Al," I said, extending the pack. She didn't look up. I put my hand on her arm. She sloughed it off. Her head was down. I could just see the expanse of her wide back, the curves of her shoulders. I touched them without thinking twice. She let me.

I smoked with one hand and touched her back with the other. She began to tremble. I put my arms around her. Her body softened against me. She was hurt. The parent had become the child for this moment. I felt strong. There was comfort to be found in my arms.

"Hey, look at this," one cop yelled to another. "Allison found herself a baby butch. They look like two faggots." The cops laughed.

My arms took more of her into my circle to protect her, as though I could ward off their jeers and keep her safe in my embrace. I had always marveled at her strength. Now I felt the muscles in her back and shoulders and arms. I experienced the power of this stone butch, even as she slumped wearily in my arms.

The cops announced Jacqueline had posted our bail. The last words I heard from the cops were, "You'll be back. Remember what we did to your buddy."

What did they do? The questions came back again. Jacqueline looked from Al's face to mine asking the same. I had no answers. Al offered none. In the car Jacqueline held Al in a way that made it look at first glance like Al was comforting her. I sat quietly in the front seat needing comfort, too. I didn't know the gay man who drove us. "Are you OK?" he asked me.

"Sure," I answered without thinking.

He dropped us off at Al and Jackie's house. Al ate her eggs like she couldn't taste them. She didn't speak. Jacqueline looked nervously from Al to me and back again. I ate and then did the dishes. Al went into the bathroom.

"She'll be in there a long time," Jacqueline said.

How did she know? Had this happened many times before? I dried the dishes. Jacqueline turned to focus on me. "Are you OK?" she asked.

"Yeah, I'm alright," I lied.

She came closer to me. "Did they hurt you, baby?"

"No," I lied. I was mortaring a brick wall inside myself. The wall didn't protect me, and yet I watched as though it wasn't my hands placing each brick. I turned away from her to signal that I had something important to ask. "Jacqueline, am I strong enough?"

She came up behind me and turned me around by the shoulder. She pulled my face against her cheek. "Who is, honey?" she whispered. "Nobody's strong enough. You just get through it the best you can. Butches like you and Al don't have a choice. It's gonna happen to you. You just gotta try to live through it."

I was already burning with another question. "Al wants me to be tough. You and Mona and the other femmes are always telling me to stay sweet, stay tender. How can I be both?"

Jacqueline touched my cheek. "Al's right, really. It's selfish of us girls, I guess. We want you to be strong enough to survive the shit you take. We love how strong you are. But butches get the shit kicked out of their hearts too. And I guess we just sometimes wish there was a way to protect your hearts and keep you all tender for us, you know?"

I didn't. I really didn't. "Is Al tender?"

Jacqueline's face tightened. The question threatened to reveal something that could pierce Butch Al's armor. Then Jacqueline saw I really needed the answer. "She's been hurt real bad. It's hard for Al to say everything she feels. But, yeah. I don't think I could be with her if she wasn't tender with me."

We both heard Al unlock the bathroom door. Jacqueline looked apologetic. I signaled that I understood. She left the kitchen. I was alone. I had a lot to think about.

I lay down on the couch. After a while, Jackie brought me bedding. She sat down beside me and stroked my face. It felt good. She looked at me for a long time with a pained expression. I didn't know why but it scared me. I guess I figured she could see what was coming and I couldn't.

"Are you really OK, honey?" she asked.

I smiled. "Yeah."

"Do you need anything?"

Yeah. I needed a femme who loved me like she loved Al. I needed Al to tell me exactly what they were going to do to me next time and how to live through it. And I needed Jacqueline's breast. Almost as soon as the thought crossed my mind, she put my hand on her breast. She turned her head in the direction of the bedroom as though she was listening for Al. "Are you sure you're OK?" she asked one last time.

"Yeah, I'm OK," I said.

Her face softened. She touched my cheek and pulled my hand away from her breast. "You're a real butch," she said, shaking her head. I felt proud when she said that.

In the morning I woke up early and left quietly.

Butch Al and Jacqueline weren't at the bar after that. Their phone was disconnected. I heard some stories about what happened to Al. I didn't choose to believe any of them.

The summer passed. It was time for my junior year of high school to begin. As summer turned to fall I stopped going to Niagara Falls on the weekends. Just before Christmas I went back to Tifka's to see the old crowd. Yvette wasn't there. I heard she died alone in an alleyway, her throat slashed from ear to ear. Mona overdosed, purposely. No one had seen Al. Jackie was working the streets again.

I walked against a bitter wind from bar to bar along the Tenderloin strip. I heard her laughter before I saw her. There was Jacqueline in the shadow of an alley, sharing an ironic laugh with other working girls. She saw me.

Jacqueline came to me readily, smiling. I saw the glaze of heroin across her eyes. She was thin, very thin. She faced me. She opened the collar of my overcoat in order to straighten my tie. She turned my collar up against the cold. I stood with my hands buried deep in my pockets. I felt like I did the night I danced with Yvette.

We were asking each other a lot of questions with our eyes and answering them. It all happened real fast. I saw the tears just start spilling from her eyes and then she turned to go.

By the time I found my voice to speak, Jacqueline was gone.

CHAPTER 4

The note sailed across my desk and glided onto the floor. I kept an eye on Mrs. Rotondo while I bent over and picked it up. Luckily, she didn't seem to notice.

DANGER!! My parents want to know why your parents call our house looking for you. I can't cover for you any more. PLEASE FORGIVE ME!! Love until eternity—your enduring friend, Barbara.

I looked up and caught Barbara's eyes. She wrung her hands and made a face that begged forgiveness. I smiled and nodded. I mimed smoking a cigarette. Barbara nodded and smiled. She made me feel warm inside. Barbara—the girl I'd sat next to in home room for two years. Barbara—the girl who told me if I were a guy she'd be in love with me.

We met in the girl's bathroom. Two of the juniors who were smoking had already opened the windows. "Where've you been lately?" Barbara demanded to know.

"Working like crazy. I've got to get out of my parents' house or I'm gonna die. They act like they hate my guts." I took a deep drag on my cigarette. "I think they wish I was never born."

Barbara looked frightened. "Don't say that," she told me, then glanced around as if someone might hear. She took a drag of smoke into her mouth and let it trickle out as she inhaled it up her nose. "Isn't that wild? It's called a French Curl. Kevin showed me."

"Oh, shit!" someone hissed.

"Alright girls, line up!" It was Mrs. Antoinette, the scourge of girls who long for nicotine. She ordered us to line up so she could smell our breath. Since she hadn't actually seen me, I took a chance and slipped out the door. The halls were deserted. Within minutes a maddening bell would ring and the halls would be jammed with kids using their notebooks in front of them like shields in battle.

I guess the summer had changed me. Otherwise I would never have snapped the iron bands of habit and left the building during school hours. I wanted to run around the track as fast as I could, to sweat out the sticky sensation of imprisonment. But the boys were in football practice in the middle of the field, and a group of girls were trying out for cheerleading. So I climbed up into the bleachers and walked to the far end.

A red-tailed hawk glided above the trees, an unusual sight in the city. There was no place to go; there was nothing to do. Whatever was going to happen in my life I wanted it to hurry up. I wished I could play quarterback on the football team. I could imagine the weight of the equipment and the uniform tight across my chest. I put my hand against my large breasts.

I noticed that five of the eight girls trying out as cheerleaders were blonde. I didn't know there were five blondes in the whole school. Almost half the school was white, Jewish, and middle class. The other half was Negro and working class. My family was Jewish and working class. I fell into a lonely social abyss. The few friends I had in the school were from families who worked to make ends meet.

I watched the cheerleaders leave the field. They looked over their shoulders to see if the boys noticed.

Football practice ended. Some of the white boys stayed on the field. One of them, Bobby, nodded toward me with his head. I got up to leave. "Where you goin', Jess?" he mocked me, then headed toward me. Several boys followed him.

I started to hurry across the bleachers.

"Where're you going, lezzie? I mean, Jezzie." They followed me as I rushed to get away. He indicated for one of the boys to climb the bleachers in front of me. He and the other boys came directly at me. I leaped over the bleachers and ran onto the field. Bobby tackled me; I hit the dirt hard. It all mushroomed so quickly. I couldn't make it stop.

"What'sa matter, Jess? Don't you like us?" Bobby was pushing his hand up under my dress, between my legs. I punched and kicked, but he and the other boys pinned me down. "I saw you watching us. Come on, you want it, don't you, Jezzy?"

I bit the hand nearest my mouth. "Ouch, shit, fuck!" The boy yelled and backhanded me across my face. I could taste my own blood. The expressions on their faces scared me. These were not kids anymore.

I punched Bobby's chest as hard as I could. I must have hit his equipment because

I skinned my knuckles and Bobby just laughed. He pressed his forearm against my throat. One of the boys stepped on my ankle with his cleats. I struggled and cursed them. They laughed as though this were a game.

Bobby unlaced his uniform pants and jammed his penis into my vagina. The pain traveled up to my belly, scaring the hell out of me. It felt like something ripped deep inside of me. I counted the attackers. There were six.

The one I was angriest at was Bill Turley. Everyone knew he tried out for the team because the kids teased him about being a sissy. He scuffed the grass with his cleats and waited for his turn.

Part of the nightmare was that it all seemed so matter of fact. I couldn't make it stop, I couldn't escape it, and so I pretended it wasn't happening. I looked at the sky, at how pale and placid it was. I imagined it was the ocean and the clouds were white-capped waves.

Another boy was huffing and puffing on top of me. I recognized him—Jeffrey Darling, an arrogant bully. Jeffrey grabbed my hair and yanked it back so hard I gasped. He wanted me to pay attention to the rape. He fucked me harder. "You dirty Kike bitch, you fucking bulldagger." All my crimes were listed. I was guilty as charged.

Is this how men and women have sex? I knew this wasn't making love; this was more like making hate. But was this mechanical motion what all the jokes and dirty magazines and whispers were about? This was it?

I giggled, not because what was happening was funny, but because all the fuss about sex suddenly seemed so ridiculous. Jeffrey pulled his cock out of me and slapped my face, back and forth. "It's not funny," he shouted. "It's not funny, you crazy bitch."

I heard the sound of a whistle. "Shit, it's the coach," Frank Humphrey warned the other guys. Jeffrey jumped up and pulled up his pants. All the boys scattered toward the gym.

I was alone on the field. The coach stood a distance away from me, staring. I wobbled as I tried to stand. There were grass stains on my skirt and blood and slimy stuff running down my legs. "Get out of here, you little whore," Coach Moriarty ordered.

I had to walk the long distance home since my bus pass wasn't valid this late. I didn't feel like this was my life I was living anymore. It felt more like a movie. A '57 Chevy full of boys slowed down. "See you tomorrow, lesbo," I heard Bobby yell as they passed. Was I their property now? If I wasn't strong enough to stop them once, could I ever hope to defend myself again?

I ran to the bathroom as soon as I got home and threw up in the toilet. Between my legs felt like chopped meat and the shooting pains frightened me. I took a long, long bubble bath. I asked my sister to tell my parents I was sick and went to bed. When I woke up it was time to go to school. But I couldn't, I wasn't ready!

"Now!" My mother ordered me out of bed. My whole body hurt. I tried not to think about the pain between my legs. My parents didn't seem to notice my split lip or the way I was limping a little on my ankle. I moved slow as molasses. I couldn't think clearly. "Hurry up," my mother scolded. "You're going to be late for school."

I purposely missed my bus so I could walk to school. At least if I was late I wouldn't have to face the kids before the bell rang. I forgot everything as I walked. The wind whispered in the trees. Dogs barked and birds chirped. I walked slowly, as though I wasn't on my way to any place in particular.

Then the school building loomed over me like a medieval castle, and all the memories flooded back in a sickening rush. Did the kids already know? The way they whispered behind their hands as I passed in the hallway after first-period class made me think they did. I thought maybe I was being paranoid until one of the girls called out, "Jess, Bobby and Jeffrey are looking for you." They all laughed. I felt like what happened was my fault.

I ducked into my history class just as the bell rang. Mrs. Duncan spoke the dreaded words: "All right, class, tear off a half sheet of paper and number from one to ten. This is a test. Question number one: what year was the Magna Carta signed?"

I tried to remember if she'd ever taught us what the hell the Magna Carta even was. Ten facts floating in a vacuum. I chewed my pencil and stared at the blank piece of paper in front of me. I raised my hand and asked for a bathroom pass. "You can go as soon as you finish the test, Miss Goldberg."

"Um, please Mrs. Duncan. It's an emergency."

"Yeah," said Kevin Manley, "she has to go find Bobby."

I heard the guffaws behind me as I left the classroom in a panic. I ran through the halls looking for someone to help me. I had to talk to someone. I ran upstairs to the cafeteria, looking for my friend Karla from gym class. When the bell rang I saw Karla in the crush of kids going in and out of the double doors. "Karla," I yelled, "I have to talk to you."

"What's up?"

"I've gotta talk to you." We made our way to the lunch line.

"What are they serving today?" Karla asked me. "Can you see?"

"Dreck on rice and shit on a shingle."

"Yum! Same as yesterday."

"And the day before." It was such a relief to laugh with her.

We got our trays and winced as the school dietitian dumped a glop of something on each of our plates. We picked up cartons of milk and paid for our lunches. "Can we talk?" I asked her.

"Sure," she said. "How about after lunch?"

"Why not now?"

Karla looked at me blankly. "Can I sit with you?" I pressed.

She continued to stare at me. "Girl, have you gone out of your cotton-pickin' mind?" I looked confused. "There's a seating arrangement here. Or haven't you noticed?"

The moment she said it I realized it was true. I looked around the lunchroom like I'd never really seen it before. The cafeteria was absolutely, right down the middle, segregated. "Get the picture, honey? Where you been?"

"Can I sit with you anyway?"

Karla tilted her head back and narrowed her eyes at me. "It's a free country," she said as she turned on her heel and walked away.

"Hello, white girl! You new in town?" Darnell teased as he moved over to let me sit down next to Karla.

I laughed. There was no other sound in the huge room. You could've heard a pin drop. My stomach tightened, and the food on my plate looked more disgusting than usual.

"Karla," I sat down next to her. "I really need to talk to you, really bad."

"Uh oh," someone whispered at our table.

Mrs. Benson was racing toward our table. "Young lady, what are you doing?"

I took a deep breath. "I'm eating lunch, Mrs. Benson."

Everyone at the table tried to stifle giggles, but when milk sprayed out of Darnell's nose, well, it just couldn't be controlled.

"Come with me, young lady," Mrs. Benson told me.

"Why?" I wanted to know. "I didn't do anything." She stormed away.

"That was easy," Darnell said.

"Too easy," Karla answered.

"Karla, I really need to talk to you." I told her.

"Uh-oh," Darryl said, "here comes Jim Crow." Actually, his name was Moriarty. The coach was headed right for me.

I was waiting for him to say something to me, but he didn't. He grabbed me by the arms, digging his fingers into my flesh. Moriarty half dragged me to the door of the cafeteria. "You little slut," he whispered.

"I'll take care of this, Coach," Miss Moore, the assistant principal, intervened. She put her arm around me and led me out into the hall. "Child," she said, "you are in a whole lot of trouble. What the hell were you doing?"

"Nothing, Miss Moore. I didn't do anything. I was just trying to talk to Karla."

She smiled at me. "Sometimes you don't have to do anything wrong to be in hot water."

All of my panic and fear welled up in my eyes. I wanted so badly to open up to Miss Moore.

"Honey, it's not all that bad," she reassured me. I couldn't speak. "Are you OK, Jess? Are you in trouble?" She looked at my swollen lip; no one else had noticed. "Do you want to talk, Jess?"

I did want to talk. But my mouth wouldn't move.

"Here's the other troublemaker," Moriarty said. He had Karla in his grip.

Miss Moore pulled Karla close to her. "I'll take care of this, Coach. You go back to being lunch monitor."

He looked at her with open hatred. I could see what a racist he was.

"C'mon girls." Miss Moore put her arm around each of us. "I'll explain to the principal that you didn't mean any harm."

Karla and I leaned forward and looked at each other. "I'm sorry," I told her, "I didn't mean to get you in trouble."

Miss Moore stopped walking. "You girls didn't do anything wrong. You came up against an unspoken rule that needs changing. I just want you both to survive it."

When the principal, Mr. Donatto, finally called me into his office, Miss Moore asked if she could come in too. He knitted his thick eyebrows together. "I'd prefer it if you didn't, Suzanne."

Mr. Donatto shut the door and motioned for me to sit down. I felt alone in a hostile world. He slumped in his chair and pressed his fingertips together. I looked at the painting of George Washington on the wall and wondered whether he was wearing a white sheepskin coat or the painting was never finished. Mr. Donatto cleared his throat. I knew he was ready.

"I've been told you made some trouble in the lunchroom today, young lady. Would you care to explain yourself?"

I shrugged my shoulders. "I didn't do anything."

Donatto leaned back in his chair. "The world is a very complicated place. More complex than you kids realize." Oh god, I thought. Here comes the lecture. "In some schools there are fights between the colored children and the white students. Did you know that?"

I shook my head.

"I'm proud that we have good relations between the races at this school. That's not been easy since the school district changed. We want to keep things calm, do you understand?"

"I don't know why I can't eat lunch with my friends. We're not fighting."

Donnato's jaw clenched. "The cafeteria is the way it is because the students are most comfortable with the arrangement."

"Well, I'm not." I wondered who was controlling my mouth. Donnato slammed his palm on the desk.

Miss Moore opened the door. "Can I be of help, sir?"

"Get out and shut the door," he shouted at her. He turned back to me and took a deep breath. "I want you to understand that what we want is good relations between the students."

"Then why can't I eat lunch with my friends?"

Donnato came over to me and leaned so close I could feel his breath on my face. "Young lady, you listen to me and you listen to me good. I'm trying to hold this school together and I'll be damned if I'm going to let a little troublemaker like you undo all my hard work. Do you understand me?" I blinked as little bits of spit hit my face. "You are suspended for one week."

Suspended? For what? "I wanted to quit anyway," I told him.

He smirked. "You can't quit until you're sixteen."

"I can't quit but you can suspend me?"

"That's right, young lady. Miss Moore," Donatto yelled, "this student has been suspended. See that she leaves the building immediately."

Miss Moore was standing outside the door. She smiled at me and put her hand on my shoulder. "You OK?" she asked.

"Sure," I said.

"This will blow over," she assured me.

I made a pleading face. "Let me just see Mrs. Noble and Miss Candi, please? Then I'll go." Miss Moore nodded.

I wanted to talk to her so badly, but I felt as though I was standing in a boat that was drifting away from everyone. I said goodbye and walked away.

Mrs. Noble was marking test papers. She looked up as I came into the classroom. "I heard," she said, and continued to correct papers.

I sat on top of a desk in front of hers. "I came to say goodbye."

Mrs. Noble looked up and took off her glasses. "You're quitting school over this?"

I shrugged. "They suspended me, but I'm not coming back."

"They suspended you? Over the lunchroom incident?" Mrs. Noble rubbed her eyes and slipped her glasses back on.

"Do you think I did something wrong?"

She sat back in her chair. "When you do something out of conviction, my dear, it should be because you believe it's the right thing to do. If you look for approval from everyone, you'll never be able to act."

I felt criticized. "I'm not asking everybody, I was just asking you," I sulked.

Mrs. Noble shook her head. "Just think about coming back. You must go to college."

I shrugged. "I'm never gonna finish high school. I'm going into the factories."

"You need skills, even to be a laborer."

I shrugged. "I can't afford college, that's one thing. My parents aren't going to spend a dime on me or co-sign a loan either."

She ran her hands through her hair. I noticed for the first time how gray it was. "What do you want to do with your life?" she asked me.

I thought about it. "I want a good job, a union job. I'd really like to get into the steel plant, or Chevy."

"I guess it wasn't fair of me to want you to want more."

"Like what?" I said, angry that I was now a disappointment to her, too.

"I could see you becoming a great American poet, or a fiery labor leader, or discovering the cure for cancer." She took off her glasses and wiped them with a Kleenex. "I wanted you to help change the world."

I laughed. She had no idea how powerless I really was. "I can't change anything," I told her. I toyed with telling her what had happened on the football field, but I just couldn't find the words to begin.

"Do you know what it takes to change the world, Jess?" I shook my head. "You have to figure out what you really believe in and then find other people who feel the same way. The only thing you have to do alone is to decide what's important to you."

I nodded and slid off the desk. "I'd better be going, Mrs. Noble, before they send a posse to eject me from the school grounds."

She stood up and took my face in her hands. She kissed me on the forehead. For some reason it made me think about how it felt in jail with Al and Mona—about moments when you're being torn away from people you love and you feel real close to them.

"Come back and visit," Mrs. Noble said.

"Sure," I lied.

I headed toward the gym to say goodbye to Miss Candi. Miss Johnson stopped me in the hallway. "Where's your hall pass, young lady?"

"I don't need one anymore. I'm suspended." I sounded cheerful.

Only hours before I had felt imprisoned in these halls. Now that I was leaving, the school felt smaller. I wandered through the corridors like an alumna. I could hear the off-key strains of John Philip Sousa coming from the auditorium. I had forgotten there was an assembly last period. I guessed I didn't need to go. As the bell rang, doors flew open and students flowed into the corridors. I waited for the crowd to thin out before I tried to struggle upstream to the gym.

There was no one in the girls' gym when I got there. I took my sneakers and shorts out of my locker and put them on. I started playing on the monkey ropes, climbing up one and then across the others. When I shinnied down, I felt so pent-up I was afraid I'd explode. I ran around the indoor track until I almost dropped.

As I stopped I saw Miss Candi looking at me. She had come back to the gym office for something and saw me running. "How long have you been watching me?"

She shrugged. "I heard you've been suspended."

"Do you think I did something wrong, Miss Candi?" Even as I said it I remembered what Mrs. Noble explained about needing approval.

"I just don't believe in rocking the boat, that's all," she said, looking away.

"Wow," I sighed in disappointment. "Well, Miss Candi, I just came to say goodbye."

I walked past the auto shop—that's the class I wanted. Instead they'd had me making popovers with lemon sauce in cooking class. How did Mrs. Noble think I could ever change this world by making popovers?

Over the main entrance to the school the words *Optima futura* were carved in stone. *The best is yet to be.* I hoped that was true.

"Hey," Darnell yelled from the second-floor detention room. "Way to go!" I waved to him. "Meet us later," he yelled. A teacher pulled him inside and shut the window.

"Jess!" I heard Karla call my name. "Jess, wait up!"

"They suspended me," I told her.

"Me too," she said. "For two weeks."

"Two weeks? They only suspended me for one! I'm quittin', though."

Karla whistled through her teeth. "Shit, are you sure about that?"

I nodded. "I can't take it anymore."

"Jess," Karla said, "with all the shit that went down I forgot to ask you what's up. You said you needed to talk."

That moment was a turning point in my life. I felt like a dam ready to burst but I heard myself say, "Aw, it wasn't that important."

Karla looked concerned. "Are you sure?"

I nodded, feeling the last brick of the wall go up inside of me that might never come down again.

"We're going down to Jefferson," Karla said. "Wanna come?" I shook my head and hugged her goodbye.

I didn't want to face my parents. I knew they wouldn't be home from work yet, if I hurried.

As soon as I got home I took two pillowcases and stuffed all my pants and shirts into them. I reached deep into my closet and pulled out the backpack that contained the tie and jacket Al and Jacqueline had bought me.

The ring! I took it out of my mother's jewelry case and slipped it on my left hand.

I hurried, afraid my parents would come home and catch me. I found a piece of paper and a pencil. I was sweating and my hand shook.

Dear Mom and Dad, I wrote.

"Whatcha doing?" Rachel asked me.

"Shhh!" I continued to write. *I got kicked out of school. It's not my fault, in case you care. I'm almost sixteen. I was going to quit anyway. I have a job and money. I'm leaving. Please don't come after me. I don't want to live here anymore.*

I didn't know what else to write. They could find me at my job if they wanted to, but there was a chance that they'd be as happy to be rid of me as I'd be relieved to be gone.

"Whatcha doing?" Rachel asked me again. Her lip trembled.

"Shhh, don't cry," I told her. I gave her a hug. "I'm running away from home."

She shook her head. "You can't," she said.

I nodded my head. "I gotta try. I'm going crazy here."

"I'll tell," Rachel threatened.

I rushed out the door, afraid to be caught by my parents at the last moment. They could use force to bring me back, have me arrested or commit me to an institution. Or they could let me go. It was up to them—I'd learned that. I ran down the street until my lungs ached. When I was blocks away I leaned up against a lamppost and caught my breath. I felt free. Free to explore what freedom meant. I looked at my watch. It was time to go to work. I was almost sixteen years old. I had thirty-seven dollars in my pocket.

"You're late," my foreman told me as I punched in.

"Sorry," I said, and started the machine up right away.

"Damn kid," he told Gloria.

She kept her head down until he walked away. Then she looked up and smiled. "Tough day, Jess?"

I laughed. "I got kicked out of school and ran away from home."

She whistled and shook her head. "I'd take you home with me, but my husband keeps trying to give away the kids we already got."

I asked Eddie if I could work a double. "I'll let you know later," he said. At 11:00 P.M. the work ran out and he sent me home. I tried to sleep sitting up at the bus station, but the cops kept coming by and asking me to show them my ticket. I bought a ticket for Niagara Falls, but they woke me every time a bus left for the Falls and wanted to know why I wasn't on it. I walked around and ate breakfast and drank coffee and walked around some more. At noon I went to a movie matinee. When I woke up, I was late for work.

Eddie warned me not to be late again.

"You look like hell," Gloria whispered.

"Thanks a lot." I started thinking. "Hey, Gloria, remember when you told me about that bar your brother went to in the Falls?"

Gloria tensed. "Yeah, so?"

"So does he know of any bars like that here in town?" She shrugged. "It's important, Gloria. Honest to god, I really need to know."

Gloria looked nervous. She cleaned her inky hands on her apron as though she wanted to wipe her hands of the whole topic. At lunchtime she pressed a piece of paper into my hand.

"What's this?" The slip of paper had the word *Abba's* written on it.

"I called my brother. I asked him where he goes. He said he used to go there."

I smiled from ear to ear. "Do you know where it is?"

"What do I have to do, drive you there?"

"OK." I put up my hands in surrender. "Just asking."

I called information and got the address. After my shift I washed up in the bathroom and changed into clean clothes. I looked at the ring on my finger. It fit snugly. I pledged to never take it off. Maybe now it was time for the ring to reveal to me the secrets of surviving my own life. I raced downtown to Abba's and then stood outside, pacing and smoking. I was just as scared to go into this bar as I'd been to enter Tifka's. Only this time I was carrying everything I owned in two pillowcases. Where would I go if I was rejected here?

I took a deep breath and walked into Abba's. It was real crowded inside, which made me feel anonymous and safe. I squeezed in at the bar. "A Genny," I called out to the bartender.

She narrowed her eyes. "Let's see some ID."

"They never asked me at Tifka's," I protested.

She shrugged. "So go get a beer at Tifka's," she said as she walked away. I hit the bar with my fist.

"Havin' a hard day, kid?" one of the butches at the bar asked me.

"A hard day?" My laughter sounded shrill. "I got kicked out of school, got no place to live, and I'm gonna lose my goddamn job if I can't find a place to sleep so I can be on time."

She pursed her lips, nodded, and took a swig of her beer. "You can stay at our place for a while if you want," she said casually.

"Are you fucking with me?" I demanded.

She shook her head. "You need a place to stay? My girlfriend and I have an apartment over our garage. You can stay there if you want, it's up to you." She signaled to the bartender. "Meg, get the kid a beer, on me, OK?"

We introduced ourselves. "Jes' what?" she asked.

"Jess, that's my name. Just Jess."

Toni snorted, "Jes' Jess, huh?"

Meg slammed a bottle of beer in front of me. "Thanks for the beer, Toni." I saluted her with the bottle. "Can I move in tonight?"

Toni laughed. "Yeah, I guess so. If I'm not too drunk to get the key in the door. Hey, Betty!"

Toni's girlfriend came out of the bathroom and stood beside her. "Hey, Betty, meet Dondi. This kid's an orphan. Parents died in a flaming car wreck, you know?" Toni laughed and took a swig of beer.

Betty pulled away from Toni. "That's not funny."

I intervened. "Toni said you got a place I could stay. I really need a place to sleep, I mean real bad." Betty looked at Toni, shrugged, and walked away.

"It's OK with her," Toni said. "I'm going back to sit with Betty. I'll find you before we leave."

I finished my beer and put my head down on the bar. The room was spinning and I wanted to sleep so badly. Meg rapped her knuckles on the bar near my head. "You drunk or something?"

"No, I'm just working round the clock," I told her. I didn't think she liked me. Then she brought me another beer.

"I didn't order one."

"It's on the house," she said. Go figure.

As the crowd started thinning out I found an empty chair near the noisy backroom, leaned my head against the wall, and fell asleep. When I awoke, Betty was tugging on my sleeve, telling me it was time to go home. Toni sang "Roll Me Over in the Clover" as Betty tried to get her into the car. I lay down on the back seat and immediately fell asleep again.

"C'mon, wake up," Betty urged me. We were in their driveway. Betty struggled to prop Toni up against the car. "Don't give me two problems to deal with," Betty told me curtly. I got out of the car and helped her get Toni upstairs.

"You can sleep on the couch tonight," Betty said.

"Who's the kid?" Toni demanded to know. "What's this, your new butch?"

"You invited the kid to live in the garage apartment, remember?" Betty snapped.

I curled up on the couch and tried to disappear. After a while Betty came out and threw a blanket over me.

"If I could just get some sleep tonight, I'll be out of here," I told her.

"It's OK," she said wearily. "Don't worry, it'll be alright." I clung to that little bit of reassurance.

Lying there in the dark I started realizing I was on my own: no more school, no more parents—unless they came after me. I gagged on shame as I recalled what happened to me on the football field. I was afraid I was going to throw up and I hadn't asked where their bathroom was. I wished this was Al and Jackie's couch. I wanted to wake up in their home. Then I could tell Jacqueline what had happened to me on the football field. Would I have told her? I realized I might not have told Jackie or Al what the boys did to me. I felt too ashamed.

I made a vow to myself before I fell asleep. I promised myself I would never wear a dress again, and I'd never let anyone rape me ever again, no matter what.

As it turned out, I could only keep one of those promises.

CHAPTER 5

Hey kid, what's up?" Meg called out as she wiped down the bar. Familiar faces softened as they welcomed me. I had become a regular at Abba's.

"Hey, Meg. Gimme a beer, will ya?"

"Sure, kid, coming right up."

I sat down next to Edwina. "Hey, Ed, can I buy you a beer?"

"Yeah," she laughed, "why would I say no?"

It was Friday night. I had money in my pocket and I was feeling fine.

"Hey, what about me?" Butch Jan laughed.

"And a beer for my elder, Meg."

"Hey, watch that elder shit," Jan said.

I felt a hand on my shoulder. Judging from the length of the red-painted nails, it had to be Peaches. "Hi, honey," she kissed me gently on the ear.

I sighed with pleasure. "And a drink for Peaches," I called out to Meg.

"Child, you're in one damn good mood tonight," Peaches said. "You get lucky with some girl or something?"

I blushed. She had hit a sore spot. "I just feel so damn good. I got a job and a motorcycle and friends."

Ed whistled. "You got a bike?"

"Yes," I shouted, "yes, yes! Toni sold me her old Norton. We went out to the supermarket parking lot Sunday, and I practiced till she got mad and went home without me."

Ed smiled. "Wow. Big bike." She slapped my open palm.

"Jesus, Ed, you know what I did after I registered it downtown yesterday? I mean when I actually realized it was mine? I got on that bike and I rode it two hundred miles out and two hundred miles back."

Everyone roared. I nodded. "Something happened to me. I finally felt really free. I'm so excited. I love that bike. I mean, I actually love it. I love that bike so fucking much I can't even explain it." All the butches who rode motorcycles nodded to themselves. Jan and Edwin clapped me on my shoulders.

"Things are lookin up for you, kid. I'm happy for you," Jan said. "Meg, set up another one for young Marlon Brando, here."

The ring must be working! " 'The Avengers' on yet?" I asked.

Meg shook her head. "Fifteen more minutes. God, I can't wait to see what Diana Rigg's wearing this time."

I sighed. "I hope it's that leather jumpsuit again. I think I'm falling in love with her."

Meg laughed. "Get in line."

The place was starting to fill up. A young guy we'd never seen before came in and ordered a gin and tonic. Meg had just placed the glass in front of him when an older guy came in and flipped open a badge. Uniformed cops rushed in behind him. The young guy was a plant.

"You've just served a minor. Alright ladies, gentlemen, leave your drinks on the bar and take out some ID, this is a bust."

Jan and Edwin each grabbed a handful of my shirt and dragged me out the back door. "Out of here, now, get out of here," they were yelling as I fumbled with my motorcycle. A couple of cops fanned out around the parking lot. My legs felt like jelly. I couldn't kick-start the bike.

"Get the fuck out of here," they shouted at me.

Two uniformed cops headed toward me. One reached for his gun. "Off that bike," he ordered.

"C'mon, c'mon," I crooned to myself.

One good kick and the bike roared to life. I popped the clutch and did an unintentional wheelie out of the parking lot. As soon as I got to Toni and Betty's house I banged on their kitchen door. Betty looked alarmed. "What's wrong?"

"The bar, everybody, they're busted."

"Calm down," Toni put her hand on my shoulder. "Calm down and tell us what happened." I sputtered as I described the bust. "How can we find out what happened to everybody?" I asked them.

"We'll find out soon enough, when that phone rings," Betty said. The phone rang.

Betty listened quietly. "Nobody got busted except Meg," she told us. "Butch Jan and Ed got roughed up a little."

I rubbed my forehead with my hand. "Are they hurt bad?" She shrugged. I felt guilty. "I think they got it worse because they got me out of there."

Betty leaned on the kitchen table and held her head in both hands. Toni went to the refrigerator. "Want a beer, kid?"

"Naw, thanks," I told Toni.

"Suit yourself."

Fear nagged at me as I fell asleep that evening. But the real terror didn't surface until I woke up in the middle of the night. I sat bolt upright, soaking wet, remembering the bust at Tifka's. I had grown an inch or two since then. The next time the police got their hands on me, my age wouldn't save me. Fear boiled in the back of my throat. It was going to happen to me. I knew that. But I couldn't change the way I was. It felt like driving toward the edge of a cliff and seeing what's coming but not being able to brake.

I wished Al was around. I wished Jacqueline would tuck me in on their couch, kiss my forehead, and tell me everything would be alright.

The owner of Abba's had been so deeply in debt a couple of years ago that he had to hand carry beer in by the case—the Mob wouldn't allow deliveries until he paid up. So he put out the word that the bar was going gay. He made money hand over fist off us. We were a lucrative and captive market. Usually only one club was open to us at a time. Other owners wanted our business for a while. But Abba's owner got greedy, so the Mob had him busted and shut down.

The new bar was closer to the Tenderloin strip in downtown Buffalo. It was called the Malibou—a jazz bar that would welcome us after the 1:00 A.M. show ended. Organized crime owned the Malibou, too. But a lesbian ran it. We figured that would make a difference. Her name was Gert. She wanted us to call her Aunt Gertie, but it made us feel like a Girl Scout troop—so we called her Cookie.

The new club had a bigger dance floor, but it only had one exit. It did have a pool table, though, and Edwin and I played for hours till the sun came up.

Ed waited for her girlfriend, Darlene, until dawn. Darlene danced nearby at a bar on Chippewa Street. Just down the block from the Malibou was a hotel where a lot of the pros—female and male—used to take their tricks. At dawn all the working girls got off their shift and filled the Malibou, which never seemed to close, or went to a restaurant near the bus station for breakfast.

I began to notice sometimes Ed didn't come in on weekends. What else was there in life besides the plants and the bars?

"Hey, Ed," I asked her one morning. "Where were you last weekend?"

She looked up from the pool shot she was lining up. "At a different club."

Her answer surprised me. There was only one club open at a time, as far as I knew.

"Yeah?" I asked her. "Where?"

"On the East Side," she said, chalking up.

"You mean it's a Negro club?"

"Black," she said as she whacked a high ball and sunk it. "It's a Black club."

I took in all of this new information as Ed lined up her next shot. "Shit," she said as she missed it.

"Is it different from this club?" I asked as I surveyed the table.

"Yes and no." Ed wasn't giving up much this morning.

I shrugged and indicated the far corner. I missed the shot. Ed smiled and patted me on the back. I had a lot of questions, but I didn't know how to ask.

Edwin sunk the eight ball by mistake. "Shit," she hissed, "shit." She looked me up and down. "What?" she demanded. I shrugged.

"Look," she said. "I work all day with these old bulls at the plant. I like coming in here and spending some time with y'all. But I like being with my own people too, you understand? Besides, Darlene and I wouldn't last a month if I hung out on the East Side." I shook my head. I didn't understand.

"Darlene doesn't worry about me being here. If I spent this much time at my own clubs, well, let's just say there'd be too much temptation."

"You hungry?" I asked her.

"Naw, man, I'm just human." She sounded defensive.

I laughed. "No, I mean you wanna get some breakfast?"

She slapped me on the shoulder. "Let's go."

We met Darlene and the other girls at the restaurant. They were all excited, something about a fight with a customer that all the girls jumped into.

"Hey, Ed," I asked her over coffee as Darlene reenacted her role in the brawl, "you think I could go with you some time? I mean, I don't know if it's OK to ask or not."

Ed looked taken aback. "Why? Why you want to go to my club?"

"I don't know, Ed. You're my friend, you know?"

She shrugged. "So?"

"So this morning I realized how much of you I don't know, that's all. I guess I'd like to meet you on your own turf."

Darlene tugged on Ed's sleeve, "Baby, you should have been there. We kicked this guy's ass all the way to kingdom come! He was beggin' us for mercy."

"I've got to think about it. I don't know," Ed said.

"Fair enough. Just asking."

Ed stopped coming to the Malibou soon afterward. I asked Grant what was up, but all she said was that Ed "had a chip on her shoulder" ever since Malcolm X was killed in New York City. I wanted to call Ed and talk to her, but Meg told me not to. She told me the butches at the auto plant said Ed was real angry and it was best to just leave her alone. That didn't feel right to me, but the advice had come down from the old bulls, so I listened.

It was springtime when I finally ran into Ed at the diner. I was so happy to see her I reached out my arms to hug her. She eyed me guardedly, as though examining me for the first time. I feared she wouldn't like what she saw. After a moment she opened her arms to me. Hugging her felt like coming home.

Ed started coming back to the Malibou. Out of the blue one morning she said, "I thought about it."

Funny how I knew exactly what she meant—about me going to the club with her.

"I didn't know how I'd feel about taking you, you know? But next Saturday night is an anniversary party for two women. One of them is white. I don't know, I thought if you wanted to go. . ."

I did. We decided to take Ed's car.

On Saturday night Ed picked me up late. We rode in silence.

"You nervous?" she asked me.

I nodded. She snorted and shook her head. "Maybe this was a mistake."

"No," I told her. "Not for the reasons you think. I'm always scared before I go to a new club, any club. You ever feel that way?"

"No," Edwin said. "Well, yes, maybe. I don't know."

"You nervous, Ed? About going to the club with a white butch, I mean."

"Yeah, maybe a little," she said as she checked the rearview mirror. Ed stopped at a red light and offered me a cigarette. "I like you though, you know."

I looked out the car window and smiled. "I like you too, Ed. A lot."

I realized I'd hung out on the edges of the Black community with friends after school, but I'd never been deep in the heart of the East Side. "Buffalo is like two cities," I said. "I'll bet a lot of white people have never even been to this city."

Ed laughed bitterly and nodded. "Segregation is alive and well in Buffalo. That's it," Ed added, pointing to a building.

"Where?"

"You'll see." Ed parked the car on a nearby side street.

We approached the door. Ed knocked hard. An eye appeared at the peep hole. As the door opened, waves of loud music flowed over us. The joint was packed wall-to-wall. A lot of butches immediately came over to welcome Ed and shook her hand or hugged her shoulders. She gestured toward me and shouted something in their ears, but it was too loud to hear much. Several women beckoned us to share their table and each shook my hand as I sat down. Ed ordered us beers and sat down next to me.

"Daisy's already got her eye on you," Ed yelled in my ear. "The woman sitting directly across the dance floor from us, in the blue dress. She's checking you out."

I smiled at Daisy. She dropped her eyes and then boldly met mine. After a few minutes she whispered something to her girlfriend and stood up. She was wearing blue spike heels that matched her dress. With a steady step, she made her way directly to our table.

"Lord have mercy on your soul, girl," Ed shouted at me as I rose to meet Daisy. Daisy put out her hand and tugged me toward the dance floor. Edwin grabbed my other hand and pulled me down near her ear. "Are you still uptight?" she yelled.

"I'm adjusting," I shouted back over my shoulder.

"I don't believe you back there," Ed said to me hours later as we left the club. "*I'm adjusting,*" she mimicked me with a laugh and punched my shoulder. "Girl, you're just lucky that Daisy's ex wasn't there. She would have kicked your mutherfuckin' white ass."

She was interrupted by a hand on her shoulder that spun her around. I was pushed hard from behind. When I turned I caught a glimpse of a cop car with both doors open. Two cops were pushing us with their nightsticks. "Up against the wall, girls." They pushed us into an alley. Ed put her hand on the back of my shoulder as reassurance.

"Keep your hands to yourself, bulldagger," one cop yelled as he slammed her against the wall.

Even as I was shoved against the brick wall I could still feel the comfort of her hand as it had briefly touched my shoulder.

"Spread your legs, girls. Wider." One of the cops grabbed a handful of my hair and jerked my head backward as he kicked my legs apart with his boot. He took my wallet out of my back pocket and opened it.

I looked over at Ed. The cop was patting her down and running his hands up her thighs. He pulled her wallet out of her pocket, took out the money, and stuffed it in his own pocket.

"Eyes straight ahead," the cop behind me had his mouth close to my ear.

The other cop began shouting at Ed. "You think you're a guy, huh? You think you can take it like a guy? We'll see. What's these?" he said. He yanked up her shirt and pulled her binder down around her waist. He grabbed her breasts so hard she gasped.

"Leave her alone," I yelled.

"Shut up, you fuckin' pervert," the cop behind me shouted and bashed my face against the wall. I saw a kaleidoscope of colors.

Ed and I spun around and looked at each other for a split second. Funny, it seemed as though we had plenty of time to consult. There are times, the old bulls told me, when it's best to take your beating and hope the cops will leave you on the ground when they're done with you. Other times your life may be in danger, or your sanity, and it's worth it to try to fight back. It's a tough call.

In the blink of an eye, Ed and I decided to fight. We each punched and kicked the nearest cop. For just a moment things started looking up for us. I kicked the cop in front of me in the shins over and over again. Ed got the other cop in the groin and was hitting him on the head with both her fists.

As one cop lunged at me, the point of his nightstick caught me squarely in the solar plexus. I crashed against the wall, unable to breath. Then I heard a sickening thud as a nightstick connected with Ed's skull. I vomited. The cops beat us until I found myself wondering through the pain why they weren't exhausted from the effort. Suddenly we heard voices shouting nearby.

"C'mon," one cop said to the other.

Ed and I were on the ground. I could see the boot of the cop standing over me pull back. "You fuckin' traitor," he spat, as his boot cracked my rib for punctuation.

The next thing I remember was light glowing in the sky beyond the alley. The pavement felt cold and hard against my cheek. Ed was lying next to me, her face turned away. I stretched out my fingers to touch her, but I couldn't reach. My hand rested in the pool of blood around her head.

"Ed," I whispered, "Ed, please wake up. Oh god, please don't be dead."

"What," she moaned.

"We got to get out of here, Ed."

"OK," she said, "you pull the car up."

"Don't make me laugh," I told her. "I can hardly breathe." I passed out again.

Darlene told us later that a family on their way to church found us. They got some people to help get us to their home nearby. They didn't take us to the hospital because they didn't know if we were in trouble with the law or not. When Edwin came to, she gave them Darlene's number. Darlene and her friends came and got us. Darlene took care of both of us at their apartment for a week before Ed or I were really coherent.

"Where's Ed, is she OK?" was the first thing I remember asking Darlene.

"That's the first thing she asked me—how you were," Darlene answered. "Alive. You're both alive, you stupid motherfuckers."

Neither of us ever saw an emergency room doctor for fear they'd call the cops to see if we were in any trouble. When Ed and I could sit up and even walk a little, we began recuperating in the living room together during the days while Darlene slept. The couch opened up as a bed.

Ed gave me *The Ballot and the Bullet* by Malcolm X. She encouraged me to read W.E.B. Du Bois and James Baldwin. But we each had a headache so bad we could hardly read the newspaper. All day long we lay next to each other and watched television: "Get Smart," "The Beverly Hillbillies," "Green Acres." We healed in spite of it.

Ed got disability pay during her absence. I lost my job as a printer.

When Ed and I finally showed up at the Malibou a month later, someone pulled the plug on the jukebox and everyone rushed up to hug us. "No, wait, gently," we shouted, both backing up toward the door. "Notice the resemblance?" I asked, as Ed and I put our faces near each other. We had matching gashes over our right eyebrows.

Speaking for myself, I lost a lot of confidence after that beating. The pain in my rib cage reminded me with every breath how vulnerable I really was.

I propped myself up at a back table and watched all my friends dancing together. It felt good to be back home. Peaches sat down next to me, draped her arm around my shoulders, and planted a long sweet kiss on my cheek.

Cookie offered me a job as bouncer on the weekends. I held my ribs and winced.

She said I could wait on tables until I healed, if I wanted to. I sure needed the money.

I watched Justine, a stunning drag queen, going from table to table with an empty Maxwell House coffee can, collecting money.

She came over to the table where Peaches and I were sitting and began counting out the bills. "You don't have to contribute, darlin'."

"What's it for?" I asked.

"For your new suit," she answered, and continued counting the bills.

"Whose new suit?"

"Your new suit, honey. You can't expect to be Master of Ceremonies of the Monte Carlo Night Drag Show Extravaganza in that tacky old outfit, do you?" I looked bewildered.

"We're taking you out and buying you a new suit," Peaches explained. "You're going to emcee the drag show next month."

"That's what I just told you," Justine sounded annoyed.

"I don't know how to be an emcee."

"Don't worry, darlin' " Justine laughed, "you're not the star."

Peaches threw her head back. "We are!"

"But you are going to look divine," Justine said, waving a wad of bills.

I had heard horror stories about butches and their femmes trying to shop for a suit at Kleinhan's clothing store. But this time Kleinhan's was in for some discomfort as three powerful queens in full drag helped me pick it out.

"No," Justine shook her head emphatically. "She's an emcee, not a fucking undertaker."

"Earth tones," Georgetta turned my face in her hands, "because of her coloring."

"No, no, no," Peaches said, "this is it." She held up a dark blue gabardine suit.

"Yes," Justine sighed as I came out of the dressing room. "Yes!"

"Ooh, honey, I just might swing for you," Georgetta exclaimed.

Peaches fussed with my lapels. "Yes, yes, yes."

"We'll take it," Georgetta told the salesman, who looked visibly annoyed. "Tailor it for the child. And make it look nice!"

The salesman pulled the tape measure from around his neck and tried to chalk the trousers and jacket without touching me. Finally he straightened up. "You can pick it up in one week," he announced.

"We can pick it up today," Georgetta declared. "We'll just walk around the store trying things on till it's ready.

"No," the salesman blurted. "Come back in two hours. Just leave now. Just leave."

"We'll be back in an hour, darlin'," Justine said over her shoulder.

"See you." Georgetta blew him a kiss.

"C'mon." Peaches waved for me to follow. "It's our turn." They steered me toward the store next door. We were headed for the lingerie department.

I shook my head. "I gotta use the bathroom. God, I wish I could wait, but I can't."

Justine touched my cheek. "Sorry, darlin'."

Peaches drew herself up to her full height. "C'mon. We'll all go in together with her."

"No," I held up both hands. "I'm afraid we'll all get busted." My bladder ached. I wished I hadn't waited so long. I took a deep breath and pushed open the door to the women's bathroom.

Two women were freshening their makeup in front of the mirror. One glanced at the other and finished applying her lipstick. "Is that a man or a woman?" she said to her friend as I passed them.

The other woman turned to me. "This is the women's bathroom," she informed me.

I nodded. "I know."

I locked the stall door behind me. Their laughter cut me to the bone. "You don't really know if that's a man or not," one woman said to the other. "We should call security and make sure."

I flushed the toilet and fumbled with my zipper in fear. Maybe it was just an idle threat. Maybe they really would call security. I hurried out of the bathroom as soon as I heard both women leave.

"You OK, darlin'?" Justine asked. I nodded. She smiled. "You took ten years off those girls' lives."

I forced myself to smile. "Naw. They never would have made fun of a guy like that. I was afraid they might call the cops on me. They took ten years off my life."

"C'mon." Peaches impatiently tugged on my sleeve. "It's high femme time." She dragged me toward the lingerie department.

"What do you think?" Georgetta held up a red silk nightie.

"Black," I told her. "That black lace one."

"Lord, this boy's got taste," she said.

Peaches sighed. "It's funny, seeing you trying on that suit, all excited and everything. I remember my father making me buy a suit for Sunday service. When I dreamed of dressing up, child, it wasn't no suit. I'll tell you that much. I dreamt about something, you know, tasteful—with spaghetti straps. Kinda low cut," she drew a finger across her bodice. "I felt like a ballerina in a three-piece suit."

Georgetta snorted. "More like a fairy." Peaches threw back her head and dragged me away.

We went back to Kleinhan's an hour later. The suit was ready.

"We have enough money left over to pick out a shirt and tie," Georgetta announced.

Justine held up a powder blue dress shirt. It was more beautiful than any shirt my father ever owned. The buttons were sky blue with white swirls, like clouds. Peaches and Georgetta settled on a burgundy silk tie.

The salesmen held their heads in their hands as though they all had headaches. Well, better them than us.

"I can't thank you all enough," I told them.

"Yes you can, honey. You best pick me as the winner of that drag show."

"She can see I'm the fairest of them all."

"Oh, please child, don't make me laugh."

I held up both my hands. "Wait," I protested, "you never told me I was going to judge the drag show."

"Well, darlin'," Justine smiled, "it's a month away. Don't you worry your handsome little head about it."

The month passed quickly. I tried to avoid all the squabbles between contestants over how the show should be run. I arrived at the Malibou a little late the night of the show. I took off my helmet and sat on my Norton in the back parking lot, smoking a cigarette.

"Child, where have you been?" Peaches demanded as she rocked from side to side in her high heels on the gravel.

"I'm coming," I shouted, grinding out my cigarette. "I'll be right there."

Everyone stopped and stared as I walked in the door. "You look good enough to eat," Peaches said, smoothing my lapels.

Georgetta clasped her hands in front of her. "I think I'm falling in love."

"Yeah, she says that after every blow job," Justine muttered.

Cookie went over the program with me. I chewed at my thumbnail as she spoke. I'd spent my whole life wishing I could be invisible. How was I going to climb up on a stage, with a spotlight on me? When I got up on the runway it was dark in the club. After the spotlight hit me, I could hardly see the crowd.

"Sing something," one of the butches shouted out.

"What do I look like, fucking Bert Parks?" I yelled back. "OK," I began to sing, "Here she comes, Mis-cell-an-eous."

"Boo!"

"Listen up now," I pleaded, "this is serious."

"This ain't serious, this is a drag show," someone yelled.

"Yeah," I said. "This is serious." I realized what I wanted to say. "You know, all our lives they've told us the way we are isn't right."

I heard some murmurs, "Yeah!"

"Well, this is our home. We're family."

There was a ripple of applause from the audience. "You're goddamn right," one of the drag queens behind me shouted.

"So tonight we're going to celebrate the way we are. It's not only OK, it's beautiful. And I want you all to make our gorgeous sisters in this show feel how much we love and respect them." The crowd roared in approval. Justine and Peaches ran out and kissed me and then ran backstage to await their cues.

I flipped through the index cards Cookie had given me. "Will you please welcome tonight, Miss Diana Ross, singing 'Stop in the Name of Love.' " The music swelled, and I stepped aside.

Peaches' dress shimmered as the spotlight illuminated her. What a breath-takingly beautiful human being.

"Stop in the name of love," she grabbed a fistful of my tie as she sang, "before you break my heart." Her lips were close to mine. I gasped, caught up in the power of her performance.

The applause was thunderous.

"Get the kid a towel," someone yelled as I wiped my forehead with the back of my hand.

"Will you please welcome Miss Barbara Lewis, singing 'Hello Stranger.' "

Justine walked straight toward me—slow, absolutely steady on her spike heels as the music rose. "Hello stranger," she draped one arm over my shoulder, "it seems like a mighty long time." I could get to like this.

The next performer was Georgetta's boyfriend, Booker. I'd never seen Booker try on drag before. Even in a dress I still thought of Booker as *he.* Booker was also doing "Stop in the Name of Love." Georgetta peeked out from behind the stage wall to watch. "Wouldn't you just know it," she whispered to me. "You think you married a real man and you find out you've got a sister who borrows your lipstick and won't return it." I chuckled.

"Lord have mercy," she said, "that girl's in trouble." The strap on Booker's dress slipped down every time he lifted his arm to sing "Stop!" It could have been very sexy, but he was so nervous he kept trying to hike up the strap.

"Help her," Georgetta said to me.

I handed Georgetta the mike and walked out on stage in front of Booker. I got down on one knee in front of him and pretended he was singing to me. Then I circled behind him and pulled down his strap seductively. "Leave it," I whispered, as I kissed his shoulder. Booker pushed me away dramatically, singing, *Before you break my heart.* The crowd roared its approval. Everybody was really enjoying the way Booker was pulling off this act.

None of us saw the red light flashing.

The music died and everyone groaned. Then the police flooded into the club. I held my hand up to shield my eyes from the spotlight, but I still I couldn't see what was happening. I heard shouting and tables and chairs overturning. I remembered there was only one door—there was no escape this time. At sixteen years old I was still underage.

I slowly took off my new blue suit coat, folded it neatly, and put it on the piano at the back of the stage. For a moment I considered taking off my tie, thinking somehow it might go easier for me if I did. But, of course, it wouldn't have. In fact, the tie made me feel stronger in order to face whatever lay ahead of me. I rolled up my sleeves and stepped off the stage. A cop grabbed me and cuffed my hands tightly behind my back. Another cop was smacking Booker, who was sobbing.

The police van was backed right up to the door of the club. The cops roughed us up as they shoved us in. Some of the drag queens bantered nervously on the way to the precinct, making jokes to relieve the tension. I rode in silence.

We were all put together in one huge holding cell. My cuffed hands felt swollen and cold from lack of circulation. I waited in the cell. Two cops opened the door. They were laughing and talking to themselves. I wasn't listening. "What do you want, a fucking invitation? Now!" one of them commanded.

"C'mon, Jesse," a cop taunted me, "let's have a pretty smile for the camera. You're such a pretty girl. Isn't she pretty, guys?" They snapped my mug shot. One of the cops loosened my tie. As he ripped open my new dress shirt, the sky blue buttons bounced and rolled across the floor. He pulled up my T-shirt, exposing my breasts. My hands were cuffed behind my back. I was flat up against a wall.

"I don't think she likes you, Gary," another cop said. "Maybe she'd like me better." He crossed the room. My knees were wobbling. *Lt. Mulroney,* that's what his badge read. He saw me looking at it and slapped me hard across the face. His hand clamped on my face like a vise. "Suck my cock," he said quietly.

There wasn't a sound in the room. I didn't move. No one said anything. I almost got the feeling it could stay that way, all action frozen, but it didn't. Mulroney was fingering his crotch. "Suck my cock, bulldagger." Someone hit the side of my knee with a nightstick. My knees buckled more from fear than pain. Mulroney grabbed me by the collar and dragged me several feet away to a steel toilet. There was a piece of unflushed shit floating in the water. "Either eat me or eat my shit, bulldagger. It's up to you." I was too frightened to think or move.

I held my breath the first time he shoved my head in the toilet. The second time he held me under so long I sucked in water and felt the hard shape of the shit against my tongue. When Mulroney pulled my head back out of the toilet I spewed vomit all over him. I gagged and retched over and over again.

"Aw shit, fuck, get her out of here," the cops yelled to each other as I lay heaving.

"No," Mulroney said, "handcuff her over there, on top of the desk."

They lifted me and threw me on my back across the desk and handcuffed my hands over my head. As one cop pulled off my trousers I tried to calm the spasms in my stomach so I wouldn't choke to death on my own vomit.

"Aw, ain't that cute, BVD's," one cop called out to another. "Fuckin' pervert."

I looked at the light on the ceiling, a large yellow bulb burning behind a metal mesh. The light reminded me of the endless stream of television westerns I saw after we moved up north. Whenever anyone was lost in the desert the only image shown was a glaring sun—all the beauty of the desert reduced to that one impression. Staring at that jail light bulb rescued me from watching my own degradation: I just went away.

I found myself standing in the desert. The sky was streaked with color. Every shift of light cast a different hue across the wilderness: salmon, rose, lavender. The scent of sage was overpowering. Even before I saw the golden eagle gliding in the updraft above me, I heard it scream, as clearly as if it had come from my own throat. I longed to soar in flight with the eagle, but I felt rooted to the earth. The mountains rose to meet me. I walked toward them, seeking sanctuary, but something held me back.

"Fuck it," Mulroney spat. "Turn her over, her cunt's too fuckin' loose."

"Jeez Lieutenant, how come these fuckin' bulldaggers don't fuck men and they got such big cunts?"

"Ask your wife," Mulroney said. The other cops laughed.

I panicked. I tried to return to the desert but I couldn't find that floating opening between the dimensions I'd passed through before. An explosion of pain in my body catapulted me back.

I was standing on the desert floor again, but this time the sands had cooled. The sky was overcast, threatening to storm. The air pressure was unbearable. It was hard to breathe. From a distance I heard the eagle scream again. The sky was growing as dark as the mountains. Wind blew through my hair.

I closed my eyes and turned my face up to the desert sky. And then, finally, it released—the welcome relief of warm rain down my cheeks.

CHAPTER 6

The ring was gone. The only tangible proof it had ever existed were the blood blisters on my ring finger; the cops must have pried it off while my hands were cuffed and swollen. The ring was gone. I sat in my apartment and stared out the window. I couldn't tell how long I'd been awake.

Justine and Peaches had bailed me out. I recalled they told me there were no charges filed against any of us. Justine wanted to come upstairs with me when I got home, but I was adamant: I wanted to be alone.

The first thing I did was take a bath. I put my head back and tried to luxuriate in the tub. Then I noticed the water turning deeper shades of pink and a current of red water between my legs. I instantly recalled the feel of the hard piece of shit against my tongue and I climbed out of the bathtub in a panic, just making it to the toilet in time.

Now I was tranquil. I didn't feel much of anything at all. But even through this blessed serenity I grieved for the ring that would have protected me, or at least offered me its wisdom. The ring was gone. There was nothing to hope for now. The ring was gone.

Betty knocked on the door and let herself in. She noticed the plate of fried chicken she'd brought me last night was untouched. The chicken looked like human limbs, and

I couldn't bring myself to bite into flesh. The thought had sent me flying into the bathroom, retching.

"I brought you some apple pie," Betty said. She had bright yellow calico in her hands. "I thought I'd make some curtains for this window, if that's OK?" I'd lived without curtains since I'd moved in more than six months ago. I nodded. Betty began to sew. From time to time she glanced up at me. I knew she had probably been sewing in my room for several hours when she stood to iron the curtains, but it seemed like seconds.

The curtains were real pretty, but my face wouldn't move, even to smile. Betty came over and sat down near me. "You should eat something," she said. I looked up to acknowledge I'd heard her. She moved toward the front door to leave and then stopped. "I know," she said. "You don't think anyone knows. You can't believe anyone would understand. But I do know." I shook my head slowly—she didn't know.

Betty knelt down in front of me. As we made eye contact I felt a sudden jolt of emotional electricity. I saw everything I was feeling in Betty's eyes, as though I were looking at my own reflection. I looked away in horror. Betty nodded and squeezed my knee. "I do know," she said, getting up to leave. "I do understand."

I didn't move from the couch. Darkness settled over the room. There was another knock at the door. I wished everyone would go away and leave me alone.

Peaches came in, dressed to kill. "My date was a dud," she said, and went into the kitchen. A moment later she brought out two pints of vanilla ice cream with a spoon sticking out of each. She sat down next to me on the couch and offered me one. The ice cream tasted so sweet and cool going down my throat it made my eyes sting with tears.

Peaches stroked my hair. I was thinking about how the world looks when it's buried in deep snow drifts—every twig and telephone line outlined with inches of snow, sparkling in the moonlight. Silent and still. Muffled. That's how the world seemed to me now. I wished I could tell Peaches or Betty how peaceful I felt, but I couldn't speak.

"You're afraid to sleep, aren't you child?" Peaches' voice was so soft. "But Miss Peaches is here with you now. You gonna sleep safe in her arms tonight. I won't let anything hurt you."

She disappeared into the bedroom. A moment later she came out and led me to my bed. She'd changed the sheets; they were fresh and clean. She put me down like a child and lay next to me. I could taste vomit rise in my throat, but she gently pulled me to her body. My lips found the curve of her breast. "That's hormones made them swell up like that, but they're mine now." She kissed my hair.

She sang a song in a voice so satiny smooth that I trusted the sound and followed it right into sleep.

Edwin brought over my blue suit coat. She found the matching trousers in a pile by my bathroom door and took them both to the dry cleaners for me.

When I didn't show up at the Malibou the next Friday, Ed and Georgetta and Peaches came by and picked me up. Cookie threw me a towel when I arrived and told me to start waiting on tables. I moved in numbness for several weeks, unable to feel the sensation of temperature, hot or cold. The world seemed distant.

One night at work a guy beckoned me over to his table and told me to take the french fries back to the kitchen. He said they were cold. I took them to Cookie, but she said she was too busy. I brought the french fries back to the guy and apologized. He picked up a glass of water and poured its contents all over the french fries. "They're cold," he said.

He opened a traveling case, pulled out a huge snake, and coiled it around his neck. And then he bit off a chunk of the water glass and chewed it. "The french fries are cold," he repeated.

"Cookie," I yelled as I skidded into the kitchen. "Give me some hot french fries, and I mean now!" She started to protest. "Now, goddamn it. I want them now!"

The guy left me a great tip.

"You didn't know who that guy was?" Booker doubled over laughing. Everyone chuckled. "That was Razor Man. He performs at a club near here."

I threw down my towel. "This job is fucked up," I protested, but even I started to smile.

"What's so funny?" Toni said behind me. I turned around to explain, but her face was all twisted up in anger. "I said, what's so goddamn funny?" she demanded.

One of the butches tried to pull her back, "Come on Toni, blow it off."

She yanked free and staggered toward me. "You think you're funny?"

"What the hell, Toni," I said, flustered.

A group of pros came in the door and I started to walk over to say hello, but Toni spun me around. "You think I don't know what's going on with you and my femme?"

Everyone sucked in their breath. I felt stunned. "Toni, what the hell are you talking about?"

"You think I don't know, don't you?"

Betty started toward Toni, but Angie, one of the pros who had just walked in, held her back.

"Step outside you chickenshit bastard." Toni spat on the floor.

I sure as hell didn't want to fight Toni, so I went outside to talk to her. Everyone followed me out to listen. "Toni," I appealed to her.

"Shut up and fight, you fuckin' bastard. Come on, you chickenshit son-of-a-bitch."

"Look, Toni," I said, "if you want to hit me, you go ahead. If it'll make you feel better, I won't stop you. But why would I want to hit you? You helped me out when I needed it. You know damn well I'd never disrespect you or Betty."

I caught Betty's eye and she looked at me apologetically. "Don't you be looking at my femme, you motherfucker!" Toni sputtered.

"Toni, I'm telling you I wouldn't do anything, ever, to disrespect you."

"Get out of my fucking house," she yelled at me. She was reeling. "Get out!"

Angie was behind me. "C'mon, baby." She tugged on my arm. "It's only gonna get worse out here. C'mon," she said, pulling me back into the bar.

Grant and Edwin offered to help me pack up my stuff and bring it back. "Hell," I told them, "I still only need a couple of pillowcases for all my stuff. I can bring it back on the bike."

When I got back to the club with my things, I found a stool at the end of the bar and nursed a beer. Angie sat down next to me. "You got a place to stay tonight?" She stubbed out her cigarette. I shook my head. "Look," she patted my arm. "I'm tired, I want to go home and to bed—to sleep. You need a place to sack out for the night, fine. Just don't get any funny ideas."

"You been turning tricks all night?" I asked her.

Angie eyed me distrustfully. "Yeah."

"Then why on earth would I think you were dying for someone to take you home and fuck you?"

Angie tossed back her whiskey and laughed. "C'mon, baby, I'll buy you breakfast for that one."

"Tell me the truth," Angie said as she buttered her toast. "No bullshit. How come you didn't fight her? Was it really cause she's your friend or were you scared?"

I shook my head. "She's not like my best friend or anything, but she helped me out a lot. I don't want to hit her, that's all. She was drunk."

Angie smirked at me. "So were you fuckin' around with Betty?"

I shook my head. "I don't play that game."

She watched my face as she poked her eggs with a fork. "How old are you, baby?"

"How old were you when you were my age?" I felt annoyed.

She leaned back against the booth. "I guess the streets made us old before our time, huh, kid?"

"I'm not a kid." My voice sounded hard.

"I'm sorry," she sounded like she meant it. "You're right, you aren't a kid."

I yawned and rubbed my eyes. She laughed. "Am I keeping you up?"

Angie glanced over at an older pro who was paying her check at the register. "You know," she told me, "when I was a little girl I remember being in a restaurant with my mother and stepfather and I saw a woman who looked something like her."

"She's beautiful, isn't she?" I said.

Angie looked at me and cocked her head. "You like tough women, don't you, butch?" I smiled and stabbed my eggs with my fork.

"I remember," Angie continued, "my stepfather said, 'Dirty, filthy whore,' right out loud as the woman paid her bill. Everyone in the restaurant heard him say it. But that woman just paid her bill and took a toothpick and walked out real slow, like she never heard him at all. *That's gonna be me when I grow up,*" I thought.

I nodded. "That's like the time I was about fourteen and I saw this he-she." Angie rested her chin on the heel of her hand as she listened. "I'd forgotten about this. My parents dragged me along while they shopped. You know how crowded and loud the stores are before Christmas? All of a sudden, everything got real quiet. The cash registers stopped ringing and nobody moved. Everybody was staring at the jewelry department. There's this couple—a he-she and a femme. All they were doing was looking at rings, you know?" Angie sat back and exhaled slowly. "Everyone was glaring at them. The pressure just popped those two women out the door like corks. I wanted to run out after them and beg them to take me with them. And all the while I was thinking, *Oh shit, that's gonna be me.*"

Angie shook her head. "It's tough when you see it coming, ain't it?"

"Yeah," I said, "it's like driving on a single-lane highway and seeing an eighteen-wheeler heading right for you."

She winced. "C'mon," she told me, "I got to get some sleep."

Angie's apartment was more like a home than mine had been. "I like that kind of material you got for curtains in the kitchen." I asked her, "What do you call that?"

"Muslin," she said. She got two bottles out of the refrigerator. "Listen, if you need a place, this apartment might be available—very, very soon, if you know what I mean."

I cocked my head. "Like tomorrow?"

She laughed. "Maybe sooner, who knows?"

I drank my beer and lit a cigarette. I threw the pack on the kitchen table. Angie took one and sat down across from me. "I'm gonna be in a little trouble soon, you know?" I nodded. "So, if you want this place, it's cheap."

"You know," I told her, "I don't even know how to pay bills, or how any of that works. I never lived any place except for Toni and Betty's."

Angie rested her hand on my arm. "I'm gonna give you a piece of advice—you don't have to take it. Get yourself a factory job so you don't end up spending your whole life in the bars. Life in the Tenderloin's like lickin' a razor blade, you know what I mean? I'm not saying the plants are heaven, or anything, but maybe you can get into a plant with the other butches, pay your bills, settle down with a girl."

I shrugged. "I know I got some growing up to do."

Angie smiled and shook her head. "No, baby. I'm talking about staying young. I don't want you to have to grow up too fast. I got old the night I first got busted—I was thirteen. The cop kept yelling at me to give him a blow job and he beat the shit out of me when I didn't. I just didn't know what he meant by a blow job. It wasn't like I'd never had to do it before."

I got up and walked over to the sink. I felt like I was going to throw up. Angie got up and put her hands on my shoulders, "I'm sorry, that was a stupid story to tell anybody." I couldn't turn around and face her. "C'mon, baby, come sit down," she tugged on me gently. "You're OK," she said as she turned me around. "Are you OK?" I smiled at her, but it wasn't convincing. She ran her fingers through my hair. "You're not OK, are you?"

I was so relieved she said it out loud that I started to cry. She held me against her shoulder and rocked me. She pushed me back against the sink and looked at my face, "You want to talk?" I shook my head. "OK," she whispered, "it's OK. It's just, sometimes it's good to talk about stuff." She held my chin in her hand. I tried to pull my face away, but she wouldn't let me. "You know," she said, "maybe it's a little bit easier for femmes to talk to each other about this stuff than it is for butches, what do you think?" I shrugged my shoulders. I felt trapped and sick.

"Who hurt you, baby? The cops?" She watched my face. "Who else?" she concluded out loud. "Aw, baby, you're already old, too," she crooned as she held me tightly against her. I buried my face in the safety of her neck. "C'mere baby, sit down." She pulled a kitchen chair up next to me.

"I'm OK," I said.

"Uh-uh. You're not talking to the butches now. Do you open up to your girlfriend?"

"I don't have a girlfriend," I reluctantly admitted.

Angie looked surprised, which made me feel flattered. Then she smiled coyly. "Have you ever opened up to a girlfriend?"

I felt like a pinned down butterfly. "I. . ."

She shook her head and looked me in the eye. "You never had a girlfriend?" I looked down at my lap in embarrassment. "How did a good-looking young butch like you ever escape all those hungry femmes out there?" she teased me, lifting my chin. "How many times you been busted, baby?"

I shrugged. "A couple."

She nodded, "It gets harder when you know what's coming, doesn't it?" I let her see into my eyes. "Baby," she sat on my lap. She pulled my face against her breasts. "Baby, I'm sorry they hurt you. But more than anything, I'm sorry you got no place to go with it. Bring it to me now. It's OK." She held me inside her warmth. Without words I told her everything I felt. Without saying anything she let me know she understood.

Then my lips brushed against her breast and a sound escaped her throat. We looked at each other, startled. She had a frightened, frozen look on her face, like a deer caught in headlights. That's when I realized sex is very powerful.

Angie took a handful of my hair in her fist and pulled my head back slowly. She brought her mouth close to mine, until I could feel the warmth of her breath. A grunting sound came from my throat. Angie smiled. She pulled my head back further and ran her fingernails lightly down my throat. I ached from my waist to my knees.

She kissed me with her whole mouth. I used to think it was disgusting that adults licked each other's tongues. I figured it might not even be true. But what Angie's tongue was doing to mine set my whole body on fire. I strained to take more of her tongue with mine.

Suddenly she pulled my head back again and looked at me with a strange, wild look on her face. I felt scared, and she must have realized it because she smiled and pulled me closer. My hands kneaded her waist and my lips found her hardened nipple.

Without a word she stood up and took me by the hand. In her bedroom she kissed me, pushed me away, looked at me, and kissed me again.

Her hand slid down my waist to my crotch and I pulled away. "You're not packing?" she asked. I didn't know what that meant. "It's OK," she said, going to her dresser drawer. She muttered to herself, "If I don't have a harness in here, I'm going to kill myself."

I realized she was looking for a dildo. I couldn't remember anything Al had taught me—not a word. All I remembered was Jacqueline's warning: *You could make a woman feel real good with it or you could make her remember all the ways she's ever been hurt.*

"What's the matter, baby?" Angie asked. We both looked down at the dildo and the harness in her hands. Angie's face passed through a series of expressions I couldn't read. "It's OK," she said as I started to turn away. "C'mere, baby," she coaxed me. Angie turned me around, "I'll show you how."

Those were the most comforting words I ever heard.

She went over to the radio and turned the dial until she heard Nat King Cole's silky voice singing "Unforgettable." She came into my arms. "Dance with me, baby. You know how to make me feel good. Feel how I'm following you?" she whispered in my ear. "That's what I want you to do for me when we fuck. I want you to slow dance with me. I want you to follow me like I'm following you. C'mere."

She tossed the dildo aside, lay down on the mattress, and pulled me on top of her. "Listen to the music. Feel how I'm moving? Move with me," she said. I did. She taught me a new dance. When that song ended another slow song came on, the one from the movie with Humphrey Bogart—*Casablanca.* When it got to the part where the man sang, *Woman needs man and man must have his mate,* we laughed together.

Angie rolled me over and began unbuttoning my shirt, leaving my T-shirt on. She got up on her knees and slowly fingered the button on my pants. She slid my pants off but left on my BVD's. I struggled to slip on the harness and the dildo. Angie pushed me back on the pillow and took the rubber cock in both her hands. The way she touched it mesmerized me. "Feel how I'm touching you?" she whispered with a smile. She ran her nails down the sides of my T-shirt and up my thighs. Her mouth was very near my cock. "If you're going to fuck me with this," she said, stroking it, "then I want you to feel it. This is an act of sweet imagination." She took the head of the cock in her lips and began to move her mouth up and down the length of it.

When she finally spoke, *Now* was all she said.

Angie rolled over on her back as I fumbled with her clothing. I touched her with an adolescent's lack of grace. At first I thought she was being very patient about it. Then I wondered if my clumsiness allowed her to be more excited with me than she could have been if I was experienced. When I was fearful or unsure, she became more present in our lovemaking, encouraging me. When I got excited like a colt, she guided me back under control.

No amount of advice I'd ever received from the older butches, however, prepared me for the moment when I knelt between Angie's legs and had no idea of what to do. "Wait," she said, pressing her fingertips against my thighs, "let me." She gently guided the cock inside of herself. "Wait," she repeated, "don't push. Be gentle. Let me get used to you inside of me before you move."

I carefully lay on top of Angie. After a moment her body relaxed against me. "Yes," Angie said as I moved with her, following her lead. I found if I tried to think about what I was doing, I lost the rhythm of her body. So I stopped thinking. "Yes." She grew more excited. Angie became wilder in my arms. It scared me, I didn't know what was happening. Suddenly she started to cry out and yanked my hair. I stopped moving. There was a long pause. Her body slumped beneath me. One of her arms flopped over her head against the pillow in annoyance. "Why did you stop?" she asked quietly.

"I thought I was hurting you."

"Hurting me?" Her voice rose a bit. "Haven't you ever?" She stopped mid-sentence. "Sweetheart," she said to me, searching my face for the truth, "have you ever been with a woman before?"

So much blood pumped into my face that the room spun around. I turned away from her, but I was still inside of her. "Wait," she said putting her hands firmly on my ass. "Pull out of me gently, careful, ah, OK."

Angie got up slowly and brought back a pack of cigarettes, matches, an ashtray, and a bottle of whiskey. "I'm sorry," she said. I turned away from her. "Listen to me, Jess. I'm sorry. I didn't know you'd never been with a woman before. The first time should be special. It's sort of a big responsibility, you know? C'mere, baby," she pulled me against her. I lay quietly in her arms. Billie Holiday was singing on the radio. We both felt how close my mouth was to her breast at the same moment, and something flared between us.

"Roll over," she told me. I did. "Relax. I won't hurt you." She straddled my waist and began to massage my shoulders through my T-shirt. I could feel the strength of the muscles in her thighs. I rolled over and she stayed over me. I reached up for her face and pulled her down to kiss me.

She gave me another chance. I did better that time.

We held each other for a long time without speaking. Then she laughed. "That," she said, "was great. That was really wonderful." It was so nice of her to say that. She guided me out of her slowly, then kissed me all over my face and made me laugh. "You're really very sweet," she told me, "you know that?"

I blushed, which made her laugh and kiss me all over my flushed face again.

"You really are pretty," I told her. She made a face and leaned over for a cigarette. I shook my head. "How come you make your living from your looks and you don't know how beautiful you are?"

"That's why," she laughed bitterly. "Whatever it is they find attractive, you figure it must be pretty ugly. You know?" I didn't, but I nodded.

"Will you respect me in the morning?" she demanded.

"Will you marry me?" I asked her.

We both laughed and hugged each other, but the sad thing is, I think we were each kind of serious.

Angie looked at me long and hard. "What?" I was worried. "What?"

She ran her hands through my hair. "I just wish I could make you feel that good. You're stone already, aren't you?" I dropped my eyes. She lifted my chin up and looked me in the eyes. "Don't be ashamed of being stone with a pro, honey. We're in a stone profession. It's just that you don't have to get stuck in being stone, either. It's OK if you find a femme you can trust in bed and you want to say that you need something, or you want to be touched. Do you know what I mean?"

I shrugged. She kept talking. "I remember when I was a little kid, I saw a bunch of the older kids in a circle in the playground. I went over to see what they were doing." I got up on one elbow to listen. "There was this big beetle. The kids were poking it with a stick. The bug just kind of curled up to protect itself." She snorted, "God knows I been poked with enough sticks." I kissed her on the forehead.

"God," she said, "by the time we're old enough to have sex, we're already too ashamed to be touched. Ain't that a crime?" I shrugged.

"Will you trust me a little?" she asked. I tensed. "I won't touch you any place you've been hurt, I promise. Turn over, baby," she whispered.

She lifted the back of my T-shirt. "God, your back looks like raw hamburger. Did I do that to you?" I laughed. "God, it's bleeding a little. Did I hurt you?" I shook my head. "What a butch," she laughed. Angie's hands rubbed all the soreness out of my shoulders and lower back. She slid her nails down my back and sides, and soon her mouth followed the same trail. I clenched the pillowcase in my fists. I knew it pleased her that I writhed under her touch.

As her hand ran up my thigh, I froze. "I'm sorry, baby, it's OK," she reassured me. I rolled over and she came into my arms. "Usually it's me that reacts like that," she said. "It's strange. It's like being on the other side of the looking glass, you know?" I didn't, but I could feel myself drift irresistibly toward sleep.

"Sleep now, baby," Angie cooed in my ear. "You're safe here."

"Angie," I asked her as I slipped into sleep, "will you be here when I wake up?"

"Sleep now, baby," she answered.

CHAPTER 7

It was time to find a factory job. The butches urged me to try to get into steel or auto. Of course I already knew that. I wasn't a damn fool. The strength of the unions in those heavy industries had won liveable wages and decent benefits.

But Edwin said there was more to it than that. The trade unions safeguarded job security. She told me that unlike a nonunion shop if she had a run-in with a jerk on the plant floor, it didn't signal her last day on the job. You couldn't be fired just because some foreman didn't like your face. With union protection, all the butches agreed, a he-she could carve out a niche, and begin earning valuable seniority.

In the meantime, while I was waiting for an opening, I had to work through the temporary labor agencies at minimum wage. In early autumn the agency sent me to a one-day job on the loading docks of a frozen food plant. My heart leaped when I saw Grant walking into the factory ahead of me. I caught up to her and shook her hand.

Unloading trucks on the docks was male turf. It meant a lot to have another butch watch your back. Grant dug her gloved hands deep inside the pockets of her blue Navy coat. "Brrr," she shivered. "I'm freezin' my ass off out here, let's get inside." Then she sauntered very slowly toward the loading docks. She never hurried. She was so cool.

One of the truckers shouted, "He-shes at high noon!" Several guys peered out from inside the plant and shook their heads in disgust. It was going to be a long shift. I was glad we walked slowly, like we owned the god damn parking lot.

We climbed up on the dock. The foreman came out to look us over. Grant took off her glove and extended her hand. At first the foreman looked like he wasn't going to shake her hand, but he did. What little respect Grant got, she earned.

The afternoon was waning. The sun dipped low in the winter sky. A brutal wind blew off the frozen lake. The huge semi we were unloading served to block the wind, but not the cold. I shivered. We were told we would unload two of these long, long trucks during the shift. We both nodded. Personally, I had my doubts.

We worked in silence with two guys. Neither of the men spoke a word to us. They hardly spoke to each other. When Grant and I had to get around the men, we all dropped our eyes. It was harder to bear than a storm of insults.

The cartons of frozen food weren't as heavy as I thought, not for the first three or four hours. After that, they felt like they were filled with cold steel. My muscles ached and burned. I felt elated as the truck load emptied. I worked faster. Grant slowed me down with a well-intentioned glare. I had forgotten another semi was coming until I saw it parked, waiting in the lot.

We had a ten-minute breather as one truck pulled away and the other backed in. Then we began unloading the endless rows of cartons in its trailer.

Sweat ran in rivulets between my breasts. But my head was frozen and my ears burned like fire. That's when I noticed with horror that both of the men we were working with were missing pieces of their ears. Frostbite.

In some plants the men were missing a finger down to the second joint, or a thumb. Out here on the docks, which butt up against the frozen lake, the men gave up little exposed pieces of their bodies. It frightened me. I wondered what I would be forced to sacrifice in order to survive.

I shuddered. Grant gave me a slight push that made me focus again on the task at hand. She looked me up and down to make sure I was alright. She wouldn't ask out loud. In order to be safe on men's terrain it was necessary to work with dignity, as though the job was effortless. I also didn't want Grant to see me cold and scared and tired. She seemed fine. She wasn't even breathing hard.

When the shift finally ended we got the night foreman to sign our timecards and hightailed it out to the parking lot. We sat in Grant's car smoking cigarettes in silence. My arms trembled with exhaustion. It was the first real break we'd had in eight hours. Our smoky breath formed ice crystals on the windshield. Grant revved up the engine and turned the radio on low as we waited for the car to warm up.

"Wasn't too bad," I said casually, "huh?"

"Are you kidding?" she asked me incredulously. "Halfway through I thought I'd die."

I registered shock. "For real? You made it look so easy!"

She laughed. "You must be joking. The only thing that got me through was it looked like it wasn't bothering you much. I figured I had to show you an old butch like me could still keep up with a young punk like you!"

For a moment I felt uneasy. If she relied on me, she had no idea what a thin reed she leaned on. Then I flushed with gratitude as I realized how she was holding me up, even at this moment. "You pulled it off, kid," she punched my shoulder lightly. "Jesus," she added, as a look of fear crossed her face. "Did you see the ears on those guys?"

We finished our cigarettes in silence, lost in similar thoughts.

It was always hard the first day I started working at a new factory; it wasn't easy for anyone. It took a while for a new person to be accepted into the community of a plant. Before coworkers invested their caring in you they wanted to know if you were staying. Many workers never came back after the first day, or couldn't make quota. Others made it almost to the eve of the ninety days required to join the union, only to be laid off.

I planned to stay at this bindery, if I could. I easily made quota the first day, feeding machines and packing skids. By day two I slowed down. If quota was made too effortlessly, the foreman would raise it.

I was being watched and I knew it. The first day I wore sunglasses, defensively, all day long. I didn't take off my denim jacket and kept it buttoned up over my black T-shirt.

This was a small sweatshop with a company union and I was the only he-she in the plant. If this were a big plant, I would be one of many he-shes, so many we would have our own baseball or bowling teams within the factory complex. There I would probably have bound my breasts at work, worn a white T-shirt with no jacket, and found my place among our own smaller societal structure within the life of the plant.

But despite the fact that I hadn't yet been initiated into this society, kindnesses were not withheld. At lunch I bought a bottle of pop from the machine near the time clock and sat down on a skid to eat my baloney sandwich. Muriel, one of the older Native women who worked near me on the line, offered me half her apple. I stood and thanked her. I ate it appreciatively. Each morning for the next week Muriel offered me coffee from her thermos. Everyone watched us, weighing everything they could observe.

Those moments before the whistle blew in the morning were precious because they were ours. Only the *kerchunk* of the time clock stole the last one from us. We all dragged ourselves out of bed a little earlier in the mornings to be at the plant a quarter hour before we had to punch in. We drank coffee and ate rolls, talked and laughed.

We talked all day long too. The owners only rented our hands, not our brains. But even talking had to be negotiated when it was on the bosses' time. If we seemed to be having too much fun, laughing and enjoying ourselves too much, the foreman would come up behind us and hit the solid wooden worktables with a lead pipe while he growled, "Get to work." Then we'd all look at our hands as we worked and press our lips together in silent anger. I think the foreman sometimes got nervous after he'd done that, sensing the murderous glances he received moments after he turned his back. But he was assigned to keep us under control. That required keeping us divided.

We came from many different nationalities and backgrounds. About half the women on the line were from the Six Nations. Most were Mohawk or Seneca. What we shared in common was that we worked cooperatively, day in and day out. So we remembered to ask about each other's back or foot pains, family crises. We shared small bits of our culture, favorite foods, or revealed an embarrassing moment. It was just this potential for solidarity the foreman was always looking to sabotage. It was done in little ways, all the time: a whispered lie, a cruel suggestion, a vulgar joke. But it was hard to split us up. The conveyor belt held us together.

Within weeks I was welcomed into the circle, teased, pelted with questions. My differences were taken into account, my sameness sought out. We worked together, we talked, we listened.

And then there were songs. When the whistle first blew in the mornings there was a shared physical letdown among all the women and men who worked between its imperative commands. We lumbered to our feet, stood silently in line to punch in, and took our places on the assembly line—next to each other, facing each other. We worked the first few moments in heavy silence. Then the weight was lifted by the voice of one of the Native women. They were social songs, happy songs that made you feel real good to hear them, even if you had no idea what the words meant.

I listened to the songs, trying to hear the boundaries of each word, the patterns and repetitions. Sometimes one of the women would explain to us later what the song meant, or for which occasion or time of year it was sung.

There was one song I loved the best. I found myself humming it after I punched out in the afternoons. One day, without thinking, I sang along. The women pretended not to notice, but they smiled at each other with their eyes, and sang a little louder to allow me to raise my own voice a bit. After that I started looking forward to the songs in the morning. Some of the other non-Native women learned songs, too. It felt good to sing together.

One wintry Friday night, before we punched out, Muriel invited me to go to an indoor pow-wow on Sunday. I said yes, of course. I felt honored.

There were a few other Black and white workers at the social—friendships too valuable to explore solely on company time. I began to go regularly and got strung out on fry bread and corn soup.

Once or twice I was cajoled to get up and join a round dance. I must say that although the pounding of the drum resounded in my heart, it never got as far down as my feet. I felt awkward dancing and self-conscious about being so butch.

Of course, Muriel's daughter Yvonne being there made me self-conscious too. I had a fierce crush on Yvonne. She worked in the front office of the same factory. Everyone knew she was the girlfriend of a local organized crime boss. That didn't stop us from knowing where each other was in the room during those socials. I think all the women noticed right away.

I'd already decided I wasn't even going to think about approaching Yvonne, even though she seemed to like me. Some of the older butches had warned me that sometimes on a job the guys would pressure one of the women to sleep with a he-she, as a joke, and then come back and tell everyone about it. That was the last day on the job for the butch, who usually left in shame. But sooner or later the stigma also came back around and stuck on the woman who slept with one of us, and she had to leave too.

I was afraid of this at first with Yvonne, but she wasn't like that at all. One night when a group of us went out after work and got drunk, she told me her boyfriend had suggested he wanted to watch us make love and she had told him to fuck off. Once that had been said out loud, however, it was hard not to think about making love with Yvonne.

Just before Christmas the crew from work went to a bar near the plant for a few beers. There was a heavy snowstorm outside. Inside, we drank and laughed. By the time we left, the snow had nearly covered the cars. I heated the car door key to Muriel's old Dodge with my lighter to defrost it. When I finally got the car door open, Yvonne kissed me right on the mouth. She left me in that parking lot, stunned and excited.

The next night I went to the Malibou and wondered the whole time what it would be like to bring Yvonne there.

I was happy at the plant, flirting with Yvonne, listening to Muriel's stories, waiting for the next social. On Friday nights we drank at the bar where we cashed our checks. Saturday nights I spent at the gay bar. I was feeling just fine.

Then one day, when the plant whistle blew, silence hung heavy in the air. I looked from face to face. Something was up. Muriel spoke first. "Today you start the song," she suggested casually, "any song you want." I looked around in disbelief, but she was serious. I felt the blood rise in my face. I didn't want to call attention to myself. I didn't want to hear my voice rise alone, even for a minute, above the sounds of the machines and the other women. In fact, I realized I felt ashamed of my own voice. "I can't," I protested. I felt near tears. No one said a word. They just kept working in silence. By lunchtime I realized there would be no songs until I began one.

Why? I wondered. *Why are the women doing this to me? Are they making fun of me?* I knew it wasn't true. They noticed how quietly I mouthed the words to songs. They were inviting my voice to join theirs. They were honoring me again.

That night I lay awake in panic. The daily routine wouldn't resume until I sang alone. My throat clenched at the very idea. I thought about calling in sick, but it was too cowardly and it wouldn't change anything. No one was going to forget I was asked to start the first song. Besides, the next day was Christmas Eve. I would lose my holiday pay if I called in sick. And immediately after the holiday I was eligible to join the union.

In the morning I tried to act normal at work. I was welcomed as usual. When Yvonne came in, I wondered if she had heard. Her smile let me know she had. The whistle blew. Each of us punched in. We took our places on the line. The tension was thick. I cleared my throat several times. Muriel watched her hands while she worked; she smiled gently.

This was it. I would try to find my voice and be proud of it. After several false starts my voice began to rise, singing the song I loved most—the first song I'd learned. Almost immediately the other women lifted their voices up with mine to spare me any pain. We all smiled at each other and sang with tears in our eyes.

After lunch the foreman called me into his office and handed me a pink slip. "Sorry," he said. He escorted me to my locker to get my things. I wasn't allowed to say goodbye to anyone.

I actually felt embarrassed about being fired. I knew it was because I was so close to getting into the union. And I knew management had been watching the growing solidarity with great trepidation. But my shame rekindled as I realized the foremen probably heard my voice rising alone in song.

I walked home in the snow. The deep drifts muffled all the sounds of the city. I felt pretty low. Immediately after the holiday I'd have to begin job-hunting all over again. When I got home I hoped the phone would ring. It didn't. I had nothing to look forward to except watching the "Perry Como Christmas Special." That made me feel much worse. Drinking didn't help either, not that it ever did.

I was thinking about going out to the Malibou when I heard footsteps thumping up the stairs. I opened the door. There was Muriel, Yvonne, and some of the other Native women from the plant. They brought me food and a few wrapped presents. They were on their way to a social. I was invited. Muriel watched my face with mock solemnity as she said, "Now you learn to dance."

CHAPTER 8

"You made Grade Five?" A butch cheer went up in the plant cafeteria. "Alright! Way to go!" All the butches clapped me on the back and shook my hand. I felt euphoric.

Butch Jan put an arm around me. "You done good, kid," she said. I blushed.

"How'd you do it?" Frankie wanted to know. Actually, I didn't know why I'd been selected for the job. Maybe it was for the same reason a lot of factory jobs were opening to us: all the young guys were getting drafted left and right.

I'd been at this bindery for six months. It was a huge factory. Grant and I both got jobs around the same time. Two months later, when the educational materials division opened, seven more butches had been among those hired. Nine of us. Almost the whole team I'd played softball with last summer. Nine of us—it was heaven.

Since I'd been in the plant for a while, I knew the ropes and was already in the union. So occasionally the other butches came to me for advice about problems on their floor or about the union. I enjoyed the unprecedented reversal of roles.

I worked with Jan in the trimming and folding division. Giant machines folded huge pieces of paper stock that were then trimmed into pages. Stacks of pages were loaded on skids near the massive collating machine. Women ran from the skids to feed fresh pages into the pockets of the collator. The pages dropped onto a moving belt. The women at the end added cover sheets and stapled them. I stacked the finished booklets onto skids.

Every once in a while I got pulled from this work to help unload the trucks bringing in skids of fresh paper. I looked forward to it because it meant driving a forklift. The only part I didn't like was feeling a little distanced from the other women. Not one of my coworkers was ever taken off the line for any other task.

One morning the foreman replaced me on the line. "Goldberg, come on," Jack commanded. I followed him into the shipping department. "Wait here," he said.

Tommy made a face behind Jack's back. "I hate that guy," he told me after Jack left. "He reminds me of this officer I had in the Navy, always ragging me. I hated his guts."

I nodded, but I didn't speak. Tommy was OK, but I didn't know if he'd repeat anything I said.

Tommy looked at the clock. "Almost break time," he said. "God, I hated the Navy. Two years of my life they stole from me. I used to watch the clock all day. They could force me to do anything, but they couldn't stop time. Sooner or later they had to let me out."

I shrugged. "So why'd you join?"

"Are you kidding?" he asked me. "So I wouldn't get drafted into the Army. LBJ's sending any guy who can walk over to Nam."

Jack came around the corner with Kevin, his assistant, and Jim Boney. Damn, I hated Jim Boney.

"Hey, Tommy, you makin' a real woman out of Jess?" Boney taunted. Tommy leered and grabbed his own crotch.

"C'mon," Jack ordered me to follow him.

I looked back at Tommy. He mouthed the words, *I'm sorry.*

I mouthed the words, *Fuck you.*

Jack led me to a giant folding machine that was idle. I watched as he took out his tools. "Now watch," he ordered as he began to set the machine for a different-size fold. I couldn't believe it. This was an apprentice job. No one else was allowed to learn the mysteries of setting up a job or repairing the machines. Apprenticing led to a journeyman's card. My hopes fluttered.

"You set the vertical, same way," Jack said. He grabbed a rag and wiped oil off his hands as I tried to set the vertical folds. "No, like this," he corrected. The lunch whistle interrupted us. "After lunch," he said. I flew up to the cafeteria.

Why do triumphant moments have to be so fleeting? Just when all the congratulations had died down, Duffy, the chief shop steward, approached our table. "Goldberg, can I talk to you a minute?"

I motioned to the chair next to me, "Sure."

He gestured toward the door. By the time we got out in the hall, I had a feeling I knew what this was about. "Duffy, don't tell me there's some fucking reason why I can't bust the barrier to a number five grade."

He folded his arms and looked at the floor. "Listen, Goldberg, I know you want that grade, and you deserve it. No woman in this plant has ever gone higher than a four, and none of the guys, except one, have ever worked lower than a five. It ain't right."

I narrowed my eyes. "So?"

He sighed. "So I'd be willing to file a grievance to get you or any of the other women a Grade Five job. Just not that job."

I wanted to punch him out. "Why the fuck not, Duffy?" He put his arm lightly on my shoulder. I shook it off. My fists were balled up at my sides.

"Listen, Goldberg, Jack and Boney are setting you up."

I was confused. "What's Jim Boney got to do with this?"

Duffy pulled out a pack of cigarettes and offered me one. I took it. "You know Leroy? Well, he's a Grade Four. Most of the time they have him sweeping up."

I exhaled slowly. "Shit, I didn't know that."

Duffy nodded. "He's been bidding for that Grade Five job now for more than a year. When Freddie got drafted last month, Leroy told Jack he wanted the job. Jack kept stalling him. Leroy finally came to me and asked me to help him fight for the job, so we filed a grievance." The picture was coming into focus.

"Jack is using you. Boney's a union man, but he's such a fucking racist he'd rather block with Jack than work with a Black guy. Leroy deserves that job," Duffy added.

"Well so do I," I argued, but I said it without much steam.

Duffy could see me wrestling with what he said. "Yeah, you do. And I'll help you push to get a higher grade job if you want to fight for it, just not this job. Stick with me on this one, Goldberg. It's really important for the union right now."

"Why now?" I asked.

"Our contract's up at the end of October. The company will do anything to split us up right now to make it harder for us to strike if we have to. We need to stick together."

I sulked. "Look, Duffy, I'm for the union, you know that. But butches can't even come to union meetings."

Duffy looked confused. I explained to him that we were allowed to drink downstairs at the union hall, but we weren't allowed to go upstairs to the meeting.

"Who says?" he wanted to know.

"That's the way it is. That's the way it's always been, as far as I've heard."

Duffy put his arm around my shoulder. "Look, help Leroy win this one. As soon as the strike's over, you get the butches together, and I'll get as many of the stewards as possible, and we'll all go into the ratification meeting as a group and insist on your right to be there."

It sounded like change. "I guess," I told him. "But how come we have to wait till after the strike?"

He knitted his eyebrows. "Well, we don't. It's just that there's gonna be an explosion about Leroy, one way or the other. I'm trying to hold things together this summer, so that we're strong if we need to strike, you know?"

I shrugged and nodded. The lunch whistle blew. I panicked. "What do I tell Jack now?"

Jack came around the corner as I spoke. "You ready?" he asked me.

I took a deep breath. "I don't feel good, Jack. I'm punching out and going home."

Jack glared at Duffy. "Suit yourself."

Duffy whistled as Jack left. "You're alright, Goldberg."

I smiled grudgingly. "Call me Jess."

The next morning when the whistle blew I took my place at the collating machine, ready to feed the pockets. I could see Duffy and Leroy talking to Jack. Duffy was waving his arms and yelling over the din of the machinery. Jack had his hands on his hips and his face was all red and blustery.

When I looked over a few minutes later, Leroy was working on a machine with Jack's assistant. I had to hand it to Leroy, these guys weren't going to make life easy for him. As it turned out, they weren't too pleased with me, either.

"You son-of-a-bitch," Jack yelled in my ear as he walked past me. Jim Boney was glaring at me from across the room. Jan was on the other end of the collating line, watching everything.

The hardest part was telling the butches at lunchtime that I was back to Grade Four. "It ain't right," Grant said sullenly. Johnny and Frankie glanced at each other and shook their heads. Jan just watched the situation unfolding. I told everybody about the promise Duffy made to get all the butches into the union meetings.

"Big deal," Grant laughed. "This kid's like Jack and the Beanstalk, you know? She trades a cow for a magic bean. Fuck that shit. I don't want to be part of no union that doesn't want me."

My face burned. "We can't just say 'fuck the union,' we're in it. The contract's up in October. What are we gonna do, go into the plant manager's office one at a time and negotiate? We don't have a choice. We've gotta make the guys see that they need us too."

Grant thumped her fist on the table. "I got a choice," she said. "I don't want no part of this union. You sold out, kid. Fuck you."

The whistle blew. Lunch was over. Everyone got up and went back to work. I stayed at the table for a moment, trying to remember what it was like to feel so good the day before. I would have done almost anything to get back the respect I lost. Jan was still at the table. She stood up and put her hand on my shoulder, "C'mon, kid, we're late."

I stood up and sighed. I felt defeated and raw. Jan looked me in the face. "Life's complicated, ain't it, kid?" I nodded, unable to look her in the eye. She gently touched my cheek with her calloused hand. "I think you did the right thing."

I remembered something my English teacher told me about not looking for approval for doing what you think is right. But I needed Jan's approval so much at the moment that my eyes welled up with tears of gratitude.

From that day forward, Jim Boney began to bait me mercilessly. "Hey, suck this," he'd shout at me across the shop floor. Nobody wanted to take him on, partly because he held sway as a bully and partly because he was so tight with the foreman.

"What am I gonna do, Jan?" I moaned over a beer.

"You've gotta fight him," Jan told me. I didn't want to fight Jim Boney. I was afraid of him. "There's no other way to stop him," Jan said. I knew she was right.

Two weeks later, Jim Boney pushed me too far. I was bending over to grab some sheets off the skid and I felt something on the back of my thigh. I swatted behind me and touched flesh. Jim Boney had pulled his cock out of his pants and rubbed it up against my jeans. I felt dizzy with fear and nausea. The worst part was that Jim Boney saw the look and recognized it. He and Jack laughed at me.

All the women were watching, instead of working, so the booklets spilled off the end of the line and scattered on the floor. Jack shut the machine down. It got real quiet.

Leroy called Jim Boney an asshole and told him to put his little dick back in his pants. Boney pushed Leroy, and they squared off to fight.

"Your fight's with me, Jim Boney," I shouted. This burst of bravado startled me as much as it did everyone else. They were brave words, born of fear. "C'mon, you want a fight? Let's go."

Everybody looked at Boney. He smirked at me in such a smarmy way that I knew he wanted to reduce me to the same helplessness I'd felt minutes before, but I refused. "C'mon," I told him. "What are you afraid of, huh? Getting your ass whipped by a bull-dagger?"

Duffy came running up and then stopped in his tracks. He watched the standoff. Jim Boney lunged forward, and Jack and Kevin held him back. But I could tell Boney wasn't struggling too hard to get to me. I didn't know why Boney wasn't eager to fight me, but it emboldened me. "I've had it up to here with your shit, Boney. We all have. Do your fucking job and leave me alone or else I'm gonna pound the shit out of you."

Jack and Kevin looked at Boney to see what he'd do. They let go of his arms. Boney waved his arm at me as though he were disgusted and turned away. "She ain't worth it," he told them. "She ain't worth shit."

As Boney walked away, Duffy shouted at him, "She's a better union man than you are, Boney!"

Jan shook my hand. Duffy clapped me on the back.

"Atta girl." Sammy, the truck driver, patted my shoulder. "He's a jerk."

Walter, the repairman, caught my eye and nodded his head once in my direction.

"Alright," Jack yelled as he turned the machinery back on, "get back to work, all of you."

None of us would have attended the union picnic if it wasn't for Duffy. It was his idea that I should organize all the butches to come. "And you can bring all your girlfriends," he added. "Jess, do you have a girlfriend?" The look on my face answered him. I knew he was just trying to get to know me better, but that was not a great place to start.

"Jess," he said, "did I say it right? *Girlfriends,* I mean."

I laughed. "You're alright, Duffy."

The other butches weren't all that wild about coming, but Jan understood it would be a breakthrough and she promised her lover Edna would come as well. Once Jan said yes, the other butches agreed.

We brought our baseball equipment. Once Abba's reopened in the spring we had formed the Abba Dabba Do's softball team.

Jan and Edna and I sat under a tree. Duffy brought us bottles of beer. "I like him," Edna said, after he left.

I smiled. "I do too."

Jan patted my shoulder and told Edna, "The kid's becoming a real union organizer."

"Aw, I am not," I demurred.

"Hey, kid," Jan told me. "We can use all the unity we can get. You been doing real good on this job trying to hold everything together. Take a few bows, OK?" I swelled with pride.

Edna stood up. "I need a cup," she said.

I studied Jan as she watched Edna walk away. Her face was filled with pain. I'd unconsciously noticed the weight of Jan's sadness lately, but I hadn't really thought about it. Jan looked at me, and she let me see a little farther into her eyes than usual. I tried to show her how much I cared about her before I spoke. "You OK?" I asked her.

Jan shook her head slowly. "I think I'm losing her," she said.

My stomach clenched. Jan slapped my thigh. "I'm gonna get another beer, you want one?"

I stood up with her. "No, but," I rested my hand on her arm, "if you ever need to talk, you know. . . ." Jan smiled and walked away.

Duffy sat down next to me. "Hey, Jess, you're the only one I know who I could ask this question." I felt flattered.

"I wanted to ask you about Ethel and Laverne," Duffy said.

I looked around. "Are they here?" Duffy shook his head. "Too bad," I told him, "I always wanted to meet their husbands."

Duffy spoke carefully. "What's the story with Ethel and Laverne? Are they lovers?"

"Naw, they're both married. You know that."

Duffy fumbled for words. "Yeah, but aren't they butches?"

I understood what he was driving at. "Well, they're he-shes, but they're not butches."

Duffy laughed and shook his head. "I don't get it."

I shrugged. "There's not much to get, really. I mean they look like Spencer Tracy and Montgomery Clift, but they really seem to love the guys they married."

Duffy shook his head. "But they're inseparable. Don't you think maybe they're lovers and they're afraid to let people know?"

I thought about it for a moment. "Jeez, Duffy, it's not like they're getting off much easier by being married—they're still he-shes. They've gotta deal with the same shit butches do. Imagine Laverne going into the ladies room at the movies. Or Ethel at a bridal shower. I don't think people who give them a rough time give a fuck who they sleep with. It's probably harder for them, too," I added. "They don't have a place to go like we do—I mean like the bars. All they got is their husbands and each other."

Duffy smiled and shook his head. "The way Ethel and Laverne are with each other, I was sure they were lovers."

"Oh, they love each other alright. You can see that. But it doesn't necessarily mean they're hot and bothered for each other. They really understand each other. Maybe each of them just likes looking in the other's mirror and seeing a reflection that smiles back."

Duffy put his arm around my shoulder and hugged me. "You're very smart about people," he said.

I blushed with pride and pulled away in embarrassment. "I'm gonna get some food."

I heard Grant's voice rising before I saw the confrontation. She was shouting, nose to nose, with Jim Boney. "What do you mean you don't want no fucking girls on your team?" she yelled.

Boney shouted in the direction of the other guys, "Cause we want to win, don't we guys?" He smacked his fist into his first base mitt.

"Hey, Boney," I called out as I strode toward them, "you talking about softball? We'll kick your ass!"

A silence fell over the picnic. For one thing, everyone knew this was about a lot more than a softball game. On the other hand, baseball was sacred to these guys. The thought of playing against girls bordered on heresy. If they won, where was the victory? If they lost. . . it was too humiliating for them to consider.

Even the butches stared at me with a horrified look on their faces. But it was too late, my boast hung in the air. "C'mon, Boney," I said. "We'll challenge you to three innings, and we'll whip you, too."

Boney sneered. "Bet you won't, *Goldberg*." The way he said my name made me realize how much he also hated me as a Jew.

I smiled. "Bet you your glove we will." The grin melted off Boney's face. He loved his first base mitt the way most people love their puppy dogs. He kept it in his locker at work every day, even in the wintertime.

"And if you lose?" he countered. All eyes turned toward me. The smile grew back on Boney's face. "If you lose, Goldberg, you gotta kiss me."

"Ewww, yecch," everyone moaned. Some of them spit on the ground for emphasis.

"C'mon," I told the other butches, "let's get our equipment."

Jan shook her head as we gathered on the field in a huddle.

"I don't know about this," Grant muttered.

"Look," I admitted, "I made a mistake, OK? I knew it the minute the words were out of my damn mouth. I'm sorry. All we can do is play our best game and I'll take the consequences."

Grant threw her glove down and put her hands on her hips. "We'll all pay if we lose, that's what's so fucked up about it."

Frankie intervened. "She said she was sorry. So let's win, OK?"

That was easier said than done. The men's team scored two runs in the first inning. We couldn't seem to handle the field at all. I wondered why we were playing so poorly. After all, most of the guys weren't in great shape. *We* played every week. Maybe we were intimidated because we believed they were better than us. I suddenly got a sick feeling in my stomach when I realized three innings might not be enough for a team of he-shes to overcome our fear.

"C'mon," I said as we huddled between innings. "Can't we show them we got power?"

We scored two runs, but the guys scored two also. We were two runs down. Between innings, Frankie asked what would happen if we tied. Jan exploded. "Listen to this shit," she growled. "Why don't we just admit we lost the game now, huh? Why even play another inning?" Her voice got real low and menacing. "This is no fucking joke. You just think what it'd be like to have to watch Jess kiss Jim Boney. I'm not gonna stand by and let that happen."

That was my friend, Butch Jan.

We took our positions to play, and play we did. We scored three runs—five to four, our favor. But when Frankie headed into home plate, Jim Boney smacked her on the back so hard with the ball she hit the dirt.

We all charged Boney, ready to kill him. Jack and his assistant closed ranks with Boney. No one could tell if all the men were squared off against the he-shes, or if it was just those three guys against us. Duffy rushed up between the butches and the men. "Jack, you took Frankie out, you fucking bastard. If they're down one man, so's your team. You're out of the game."

"Bullshit," Boney waved his arms around. "It was a fucking accident, that's all." We wanted to kill him.

"The bet's off," Grant shouted.

"You fucking cowards," Boney said. The bet was back on.

Duffy paced. "This is a mistake," he muttered.

"Yeah?" I asked him angrily. "Who're you rooting for?"

"The union," he shot back at me.

"Then you better hope that our team wins, not Boney's and Jack's," I told him.

Duffy mulled that over for a second and then smiled. "You're right." Duffy clapped his hands and shouted, "C'mon, Jan," as she headed to the plate.

Jan hit the ball up high in the air. We all poised and watched it fall—right into Jack's glove. It was our third out. We were up one run, but our opponents had another inning.

Sammy was up to bat first. He hit the ball smack into Grant's glove. Before he dropped the bat, he gave me a wink I could see all the way from my position on first base.

Tommy was up next. He hit a weak grounder that Grant scooped up at third base, but he made it to first.

"I'm sorry," he whispered.

"Fuck you." I was still mad at him.

Jack drove a low grounder into our weak spot in center field and loped toward my base. "After Boney gets done with you, I want sloppy seconds," Jack sneered. I tried to keep my mind on the game.

Walter was up next. He stepped up to the plate, tapped the dirt off his shoes with the bat, and wiggled his butt into position. He hit a pop-fly high into the air. We all pushed our caps back and watched it fall easily into Jan's glove. Walter pulled the brim of his cap and walked away from home plate with a spring in his step.

Boney stepped up to the plate. We directed every bit of our hatred toward him, but he seemed unscathed. He swung at the first pitch with power and missed.

"Strike one," we all yelled.

He swung angrily at the second pitch and missed.

"Strike two," we called out in elation. We began to heckle him for all we were worth.

The crack of Boney's bat against the third pitch silenced us. We all looked up in the sky as the ball seemed to float in midair. Tommy hovered around third base, as mesmerized as we were. Jack ran toward third and shouted at Tommy to run. Jim Boney slid toward first base.

The ball fell with a plop, right into Grant's glove. It was the third out, so there was no reason to throw the ball to first base—but she did. The ball landed in my glove with a whack. I braced my arms as I extended the ball and the glove towards Boney's nose, which was rapidly approaching me. There was a little snapping sound as his nose hit the ball. The game was officially over. We'd won. I didn't have to kiss Jim Boney, who was now bleeding all over first base. I would've claimed it was an accident, but no one asked.

I caught sight of Jack glaring at me—always the foreman, even at a picnic. His menacing look chilled me. But I let it go because almost all the guys from the other team came over and slapped us on the back and said they were glad we won. I realized these guys had just lost to a team of he-shes—right in front of their wives and girlfriends—but they didn't seem sore about it.

The butches were happy about winning, but they hung back a bit. I knew they were kind of peeved at me. It was a cocky challenge I had hurled at Jim Boney. It could've turned into a defeat for all the butches on the job, and they knew it. It was Jan who broke the ice. "All's well that ends well, right kid?" She put her arm around me. "I think I'd have died before I'd let you kiss that guy."

I looked shocked. "You didn't think I would've kissed him if we'd lost do you?"

Tommy ran up, out of breath. "Good game," he extended his hand. My expression was frozen, but I shook his hand. "Look, I'm sorry, OK?" he told me.

I shrugged. "You're not a bad guy, Tommy. But in front of the other guys you sink like a stone. I just don't trust you." He opened his mouth to speak, but no words came out.

Jan and I walked away. "You were pretty hard on him," she said, "but I'm sure you had a good reason."

"Attention everyone! Can I have your attention!" It was Tommy, on top of a picnic table. We all came closer. He had Jim Boney's prized baseball mitt in his hands. "On behalf of the losing team, I'd like to award the winning team this first baseman's mitt. Well," he stammered, "first base mitt." He tossed the glove to me. "You all won it fair and square."

Edna waited till Jan walked away from me before she came over. I saw the same deep pain in her eyes as she watched Jan from a distance. I wished a woman loved me that much. As Edna approached me, her mouth twisted into a teasing smile. She held my face lightly in both of her hands. "Good game, butch."

I shifted uncomfortably from foot to foot. "Aw, Edna, you know."

She nodded to silence me. "Yes, I do know, but it came out just fine."

We both noticed Duffy standing nearby, waiting to congratulate me. "You were right, Jess," he told me, as he pumped my hand. "The union did win the game. My first instincts were wrong, I'm sorry."

I got myself an ice-cold beer and a piece of fried chicken and sat down alone under a tree. The air was hot, the breeze was cool. I felt on top of the world.

CHAPTER 9

Jim Boney didn't show up for work on Monday. I was glad. I wouldn't have admitted this to anyone, but I was still scared of him. So when he called in sick Monday morning I walked around the plant feeling a little smug.

Jack pulled me off the line and led me to a die cutter, which punched school flashcards into the shape of decks. Normally one of the guys used a powerful air hose to blow away the trim before it jammed the machine. "The air hose is being fixed," Jack shouted over the roar of the machinery. "You assist Jan when she needs help loading her skids. Every once in a while, you brush the shit off the press, like this." He ran his hand across the face of the die cutter in the split second between punches. "Don't let it jam," he warned me, before he walked away.

Jan looked at the machine and back at me. "Be careful," she cautioned.

I watched the die cutter punch the decks, trying to learn its rhythm like a song. My hand darted out and quickly brushed some of the trim away. I got most of it. My hands were trembling. When you work around machines you grow to respect their mesmerizing power. I tried to stay in sync with the punch press. Just once my hand was slow. Just once was all it took.

It happened so fast. One moment my fingers were all connected to me. The next moment I could feel my ring finger lying against my palm. My blood spurted in an arc across the machine, the decks of cards stacked on skids, and the wall in front of me.

I tried not to look at my left hand, but I did. My stomach heaved before my mind could even understand what my eyes saw. I couldn't have been heard over the thunder of the machines, but it didn't matter. I couldn't make a sound. Everything took place in slow motion. Jan waved her arms and shouted. People came near but froze in horror.

It occurred to me I should go to a hospital. I knew I couldn't drive my motorcycle. As I walked to the door I wondered if I had enough bus fare. Walter and Duffy ran after me.

The next thing I remember was being in a car. Walter had his arm around me. Duffy was driving and he kept turning around to look for a sign from Walter. My whole hand was bound up in a red-soaked cloth. I felt so sorry for my finger that hot tears of grief ran down my face. I was thinking maybe I should bury it. I wondered who I should invite.

Walter lifted my injured hand up high with one of his large, gentle hands, and held me tightly against him with the other. I shook violently. "It's gonna be OK, honey," he crooned. "I seen a lot of these things happen. It's gonna be alright."

The next thing I knew I was lying on an operating table. I panicked. What if they took my clothes off? There was no one around. A fly buzzed around me and landed on my hand. My body lurched. The fly circled and landed again. This time as my injured hand jerked, my finger seemed to move in a different direction. I passed out.

It was Duffy's face I saw as I drifted back to consciousness. He was smiling, but he looked upset, too. "Duffy," I whispered, "where's my finger?"

He winced. "It's OK, Jess. They saved your finger."

I didn't think it was true. I'd seen lots of movies where they lie to injured people like that. I lifted my head slightly to look at my hand. It was covered in layers of gauze and there was some kind of metal device running from my forearm into the gauze and then emerging at the tip of where my finger would be. Duffy nodded. "Your finger's OK, Jess. The bone wasn't completely severed." He turned away as he said it. I thought maybe he was going to throw up.

I was still dressed in my bloody work clothes. "Get me out of here, Duffy."

He stopped at the pharmacy to fill my prescriptions and drove me home. When I awoke he was gone. There was a note on the nightstand explaining when I should take the pills. He also left his phone number and said I should call when I woke up. I was relieved to find I was still in my work clothes.

I called him later that night and he raced over. "Jack set you up, Jess." Duffy paced around my kitchen. "Just before he put you on that machine one of the guys saw Kevin removing the safety device. Jack could claim he took it off because the hose was on the blink, but ordering someone to put their hand in it was an out-and-out contract violation."

I had trouble following what Duffy was saying. It wasn't just that my mind was hazy with painkillers, I didn't want to understand.

"But get this, Jess," Duffy bent over the kitchen table and pounded it. "After we took you to the hospital Jack reinstalled the safety device and swears it was on all the time. The bastard set you up, Jess."

I felt woozy with fear. It reminded me of when my parents had me committed, or the cops opened my cell door. So many people in the world had so much power to control and hurt me. I shrugged as though it wasn't important to me. "Look, Duffy, it's over. Besides, the contract's up in two months. We got other things to worry about."

Duffy looked at me like I was crazy, but when he spoke his voice was calm. "No, Jess. We're going to worry a lot about this. We're going to prove what Jack did to you and we're going to tell management either he's out or we all walk out." I marveled at the idea that straight people would stand up for me, or for any he-she.

"You know," Duffy added, "I don't think I really realized how hard it is for you. I know what jerks the guys at work can be sometimes." He leaned up against the sink and folded his arms. "But when I went to the hospital with you, I saw how they treated you, how they talked about you," he rubbed his face. When he looked back up at me, I saw tears in his eyes. "I felt so helpless, you know? I kept yelling at them that you were a human being, that you mattered, and it was like they weren't even listening to me. I couldn't do anything to help you and I couldn't make them take care of you the way I wanted, you know?"

I nodded. I did know. And now I knew that Duffy did too.

Jan drove me to Abba's on Friday night. Everyone cheered when I walked in. They hung a sign on the wall in the backroom that read: *Get Well, Jess!* Frankie and Grant and Johnny told me Duffy organized a union investigation of the "accident."

I was watching Jan. She looked so sad. "Where's Edna?" I whispered to Grant. Grant drew an index finger across her throat. I waited till I saw Jan sitting alone in the back. I brought over two beers. "Can I sit with you?" She gestured towards an empty chair.

"You're my friend, Jan," I told her, "and I love you." She looked surprised when I said that. "If you don't want to talk about it, that's OK with me. But I can't pretend I don't know you're hurting."

Jan leaned forward and rested her elbows on the table. "I lost her. I love her and I lost her. What else is there to say?"

I shrugged. "I know you both loved each other a lot."

Jan took a swig of her beer. "Sometimes love just isn't enough," she said. I hoped she was wrong. She sighed. "The worst part is, it's my fault. I knew she was going to leave me and I just couldn't change fast enough to stop her. Who knows, maybe I'm just too old to change at all."

I didn't know what she was talking about, but I kept my mouth shut. Jan slumped. "If I tell you why she broke up with me, you promise me you'll never tell another soul?"

I thought about it before I answered her. "You can trust me," I said.

"You took long enough to answer," she said, warily.

"First I had to make sure I meant it."

Jan's voice grew hoarse. "I just couldn't let her touch me. We never talked about it. I don't even know how to talk about it. At first it was OK with her, she understood. But later she told me she prided herself on always having been able to seduce her stone lovers. That scared the shit out of me, you know?"

I was thinking how nice that would be to have a femme lover who cared enough to try.

"Anyway," Jan said, "I couldn't, and she finally left me. After all these years. Can you believe that?" She laughed ironically. "The only woman I ever loved so goddamn much it makes my teeth ache and she left me."

Jan gripped my arm. "I'd do anything to get her back." She had tears in her eyes as she spoke. "I'd get down on my godamn knees in front of the whole bar. I'd do anything. I just can't change the way I am. I don't know what's wrong with me. I just can't, you know?"

I did. I leaned forward and put my arm around her. She leaned her head against my shoulder. If Jan hadn't been drunk she might have been embarrassed.

Deep down, my insides seethed. I knew I was stone, too. It was a home alarm system that didn't seem to have an on-off switch. Once installed, the sirens went off and the gates shut, even if the intruder was loving. Would I finally find a woman who loved me and lose her because of that? If that was true, life seemed too hard to bear.

I obsessed about one thing Jan had told me: Edna prided herself on being able to seduce her stone butch lovers. I wondered how she did it. I wondered how it would feel to be touched and not be afraid. I thought about Edna a lot.

I hung out at Abba's almost every evening while I recuperated on compensation. Jan stopped going to the bar, afraid to run into Edna. Edna came to the bar on Saturdays. I looked forward to that night, all week long. When she walked through the door that Saturday night, she was all I could see. Everyone else was in black and white; only Edna was in full, living color.

She headed right toward me. I got off the bar stool as she approached. Edna reached down for my injured hand. She lightly supported the metal contraption and looked up at my face.

I shrugged. "It's better. The doctor says I'll have feeling in it," I reassured her.

"How long do you have to wear this?" she asked.

"I don't know. They'll tell me in a month." I saw concern in her eyes. I felt honored.

We both sat down and I gestured to Meg for two drinks. I reached for my wallet. Edna rested her hand on my arm. "I'm working," she said. "Let me pay."

Edna took a sip of her drink. "You're really brave," she told me.

I felt ashamed; it wasn't true. "I'm not, really," I told her honestly. "I'm scared all the time, Edna."

Her face softened. "What a brave thing to say to me."

I blushed. She put her hand over mine. Her nails shined with fresh red polish. "You know what I think?" she asked me. I leaned forward to hear. "I think everybody's scared. But if you don't let your fears stop you, that's bravery." I decided she was the wisest person I'd ever met.

Edna ran her fingers through her own hair. It was such an intimate gesture. She saw the look on my face; she dropped her eyes and smiled. Someone put a quarter in the jukebox. *You're my soul and my heart's inspiration,* the Righteous Brothers sang. *Without you, baby, what good am I?* I wondered if I had the courage to ask her to dance. "Edna," I mumbled, "wanna dance?"

At that moment the bar door opened and everyone fell silent. Standing in the doorway was a mountain of a woman. She wore a black leather jacket unzipped. Her chest was flat, and it was clear she wasn't wearing a binder. Her jeans were low slung, unbelted. She carried her riding gloves and her helmet in one hand. Rocco. Her legend preceded her.

I glanced over at Edna. She was lost in a memory I couldn't see. I watched their faces as they saw each other for the first time in years. I looked back and forth as though this was a tennis match and I didn't want to miss a stroke. I could feel how much they loved each other.

"Hello, Rocky," Edna said quietly. It sounded like a line from a movie.

"Hello, Edna," Rocco answered in a deep timbre. Their faces were close to each other and to mine. I could see the beard stubble on Rocco's chin and cheeks.

Jan once told me that Rocco had been beaten up so many times nobody could count. The last time the cops beat her she came close to dying. Jan heard that Rocco had taken hormones and had breast surgery. Now she worked as a man on a construction gang. Jan said Rocco wasn't the only he-she who'd done that. It was a fantastic tale. I'd only half believed it, but it haunted me. No matter how painful it was to be a he-she, I wondered what kind of courage was required to leave the sex you'd always known, or to live so alone.

I wanted to know Rocco. I wanted to ask her a million questions. I wanted to see the world through her eyes. But most of all, I wanted her to be different than me. I was afraid to see myself in Rocco.

I watched Edna's face. She held herself with such strength and dignity it made the pain she tried to conceal all the more obvious. I couldn't tell if she was reaching to touch Rocco's cheek or if I was just reading Edna's mind. I trembled at my nearness to two such powerful women.

Rocco touched Edna's elbow. Edna rose and led Rocco to a table in the backroom. I sat alone, shaken. I felt left out, jealous. I hungered for the attention of both women. As I stole a glance back at Edna, I longed for her to look at me that way. I wished I was so powerful that a glimpse of me could shake the leaves from her branches. And I wanted Rocco to be my friend, to reveal all the secrets of the universe we revolved in. I wanted her as a home to come to when I wasn't strong.

I strained to read their body language as they talked.

Rocco stood up. Edna held onto Rocco's leather lapels. Their lips touched briefly, then Rocco turned to go. I wished Rocco could have seen the look on Edna's face after her back was turned. It might have meant a lot to her.

Rocco was headed toward me to go out the door. I searched my brain to think of something to say to make her stop and talk. Maybe the pained look on my face made her pause in front of me. She asked me a question with her eyebrows. I couldn't find words to say what I wanted; I'm not sure I even knew.

For just a moment, doubt flickered across Rocco's face. I saw her guard begin to go up. I couldn't think of what to do, so I extended my hand to her. She looked at it, then she glanced at my other hand, all bandaged and looking like part of a robot. As she shook my hand she nodded—I'll never know why. And then she left the bar.

The sound level rose again after she'd gone. I felt empty and hollow with loss. If I ached, I knew Edna must be bleeding. I waited a decent amount of time before I went back to her. "Can I buy you a drink?" I asked her.

She looked startled. "What?" She hesitated. "Yes, thank you."

We drank in silence. I felt connected to her grief. I watched the couples dancing in the smoky darkness. Out of the blue Edna looked over at me and whispered, "I hurt." She said it so calmly and quietly I was afraid I'd misunderstood her. But I saw the pain in her eyes so I moved my chair near hers. Edna curled up against me, softly exploring my body with hers. Holding her was such a simple joy. She sighed once and then her body shook with sobs.

At first I felt embarrassed, worried what people might think. But then I gave myself to Edna, concerned only with her comfort. She trusted me enough to bring her sorrow to my arms. I kissed her hair. The scent made me lightheaded. She looked up at me. I longed to lift her chin with my hand and kiss her mouth, deeply and slowly. She saw the look in my eyes. There was no point in hiding it.

"I'll be right back," she said. Edna was in the bathroom for a long time. When she returned I offered her a cigarette and lit it for her. Edna shook her head slowly. "Just when I thought I couldn't hurt anymore, guess who walks in the door?"

I exhaled smoke and watched her face. "What did she want?" I couldn't believe I'd asked her such a personal question.

Edna blinked in surprise at my directness. "She heard Jan and I broke up. She waited a month or so and came to ask me if there was a chance we could get back together."

I lightly tapped my Zippo lighter against the whiskey glass: butch Morse code. "Is there? A chance, I mean."

Edna sighed. "People have seasons, you know? Cycles. I've just left an eight-year marriage. Rocco's been alone a long time." It hurt me to think of Rocco being lonely.

"I don't think I've ever seen a woman like Rocco before," I told her.

I could see that Edna wasn't quite sure what I meant and I realized she'd fight to the death to defend Rocco. "I wish she were my friend," I said quickly, to make her understand.

She smiled warmly and reached out to touch my arm. "Rocco would love you," Edna said.

I brightened. "You really think so?"

Edna nodded and shook her head. "You remind me of her in many ways. You're a lot like she was when she was younger." I wanted to ask her what she meant, but part of me was afraid to hear her answer.

"One time," I told her, "it was the first night I found one of our bars, that's the night I met Al."

Edna nodded. "You were a friend of Al's?" she said. A misty look clouded her eyes.

"You knew Al?" I asked her. I meant *knew* in the biblical sense. She understood the question.

"This is a small world," she answered. "This circle of people stays pretty much the same." She touched my arm. "Whatever you do now, make sure you can live with it for the rest of your life." I knew I'd better give that a lot of thought. "Anyway," she said, "I interrupted you."

I leaned forward. "When I first laid eyes on Al, it was like love at first sight, you know?" Edna's face softened.

"I mean, there's different kinds of love," I said. "I can't explain how it feels to me, but it's love. That's how I felt tonight when I saw Rocco."

Edna touched my face with her fingertips. "The more I get to know you," she said, "the more I like you." She leaned forward and kissed me lightly on the lips. I blushed from head to toe. Edna smiled.

"I've got to go home and sleep," Edna told me. "Do you want a ride?"

I shook my head. "I think I'm gonna stay for a while, thanks."

After Edna left, I replayed the whole night in my mind, over and over again.

"Scabs!" we all screamed as the cops tried to help them cross our lines and take our jobs away. Hundreds of us strained at the barricades, and the cops held the scabs back.

"Faggots!" some of our guys yelled at the strikebreakers. All the butches pulled back from the police barricades. The word seared like burning metal.

"Duffy," I pulled his arm. "What's this *faggot* shit?"

Duffy appeared torn in ten directions. "Alright," he said. "Listen up you guys. Stop with the faggot stuff. They're scabs." The men looked confused.

A light bulb lit up over Walter's head. "Aw, shit." He extended his hand to me. "We didn't mean you guys."

I shook his hand. "Listen," I said, "call them whatever you want, but don't call them faggots."

Walter nodded. "Agreed."

"You cocksuckers! You motherfuckers!" they shouted instead.

I pushed forward at the barricade. "You fucking scabs," I yelled. "You all have sex with other men."

The guys looked baffled. "What's she talking about?" Sammy wanted to know.

"You have intercourse with your own mother," I screamed.

"That's disgusting," Walter said.

Duffy intervened. "OK, they're scabs and strikebreakers. Let's call 'em what they are, alright?" Duffy glared at me, but there was a smile underneath it.

Grant pulled me aside and motioned towards Duffy. "You know that guy's a communist?"

I was stunned. "He is not," I told her.

"Oh yeah?" she asked me. "How do you know?"

Jan looked worried. "Is that true?"

"It's bullshit," I told them both. When they went back to yelling at the scabs and the cops, I stood next to Duffy. "What's up?" he asked.

I shrugged. "Are you a communist?"

I was hoping he'd laugh, or at least look startled, but instead he had a sad look in his eyes. "Do we need to talk about it now?" he asked.

"I told them it was bullshit," I said. "It is bullshit, isn't it?"

"Can we talk about it later?" he asked me again. I nodded, but I wished we could have worked it out right there. I just wanted to hear him say it wasn't true.

The cops suddenly put on their riot helmets and took out their clubs. We all tensed and gathered in front of the barricades. They were ready to bring the scabs in past us. We roared so loud that people from the nearby projects came out to watch. We rattled the barricades to remind the cops and scabs how frail the wood was and held up our signs, loosely stapled to two-by-fours.

As the scabs moved closer, one of them pulled out a blackjack and hit Frankie's fingers which were resting on the barricade. Jan got so mad when she saw that happen she cracked the scab over the head with her picket sign. The cops grabbed Jan and pulled her right over the barricades. They threw her up against the police van and roughed her up. Three strikers tried to jump the barricades to help Jan, but the cops nabbed them and handcuffed them. All four were thrown into the back of the police van.

"Duffy," I yelled, over the confusion. "Duffy, we got to get her out of there. Help her!"

Duffy worked his way through the crowd. "Jess, we got four union people in that van."

"Duffy, you don't understand. Think about it. It's different for her to get busted. Please listen." I didn't have time to explain. Duffy took my arm and looked into my face for the answer. I let him see the fear and the shame in a way I'd never voluntarily let a man see before. Duffy nodded. He understood.

Duffy pushed his way to the barricade, lifted his work boot, and kicked it over. "C'mon," he signaled the strikers.

The cops were caught off-guard as we surged past them. There were skirmishes, but most of us made it to the police wagon and surrounded it. People from the projects formed an outer circle around us. "Let them go," we rocked the van. "Let them go! Let them go!" An ashen-faced cop wearing gold bars whispered to the officers nearby. We closed in around them. Quickly they opened the van. Four sets of handcuffs were unlocked. Just as fast as they'd been busted, the four were free.

We all turned toward the group of scabs who were near the plant door. Without a cordon of police for protection they scurried like rats. Several of them ran inside the factory and attempted to hold the door shut. Some of the strikers pulled at the door, struggling to get at them. Others chased scabs down the street. The police pulled back across the street.

We set up a picket line right in front of the plant doors. "Contract! Contract!" We all cheered ourselves.

"We won," I shouted to Duffy. "We won!"

He shook his head. "We won this battle. Tomorrow will be even rougher." What a spoilsport, I thought.

I saw Jan trembling. I signaled to Duffy that I was going to get her out of there. Jan and I walked a block away to her parked car. She leaned against the car door and heaved her guts up. Her hands were shaking so bad she almost couldn't light her cigarette. I pulled out my Zippo. "I was scared back there," she said.

I nodded. "Me too."

"No," she grabbed me by the shoulder. "I mean I didn't think I could take it—not alone, not without Edna to go home to."

I flushed at the thought of going home to Edna. I pushed the thought back down. "I know, Jan," I whispered. "When you got busted, I suddenly remembered things I didn't want to think about, like they were happening to me all over again."

She looked up at me and smiled gratefully. "You understand," she said. I nodded and dropped my eyes.

Jan crowed. "I can't believe you guys got me out. It was unbelievable. I thought I was a goner and you guys got me out! Unfucking believable!" We laughed until tears streamed down our faces.

"I've gotta go back now," I told her. "Why don't you go home and get some rest."

Jan nodded. "Tomorrow morning? 7:00 A.M.?" I smiled and turned to go.

Jan called to me, "You're a real friend, you know that?"

If she only knew how I felt about Edna, she'd understand what a traitor I really was.

I was sound asleep that night when Duffy called. "You were right," he shouted. "We won it at the table tonight! And we got management to agree that Jack is out!"

I tried to climb from the depth of sleep. "What? What did you say?"

"Jess, we won!" he laughed. "The ratification meeting is tomorrow night. I want you to organize all the butches to come to the union meeting to vote, you got that?"

"Sure," I mumbled and hung up.

The next morning I called up all the butches from the plant so we could go to the meeting Tuesday night as a group. When I called Grant, she had big news. "The steel plant has to hire fifty women," she told me. "They're accepting applications Wednesday morning. I don't know about you, but I'll be camping out on the line Tuesday night. By late that night the line will stretch from Lackawanna to Tonawanda." It was a slight exaggeration, but her point was well taken.

I called Jan. "I don't know," she said. "What do you think we should do?"

"I was kind of hoping you'd tell me what we should do," I told her.

I called Duffy on Tuesday afternoon. I told him all the butches wanted the chance to get into the steel plant. There was a long silence on the line. "It's a mistake," he said.

"You don't understand," I shouted. "You don't know what it means to us to get into a big plant like that."

He tried to argue with me. "If the vote passes, at least punch in Wednesday morning or else you'll be automatically fired."

He didn't seem to realize I was already gone. "You don't understand what it would mean to work in the steel mill, do you?"

He shouted back at me. "What the hell is this about, looking tough?"

"Yeah," I yelled, "in a way. But not like you're saying it. All we got is the clothes we wear, the bikes we ride, and where we work, you know? You can ride a Honda and work in a bindery or you can ride a Harley and work at the steel plant. The other butches are gonna leave sooner or later, and I don't want to get stuck in that sweatshop with that rinky-dink union."

I knew I'd hurt him, but I couldn't find a way to retreat. "If you don't understand that, I can't explain it to you," I told him.

"Well, I think it's stupid." He sounded like a kid. That's when I knew I had really hurt him. "The company was ordered to hire fifty women, but they don't have to keep them. If five of you last the ninety days to get into the union I'll eat Jim Boney's baseball mitt."

I was riled. "It's my baseball mitt," I reminded him and hung up the phone.

Tuesday night was bitter cold. We huddled around the flames leaping out of metal barrels. It was a long, long night. My stomach tightened every time I thought about the contract ratification meeting.

"You think we made a mistake?" Jan asked me. I didn't answer.

Fuck Duffy, I thought to myself. *He doesn't understand us.*

The first fifty of us filled out applications and were told to return the next night at midnight. There was a snow squall during the day while we slept, but Jan and I were determined to get to work anyway.

We wandered through the plant as though we had just landed on this rusty corrugated planet. Sounds, muffled and loud, startled us. The blast furnace lit up the sky orange and red.

We gave the foreman our work assignment slips. He looked us up and down. "Come with me," he said, and led us outside.

The wind whipped the top layer of powdery snow into tiny tornadoes. The foreman took one of two shovels and he dug until we heard a clank of metal against metal. "Hear that? Railroad tracks." He handed us each a shovel. "Clear 'em off."

He looked at my left hand. I had wrapped a scarf around my injured hand. The cold made the metal brace burn against my skin. "You gonna be able to work?" he nodded toward my hand.

"Sure," I said. "Hey, how far down do the tracks go?"

He answered over his shoulder, "You can shovel all night long and never get to the end."

Jan and I stared at the snowdrifts. Jan threw her shovel down. It thumped softly in the snow. I braced myself, but she spoke quietly. "I'm too old for this horseshit," she said. "They're gonna make it hell for us until we quit." I knew she was right.

"C'mon," she told me. "I'll drive you home."

I sat up until dawn watching the snow fall. I knew I'd been fired the day before when I didn't punch in for the first shift after the strike officially ended. When light glowed on the horizon I walked to the bindery so I'd be there when Duffy arrived. I came out from behind the gate as soon as his car pulled in. I couldn't read the look on his face when he saw me. "What do you want?" He asked it gently, but the words were cold.

"You were right." I nearly choked on the words.

He shook his head. "I'm not glad I was right."

I shrugged. "It doesn't matter, really. I just came to tell you I'm sorry. I made a mistake."

He put his arm around me. "I made a mistake, too. I've thought a lot about it. You remember when you were bidding on the same job as Leroy?" I nodded. "Well," Duffy continued, "you were willing to step aside to make sure Leroy got that job. And you told me the butches weren't welcome at the union meeting. I asked you to wait till after the strike to deal with it. It wasn't that I thought your grievance wasn't as important. I only had so much energy to deal with everything. But maybe that's how it seemed to you. I'm sorry, Jess. If I could do it again, I'd bring Leroy and all of the butches to that next meeting and say to the guys, 'Here we all are, we're the union!' I think I made a mistake too."

Tommy and Duffy were the only two men who had ever apologized to me. "I gotta go," I told him. "You're gonna be late."

"Wait!" he held up a gloved hand. "I have something for you." He unlocked his car door and handed me a wrapped present. "After I found out we won the strike, I got this for you." Duffy looked embarrassed as he handed it to me. He took off his glove and shook my hand. "Goodbye, Jess. Thanks."

"Thanks for what?"

He smiled. "Thanks for teaching me so much." He turned and walked away.

I walked home in the snow, trying not to think about anything. When I got home I realized I was still carrying the package. It was wrapped up in an AFL-CIO newsletter and it had a gold bow that looked left over from Christmas. It was a book, an autobiography of a woman labor organizer named Mother Jones. Inside the front cover, Duffy had written: *To Jess, with great expectations.*

I went to the window and looked out over the mounds of snow, wishing I could do everything in my life once as practice and then go back and do it again.

I sat at the bar and smoked nervously, waiting for Edna to arrive. Justine raised one eyebrow. "She's not here yet?"

"Who?" I asked innocently.

Justine smiled and raised her glass in a toast. "To love," she said, "or is it lust?"

My defenses crumbled. "I just know that I wait all week to see her and when I do. . ."

"Uh-oh," Justine laughed. "Does she feel the same way?"

I shrugged. "I think she likes me."

Justine leaned forward. "So what's the problem, darlin'?"

"I don't know. She's single, I'm single. There's no law against it, right?" Justine didn't answer. "I don't know, Justine, it just doesn't feel right. I mean, Jan's my friend. She's told me stuff, confided in me. It would never be right again with me and Jan. But then when I see Edna, I want her so much it hurts." Justine didn't say a word.

"Say something," I pleaded.

Justine shrugged. "This one you've got to figure out on your own."

"Thanks a lot."

Edna walked in the door. We couldn't pretend to be casual. She held my eyes as she walked over to me. She smoothed my lapels and kissed me lightly on the lips. My heart was thumping. Edna led me by the hand into the backroom. I put my drink down on the table and started to sit down, but Edna pulled me toward the dance floor. This was a moment I'd dreamed of.

The pleasure of the dance was so exquisite, I almost couldn't stand it. I only opened my eyes once while the music was playing. I saw Jan watching us. Although she was only silhouetted, I recognized her jealous rage. In an instant, she was gone.

Edna pulled back and looked at me. "What's wrong?" she asked. My eyes brimmed with tears. She put her fingertips on my cheek and drew me closer. "Did I do something wrong?" I couldn't explain that I was afraid I'd just lost Jan, too.

Edna led me back to the table. "Edna," I began.

She shook her head. "I don't like the sound of that. You don't have to explain," she said as she gathered her purse and coat in her arms.

"Wait," I told her. "You don't understand." She dropped her coat wearily. "I want you so much, it's driving me crazy. It's just doesn't feel right." Edna didn't say a word. This was my job to try to explain.

"I can't stop thinking about you." She leaned forward and rested her hand on my uninjured arm, but she still didn't speak.

"Remember something you told me, about people having seasons? You just broke up with Jan and you're hurting. I love Jan, too—she's my friend."

Edna dropped her head and then raised it. Her eyes were filled with sadness. "I thought you were going to tell me I was too old for you."

"I don't think you're old at all, Edna. I think I'm a little too young for you. I'm not really talking about age, so much, as about being grown-up. Sometimes I imagine walking into the bar with you and being an instant elder because you're on my arm." Edna still didn't speak. She sure wasn't making this any easier for me. "And sometimes when I get so confused about what to do, I think you could make sense of the world to me." Edna smiled gently.

"But I can't be an instant elder. I can't jump over all the things I've got to learn and I can't get it all from you. I guess I'm saying that the first time I take you into my arms as a lover—and I will someday—I want to be more grown-up than I am now." I sucked in my breath. "And second of all, I love Jan, she's my friend. You told me that what I do now, I'll have to live with for the rest of my life."

"I did say that," Edna sighed wistfully. She sat back in her chair, just at a moment when I wished she'd move closer. "I'm not ready to settle down with any butch," she told me. "But if I were, I'd be honored to walk into the bar on your arm. If anyone had told me I could hurt as much as I do and still be so attracted to you, I'd have thought they were crazy."

I blushed. These were the words I'd waited to hear. She smiled. "And I am very flattered that a young butch like you would pay me such attention. You made me feel beautiful at a time when I didn't think I was. But I don't think I really realized what you were made of until I just heard what you said. I love butches," she squeezed my arm. Her words were like a fire I warmed my hands in front of.

"I love Rocco and Jan for being willing to take on the whole world rather than make a lie out of their lives. And somehow they still manage to be honorable women. They were loyal to me and to their friends." I nodded and dropped my eyes.

"I respect them for it," she told me. "It's part of why I love them so much. And I see that in you."

I was afraid if we kept talking I would forget my decision and bury myself in her arms. I wanted to ask her to teach me how to let myself be touched, but I couldn't violate Jan's confidence.

Edna spoke first. "I've got to go home now."

I sighed in relief. I stood and held her coat for her. She slipped her arms into the sleeves and turned to me. She kissed me lightly on the lips. I took her waist in my hands. Her mouth opened for me and I discovered all the pleasure I'd hoped to find in its warmth.

She pulled back. So did I. She lifted my injured hand and kissed my fingertips, and then she was gone. I stood in the same spot for a long time, unable to move.

Peaches appeared at my side. "C'mon child," she said, leading me to the bar. "Set 'em up, Meg, and keep 'em coming."

Justine lifted her glass in the air to salute me. "I wouldn't have said you were wrong, but in my book you did the right thing."

I slumped on the bar. "Jan's mad at me anyway," I told them. "She saw us dancing together."

Justine stroked my hair. "She's still your friend."

"I'm afraid I've lost them both," I sighed.

Justine shook her head. "Jan will be back. And Edna was crying and smiling when she walked out of here. You must have done something right."

I shook my head. "I don't know, it doesn't feel like I'm doing anything right."

Peaches laughed, "You wait and see. The right girl is coming down the road, headed in your direction."

If that was true, I sure wished she'd hurry.

CHAPTER 10

If it wasn't for Edwin I might never have met Milli. Ed was on her way to have breakfast with Darlene one morning. "Come with?" she asked.

When Ed and I walked into that sleazy diner I was glad I'd come. The restaurant was filled with working girls—male and female. We were welcomed with a boisterous roar. I got kissed and teased. Darlene pulled Edwin down on her knee and feigned threats to all the other femmes to leave her butch alone. It was fun when we all played like that.

Darlene told me about the last television episode of "The Fugitive": the real killer is caught and David Janssen gets vindicated and can stop running.

Ed was arguing with a woman sitting across from us about the riots in Newark and Detroit. "Violence is as American as cherry pie. That's what Rap Brown says." Ed pounded her fist on the tabletop. "They're a dress rehearsal for revolution."

The woman raised both her hands in surrender. "OK, alright. Don't blow your cool."

Everyone was trying to shout over the jukebox, which was turned up real loud. The Beatles were singing "Lucy in the Sky with Diamonds." I tapped Darlene on the shoulder. "What's that song mean, anyhow?"

She laughed. "How the hell should I know?"

My eyes burned from exhaustion. I asked Edwin to come outside with me and listen while I kick-started my Norton. It wouldn't kick over whenever it was chilly and damp. I didn't know why.

It was over Ed's shoulder that I really saw Milli for the first time. She was standing there just looking at me. Ed glanced at Milli and then, like a good friend, Ed walked away.

I have a few mental photographs I can see in my mind's eye. One of them is Milli, hands on her hips, looking me up and down as if the bike and I were one lean machine. Her body language, the gleam in her eyes, the tease in her smile, all combined into an erotic femme challenge. Milli set the action into irresistible motion by lifting one eyebrow.

Without a word I took off my brown leather jacket and offered it to her. Neither of us were in any hurry. Once this dance began there was no reason to rush and every reason to take it deliciously slow. I helped her on with my jacket.

I think I fell in love with her the moment she swung her leg over the bike and settled in behind me. The way two women relate on a motorcycle is part of their sex together—and she was very, very good on a bike.

I didn't realize until she waved as we roared off that all her friends were watching us from the restaurant window, smiling those sweet, secret kind of smiles at her.

From that moment on I was her butch and she was my femme. Everybody knew it. So did we. We just fit and the sparks flew. We were both a couple of tough cookies, and together we felt unbeatable.

It wasn't just bravado. We matched each other in nerve. For a stone butch and a stone pro to survive, they have to tough it out with the world. We walked our talk and we appreciated it in each other. Slow dancing at dawn, making fierce love, leaning together as one with the motorcycle into a deep curve—it just got better and better.

One morning Milli didn't come to the bar after work as usual. Neither did Darlene or her friends. All of us were worried. Darlene finally pulled up in a car. Milli was bleeding in the back seat. Her face was all busted up. I got in and held her head on my lap. We had to take her to a goddamn veterinarian to get her arm set in a cast. We were afraid emergency room staff might have called the cops. It was an off-duty cop who beat her.

It took Milli a long, long time to get her confidence back. It changed her. Every beating changes you.

I got a day-shift job at a plastic pipe factory. Milli worked as a temp at a bindery. Everything was OK, it was just different. Then I got pink-slipped and Milli told me casually that she was thinking of going back to dancing in the clubs to get us through.

"No, no, no, no, no!" I thought that made my position perfectly clear. But the way Milli was coming around the kitchen table after me in response made me retreat.

She backed me up against the sink and came right up under my nose. "Nobody," she sputtered in rage, "nobody tells me how to run my life, not you, not anybody. You got that?" I conceded she had a point. "And when did you get so goddamn morally righteous all of a sudden?" She paced around the kitchen.

"Fuck you," I yelled. She knew it wasn't true. "You just said that to hurt me." She conceded I had a point.

"It's just so fucking dangerous for you to go back to the life," I argued. "Don't you remember why you quit?" That last thing I said was a big mistake. I realized it when she picked up the nearest dish and sent it sailing across the room in my direction. I ducked.

"You condescending, motherfucking son-of-a-bitch," she shouted. "Don't you think I know the life better than you do, you bastard?"

We were both quiet for a moment. I decided to do the dishes. Milli leaned up against the kitchen counter with her arms folded across her breasts watching me.

"I just can't stand the thought of any guy, anybody hurting you." I said it as quietly as I could.

Milli grabbed a dishtowel and started drying the dishes. It was a good sign. "How do you think I feel," she asked, "when you're bouncer at the bar on the weekends and there's a fight?" She got herself all worked up again. "For christsakes what's the fucking difference between you being a bouncer and me working as a hostess?"

"A *dancer,*" I clarified. "You know I'd be worried every fucking minute you were late from your shift."

"Well, fuck you then. That's your problem, baby, not mine." Milli did a double take at me and dropped her gaze. I thought maybe she was sorry she had said that.

"I'm sorry," she told me. "It's just I can't stand it when someone does this moral thing with me."

"Goddamn you!" Now I was yelling. "Ever since you met me you've been waiting for me to make one fucking mistake, say one wrong thing about you being a pro."

"An ex-pro," she said sarcastically.

"It's no goddamn joke. I never laid any bullshit on you about it. You know that. But every time we have a fight you're lying in wait, just hoping you'll make me so mad I'll make a mistake. Then you could leave."

Milli smiled for the first time since I came home and told her I'd been laid off. "What's so funny?" I asked sullenly.

"I like you," she said softly.

I turned back to the sink and shook my head so she could see that I was exasperated. She turned me around. There was a really warm look on her face. She kissed me on the mouth. I kissed her back. Then I turned around to finish the dishes.

She turned me around again. "We have to pay the rent. It's just for a while. I don't like it any better than you do."

I laughed. "Bullshit!"

She raised one eyebrow, daring me to pursue it.

"There's parts of the life you like a lot," I told her. "I know that."

Milli looked amazed. "Do you really know that?" I nodded. She put her arms around me. "We fit perfectly," she ran her hands up and down my back. "Remember those old spy movies where they cut a playing card into two jagged pieces? Then when the spies meet they put the two pieces together. That's how pros and stone butches are. We just fit, you know?"

She kissed me again. She was a great kisser. Then she grabbed a handful of my hair and pulled my head back and really looked at me before she spoke again. "You're the only women in the world who hurt almost the same way I do, you know?"

I did.

"And another thing," she kissed my throat. "You're the tenderest lovers in the world." She unbuttoned my shirt as she spoke. The talking was over. The conversation had just begun. We conducted electricity between our bodies.

Later, in bed, I held her in my arms and remembered our fight as if it had been a dream.

"When will you start?" I asked her.

Her body tensed. "I'll call Darlene tomorrow."

I spent all week in a panic putting in applications at the plants. If I could just get a job before the end of the week.

Thursday Milli told me real casually at dinner she was going to start work with Darlene the next night at the Pink Pussy Kat. I poked my meat loaf with a fork.

"Don't start," she warned me.

"I didn't say anything."

We ate in silence. On Friday I left for the bar in the early evening while she was still sleeping. I packed a lunch for her and stuck little red paste-on hearts on the brown paper bag.

Everybody at the bar knew I was upset. The butches patted me on the back and told me to cheer up. The femmes just kind of smoothed the lapels of my suit coat and held me in their gaze for a moment—a more complicated message. Then Justine called me across the room by curling her index finger. She grabbed me firmly by my tie and wouldn't let go. "Cut it out," she ordered.

"What?"

"I said," she gripped my tie more firmly, "cut out all this drama. She doesn't need it, honey. And if you want to lose her, this is just the way to do it."

I felt stunned. "I don't get it," I answered honestly.

"Grow up," she concluded, and let go of me.

By the time the sun came up I was excited about seeing Milli. When she arrived with the other dancers from the club, I was anxious to leave together. But they all spent a long time in the bathroom together.

Finally, each of the women came out, hesitantly leaving the camaraderie of their group and joined us, one-on-one.

Milli's head rested on my back the whole ride home. I was afraid she was asleep and might fall off on a curve.

Once we got home I ran her a hot bubble bath. I went into the bedroom to tell her it was ready, but she'd already fallen asleep. I wasn't tired.

I woke her up around 6:00 P.M. to eat dinner. I'd made her favorite meal, but she just kind of picked at it with her fork. "You OK?" I asked her.

"Yeah, sure," she answered, just like I would have.

"You coming to the bar after work?"

She was quiet for a minute. "Can I meet you at home? I'm just so tired."

I instantly grew sullen because I was scared. "What's wrong with meeting me at the bar?"

"Can we talk about this another time?" she asked me.

"Yeah, sure," I said.

That night I packed her a lunch with the little red hearts on the bag. She picked it up and smiled—at the bag, not at me.

I felt strange the next morning when the other women came to work to meet their butches. As each person asked me where Milli was I grew more defensive and angry.

Millie and I fought about it that morning. "Did it ever occur to you that I might be uncomfortable at the bar?" Milli shouted.

That had never occurred to me at all. "Why?" I asked puzzled.

"Because there's attitude toward us."

"What are you talking about? Lots of the women at the bar are pros." I was aware I was shouting and I wished I would stop.

"They're hometown girls who turn tricks to pay the rent. They're ashamed of what they do. They aren't into the life in the same way as the rest of us. We're different."

I had never thought about it. I was reeling.

"Get it, baby? That's your people, not mine." Her ice-cold tone chilled me. "My people are the women I dance with. That's who watches my back." Milli always was a pro's pro.

I grabbed my leather jacket and took the bike far outside the city limits before I pulled off the road and sat down to think.

The rest of the week we were super-polite to each other around the apartment. I couldn't get Milli to respond to me. She wouldn't play. "I don't know," I told Edwin. "I'm used to being the one who shuts down."

"Give her time," Ed said. "You both just need time."

Sunday morning I was almost asleep when Milli came in. She was in the bathroom for a long time before I realized something was wrong. She turned her face away when I came to the bathroom door. I sat down on the tile floor. "You OK?" I asked her.

"Yeah, baby. Go to sleep."

After a few minutes I got her to look at me. Her face was swollen on one side. A little trickle of blood was leaking from her split lip. I got a washcloth and ran cold water. I stood in front of her until she let me know it was alright to touch her face. She wrapped her arms tight around my waist. I dropped to my knees and held her. Then she pulled away and got up and ran a bath.

I got the message. I went to bed. I was awake when she got undressed and lay down, but I didn't show it. She knew. I think it surprised me more than her when I started to cry. She could deal with me crying about as well as I could deal with her tears. She went into the kitchen and made coffee. I stayed in bed.

She brought a cup of coffee to share and sat down on the bed. Her tone was gentler than I expected. "You remember the time I got beat up real bad and I stopped working the clubs? You know, after we met?"

"Yeah, sure." I wondered what the point was.

"Remember when you held me and told me you would protect me, you wouldn't let anyone hurt me?" I winced. Milli put her hand reassuringly on my back. "What you said wasn't wrong, baby. That's what everyone wants to hear when they've been hurt. The only problem was, you believed it yourself. You can't protect me, sweetheart. I can't protect you. I think you're having trouble dealing with that lately."

I didn't deny it. I didn't say anything. After a while I drifted to sleep. When I got up to go to work, Milli was sleeping on the couch. I covered her with an afghan. I loved her so damn much. What she said was true. I wanted to protect Milli and I knew I couldn't. I couldn't even defend myself very well. I was losing my nerve. I was scared, even at work.

The night before, just after closing time, young Sal had staggered into the bar covered with so much of his own blood we almost didn't recognize him. He was a victim of a Marine who was tying young femme gay men to lampposts and slicing them with razor blades—hundreds of small cuts. Then the Marine would go sit in the restaurant across the street from the bar, waiting to see if anyone would dare stop him.

Everyone knew he'd be skulking around, but none of us expected him to walk right into the bar on a crowded Saturday night. I hardly realized what was happening at first. The pay phone rang. Justine yelled it was for me and told me to hustle up, it was Milli. I put one finger in my ear to hear her better over the noise of the juke box when I saw the Marine cutting right through the crowd toward me. He pointed his index finger at me and mumbled.

"Take it easy," I soothed him.

Booker smashed the guy on the head with a bottle of ketchup. He said later it was the only thing he could grab in such a hurry. It did a fine job. I think it gave everyone a lift to see the Marine out cold, covered in ketchup. The following weekend we heard the Marine had been found dead. No one knew who did it.

When I got home that morning I reenacted the whole scene for Milli. Deep down I wanted so much to make love to her. I had wanted her all week. But we went to sleep still talking about what a hero Booker had been.

It was the next Friday night that we fought so bitterly. I don't even remember what started it. It doesn't really matter. What mattered was that it was the kind of fight that's so painful it takes the top layer of skin off your heart.

I tried to go for a ride. My bike wouldn't kick over. I stormed off for a walk around the block. When I came back, Milli was gone. I sat in the apartment for a long time in the dark. I was really upset. My brain wasn't working too clearly, I remember that.

That's when I realized how we were running off the rails. I suddenly felt I had to apologize to her, to explain, or I'd lose her forever. So I went down to the Pink Pussy Kat. I don't know what I was thinking.

I paced outside the club smoking a cigarette. You couldn't see inside the bar because the windows and doors were papered with shiny foil.

As I opened the door Darlene saw me immediately. She had her arm around a sailor's neck. She looked up at Milli, who was dancing in a little cage just above the bar. Milli had seen me too.

Maybe I thought Milli wore an outfit when she danced. It wasn't that it mattered, I just realized I had never wondered about it. I took in the sights and sounds and smells of the world in which she worked. I listened to the music she danced to: *I never loved a man the way that I, I loved you.*

I had been in so many sleazy bars there was something sort of familiar and commonplace about it all. I could see immediately who was working in the room. It was, of course, the women. But you could tell more by their attitude than their sex. This was, after all, a job. It paid well for women who could take care of themselves. And Milli could take care of herself.

But I knew I had made a fatal error walking in the door—the last mistake I would be allowed to make. I realized in that moment it was too late for us.

I went back to our apartment to wait for her.

Milli came home within hours. She left the apartment door open as she stormed up to me. I must have sensed what was coming because I buried my hands deep inside my pockets. She slapped me hard across my face.

"I'm sorry," was all I could say. I really, really meant it.

"I'll bet you are," Milli said. Her voice was cruel and cold because she was hurting too. "Did you get to see everything you wanted?"

"I'm sorry, baby," I tried to explain. "I didn't go there to hurt you. I wanted to start over. I made a mistake."

"You sure did," she said, but her voice was quieter. She looked at me quizzically. "What were you thinking of?" Then she stopped being angry for a moment. "How did you feel when you walked in there, Jess? Did it hurt you?"

"It's funny," I said. "I sort of felt closer to you right then. And I was thinking about how brave you all are."

"Brave?" Milli narrowed her eyes.

"Yeah. I don't think I could be strong enough to fight without my clothes on."

Milli stood and looked at me without speaking. Then she went into our bedroom and started throwing clothing into a suitcase. I didn't move from where I stood. When she came out, she acted like she was looking around for whatever else she wanted to take, but I knew she was stalling.

"Is there anything I can say?" I asked, already knowing the answer.

Milli softened her expression and came closer.

"I'm sorry, baby," I told her as the tears streamed down my face. She came into my arms for the last time.

"I know I made a big mistake tonight, Milli. I'm sorry I hurt you."

She shook her head and took my face in her hands. "It was a mistake. But that's all it was. I've made some pretty big ones with you. That's not why I'm leaving." She went over to her suitcase and took out the porcelain kitten she'd left home with fifteen years before and put it down on the coffee table near me. She came back and put one hand on my cheek. "I just don't think it's going to be much different than it is, not for now anyway," she explained. "I want to leave before we break everything."

Milli brushed my cheek with her lips, and then she walked through that open door. She was gone.

I sat down on the couch and cried because I just didn't know what else to do. I jumped up and ran downstairs and outside, but she was already gone. Besides, I didn't know how to change everything back to the way it was.

I went back upstairs, opened a bottle of beer, and sat on the edge of the bed. That's when I recalled the weekend before when Milli had called me on the pay phone at work. Just at the moment when I realized the Marine was coming toward me, I forgot—it sounded like she was crying. I just didn't remember, with all the excitement, to ask her later why she had called. Now I'd give anything to know.

The telephone rang. I ran to pick up the receiver. It was Edwin. Of course she knew. Darlene had been waiting downstairs with the car while Milli came upstairs to pack. Darlene wanted Ed to tell me how sorry she was and how much she loved me, too.

"You OK?" Edwin asked me.

"I don't think so," I told her.

There was a long silence.

"You were great together," Ed said.

"Yeah, we were, weren't we?"

"She really loved you," Ed reminded me. "Remember when you used to pack those lunches for Milli in the brown paper bags with those little red hearts on them?"

"How did you know that?" I asked. "Did the other girls tease her about it?"

"Hell no," Edwin said. "They were jealous. You made it hard on the rest of us butches. We all had to start packing 'love lunches.' Anyway, promise you won't tell Darlene this?" I promised.

"Milli told Darlene that she thought she might have been loved once or twice in her life, but nobody had ever cared about her as good as you did."

I took a deep breath. "Did she say that a long time ago?"

"Nah," Ed said, catching my drift, "recently."

"Ed, I hurt."

"I know," Ed said gently. "I'm sort of in the same boat. Things are kind of rough right now with me and Darlene."

"Why is it so hard?" I felt confused.

"I don't know," Ed sighed. "I guess love's never easy. But it's different between a butch and a pro." Ed sounded lost in her own thoughts. "It's love with no illusions."

There was a long silence. We both took a deep breath.

"My bike isn't running."

"Go to work tonight," Edwin advised. "I'll meet you there in the morning and we'll take a look at it."

"Ed," I said, "I really fucked up this time."

"Nah," she reassured me, "you just got a little more growing up to do."

"I don't know if I can do it," I told her.

My friend laughed. "You got no choice."

CHAPTER 11

I stopped going to the bar for a few weeks. I'd heard Milli left town, but I just didn't feel like seeing anybody. I got two temp jobs in order to pay for some major repairs on my Norton and to keep me busy. My life felt so hollow after I lost Milli.

During the day I packed cartons of milk at the dairy on Niagara Street.

At night I worked at the plastic pipe factory in South Buffalo. We'd dump huge twenty-five-pound bags filled with powder into extrusion machines, and plastic pipe would push out the other end. The first day I started there my pocket watch stopped ten minutes after the shift started—it was jammed with powder. I got coated from head to foot with that dust.

After a couple of weeks I was exhausted from working doubles. I saved up more than enough to fix my bike and I couldn't think of anything else I needed. So I gave notice Friday night at the pipe factory.

When I got home Saturday morning, I found Ed sitting on my front porch. She was wearing dress pants and a starched white shirt with ruby cuff links. Ed was a sight for sore eyes. She stared at me like she'd seen a ghost. "What's that green shit all over you?" Only my eyes showed under the coat of powder. "You better get cleaned up,"

Ed told me. "Don't you know about the funeral today? Old Butch Ro died."

Butch Ro was very much loved by all the old bulls. She was the elders' elder. She had worked in the Chevy plant longer than anybody could remember. I could hardly imagine the depth of grief the older butches were feeling. They had loved each other so long and shared so much together.

Ro and her lover almost never went out to the bars. I'd only seen them once in Niagara Falls at Tifka's. But whether I had known her or not, it was important for me to attend her funeral. All the butches would be there. It was a sign of respect for the role she played in our community.

I showered while Ed made coffee. She shouted something about dressing up as I was drying off. "What?" I called from the bathroom.

"We're supposed to dress up," Ed yelled.

"Yeah, of course."

"No," she shouted. "You know, like girls."

I put on a robe and came into the kitchen to make sure I'd heard her right. "Says who?"

"The old bulls said so." Ed shrugged. "But I don't put on a dress for nobody!" She told me we were going to a funeral home to see a body, not knocking on heaven's gate to get let in.

I couldn't put on a dress. I shuddered at the thought. Besides, it was a moot point—I didn't own one. But if the word had come down from the older butches, something must be up.

"C'mon, hurry up and get dressed," Ed urged me. "Everybody's probably already there by now."

It was too late to call up anyone for advice. I put on my blue suit, a white shirt, and dark tie.

Ed drove her car to the funeral home. I followed on my motorcycle. Once we arrived, I sat on my bike in the parking lot. I wanted to show my respect for Butch Ro, but I wished I didn't have to go in. "What's with you, Jess?" Ed asked me in exasperation.

"I don't know," I told her. I felt a sense of dread.

When we got inside, it took a minute to find the right room. Then I knew we had found it. There, around the open casket, were Butch Ro's lifelong friends. All of them were wearing dresses. That's how much they loved her.

These were burly, big-shouldered he-shes who carried their womanhood in work-roughened hands. They could playfully slap you on the back and send you halfway across the room. Their forearms and biceps were covered with tattoos. These powerful butch women were comfortable in work chinos. Their spirit roared to life when they wore double-breasted suits.

Wearing dresses was an excruciating humiliation for them. Many of their dresses were old, from another era when occasional retreats were still necessary. The dresses were outdated, white, frilly, lace, low-cut, plain. The shoes were old or borrowed: patent leather, loafers, sandals. This clothing degraded their spirit, ridiculed who they were. Yet it was in this painful drag they were forced to say their last goodbye to the friend they loved so much.

Ro's femme, Alice, greeted each one of them. You could see how much she longed to fall against their solid bodies, to feel the gentle strength of their arms. Instead she respectfully refused to acknowledge the pain they all shared together. She held in her own. Ro—the butch Alice had loved for almost thirty years—lay in the casket next to her, laid out in a pink dress and holding a bunch of pink-and-white flowers.

What cruel hand controlled this scene? I saw them just as they saw Ed and me. It was Ro's family—father, mother, and brothers. They saw us the moment we walked in and whispered in the funeral director's ear. In a flash, the director announced the funeral home was closing and we all had to leave. Just like that.

Ed and I went to the local diner for coffee. We were sitting there when all the older butches came filing in past us. Each of them had found a place to change clothes, even if it meant crouching down in the backseat of a car. When they saw us, they all headed straight for the opposite side of the diner.

Jan charged at me with murder in her eyes, but the other women restrained her. Butch Jan—the elder I wanted to turn to for advice. Butch Jan—my friend.

Jan had been cool to me for a long time, ever since the night she saw me dancing with Edna. Now she really hated me.

A few minutes later Alice came in, supported by a butch on each side.

Ed and I were completely isolated. I wanted to leave. It was too painful. After a few minutes Alice came over to us, like an emissary. I felt bad that she had to play diplomat at a time when her grief was so unbearable, but I knew the butches were too angry to speak to us. I stood as she approached our table. I took her hand; she kissed my cheek.

"The old butches are pretty mad at you two," she explained gently. "Some of them feel like you spoiled it. See, they figured if they could make such a sacrifice to say goodbye to Ro, you young ones could, too. It's not your fault, really. But you two better keep a low profile for a while, if you know what I mean."

Alice's anguish was so discernible that I ached to reach out and hold her, but she wouldn't have let me. I understood. It was easy for me to feel strong, to give of myself, dressed the way I was. For the butches who were watching us from across the diner, it had been painful and hard. Alice kissed my cheek lightly. "It'll blow over, you'll see," she whispered. I hoped she was right.

I figured I'd take Alice's advice and lay low for a week or two, until I got some sign it was alright to appear at the bar again. But weeks of exile passed without a single phone call that would signal the ice had thawed.

Mornings grew chilly. Autumn was in the air. There weren't many jobs. The temp agency sent me to the cannery at Four Corners. It was an unpaid two-hour ride each way.

I boarded the company bus at 4:45 A.M. It was cold and damp. Someone passed a bottle of whiskey around. I reached for the bottle and drank as I looked out the window.

"Hey," I heard Butch Jan's voice growl, "are you gonna share that, or what?" She was kneeling on the seat in front of me. I held my breath. Jan leaned forward and grabbed a handful of my jacket. "Do you get it yet?" she demanded. Her face contorted with shifting emotions.

I nodded. "Yes, I think I understood right away. I just didn't know what to do. I'm sorry. I'm so sorry I messed it up for all of you to say goodbye to Ro."

Jan let go of my jacket and smoothed the leather. "Ah, it wasn't your fault," she said. "The next day at the burial the family made us stay one hundred yards away from the grave. That wasn't your fault either."

I leaned closer to her. "Listen, Jan," I whispered, "I'm sorry about everything, you know what I mean?" We both knew I had shifted the conversation to the night Jan saw Edna and I dancing together. "It wasn't like you think, really."

Jan looked out the window like she was daydreaming. I waited. Jan smiled and reached for the bottle of whiskey. "It's OK." She took a slug and shivered. "No harm done. You ever work at the cannery before?" I shook my head.

She smiled and patted my cheek roughly. "I'll show you the ropes." With those kind words she welcomed me back to the only real family I'd ever known.

CHAPTER 12

I still remember the moment Jan and I walked into the cannery and I saw Theresa, standing right there in front of me. She was working on a machine, coring apples. I was trying to get a better look at her, wondering what color her hair was under that white paper net. "You coming or not?" the foreman asked me. I hung back for a moment. Her smile told me she already knew she had my complete attention.

Even when we were filling out forms in the foreman's office, I still felt floored and flustered. Theresa never stopped affecting me just that much. The foreman noticed, but he must not have cared because he assigned me to work on the line near her.

I watched as each woman put an apple on a spindle and pressed a foot pedal. The apples spun around and were peeled and cored in the process. All of it landed on a conveyor belt headed toward me. Just past me, the conveyor split into two belts.

The foreman handed me a stick. I looked at it stupidly. He told me to hit the cores and peels one way, the apples another. "That's it?" I asked. He snorted and walked away.

Thus began my short-lived career as an apple-hitter.

I knew Theresa was watching so I wanted to do it suavely, but that was kind of stretching it, considering the task.

"What are you doing?" she asked me.

I shrugged. "I'm inspecting the apples—you know, quality of the fruit, worm holes, efficiency of the coring and peeling operation."

She threw her head back and smiled. "You mean you're an apple-bopper?"

"Yeah," I laughed. "Something like that."

"Hey you, asshole!" someone at the end of the conveyor belts yelled. OK, so I had let a few peels go down the apple belt. Big deal!

Theresa laughed softly and went back to her work. She was playing with me. This flirtation was one of life's unexpected pleasures. Almost as soon as it started, it ended. The foreman announced he was moving me. "I could do a better job hitting these apples," I insisted.

I followed him to another part of the plant where the actual canning was done. The noise terrified me. The foreman pointed to a Y-shaped conveyor belt running parallel to the ceiling. I saw a guy up there straddling a giant pipe near the point where the conveyor belt split into two. Every few seconds a carton came down the single belt. He diverted them alternately one way or another. I was replacing him.

The foreman showed me a metal pole with footholds. I waited for the guy who was already up there to climb down, but he swung down from pipe to pipe, brushed off his hands, and walked away. I assumed he had been doing this job for a while.

I had hoped I could climb above the din, but both the height and the roar made me nauseous. This job looked like it required all the skill and judgment of apple-bopping. But although it wasn't a complex task, it sure wasn't as easy as it first appeared. The cartons were packed with heavy cans of applesauce. They hurtled at me with tremendous velocity, and I had to hit them to divert them. I nearly fell off. I learned to hit the boxes from an angle, not head-on.

After I got the hang of it I realized what an interesting vantage point I had. I'd never seen the life of a factory from a bird's-eye view. The arrangement of the machines, the sequence and interrelatedness of tasks, the organized scurrying of workers.

I noticed a ruckus near the women's bathroom—Butch Jan squared off with two women and a man. It was a fight I'd engaged in many times, but never watched safely as a third party. Jan stood with hands on hips and her mouth moving like she was shouting. I could see how defensive and embarrassed she felt by watching her body.

I never would have heard the foreman yelling for me below. He banged a hammer against a metal pipe connected to the one I was sitting on. The vibration startled me, and the next box almost took me over and down. He pointed to his watch. It must be lunchtime.

I met up with Jan in the cafeteria. She was upset because some women in the bathroom claimed they thought she was a man. They said God didn't create women to look like men. "Then explain me," Jan answered them. I laughed as she told the story, but it really wasn't funny.

I saw that good-looking femme come in, but Jan was sputtering mad and I wanted to hear her out. "They said they thought I was a man when they saw my tattoos." Jan hit the lunch table. "I said, 'If you really thought I was a man you'd of run out of the bathroom yelling.' " I nodded. She was right.

The woman sat at a table with her friends. I swore she was checking me out. Jan glanced over her shoulder to see what I was looking at. "See something you like on the menu?" Jan laughed.

I squirmed in my seat. "Aw, you know. She's probably just playing with me."

"Like hell she is." Jan sounded in the know.

"Whaddya mean?" I shot back.

"I heard she asked someone what your name was."

"You're kidding me. I don't believe it."

Jan looked wounded. "No, really."

I got my hopes up. Then they sank. "Oh, it probably doesn't mean a thing," I concluded.

Jan smiled like there was something else. "Well, she did ask if you were single." My jaw dropped. I couldn't recover my composure. "For Christsake, be cool," Jan patted my arm.

"Jan, what's her name?"

"Theresa." I savored her name, repeating it over in my mind. When you do that, it's a sign something big is happening in your heart.

At the end of the day I looked for Theresa at the time clock, but she was hidden in the wave of hundreds of workers leaving and hundreds more entering for the next shift. I didn't talk much on the bus ride home. I just stared out the window. Jan laughed softly and shook her head.

The next day I could hardly wait to get to work. Jan and I were assigned to load trucks. It was heavy work. I was leaning up against a pole smoking a cigarette when Theresa walked by to go to the bathroom. Actually, the bathroom was in the opposite direction. I felt embarrassed because I was dripping with sweat and my white T-shirt was filthy. Theresa smiled. "I like sweaty butches," she said, as though she'd read my mind. Man, those boxes sailed out of my hands all day as though they were filled with feathers.

For the next week I didn't sleep much. I leaped out of bed as soon as the alarm rang and rode the long distance out to the cannery in excited anticipation. I saw Theresa at least twice a shift. I was floating a foot off the ground.

Then, one day, Jan pulled me aside after a break. "Got some bad news for you, kid." Theresa had been fired. The General Superintendent called her into his office to go over her six-month review. That's when he grabbed her breasts. Jan said Theresa kicked him in the shin, yelled at him, and then kicked him in the other shin. Good for her. Anyway, he fired her.

I crashed from the summit of euphoria. It was just a job after that. Worse, really, because it had been so much fun. I knew it was time to ask the temp agency for another assignment.

The following Friday night I showered and dressed up. When I got to the bar, I was glad I had. Theresa walked in the door. I had never expected to see her again. She had cajoled some friends into driving her to Buffalo to look for me. Lucky for me there was only one gay bar at a time.

The hue of Theresa's hair reminded me of the lustrous colors of a chestnut. It was well worth waiting to see. Her eyes didn't hide how happy she was to see me. I think she would have liked to hug me, but she restrained herself. So did I. I kissed the cheek she offered me.

I saw Grant near the jukebox. A moment later I heard "Stand By Your Man" playing. Thanks, Grant. I asked Theresa to dance. She took her time smoothing my collar and adjusting my tie before she led me to the dance floor. We moved beautifully together. Meg told me later we looked as good as Ginger Rogers and Fred Astaire.

All the while we were dancing, Theresa traced the back of my neck above my collar with her fingernails. She was driving me mad. I guess that was the point. I knew I was driving her crazy, too, but I was being very, very careful doing it. Sometimes when you just move a little, carefully, it's a whole lot more powerful than grinding.

When the song finished I let go of her, but Theresa pulled me back. "I wasn't trying to be mean to you at the plant. Did you think I was?"

"No, it felt good."

She smiled. "I don't think I was very nice to you. I was just teasing you, to get your attention. I liked you."

I blushed. "Nobody ever flirted with me outside a bar before—I mean in the real world, you know? It made me feel normal." She nodded like she really understood.

We talked for a while about our lives. She was a rural girl from Appleton. She came right out and told me she got friends to drive her to this bar just to look for me.

Then someone tapped Theresa on the shoulder. The women she rode to Buffalo with were leaving. She took my face in both her hands and kissed my mouth. I blushed from head to toe. She stood back and grinned at my color, proud of her work. "I'll make you dinner at my house next Saturday night if you want," she offered.

"You're on," I said, still blushing.

She scribbled her phone number down on a cocktail napkin. "Call me," she shouted over her shoulder.

"You can bet on it," I answered. I was still blushing.

You would have thought I'd won the Kentucky Derby the way everybody came over to congratulate me. I felt like a million bucks. I just wondered if I'd ever stop blushing.

It took me all day Saturday to get ready—pick out the right clothes, bathe, shower, shower again. Then there were questions like which tie, cologne or no cologne? Something so sweet took a lot of care.

I brought Theresa daffodils. When I handed them to her, her eyes filled with tears.

I had a feeling nobody had treated her like someone special before. I silently vowed to always make her feel that way.

"I'll just be a minute," she called out from the kitchen. I was glad for the time to nose around her living room and get a sense of her. One thing I could tell for sure—she loved dried wildflowers. "Ready," she called out moments later. "Do you mind eating here in the kitchen?" I'd never eaten anyplace else.

She made me a steak and mashed potatoes with gravy. God, it looked delicious. Then she put a mound of soft, green stuff on my plate.

"What's that?" I asked as politely as I could.

"Spinach," she said, locking me into her gaze. I circled it with my fork. "Is something wrong?" she asked.

"I just never eat vegetables, that's all."

Theresa took off her oven glove. She sat down on a kitchen chair next to me and took both my hands in her hands. "Never say never," she said. "We're too young to close the door to anything in our lives."

I discovered I was already in love with her. Actually, I found out spinach isn't all that bad either, if you put lots of butter and salt on it.

After dinner I helped her wash the dishes and clean up. Then, by the sink, we moved close to each other. I felt shy. That turned out to be alright. Gently, we kissed each other. Our tongues discovered a silent language to express our needs. Once we started, we never wanted to stop. That's how it began.

Within a month we rented a U-Haul trailer and moved into a new apartment together in Buffalo. Theresa negotiated with the landlord. He lived in Kenmore, so we hoped he'd never actually see me.

We got real furniture. I mean, it was Salvation Army, but it was real. Our names were printed inside a heart on the dish towel that hung on the refrigerator door handle. We got it made at Crystal Beach. It was a brave thing to do. But later we spilled loganberry juice on it, so we used it for dishes because we couldn't bring ourselves to throw it out. And there were marigolds in amber glasses on the windowsill, daisies in a green cut-glass vase on the kitchen table, fresh mint and basil growing in a flower box on the porch.

It was a home.

I grew up in leaps and bounds. I learned to reduce the anxieties of life by paying bills on time, keeping receipts and promises, doing laundry before I ran out of underwear, picking up after myself. Most importantly, I learned to say I'm sorry. This relationship was too vital to let dust accumulate in its corners.

I began to realize how emotionally wounded I was, how damaged. But Theresa could always sense when I was about to petrify like stone. She could see it coming by the way I held my body as I walked in the door. She could hear it building up in the stories of life's daily abuses—on the job, at the corner store, on the street. Those were the times she would tell me stories in bed—wonderful, sensuous, tactile fantasies about how your body feels when you're lying on sand in the sun and the ocean's waves are lapping near your toes. Or climbing worn wooden stairs to visit a quaint sunlit room where a lover awaits. The stories were relaxation therapy and sexual fantasy combined, meant to simultaneously calm and arouse me. They did both. Theresa could always melt my stone.

It was 1968. Revolution seemed to glimmer on the horizon. Millions took to the streets in protest. The world was exploding with change. Everywhere, that is, except in the factories where I worked. Every morning at dawn we punched in as usual. We only dreamed at night.

It wasn't that we didn't know there was a war raging. There were hardly any draft-age guys in the plants anymore. Coworkers who were absent for several days were assumed to have lost a husband, son, or brother. The ashen grief on their faces when they returned to work confirmed the fact.

I knew there was a war. I wasn't stupid. I just didn't know what on earth I could do about it.

It was Theresa's job as a secretary at the university that opened a window, allowing me to feel the hurricane force of change. She brought home leaflets, pamphlets, and underground newspapers. I read about Black Power and Women's Liberation. I began to understand that outrage against the war was much deeper and more organized than I'd realized. "There's campus rallies and protests almost every day now," she told me, "not just against the war, but to open up the schools to everybody."

When Theresa learned I'd never read anything in a newspaper except the comics, she ordered home subscriptions to the morning and evening papers. One day she left a copy of *The Ladder* on the couch. It was a magazine put out by a group called the Daughters of Bilitis. I didn't know who Bilitis was. I'd never seen anything about women like us in print before.

"Where'd you get this?" I shouted to her.

She called back from the kitchen, "In the mail."

"You got this sent to our address in the mail? Was it wrapped? What if someone in the building saw it?"

After a long silence, Theresa came in with a hand mirror and held it up to my face. "Did ya think you were a secret?"

Theresa needed a root canal, but she couldn't get any overtime at the University. So when the temp agency offered me a triple shift at the electronics plant, I jumped at the chance. Theresa wondered if the emergency production at the factory had something to do with the war. In any case, we needed the money so I took it.

I started the triple on Thursday evening. What a killer. By the end of the third shift I could scarcely feel the wires as I soldered. I kept burning my index finger with the red-hot iron.

Theresa was out when I got home Friday night. I left her a note, stumbled into bed, and lost consciousness. When I woke up, she was lying next to me, smoking one of my cigarettes. I knew something was up. She didn't smoke. Theresa left the room and came back with ointment and bandaids for my finger. "Did you hear Dr. King was killed?" she asked me.

I lit a cigarette and lay back down. "Yeah, I heard about it Thursday night at work. What day is today, anyway?"

"It's Saturday afternoon," she said. "There's been rioting all over the place. And Jess," Theresa sighed, "there was real trouble at the bar last night."

I felt a pang of jealousy. "You went without me?"

Theresa smoothed my hair. "It was Grant's birthday, remember?"

I smacked my forehead. "Fuck, I forgot. How was the party?"

Theresa reached for another one of my cigarettes. I grabbed her hand. "Whoa! What's going on?"

"There was a big fight last night. A fist fight," she said.

I frowned. "Are you OK?" Theresa nodded. "Cops?" I asked. She shook her head. "Well, what happened?"

Theresa took a deep breath. "The Army notified Grant's family Thursday night that her brother got killed. Grant was already drunk when she showed up to the party. At first everyone was consoling her. Then some of the older butches who did hitches in the service started talking about the war. Some of the things they were saying didn't sit right with everyone." I listened quietly.

"Grant said we ought to drop an A-bomb on Vietnam. She said no one would miss them. Ed told Grant she was a racist and said we should bring all the soldiers home. Ed said she felt like Muhammad Ali, that she didn't have any beef with the people over there. Grant called her a communist."

I shook my head and started to speak. Theresa put her finger against my lips. "It got much worse, honey," she said. "Grant said some terrible things about King being killed, about the riots. She wouldn't stop. So Ed hit her."

I crushed out my cigarette. "Oh shit."

"Anyway," Theresa continued, "Grant got Ed up against the bar, choking her. Peaches hauled off and pounded Grant on the head with her high heel. Other people got involved just because they were drunk. Ed's face got cut up. Grant got a concussion. And now Meg is saying no Blacks will be allowed back at Abba's for a while."

I couldn't believe what she was saying. "Shit, Theresa, what did you do?"

Theresa looked me dead in the eyes. "When Grant tried to hit Peaches over the head with a bar stool, I cracked Grant over the head with a beer bottle and knocked her out. I'm barred from Abba's, too."

I leaned forward and kissed her on the lips. "It sounds like a mess." I sat up. "I'd better call Ed and see if she's OK," I said.

Theresa tugged my arm. "C'mere, baby. Don't call yet."

"Why not?"

Theresa shrugged. "What are you going to say to Ed?"

"I don't know. I want to know if she's OK. I just think we all shouldn't be fighting each other. We need to stick together." Theresa nodded as though I'd confirmed something she already knew. She pulled me against her body. A wave of exhaustion rolled over me.

"Be careful," Theresa whispered. "Think first before you call Ed." I pulled back my head and studied her face. I never could read that woman's mind.

"Let's go somewhere," she said.

I moaned. "I'm too tired."

Theresa grabbed a handful of my hair and pulled my head back. "Too tired to neck with me behind a sand dune at Beaver Island?"

I knew enough to surrender early. "OK, alright. Should we take the car?"

Theresa shook her head. "Get the bike out of the garage."

"Are you crazy?" I laughed. "It's cold!"

Theresa slid her hands around my waist. "It's April, honey. Let's live like it's already spring."

The moment we swung our legs over the Norton I knew it was a good decision. It felt so good to turn into the curves together. One of Theresa's hands slid down to my thigh. I revved the engine in response. The cold wind sucked the laughter from our mouths.

We rode slowly past the island marsh. Theresa pointed to a flock of wild geese headed north. The beach itself was almost deserted. A couple of mothers meandered along the boardwalk with their toddlers.

We flopped down on the sand in front of the boardwalk. The sun was strong and warm. We could hear a radio playing faintly in the distance. *This guy's in love with you,* Herb Alpert sang. I leaned up against a dune and spread my legs. Theresa curled up between my thighs and leaned back against me. I wrapped my arms around her and closed my eyes. The sound of lapping water and cawing gulls soothed all the tightness from my muscles.

"Honey," she said. Something in her tone made my muscles tense again. "You and I never really talk about the war. I don't even know how you feel about it."

My lips were close to her cheek. "I read those leaflets you bring home."

Theresa turned to look at me. "But what do you think?"

I shrugged. "What do you mean? I hate wars. But JFK didn't ask me if I wanted to start one. They're gonna do what they want to do. Why are you asking me this?"

Theresa pulled my knees against her sides with her elbows. "I hate this war, Jess. It's got to stop. There's protest rallies on campus almost every day. If anyone from the staff gets spotted at one, we can get fired. But I'm thinking about going to the big rally next week anyway."

I whistled. "You could get fired for going?"

Theresa nodded. "I can't sit by and watch, Jess. It's gotten to the point where I feel like I've got to do something."

I lay down on my belly in the cool sand. "It's funny to hear you talk like this. You know, I didn't realize before how different our jobs are. All this stuff's going on where you work. It doesn't touch us at the factory, except when one of the guys gets drafted or killed."

Theresa nodded. "I know, honey. This is the first time in my life I've had a job where I can see what's going on in the world. All day long I hear people arguing about things that are happening. I used to just listen. But now I care. Now I've got feelings about what's going on and I want to help try to change things."

I held up one hand to stop her. "Slow down, honey." I flopped over on my back. I wondered why her words scared me so much. "Is that why you brought me out here today? To talk to me about this?" I shielded my eyes from the sun to watch her face.

She shook her head. "I brought you out here so you wouldn't call Ed right way—not till we talked first."

I frowned. "Why?"

Theresa smiled and lay so close I could feel her breath on my ear. "You know one of the things I liked best about you when I first got to know you?"

I was being handled, but gently, so I didn't mind much. "Tell me," I smiled.

Theresa laughed. "You were always the peacemaker. Whenever the butches got tanked up and hot under the collar, you found a way to step in and defuse things. I even noticed that sometimes when two of the older butches would get mad at each other they would drift over to you one at a time and you'd talk to each of them and there wasn't a fist fight."

I turned my head to look at her. "There's a point here, I'll bet."

Theresa squeezed my arm. "That's one of your strengths. The way you soothe people when they're mad at each other. Sticking together is really important sometimes. But not always."

I sat up. "What do you mean?"

Theresa sat up next to me. "Sometimes you have to take sides."

I reached for my cigarettes and lit one. Theresa took it from my hand. I lit another for myself. "Sides on what?" I asked her.

Theresa ran her fingers through my hair. "Where you stand on the war, for one thing. If you come out against the war, you'll have to take on some of the old butches. And I think that's going to be very hard for you."

I sighed. "Of course I'm against war. Who's for war?"

Theresa sighed. "Some of the butches are for the war, honey. And are you sure you're really against all wars? Are there any wars you feel different about?"

I did a double take. "Like what?"

Theresa took a long drag on her cigarette. "Ed feels like she's in a war here at home. You haven't seen the news yet. Cities are burning. There's troops in the streets."

I shrugged. "That's different."

Theresa nodded. "Yeah, it is. You have to figure out where you stand." I exhaled smoke and watched the wind lift it up and away.

Theresa watched my face with obvious concern. "I'm just saying be careful, honey. Think first before you talk to Ed or anybody else about what happened last night."

I listened to the seagulls' caws. Theresa tugged on my arm, demanding my response. "I'm listening. I'm glad you didn't let me call Ed all half-cocked. Everything's changing so fast. Sometimes I understand what's going on and then I lose the thread again. I'll think about it. I just don't know what I think."

Theresa kissed my lips. "That's a great answer. You'll figure it out. You always try to do what's right." I dropped my eyes. Theresa lifted my chin with her hand. She asked me with her eyes what I was feeling.

"I'm just scared," I told her. "All this stuff hasn't really hit me until now. But all of a sudden I'm realizing how much you've been changing, and it scares me to death. I'm afraid you're changing and I'm not."

Theresa pulled me down on top of her. I glanced around to see if anyone was around. We were alone.

"Jess," Theresa whispered, "don't be afraid to let me change. We're all changing. Who knows? You could end up changing so much you'd leave me behind."

I laughed at her words. "Never," I promised. "That'll never happen."

Before I could turn the apartment door key in our lock Theresa opened it. "How did it go?" she asked me.

I shrugged. "It was hard. I talked to Jan first. She said pretty much the same thing I did to you—we shouldn't be fighting each other. But she agreed Grant could be a real pain."

Theresa led me to the couch. "Did you talk to Meg?"

"Yeah. Jan came with me. We talked to Meg before everyone else showed up to the meeting. I told Meg even if she barred the Black butches and queens that wasn't gonna keep the peace because I would have jumped in Grant's face over the shit she said, too. Jan backed me up."

Theresa smiled. "Did you mention me?"

I laughed. "Not at that point. I told Meg by the time she excludes everyone who might be offended by Grant when she's drunk, she may as well shut down the bar. I said it would make more sense to bar Grant when she's plowed."

Theresa nodded. I lit a cigarette. "So?" she urged. "Then what?"

I sighed. "I said it wasn't just about me and Ed being friends. I told Meg I didn't think she handled it right. She said she's got a business to run. I said I know that, but I wouldn't go to an all-white bar."

Theresa slapped my shoulder. "Good for you, goddamn it. Right on!"

"Anyway, when Grant got there she apologized for taking out her anger at her brother's death on everybody else."

Theresa nodded. "Good."

I shook my head. "Well, it wasn't enough, really. She wouldn't say she was sorry for the racist shit she said. Grant shook Ed's hand. Ed told me to let it go for now."

Theresa jiggled my arm. "Did you and Ed talk?"

I smiled. "Yeah, we went over to her house afterward. I told Edwin I love her—she's my friend. I said the world was changing faster than I am and I needed to do some catching up in order to understand. Ed talked to me for a couple of hours."

Theresa began kneading my shoulders. It felt so damn good. "What did she talk about?"

I tried to remember. "So much stuff that it's hard for me to put it all together and tell you. You know, I always fall back on assuming that what Ed and I deal with every day as butches is pretty much the same, you know? Ed reminded me about what she faces every day that I don't."

Theresa smiled and nodded. "What did you say?"

I shook my head. "I didn't say anything. I listened as hard as I could. Look what Ed gave me." I showed Theresa the copy of *The Souls of Black Folk* by W.E.B. Du Bois. Theresa read the inscription: *To my friend, Jess—Love, Edwin.* Ed dotted the *i* in her name with a little heart.

When Theresa looked up I saw tears in her eyes. She pulled my head down and kissed me all over my face. "I love you, too, Jess," she whispered in my ear.

Theresa and I both heard the commotion outside the bar at once. She put down her beer bottle and ran outside. I grabbed our bottles in case we needed to break them to use as weapons. We both stopped dead in our tracks outside. Justine was on her knees. A cop stood over her. His club hung loosely at his side. I saw the blood streaming down the side of Justine's face.

It was a sultry hot evening in July. A number of people had drifted outside the bar in order to drink their beers. Two cop cars were parked in front of the bar. Four cops faced us. "Get inside, all of you," one of the cops barked. None of us moved.

The cop standing over Justine grabbed a handful of her hair. "On your feet," he ordered. She stumbled as she tried to rise and fell back onto the concrete.

Theresa slipped off her high heels. "Take your hands off her," Theresa told the cop. Her voice was low and calm. "Leave her alone." Theresa walked slowly toward the cop with the high heels at her sides. I held my breath. Georgetta took off both her stilettos and held one in each hand. She walked over to Theresa. They exchanged a look I couldn't see and stood side by side.

The cop put his hand on his gun butt. Somehow we all knew instinctively that none of the butches should move.

I heard Peaches' voice. "What's goin' on out here?" We glanced at each other. "Uh-oh," she said.

Theresa's voice was low like a moan. "Leave her alone." She and Georgetta inched forward until they flanked Justine. Theresa's arm draped across Justine's hunched shoulders. Justine grabbed Theresa and Georgetta's arms and pulled herself to her feet. When Justine wobbled, Theresa wrapped one arm around her waist to steady her.

The cop unholstered his gun. "You fucking slut," he sputtered at Theresa. "You fucking perverts," he shouted at all of us.

Another cop pulled on his arm, "C'mon, let's get out of here." Slowly, the four cops retreated.

I exhaled as the cops drove away. Theresa and Georgetta held Justine in their arms as she cried. I started to rush to Theresa but Peaches wrapped her arm around my shoulder. "Give 'em a minute, honey," she advised.

We formed a larger circle around them. Theresa turned and fell into my arms. I could feel her body trembling. "Oh god, are you OK?" I whispered into her hair.

She buried her face in my neck. "I'm not sure yet. I'll let you know in a few minutes."

"I thought he was gonna shoot you," I told her.

Theresa nodded. "I was so scared, Jess."

I smiled. "I'm so proud of you."

Theresa studied my face. "Really? I was afraid you'd think it was a really stupid thing to do."

I shook my head. "You were really brave."

"I was very scared," she sighed.

I smiled. "Somebody once told me that being brave means doing what you gotta do even though you're scared."

Theresa looked up at me. "Do you get scared, Jess?"

Her question stunned me. "Are you kidding? I'm scared all the time."

She nodded. "I thought you must be, but this is the first time you've ever said it to me."

"Really? Don't I talk to you about how I feel?" Theresa bit her lower lip and shook her head.

My face burned. "I thought you knew."

She nodded. "I do know—sometimes, most of the time. But you never talk about it."

I sighed. "I don't have any words, honey. I don't know how to talk about what I feel. I don't know if I even feel things like other people do."

Peaches gently pulled Theresa away from me. "C'mon y'all. We're gonna buy Georgetta and Theresa drinks till they can't stand up."

Ed arrived at the bar twenty minutes later. "I missed it?" she shouted. "Oh, shit. Why couldn't I have been here?"

I laughed. "Be glad you weren't. It could have gone another way. It was right on the edge."

Jan clapped me on the shoulder. "Yeah, but the femmes showed them tonight—

don't mess with us. It was like what happened in Greenwich Village a couple of weeks ago."

I frowned. "What happened?"

"Stonewall!" Grant shouted. I looked at Ed and shrugged.

Jan grinned. "The cops tried to raid a bar in Greenwich Village, but they got a fight instead. The drag queens and he-shes really kicked ass."

Grant laughed. "I heard they tried to burn the bar down with the cops barricaded inside."

I sighed. "Shit, I wish I had been there."

"Yeah," Ed thumped her fist on the bar, "that's how I feel about missing what happened tonight."

My friends converged on me the moment I set foot inside Abba's. Ed looked as excited as I was. "Let's see the ring!" she said.

I looked around. "Is Theresa here yet?"

Ed shook her head. "Not yet. C'mon, hurry up."

I pulled the silk handkerchief out of my inside jacket pocket and opened it. The gold band was studded with a tiny diamond and two small ruby chips. Everyone made the same sound at once. *Oooh!*

Ed patted me on the shoulder. "How long you two been together?"

"Close to two years."

Ed laughed. "And how long you had that ring on layaway?"

I smiled and shrugged. "A long damn time. Is everybody ready?"

Edwin nodded. "Jan and Frankie are in the bathroom getting ready. They couldn't get white dinner jackets so we all got cream color. Is that OK?"

I beamed. "It's alright with me if they all look as good as you do." Ed cuffed my shoulder. I fretted. "Does everyone know their part?"

Ed laughed. "I've been practicing "Blue Moon" so much around the house Darlene said her Valentine present could be to never hear that song again."

Frankie and Jan came out of the bathroom. "Holy cow," I called over to them. "You guys look great!" It was the truth. They beamed.

Peaches pushed her way through the crowd. "Look!" she smiled proudly. She held up a huge cardboard full moon painted blue. Peaches flipped it over—the other side was gold. I did a double take. "How come the face of the man in the moon looks so much like you, Peaches?"

Peaches drew herself up to her full height. "Where do you see a damn man? The moon is femme, child—high-in-the-sky femme—and don't you forget it."

I checked my watch. "Damn. Theresa will be here any minute."

Jan and Meg headed straight for me. They looked upset. Meg spoke first. "Oh, Jess. I feel awful about this."

My stomach clenched. "What?"

Meg rubbed her forehead. "I set up the phonograph in the back. Jan was gonna rehearse that *dip-di-dip* thing at the beginning. The needle slid across the record. At first we thought it was OK, but it's not."

I looked at Ed. "What's she saying?"

"Um," Ed winced, "I think she's saying we don't have music."

"What!" I panicked. "Oh man, this is all fucked up now."

Jan took me by the shoulders and turned me to face her. "Jess, take a deep breath." I did. "This is Valentine's Day. That's a high femme holy holiday. You been planning this thing for a long time now. Are you gonna let it all go down the drain?"

I pouted. "What the fuck can I do?"

Jan smiled. "You can sing to your girl."

"You mean really sing? In my own voice?"

Ed nodded emphatically. "Yeah! We can give you a nice *do-wah-do* backup."

"Jan," I pleaded, "I can't sing worth a damn."

Jan smiled. "I know. But this whole thing is about having the guts to tell Theresa how much you love her. Edna once told me there's nothing a butch can do to prove her love more than to risk looking foolish. I'm not saying I can do it, but I'm passing that along."

What scared me was I knew Jan was right and I knew I was going to do it.

Justine kissed me on the cheek. "Theresa's here," she whispered in my ear.

Frankie, Jan, and Ed took their positions in front of the bar. I hid behind it. Meg knelt down next to me. "I'm sorry, kid," she said.

I waved my hand. "Forget about it. If I live through this, I could care less."

After a long silence, Jan's voice boomed out. She remembered every *dip-di-dip* and *dinga-dong-ding* before she slid into a deep bass *Blue Mooonnn.*

I emerged from behind the bar. It was the look on Theresa's face that gave me the courage to raise my voice. "Blue Moon, you saw me standing alone, without a dream in my heart, without a love of my own." My voice cracked and pitched with embarrassment and emotion. Theresa chewed her lower lip and cried.

Do-wah-do, my friends backed me up.

Peaches stood behind me, waving the painted blue moon back and forth in a wide arc over my head.

I extended my hand toward Theresa. *But then you suddenly appeared before me, the only one my heart would ever hold.* I had a feeling I'd gotten the words wrong.

I suddenly whispered 'please adore me,' and when I looked the moon had turned to gold! Peaches flipped the moon to the gold side. Everyone cheered. Peaches curtsied and continued swaying with the moon.

Theresa reached for me. I finished the song dancing in her arms. *Blue Moon, now I'm no longer alone, I've got a dream in my heart, I've got a love of my own.*

Do-wah-do, the chorus was soft and smooth.

I pulled the handkerchief from my breast pocket and opened it carefully. Theresa lost it when she saw the ring. I cried, too. The moment really was perfect. I slid the ring on her finger. I had a speech all prepared about how much she meant to me but I couldn't remember the words. "I love you," I told her. "I love you so damn much."

"You're the best thing that's ever happened to me," Theresa whispered. She took my left hand in hers and ran her thumb lightly over the scar on my ring finger. "I want you to wear a band, too."

I shook my head sadly. "I thought about it, but I'd be too scared. I think if the cops ever took that ring from me I'd just go berserk."

Theresa touched her cheek. "If you're afraid to lose what you love, you'll never be able to let go and feel it. I'll put all my love for you in a ring if you'll wear it. And if someone ever takes it from you all they'll be able to steal is a metal band. Then I'll go out and get you another ring and put all my love in that one. That way you'll never lose it, Jess. OK?"

I nodded and buried my face in her neck. *Do-wah-do,* everyone in the whole bar sang to us as we swayed to their music.

It was the sweetest moment of my life.

CHAPTER 13

The police really stepped up their harassment after the birth of gay pride. Cops scribbled down our license plate numbers and photographed us as we entered the bars. We held regular dances at a gay-owned bar, using police radios to alert everyone when the cops were about to raid us. We heard about weekly gay liberation and radical women's meetings at the university, but Theresa was the only one in our crowd who knew her way around campus. It was still another world to the rest of us. Everything was changing so fast. I wondered if this was the revolution.

One day I came home from work and found Theresa stewing in anger at the kitchen table. Some of the lesbians from a newly formed group on campus had mocked her for being a femme. They told her she was brainwashed. "I'm so mad," Theresa thumped the table. "They told me that butches were male chauvinist pigs!"

I knew what male chauvinist meant, but I couldn't figure out what it had to do with us. "Don't they know we don't deal the shit, we get shit on?"

"They don't care, honey. They're not going to let us in."

"Should Jan and Grant and Edwin and I go to one of these meetings and try to explain?"

Theresa put her hand on my arm. "It won't help, honey. They're very angry at butches."

"Why?"

She thought about the question. "I think it's because they draw a line—women on one side and men on the other. So women they think look like men are the enemy. And women who look like me are sleeping with the enemy. We're too feminine for their taste."

"Wait a minute," I stopped her. "We're too masculine and you're too feminine? Whatdya have to do, put your index fingers in a meter and test in the middle?"

Theresa patted my arm. "Things are changing," she said.

"Yeah," I told her, "but sooner or later they'll change back."

"Things don't change back," she sighed, "they just keep changing."

I slapped the table. "Then fuck those people. Who needs them, anyway?"

Theresa frowned and played with my hair. "I need the movement, Jess. And so do you. Remember you once told me about a factory you worked where the guys didn't want the butches to come to the union meetings?"

I nodded. "Yeah, so?"

She smiled. "You told me Grant said to hell with the union. But you knew the union was a good thing. You said what was wrong was keeping out the butches. You tried to organize to get the butches into the union, remember?"

Theresa held me tight against the warmth of her body and kissed my hair. She gave me time to think about what she'd said, instead of shooting off my mouth. I felt scared, so I got up and started making dinner. Theresa just sat at the kitchen table looking out over our backyard.

I wish we hadn't traveled to meet friends at the bar in Rochester that weekend. If we'd just stayed home, I wouldn't have gotten busted. But that was wishful thinking.

I lay on a precinct cell floor, alone in a strange city, my mouth pressed against the cold concrete. I wondered if I was close to death because I seemed to be drifting away from the world. Only two things tethered me to life—one was the feel of cold stone against my lips, the other was the faint strains of a Beatles tune coming from a radio somewhere in the jail. *She loves you, yeah, yeah, yeah.*

I drifted in and out of consciousness. I remember Theresa propping me up against a brick wall in the precinct parking lot and assessing the damage with her eyes. She chewed her lower lip and fingered the bloody places on my shirt. "I'll never get these stains out." Indirect messages cut through my fog much more clearly than direct ones.

She held my head on her lap all the way back. Her fingertips stroked my hair as she drove, pulled my head gently into her lap as she braked.

And then I found myself in our home again. Theresa was in the next room. I settled into the warm, soapy bath water and leaned my head against the porcelain. Only my head existed, above the bubbles. The comfort softened me, but I could feel panic gnawing in my gut. Every time I came near its borders I was hurled back. Fear choked me. I needed Theresa to come and help me, but I couldn't call out to her—my throat constricted, strangling me.

My teeth ached. When I pushed against one of them with my tongue, it popped out and lay in my palm like a Chicklet in a tiny pink puddle of my own blood. I climbed out of the tub quickly, sloshing water over the sides. I slipped on the tile, lifted the toilet lid, and vomited.

As I looked in the mirror I felt sorry for the reflection—bloody, bruised, lumpy. I rinsed out my mouth with toothpaste and a handful of water. My legs quivered.

Theresa had left clean white underwear on top of the toilet tank. I dried off and slipped on a pair of BVD's. I'd just pulled the T-shirt over my head when Theresa opened the bathroom door. "I, um, just wanted to see if we have bandaids," she said. And then the terrifying image I had held back came flooding into the front of my mind: the memory of Theresa's face when I was arrested. In her eyes I had seen the pain of being overpowered and helpless. It was the way I felt almost every day of my life.

I pushed the memory back down as Theresa stood in the bathroom, searching my face with her gaze. Her eyes were red-rimmed and moist. My own eyes felt dry as dust. My breath came slow and easy, as though I was inhaling and exhaling molasses, not air. Theresa touched my face with her hand, turning my head slightly to study the swelling around my mouth.

I had no words. If I could have possibly found them, I would have brought them to her. But I couldn't find words. I watched the pattern of emotions on Theresa's face shift like sand dunes in the wind. She couldn't find words either. What would her words sound like, resonating in the air?

Theresa's bit her lower lip and squeezed her eyes shut. I sat down on the toilet seat. Theresa cleaned the wound on my mouth with peroxide. "I'm going to use two bandaids," she told me. "Just to be safe. It might need stitches." I shook my head slowly. No hospital. I needed gentleness and safety. Theresa gave me both. She took me to bed, held me, caressed me, ran her fingers through my hair and cried.

I awoke later and realized Theresa wasn't next to me. It was still dark outside. I staggered to the kitchen. My body hurt, but I knew the worst stiffness and pain would come a day later.

Theresa sat at the kitchen table, with her head in her hands. I noticed the level of whiskey left in the bottle. I pulled her head against my belly and stroked her hair. "I'm sorry," she kept repeating. "I'm so sorry." She lurched to her feet and fell heavily against me. I felt the frustration building in her body like a storm. I heard it in the small strangulated sounds from her throat. She pounded me with her fists. "I couldn't stop them. They cuffed me so fast. I just couldn't do anything," she cried.

That's exactly how I felt. We really were in this life together. We might not have the words, but we both knew exactly what we were choking on. There were so many things I wanted to tell her in that moment. Feelings worked themselves up to my throat and then stuck there, clenched like a fist.

I kissed Theresa's sweaty forehead. "It's OK," I whispered. "It'll be alright." We both smiled at the irony of my words. I took her hand and led her back to our bed. The sheets were cool. The night sky was filled with stars. Theresa looked up at me, her face soft with caring.

For a moment I almost told Theresa I was afraid I couldn't go on much longer—even with her love. Emotions moved from my throat to my mouth; the words banged against the back of my teeth. And then they ebbed. Theresa asked me a question with her eyes. I had no answers. I could find nothing to say. Since I had no words to bring the woman I loved so much, I gave her all my tenderness.

I found Theresa in the bathroom splashing her face with cold water. Her eyes were red and swollen from tear gas. I tried to hold her tight, but she was excited. She pulled away and started to tell me about what had happened on campus. All the words tumbled out on top of each other.

"The students called a strike. They took over the campus and Main Street. The cops were everywhere in riot gear. I stuck around but the tear gas got so bad I couldn't see. My friend Irma found me and drove me home. Looks like I'm not going to work for a while."

I shook my head in amazement. "Won't you get in trouble if you don't punch in?"

Theresa smiled and patted my cheek. "Would you cross a picket line?" she asked me. "Come into the kitchen, I want to show you something."

I made coffee while Theresa unrolled something she'd brought home. "Which of these posters do you like better?" Theresa asked me.

I held one up. "Do you know what this looks like?"

Theresa nodded. "That's what it is."

I did a double take. "Aren't there laws against that?"

Theresa laughed gently. "What a prude! What about this one?" It was a picture of a two naked women wrapped in each other's arms. I read the words out loud: "*Sisterhood—make it real.* What does that mean?"

Theresa smiled. "Think about it, Jess. It means women need to stick together. Can we put it up on the wall?"

I shrugged. "Sure, I guess. You're really getting into this women's lib stuff, aren't you?"

Theresa sat me on a kitchen chair and plopped down on my lap. She pushed the hair out of my eyes. "Yeah," she said, "I am. I'm realizing a lot of things about my own life—about being a woman—that I never even thought about until the women's movement."

I listened to her. "I don't feel it so much," I told her. "Maybe cause I'm a butch."

She kissed my forehead. "Butches need women's liberation, too."

I laughed. "We do?"

Theresa nodded. "Yes, you do. Anything that's good for women is good for butches."

"Oh yeah?"

"Yeah," she said. "And another thing."

I sighed wearily. "Uh-oh."

Theresa smiled. "When a woman tells me, 'If I wanted a man I'd be with a real one,' I tell her, 'I'm not with a fake man, I'm with a real butch.' " I beamed with pride. "But," Theresa added, "that doesn't mean that butches can't learn a thing or two from the women's movement about how to respect femmes."

I slid Theresa off my lap. "Hey, what are you talking about?" I got up and started washing dishes.

She turned me around by my shoulder. "I mean," she continued, "that it's time for women to start looking at how we treat each other. Femmes need to work on it with each other, too."

It was a momentary reprieve, but I took it. "What do femmes need to learn?"

Theresa thought for a moment. "How to stick together. How to be loyal to each other."

"Hmm." I weighed the information. "OK, what do butches need to learn?"

Theresa pushed me back against the sink. "The next time all you butches are sitting around talking at the bar, listen to how many times you hear the words *chicks* or *broads* or *hooters* or *headlights.*"

Theresa leaned her body against me. "Honey? You know how sometimes you say 'I'll never understand women'? Well, think about it, sweetheart—you are a woman. So what are you really saying? It's sort of like a gun with a barrel that's open on both ends. When you shoot it, you end up wounding yourself at the same time."

I turned and washed dishes in silence. Theresa wrapped her arms around me. "Honey?" she nudged.

"I'm listening. I'll think about it." I paused for a long moment. "Hey, wait a minute." I turned around and faced her. "I'm not the one who says I'll never understand women. I say I'll never understand femmes."

Theresa smiled and hooked her finger through the belt loop on my jeans and pulled my pelvis against hers.

"Oh, baby," she whispered seductively, "you're right about that."

Surprise! Our living room was filled with friends.

"Happy birthday, honey," Theresa beamed. The smile faded from her face. She held my head gently and turned it. The cut over my eye looked worse than it really was.

Theresa calmly took me by the hand. "C'mon, let's clean that up." I sat on the toilet seat. She dabbed at the cut. "What happened?"

I shrugged. "Three guys outside the 7-11. They were drunk."

"Are you OK?" she asked.

I smiled. "Yes and no."

She taped over the cut with two bandaids. "Maybe this party wasn't such a good idea," she sighed.

I grabbed her hand. "What? All the people I love in one room when I need them?"

Theresa kissed my forehead. She lifted my hand and turned it over. My knuckles were bloody and swollen. She smiled. "Right on, honey! I hope you fucked 'em up good."

I shrugged. "It was three against one, but they were really, really drunk. I did the best I could."

Theresa pulled my face gently against her belly. She kissed my hair and smoothed it with her fingertips. "You do real good, baby.

It was a great party. The mood was no longer boisterous, but we could each taste and feel how much we meant to each other.

Jan leaned against the side of the refrigerator. I got out two beers and offered her one. "You alright?" she asked.

I wanted to tell her that I didn't think I was alright at all. It was so hard to be different. The pressure never let up for a minute. I felt all messed up inside and bone weary. That's what I wanted to tell her. But the words wouldn't come.

I shrugged. "I'm twenty-one today and I feel old."

I could see the sadness in Jan's smile. "You've been through a lot. There's some age you can't count by years. You know how they cut a slice from a tree and count the rings? You got a lot of rings inside that trunk of yours. You know what? I think it's time I stopped calling you *kid.* You stopped being a kid a long time ago."

I nodded. Ed came up behind me and slid her arm across my shoulder. "Happy birthday, buddy." I wrapped my arm around her waist and pulled her close.

"Hey," Grant shouted at us. "You're all standing in front of the refrigerator. What do I have to do to get a beer around here?"

"You have to give me a hug," I demanded.

"Oh, c'mere," she laughed and put her arm around me. "Now gimme a beer."

I could hear the sound of Tammy Wynette's voice singing "Stand By Your Man." I found Theresa in the living room and reached out my hand to her. Her body settled against mine. We moved together to the music. She ran her fingers through the back of my hair. I pulled her close, asking her body for comfort. She gave it to me. Her arms felt like the only safe haven on earth. "Baby," she whispered, "are you OK?"

"Yeah," I answered. "I'm alright."

"Hi, honey," Theresa stood in the kitchen door.

I crossed my arms. "Dinner's ruined." Theresa came toward me with her arms extended. I ducked them. "Where were you?"

"Oh, baby," Theresa kissed my neck. "You forgot I was going to that meeting tonight after work, didn't you?"

"What meeting?" I pouted. "You still trying to fight your way into feminist meetings?" That hit home, as was intended.

"No, it was to raise support for the Indians at Wounded Knee. I would have thought you'd be sympathetic to that." Theresa scored a direct hit. She softened her tone. "Still no work, baby?"

I shook my head. "Nothing. I never thought the jobs would dry up for this long. My unemployment runs out in five more weeks."

Theresa nodded and stroked my hair. "We'll manage."

"Not if you keep ruining the dinners I'm cooking you. See if I slave over a hot stove for you any more."

"Don't worry sweetheart," she whispered. "It'll be OK. You'll get a job soon, you'll see."

She was wrong. By 1973 it seemed as though everyone we knew was laid off.

Theresa lost her job at the university. That dashed our hopes of taking a vacation together—and we sure needed it. The months of me scouring for work and money getting tighter were taking their toll on us. We had to get away, but all our escape routes seemed blocked.

"I don't even want to go on vacation," I told Theresa.

"Are you crazy?" she shouted. "We're gonna go nuts if we don't get out of here. We never go out, we never do anything."

I slumped at the kitchen table. "It's getting too scary out there, Theresa. It feels like it's getting worse. I hate to even go outside any more."

Theresa sat down at the kitchen table. "You're depressed, that's all. That's just another reason why we need to get away from here."

I wasn't sure what she meant by that. "I'm telling you, it's getting worse out there."

Theresa slapped the tabletop. "It's always been hard. When has it ever been easier?"

"I don't fucking believe it!" I shouted. "I'm trying to tell you I can't take it anymore, and you're saying I'm going under?"

Theresa leaned back in her chair and searched my face with her eyes. "Jess, I didn't say you were going under." The words echoed in the silence of the kitchen. I stood up and walked toward the bedroom.

"Jess, wait a minute. Where are you going?"

"To bed," I told her. "I'm really tired.

When I arrived at the temp agency at dawn, I saw two men leaning up against the entrance to the labor office on Chippewa Street.

"Hey, bulldagger," the dark-haired man called to me. His friend laughed. They were both drunk. There must not be any jobs inside again.

The blond man squeezed his crotch. "I got some work here for you, bulldagger. It's a big job, you think you can handle it?" I pushed past their laughter.

"Hi, Sammy." I called out to the dispatcher.

He smiled apologetically. "You want to wait around, Jess? Maybe by 10:30 we'll need a couple of guys." I wondered if I fit into that work category—one of the guys.

I looked around at the men who were waiting for work. Some stared into space, their nonfilter cigarettes burning dangerously close to their tobacco-stained fingers. Others glared at me with heavy-lidded anger. I had done nothing to them, but at the moment I was the nearest person to hate.

"Naw, Sammy. Call me later if you got anything. OK?"

Sammy nodded and waved. "Maybe tomorrow, Jess."

"Yeah, maybe tomorrow."

I began to shore myself up to walk past the two men who I knew were waiting for me outside. As I passed them, the dark-haired man hurled an empty pint bottle of rum at my feet. I fell backward, against the brick wall, startled.

"You fucking he-shes. You stole our jobs," he shouted as I hurried away. I wondered who I could blame.

That night I awoke from a dream. Moonlight illuminated our bedroom. I wanted to go back to the dream, but I was wide awake. I was still immersed in the feel of it.

In the dream I was walking through a town. All the windows were shuttered. There was no sign of life: I couldn't find people. No dogs barked. Everything was silent.

The town was surrounded by fields and woods. I followed a trail of wispy smoke in the sky above the forest. I found a hut in a small clearing. A small fire burned inside. I crawled inside the hut on all fours. I pressed my cheek to the warm earth floor near the fire and waited.

All the drag queens were there: Justine and Peaches and Georgetta. Butch Al was there, and Ed. There were a few other people nearby, but shadows covered their faces. I discovered Rocco sitting next to me. She reached forward and stroked my cheek. I touched my own face. I felt the rough stubble of beard. I ran my hand across the flat plain of my chest. I felt happy in my body, comfortable among friends.

"Where's the others?" I asked.

Justine nodded. "Everyone's going in different directions."

A sense of loss washed over me. "We'll never find each other again."

Peaches laughed gently. "We'll find each other, child. Don't you worry."

I leaned forward and squeezed Peaches' hand in mine. "Please don't forget me. Please don't any of you forget me. I don't want to disappear."

Peaches put her arm around my shoulder and pulled me closer. "You're one of us, child. You always will be."

I felt panicky. "Do I really belong here with you?" Affectionate laughter rose to answer my question. One by one each person in the hut hugged me. I felt safe and loved in their arms.

I looked up. The hut had no roof. The stars winked on and off like fireflies. The air was cool and scented with eucalyptus. I crossed my legs in front of the fire and warmed myself in pleasure.

"Where's Theresa?" I asked.

I woke up without hearing the answer.

"Honey, wake up. Please." I shook Theresa gently.

She lifted her head off the pillow. "What is it, Jess? What's wrong?"

"I just had this really amazing dream." Theresa rubbed her eyes. "I was in a place that felt very old, out in the woods. I was with Peaches and Justine and Georgetta. And Rocco was sitting next to me." I didn't know how to describe the feeling of the dream to Theresa. "I felt like I belonged with them, you know?"

I could feel Theresa's hand sweep once gently across the back of my T-shirt, then she began to drift back to sleep. "Theresa," I shook her, insistently. She moaned. "I forgot to tell you this part. In the dream I had a beard and my chest was flat. It made me so happy. It was like a part of me that I can't explain, you know?"

Theresa shook her head. "What's it mean, honey?"

I crushed out my cigarette. "It was about something old in me. It was about growing up different. All my life I didn't want to feel different. But in the dream I liked it and I was with other people who were different like me."

Theresa nodded. "But you told me that's how you felt when you found the bars."

I thought about it for a moment. "That's true. It was like that. But in the dream it wasn't about being gay. It was about being a man or a woman. Do you know what I mean? I always feel like I have to prove I'm like other women, but in the dream I didn't feel that way. I'm not even sure I felt like a woman."

The moonlight illuminated Theresa's frown. "Did you feel like a man?"

I shook my head. "No. That's the strange part. I didn't feel like a woman or a man, and I liked how I was different."

Theresa didn't respond right away. "You're going through a lot of changes right now, Jess."

"Yeah, but what do think about my dream?"

Theresa tossed a pillow at me. "I think we should go back to sleep."

Whatever kind of response I'd wanted from Theresa, that wasn't it. But the subject wasn't put to rest so easily.

Toward the end of the summer Edwin and Grant came over to our house. Jan dropped by later with some shopping bags. Jan and her new lover, Katie, looked real uncomfortable, like they'd been fighting.

"This is a real crisis," Grant stressed. "We either got to change how we look or we're gonna starve to death! Katie got some wigs and some makeup. There's a few jobs, like in the department stores. Jesus, I don't know about you, but I need work. It's only for a while, until the plants reopen." Katie and Theresa retreated to the kitchen.

Four stone butches trying on fashion wigs. It was like Halloween, only it was creepy and painful. The wigs made us look like we were making fun of ourselves.

Grant told me, "I put one on, now it's your turn, Jess." Edwin shook her head while she held up a mirror for me to see.

I threw the wig on the floor. "I look more like a he-she with the wig on than with a goddam DA."

"Well have it your own damn way," Grant yelled.

"Leave me alone, Grant," I shouted back at her. "You think you're the only one who's scared?"

Grant faced me nose to nose. "What the fuck am I gonna do if I get evicted, huh?"

I didn't want to fight with her. "Look, Grant, if it works for you then do it. But nobody's gonna hire me with that fucking wig on. And makeup's not gonna do it, either. I need a bushel basket to hide who I am."

Jan got up and left, just like that. Ed went into the kitchen to tell Katie that Jan had left. Grant and I grudgingly shook hands.

"Honey," I said to Theresa, "if you don't mind, Ed and Grant and I are gonna look for Jan and maybe grab a couple of beers, OK?" I knew Theresa wanted me to stay, but Katie was real upset, too, so Theresa just nodded.

The four of us sat in silence around the table in the backroom of a neighborhood bar on the West Side. It was pretty empty. Jan, Grant, Edwin, and I didn't look at each other. We stared at our beer bottles as though the answers we searched for could be found there.

"I've been dreaming a lot lately," I said. "I had this nightmare last night that I was being chased by something to the edge of a cliff. I'm scared of what's coming behind me; I don't know what's ahead of me. And suddenly I decide I'd rather jump than wait for it to catch up to me."

"What's it mean?" Grant asked me.

"You know," I told her.

Grant shrugged. "I know how it feels. I don't know what it means."

I looked at Ed. She knew what I was talking about. I knew she did. "I've been thinking about Rocco," I said.

Jan sighed and nodded. She used her thumbnail to scrape the label off her beer bottle. "I knew that's what you were talking about."

I nodded. "I can't help thinking maybe I'd be safe, you know?" Ed still wouldn't look at me.

Grant nodded. "God help me, I've been thinking about it, too. You know Ginni? She got on a sex-change program, now she calls herself Jimmy."

Edwin glared at Grant. "He asked us to call him he—remember? We ought to do it."

Jan put her beer bottle down on the table. "Yeah, but I'm not like Jimmy. Jimmy told me he knew he was a guy even when he was little. I'm not a guy."

Grant leaned forward. "How do you know that? How do you know we aren't? We aren't real women are we?"

Edwin shook her head. "I don't know what the hell I am."

I leaned over and put my arm around her shoulder. "You're my friend."

Ed laughed sardonically. "Oh, great. Like I can really pay my rent with that."

I smacked her on the shoulder. "Fuck you."

Grant went to the bar to get another round of drinks; Jan went to the bathroom. I watched as she opened the door marked Ladies. No women ran out, and no men ran in to drag her out, so I figured she was OK.

Ed punched me on the shoulder. "I'm sorry," she said.

"How long we been friends, Ed?" She dropped her eyes. "So how come you can't tell me what's going on with you? You know I've figured it out, but you won't talk to me."

Ed shrugged. "I feel ashamed."

"Ashamed you're doing it, or just ashamed?"

Grant came back to the table balancing four beers. Jan returned a moment later. Ed rubbed her eyes over and over again.

"What's going on?" Grant asked.

I looked at Ed. "It's no shame," I told her.

Ed nodded. "Yeah, I know."

"We're all at this same crossroads, not just you," I reminded her. "If you can't open up to your friend, who the hell can you talk to?"

Ed sighed. "I know I've got to talk about it."

"Will somebody tell me what the hell's going on around here?" Grant wailed.

Ed sighed. "I started on male hormones. I got them from this creepy quack."

"Holy shit," Grant said. "Wow. Hey, how the hell did you know, Jess?"

I shrugged. "Your voice is changing, Ed. Just a little bit. I can hear it. Besides, I oughta know, I'm wrestling with the same shit myself."

Grant rapped the table with her fist in time to the music playing on the jukebox. "Hey, Ed. Can you give me the name of that doctor? I'm not saying I'm gonna do anything. I wouldn't mind having some options, though. You know what I mean?" Ed nodded.

I thumped the table in frustration. "I wish I could talk to Rocco. Does anybody know where she is?" Heads shook no. "What happens? Does it just last for a little while? I mean can you go back to being a butch later, when it's safe to come out?"

Grant smiled sadly. "I saw this movie once. It was about this guy with a disease there was no cure for. So these scientists froze him. Later in the future they found a cure for the disease so these other doctors brought him back and cured him. The only thing was, he was from the past. He didn't fit anymore."

I fought back tears. "Yeah, but we're not sick."

Jan nodded her head. "Yeah, and what makes you think it'll ever be safe again? It may be over for people like us. We may be stuck out here forever."

Jan's head dropped low. "My sister says I can move out to Olean with her and her husband. They run a little dairy. The thing is, they said it's only OK if I move out there alone, without Katie. They said they don't want their daughters to see anything perverted." Jan banged her fist on the table. "I'm forty-four fucking years old and my little sister's treating me like she's my mother. It's not right. None of this is right."

I nodded. "What are you gonna do?"

She shrugged. "I don't know yet." She put her arm around my shoulder. "I'm supposed to be the old bull. But now I wish I had someone older to talk to. I wish Butch

Ro was still alive. She'd know what we should do."

I smiled sadly. "I don't think so, Jan. I don't think any of us knows what to do."

Grant stood up. "I'm going to buy a case of beer and go home to watch TV. You guys wanna come over?" I shook my head. Grant and Jan left together.

Ed put on her jacket. "Hey, Ed," I told her. "We gotta talk, man. If you don't talk you'll explode. And I really got to talk to you. I'm scared, Ed."

Ed chewed her lower lip and stared at the floor. "Remember that book I gave you?"

I hoped she wouldn't quiz me on it. I'd appreciated the gift, but I hadn't read it. "Yeah. The book by Du Bois?"

Ed nodded. "There's this paragraph I marked for you. I carry it in my wallet. Read it. That's how I feel. I couldn't say it any better."

I stood so close to her I could smell the delicate scent of her skin and her hair. "Ed," I whispered. "I don't want to lose you. You're my friend. I love you so much."

Ed firmly pushed me away. "I gotta go," she said. "I'll call you."

"Ed, um, what about the name of that doctor?"

Ed sighed and jotted his name and address on a bar napkin. "Good luck," she said.

I punched her shoulder lightly. "Thanks. I need it."

It wasn't right, how long I had stayed out. I came home tanked up, not expecting Theresa to be waiting for me. She sat so quietly on the couch in the dark I nearly went through the roof when she spoke. "Where have you been?" Something in her voice frightened me.

I sat on the couch near her. I wanted to touch her but I began to realize how angry she was with me. After a while she reached out and brought my full weight against her. She was more upset than mad.

"I'm sorry, baby, really," I told her. "I was only thinking about myself and I'm sorry."

She nodded. "Where have you been?"

I didn't answer for a long time. I was drunk and confused. "I know where I've been, I just don't know where I'm going." It was all I could think to say.

She looked at my face, trying to read all my thoughts and feelings. I don't know if she found what she was looking for, but afterward she stroked my head.

"You remember I told you about Butch Al and Jacqueline?" She winced. "Theresa, I'm beginning to feel like I'm going under, too."

Theresa looked at me. She seemed calm and worried at the same time.

"Jan and Grant and Ed and I talked most of the night," I explained.

"Seems like it," Theresa smiled. "What'd you talk about?"

"Honey, I can't survive as a he-she much longer. I can't keep taking the system head-on this way. I'm not gonna make it." Theresa held me tighter. She didn't say a word. "We were talking about maybe starting on hormones, male hormones. I was thinking I might try to pass as a guy."

I waited for Theresa to speak. I could hear her breathing, deep and even. I stroked her shoulder and arm with my hand, feeling the definition of each muscle. "Honey, we've got to talk about it," I said. She sat in silence with me for a long time. Then she got up without a word and went to bed.

For weeks we didn't talk about it. We didn't talk much at all. But we found little things to argue about, small explosions that threatened to ignite big ones.

When I shut down sexually, Theresa could always melt my stone. But when I turned into one big emotional rock, when I completely shut down like a slab of granite and needed her to chip away until I was free, she railed against me. It didn't work. I was still trapped in stone.

"Talk to me," she shouted.

"I'm watching TV!" I lied.

She got up and stood in front of the television. "You're not talking to me."

I exhaled dramatically in exasperation. "Fine. Now you want to talk. Great. Let's talk." My tone was flat and closed like a door still slammed shut.

"Never mind," Theresa stormed out of the room.

I continued to stare at the television. She banged the bedroom door. Now both our doors were shut.

I snapped off the television and smoked in silence. The stone walls around me melted, leaving me feeling vulnerable and raw. Now that Theresa had retreated from her frontal assault, I remembered how much I needed her.

Suddenly I panicked. Maybe I'd already lost her, but I just didn't realize it. I got up and walked slowly toward the bedroom. Theresa opened the bedroom door and walked toward me. We embraced each other feverishly. "I'm sorry, baby," I told her. "When I get like that I don't know how to get out of it."

Theresa squeezed me in her arms. "I know, Jess. I'm sorry too."

I could hear the faint strains of Marvin Gaye on someone's radio outside. "You know what I wish?" I asked her. "I wish there was still a gay bar where we could go dancing, like we used to."

Theresa sighed. "They have lesbian dances on campus. I wish we could go there. I wish we could go somewhere and be welcome."

We held each other and swayed to the sound. Theresa pulled slightly away from me. She looked me up and down with a smile and hooked her finger in my belt. She gently pulled me toward our bedroom. "Let's get it on," she sang quietly.

We fought and we made love in order to make up. It became an alarming pattern.

"You're a woman!" Theresa shouted at breakfast. She pushed her plate away. Her part-time temp work had put that meal on the table.

"No I'm not," I yelled back at her. "I'm a he-she. That's different."

Theresa slapped the table in anger. "That's a terrible word. They call you that to hurt you."

I leaned forward. "But I've listened. They don't call the Saturday-night butches he-shes. It means something. It's a way we're different. It doesn't just mean we're. . . lesbians."

Theresa frowned. "What's the matter?"

I shrugged. "Nothing, I just never said that word before. It sounds so easy when you say it. But to me it sounds too much like lezzie and lesbo. That's a tough word for me to wrap my tongue around." Theresa and I smiled at each other in spite of ourselves.

"Honey," my tone had changed, "I've got to do something. I've been fighting to defend who I am all my life. I'm tired. I just don't know how to go on anymore. This is the only way I can think of I can still be me and survive. I just don't know any other way."

Theresa sat back in her chair. "I'm a woman, Jess. I love you because you're a woman, too. I made up my mind when I was growing up that I was not going to betray my desire by resigning myself to marrying a dirt farmer or the boy at the service station. Do you understand?"

I shook my head sadly. "Do you wish I wasn't a butch?"

She smiled. "No. I love your butchness. I just don't want to be some man's wife, even if that man's a woman."

I turned up my palms. "Then what should I do?"

She shook her head. "I just don't know."

Theresa asked me to pick up our dry cleaning and to go grocery shopping while she was at work. But the moment she left the house, I felt lost. I wandered into the backyard and knelt down beside Theresa's garden.

By the time the sun was directly overhead I was sitting between the rows of squash blossoms and tomato vines. This garden was a part of Theresa I didn't know. And I began to realize this little patch of ground was a postage-stamp memory of the country soil in which she'd grown. Where was I when Theresa had planted this garden in the spring? Now it was overrun.

I thought about the way things grow in their seasons and how much takes place underground. I thought about the things a gardener can't control, like weather and critters.

The sound of Theresa's footsteps in the grass behind me was familiar, but it startled me nonetheless. I hadn't realized it was late afternoon.

I remembered earlier in the summer I'd found her working in her garden, sweaty and flushed with heat. I laid her down in the grass nearby and pressed her body into the dirt with my hips and kissed her mouth until she made small sounds of desire I recognized.

"Jess?" Theresa's voice interrupted the memory. "What are you doing in my garden?"

I sighed. "Just thinking."

"Did you pick up the dry cleaning?" she asked. "Or the groceries?" I shook my head. "Have you been sitting there all day?" I nodded.

"Damn it, Jess." Theresa muttered angrily as she walked away. "I could use a little help around here."

Ed and I kept an eye on the guys near us at the bar. "What's it like, Ed?" I pressed.

She shrugged. "It's not much different. Not yet, anyway." Her voice had deepened. She had wispy facial hair.

"Can you pass?" I asked her.

Ed shook her head. "It's like I'm not taken for a man or a woman anymore. They see me as something in between. That's scary. I wish I could hurry up and get to the part where they just think I'm a man."

"But Ed, people always act like we're half-woman, half-man."

"It's true. But now they don't know what I am and it drives them nuts. I'm telling you, Jess, if it doesn't change soon, I can't take it much longer. I'm doubling the shots of hormones just to try to make it work faster."

I put my hand on her shoulder. Two men turned and looked at us. I dropped my hand. "How's Darlene dealing with it?"

Ed slowly turned her face toward me. The sadness in her eyes frightened me. "We don't talk about it," Ed said.

I shook my head in disbelief. "You don't talk about it? How can you ignore something that big? Wait a minute, what am I talking about? Theresa and I aren't exactly communicating either."

Ed and I sat in silence, nursing our beers. I felt comforted by her presence. The bar began filling up with men. It was time to leave.

"You know the worst part of not talking to Theresa," I said to Ed as we parted, "I really don't even know what it is I want to say."

Theresa was already asleep when I got home that night. I crawled into bed and curled up against her. "Theresa," I whispered, "there's so many things I've been trying to tell you, but I don't know how."

She sighed in her sleep. "I get this feeling that the next fight will take me down and I'll die and my life won't have meant anything. Some days when you kiss me goodbye at the door I get so mad at you because you act like I'm coming home for sure and I want you to say goodbye to me like we might never see each other again."

I bit my lower lip. "I don't feel like I'm worth anything. It's only when you love me that I feel worth anything at all. And I'm afraid I'm losing you. What would I do if you left me?"

I tried to cry quietly, so I wouldn't wake her. "I'm so sorry for the times I've been such a jerk. But I love you so much. Maybe too much. Please don't leave me, baby. Please don't go."

Theresa rolled over and touched my face. I wiped away my tears. "Jess, did you say something?" Theresa's voice was hoarse with sleep.

"No, honey," I stroked her hair and kissed her cheek. "Go back to sleep."

Theresa watched me from the kitchen doorway as I repotted the spider plant. "There's a bigger pot under the sink," she reminded me.

I shook my head. "This one does better when it's rootbound. The more pressure on its roots, the more it thrives."

Theresa came up behind me and wrapped her arms around my waist. "Is that like us, honey?" I didn't answer. Theresa turned me around to face her. I couldn't look her in the eyes. "What is it, baby?" she pressed.

I shrugged. "I don't think I have feelings like other people do. Sometimes you want me to talk to you about how I feel and I can't figure out if I'm like other people inside. Maybe I don't have real feelings."

Theresa didn't answer at first. She lay her head on my shoulder and pulled me close. "Sit down, baby," she sighed. She pulled a kitchen chair close to mine. "Oh, you have feelings, honey. I think you can feel love, maybe more than other people."

She took my hand in hers. "There's so much going on in your heart it scares me sometimes because I'm afraid you'll explode if you don't have some sort of safety valve. I think anger is real hard for you. Maybe your own rage scares you. And I think humiliation is a rough feeling for anyone to deal with, and I think you feel that way a lot."

I almost couldn't stand to listen to her words. My temperature rose and I felt dizzy. Theresa pulled me closer and brushed my cheek with her lips. "Take it easy, honey," she whispered.

I pulled back. "But maybe I don't have feelings like other people. Maybe the way I grew up changed me inside. Maybe I'm like the plant: my feelings got so choked up that I grew in a different way."

Theresa smiled as she weighed the thought. "Yeah, maybe it's what makes you so sensitive to other peoples' feelings. Sometimes you see so much about people that it used to make me feel naked around you."

I sighed. "Why do feelings have to be such a big deal?"

Theresa smiled. "You mean *your* feelings, honey. You always treat other people's feelings like they're a big deal. It's a hard place for you, sweetheart. But don't leave me out here alone."

I frowned. "What do you mean?"

"I mean," Theresa said gently, "that I have feelings about what happens to us, too. And you're the only person I can really go to about them, and sometimes you're not home. Remember last year when we went to buy you a new suit?" she asked. I winced in pain and turned away from the memory. "Jess," Theresa summoned me back. "It was a nightmare. I was there too, remember? We both felt humiliated. When we got home there was nobody in the world for me to turn to about it except you. But you had already shut down, and I knew it would be days or weeks before you relaxed again. I needed you."

I stared at my hands, clasped loosely on my lap. "You know how I feel sometimes,

Theresa? Like I don't have anything to give you. I would give you anything that was in my power, but I don't feel like I have gifts for you. I mean that. You're the strong one, you're the one who holds everything together, you get us through. All I can do is make love to you."

Theresa separated my hands. "Just love me, Jess. And please, please try to let me in sometimes."

"I've been trying to tell you what I've wrestling with lately, but you haven't wanted to talk about it." I shrugged. "I can't go on much longer without something changing."

Theresa sighed. "I'm a femme, Jess. I want to be with a butch. And I'm starting to feel like part of the women's movement, even though I can't be all the parts of who I am at the same time. My world's expanding."

"Great," I snorted. "Mine's shrinking. But the hormones are like the looking glass for me. If I pass through it, my world could open up, too."

Theresa shook her head. "I don't want to be with a man, Jess. I won't do it."

"I'd still be a butch," I protested. "Even on hormones." Then I said something I really feared, but regretted having spoken out loud. "Maybe you'd like it if I was a guy. It would be easier to be with me."

Theresa leaned back against the chair, the warmth in her face cooled. "I put on lipstick and high heels and walk down the street arm in arm with you, Jess. This is my life, and I'm damn brave to love who I love. Don't try to take who I am away from me."

My chin trembled. "Well, what do think's being taken away from me? What the fuck am I going to do, Theresa? Tell me, what can I do?"

I sat stiffly as she wrapped her arms around me. "I don't know, Jess," she whispered. "I just don't know anymore."

Theresa and I sat on the couch together for a long time without talking. We were both worn down and weary from months of low-level arguing and distance.

"You've made up your mind, haven't you?" she asked. I knew her tone was colder than she meant it to sound.

I nodded. "Yeah, I sorted through hundreds of options." I hadn't meant to sound so sarcastic. "God, Theresa, I'm so scared. I don't want to die and I don't know how to live. I'm really afraid."

Theresa pulled me close. She squeezed me so tight I could hardly breathe. "I'd do anything to be strong enough to protect you," she said. "I'd do anything if I could only keep you safe with me." She put her fingers on my lips to silence me. "Maybe I do understand what you're saying. I just don't want to admit that I think you're right."

I was relieved. I tried to hug her, but her body was limp. I pulled back to examine her face. She wasn't done talking yet.

"I'm scared, too," she continued. "If I'm not with a butch everyone just assumes I'm straight. It's like I'm passing too, against my will. I'm sick of the world thinking I'm straight. I've worked hard to be discriminated against as a lesbian." We both smiled.

"You've made your decision," she said, "I know you have. I'm not really surprised. I've been so damned afraid for you." The tears began to flow down her face. I tried to wipe them, but she pushed my hands back and held them tightly in her own. "But I can't do it, Jess. I can't go out with you in the world and pretend that you're a man. I can't pass as a straight woman and be happy. I can't live as the scared couple in apartment 3G who can't trust people enough to have friends. I can't live like a fugitive with you. I wouldn't be able to survive it, Jess. Please try to understand, sweetheart."

I pulled away from her. "What are you saying?" She just shook her head. I stood up slowly. "What are you saying? You won't stay with me? Why? That's how much you love me?"

Theresa stood up and moved toward me. "Please, honey. I can't. I just can't stay with you if you do this."

Rage boiled in my throat. "If you loved me. . ."

Theresa's face was cold and angry. "Don't you ever say that to me again."

My eyes filled with angry tears. "Well it's true, isn't it?"

All the steam leaked out of me when Theresa started to cry. She buried her face in my neck. "It doesn't mean I don't love you. I love you so much I don't know what to do. I just can't go with you. I'm trying to understand you. Can't you try to understand me?"

I shook my head. "How come nobody ever gives me any choices in life? I can't go on living this way, but you won't go through the only door that's open for me. Thanks a lot."

Theresa punched me hard in the shoulder. I grabbed her wrists. We struggled until we fell wearily against each other. We sat down next to each other on the couch. "I don't know how else you'll survive," Theresa said. "I just can't do it." My throat tightened. I hoped I could change her mind. "Don't try to change my mind," she added. She always could read mine. "And I won't try to change yours, OK?"

I looked at her incredulously. "Please, honey, don't leave me now. I'm scared. It's too hard. Please!"

Theresa jumped to her feet. "Stop it," she demanded. It hurt her too much. I pulled myself back in.

I went over to her and gently turned her to face me. "What do you want me to do?" I asked her.

She said it simply: "You'd better leave."

It was strange the way I loved her so much and yet felt so far away. "You're serious?"

She nodded and walked over to the window, as if she could see out into the darkness. "I'll pack up the things you need. Your friends will help you."

I kept feeling this couldn't be happening. "Please," I said. "Can't we try? I need you!"

"I don't know what to do either," Theresa told me. "I just have to find my own way now. I feel like I'm going under, too. This time we can't rescue each other."

I looked at the floor. "What if I don't take the hormones and pass?"

"Then you'll probably be killed on the street or take your own life out of madness, I don't know." We stood in silence.

"When do you want me to leave?"

"Tonight," Theresa said, and she broke down and sobbed. I held her tightly in my arms, for the last time.

She was right. Once we both understood that we couldn't continue, I had to leave. The pain was already unbearable. Theresa stroked my face and repeated, "I love you so much." I nodded as tears streamed down my face. I knew it was true, but part of me raged against her for not loving me enough to stay together.

I went in the bedroom and stuffed some clothing in a backpack. I knew she would pack up my other things with care.

Theresa walked me to our door. We couldn't hold back our tears, but we were trying not to sob. "Part of me wants to go with you," she said. "But if I did, I'd be living your life, not mine. I'd end up resenting you for my decision." She stroked my face as she spoke. Her fingertips felt so good against my skin.

I looked down at the floor. "There's so many things I wish I had told you. I never could find the words."

She smiled and nodded. "Write me a letter someday."

"I won't know where to send it."

"Write it anyway," she said.

"Is this really it?" I asked her. She nodded.

We kissed each other as deeply as we could. Then we parted physically. I walked outside the door and turned to look back at her. She smiled, almost apologetically. I nodded. She closed the door.

Suddenly I thought of things I needed to say to her, but I knew she didn't need to hear them just then. I sat on the landing for a while. But it occurred to me Theresa might call a friend to console her and I didn't want to be on our stairs.

I went downstairs and out into the backyard. I overturned a wooden milk crate and sat down on it. The sky was black and strewn with stars. I felt alone on the planet. I was so scared I could hardly breathe. I didn't know where I was headed. I didn't know what to do with my life. I couldn't even figure out what direction to begin walking.

I sat on that crate all night long, looking up into the sky. Sometimes I cried, sometimes I just sat. I strained to look into my future, trying to picture the road ahead of me, searching for a glimpse of who I would become.

All I could see was the night sky and the stars above me.

CHAPTER 14

The night sky lightened from black to indigo. I was still sitting on the crate in our backyard. Soon the sun would rise. I didn't want to be there when Theresa and the rest of the world began their day.

I swung my leg over my Norton and kick-started it. As the engine roared to life between my legs, I fastened my helmet and flipped down the visor. Now this was the place I found my mobility and my safety—on this bike, under this helmet.

As dawn streaked the sky I rode through a maze of silent city streets. Mist clung to the asphalt, suspended like smoke. A light rain began to fall. I rode into my own future as though it was only a dream. Rain fell harder, pelting me. Water beaded on my helmet, ran in little rivulets down the back of my neck, and soaked my shirt beneath my leather jacket. Wet denim stretched taut and cold across my thighs. Every street corner was a new crisis. Turn left? Turn right? Go straight?

Hunger finally pulled me off the streets and into Loblaw's supermarket. I called Jan's house. No answer. I didn't want to call Ed this early because Darlene would be sleeping.

I filled a plastic bag with bing cherries and walked up and down the aisles eating them. My jeans stuck to my legs as I moved. I followed women who pushed shopping carts filled with cereals and children.

Those who stared at me made sure I registered their disgust before they turned away. I did.

"Jess?" The voice startled me. I turned and faced a woman who looked familiar. One child wound around her legs. The other held her hand and stared at me. "It's me—Gloria. Remember? We worked together at the print shop. You used to work there after school."

I nodded, but my mind felt swaddled in gauze. I tried to follow her words as they shot past me: Gloria was divorced, the foreman put the moves on her, she quit. What was happening with me?

Her last question startled me. I shrugged. "I'm looking for a place to stay so I can try to find some work and get an apartment. By the way," I told her, "I've always wanted to thank you for giving me the names of those bars. It changed my life."

Gloria glanced nervously at her children. "This is Scotty and this is Kim. Say hello to Jess. Jess and Mommy used to work together."

Scotty hid behind Gloria's legs. Kim maintained her slack-jaw stare. Her gaze unnerved me, but there wasn't the slightest hostility in it. Kim's face was filled with wonder, as though I was a shower of fireworks exploding in a dark sky.

"You can stay with us tonight, if you have no place to go. On the couch, I mean." Gloria gave me her address. "After 7:30," she said, "after I put the kids to bed." That left a long time to kill.

I stopped for gas. The line of cars snaked down the block. Newspaper headlines blaring about a gas shortage had panicked everyone. "You must be joking," I complained to the attendant when I saw how much a tankful cost.

"Don't blame me," he said. "Blame the Arabs. They got us by the balls."

"Oh, c'mon," I told him, pointing to the river. "There's tankers full of oil anchored out there just waiting for the prices to shoot sky high." I knew—I'd tried to get the temp agency to send me out there to clean the ballast holds, but the agency said it was a man's job.

Once I got on I-190 headed north I really opened up the throttle, hearing everything I was feeling in the engine's growl.

Late in the afternoon I headed back to the city. I stopped at a West Side pizzeria for chicken wings. I stood at the counter growing impatient, but the man behind it wouldn't wait on me. I turned around to see what he was looking at. I saw a table filled with jocks staring at me.

I rapped on the counter. "Excuse me."

"What do we have here?" I heard a man's voice behind me say. It was time to leave.

One of the guys blocked the only exit. I pushed past him real hard and ran outside to the parking lot. I jumped on my bike, but it was too late. They were almost on top of me. My bike toppled as I leaped off it. I left it lying on the asphalt and ran. My lungs ached as though they might explode, but I didn't stop running for several blocks. I finally sat down under a tree, gasping for air. I wondered when it would be safe to return for my bike.

It was almost dusk when I went back. I stood across the street from the restaurant. I couldn't see anyone inside except the guy behind the counter. I found my Norton in the parking lot. There wasn't much on the bike that wasn't smashed or twisted. They must have worked it over with a tire iron or a baseball bat. I wondered how they had shredded the thick rubber tires.

I knew it was only a motorcycle, but I felt like a ghost looking down at my own mutilated body on the asphalt. I walked away from the wreckage. It was beyond salvation.

It took me forever to get out to Gloria's house. You could die before a bus comes in Buffalo. I didn't tell her what happened, it was already awkward between us. I asked if I could use her phone. She said yes, if I wasn't on too long. She was expecting a call.

I rang up Edwin. Her voice sounded hollow and distant. Darlene had packed her things and moved out.

"Oh god, I'm so sorry," I told Ed. "Me and Theresa broke up, too." We sat in silence. I had no wheels to get to her. "Can you pick me up, Ed?"

"Darlene took the car," Ed said.

"She took the car? It was that bad?"

Ed sounded the same way I felt. Numb and detached. "No, I gave her the car to take." Gloria caught my eye and looked at her watch.

"Ed, I got no bike. I'll tell you what happened later. I'll call you, OK? Hang on. Are you alright?" I'm not sure what she answered.

Gloria called her girlfriend. I could hear her crying softly in the kitchen as they talked.

I lay down on the couch. I'd spent a lot of my life on other peoples' couches. I hadn't really let myself feel anything about breaking up with Theresa until that moment. I almost cried out loud, but I clamped my emotions like a tourniquet. I had no privacy here, no space anywhere in the world where it was safe to grieve, so I pushed it down and found the only escape route open to me: sleep.

I awoke to the slam-bam sounds of cartoons. My eyes burned. They felt swollen shut. Kim and Scotty sat on the floor, leaning up against the couch I slept on. Kim glanced over her shoulder at me.

"Is he awake?" Scotty asked.

"Yeah," Kim answered, "she is."

"You're better off without her, kid," Grant told me. "She was a fucking communist."

I sucked in a deep breath of air. "Grant, don't. I love Theresa. I'm real upset and sore right now. Be very careful where you push."

Grant shrugged. "Well, it's time to get over her and move on." The whistle blasted. Grant and I headed for the lunchroom through skids stacked so high with boxes they reminded me of desert buttes.

I was glad to have a job. The recession was deepening. Ford, Chrysler, and General Motors had just announced massive layoffs.

Grant tipped me off about this steady temp work at the box factory. We punch-cut corrugated cardboard, pizza boxes—all kinds of boxes. My head hurt from the endless staccato of the jackhammers used to chisel away the trim.

"So did you get your own place yet?" Grant asked.

I nodded. "Yeah. I ended up at Gloria's for a month before I saved up enough money."

Grant smiled. "She let you stay that long? Maybe she likes you."

I shook my head. "Naw, it just worked out for her, too. She works nights. I drove the kids to school in her car and picked them up so she could sleep when she got home. Then I worked second shift. It was perfect. I like her kids. I still take the kids out on the weekend sometimes."

Grant grinned. "Sounds real homey."

"Aw, Grant. Change the subject. Hey, have you heard from Ed?" We both looked up at each other, startled. I had forgotten for a moment about the bar fight, when Grant had lashed out at Ed in misdirected rage. I loathed the part of Grant that was so mean-spirited and hateful.

Grant watched me remember. "Ed never liked me," she said. "She doesn't like me cause I'm white."

I shook my head. "Oh, that's not true, Grant. She's mad at you for the things you said to her the night you fought her in the bar."

Grant dropped her eyes. "Jesus, I said I was sorry."

"C'mon, Grant!" I slapped the tabletop. "What if some guy called you a pervert or a freak and then later he told you he was sorry he raised his voice? I don't get it, Grant. I've watched you at work; you're friendly with everybody."

Grant rubbed her eyes. "Well, sometimes my mouth just doesn't know as much as the rest of me, especially when I've had a few too many." She shrugged. "I'm a real fuck-up sometimes." I wondered who Grant was under all those layers of hurt and anger.

Grant leaned back in her chair. "Are you going through with it?"

I knew what she meant—hormones. "Yeah. I don't know what else to do."

Grant poured me coffee from her thermos. "It would be a lot easier if we went to the sex-change clinic. They give you hormones for free. The only thing is you have to take all these tests and they interview your family and everything."

I shrugged. "Yeah, but I just want the hormones. And the surgery."

Grant widened her eyes. "What kind of surgery?"

I made a face. "What kind do you think? I don't want to have breasts like this anymore."

Grant whistled low. "How do you know you're not a transsexual? Maybe you should go to the program and find out."

I shook my head. "I've seen about it on TV. I don't feel like a man trapped in a woman's body. I just feel trapped."

Grant sipped her coffee. "I don't know. Maybe I am really a guy and I was just born wrong. That might explain a lot of stuff."

"So why don't you go to the program?" I asked her.

She smiled wistfully. "Because what if I'm not? What if it turned out I'm something even worse than I thought? Maybe it's better not to know."

I smiled and put my hand on top of hers. She looked around and pulled her hand away. I sighed. "I don't know what the fuck I am. I just don't want to be different any more. There's no place to hide. I just want everything to stop hurting so much."

The whistle blew again. Grant stood up to go back to work. "I almost got enough money together for the hormones. How about you?"

I shrugged. "If we can get in a few doubles, I'll have the money soon."

"I'll wait for you," Grant said. For just a moment her hand rested on my shoulder.

"Will you help me put together my Texaco station?" Scotty held up a bag full of colorful plastic pieces. I sprawled out on the rug and spread out the parts.

"How do you know where the pieces go?" Scotty asked.

I held up the instructions. "I've got this. It's like a map. It tells me this is A and this is B and these two go together." They didn't. "I mean this is A and maybe this is B." They weren't. I worked in silence.

A commercial for pet rocks flashed across the television screen. Scotty looked mournful. "I wish I had a pet rock."

"A pet rock?" I laughed. "What's that?" He pointed at the TV. I stroked his head. "Don't worry, I'll get you a really good rock."

Scotty rolled over on his belly and watched me very closely. "You're not supposed to glue them together until you know where they go and you gotta put a newspaper on the rug," he advised me. "You know what I'm gonna be when I grow up?"

I held up a tiny gas pump and something unrecognizable. For some reason they fit together. "What?"

"I'm gonna be the wind."

Kim rolled her eyes. "He's really weird. He sits outside and waits to feel the wind."

I smiled at Scotty. "That's not weird. If you grow up and become the wind, I'll take off my helmet while I'm riding a motorcycle and you can blow through my hair."

Kim shook her head. "That's dangerous."

I nodded. "Yeah, you're right. Why don't you become the sunshine, Scotty? Then you could keep me warm."

Scotty shook his head emphatically from side to side. "No, the wind."

Kim looked far away. "Hey, Kim?" I asked her. "What do you want to be when you grow up?

"I don't know," she answered.

"That's alright," I told her. "You don't have to know now."

Kim looked worried. "My mother says I should be something special when I grow up."

I cupped her head with my hand. "You already are," I said.

Her expression flickered as she watched my face. Then her smile began to grow like a dry sea sponge in water until it filled her whole face.

Gloria came home from work early, gripped with a stomach flu. She asked me to stay overnight and drop the kids off at school in the morning. She looked green around the gills. When I urged her to go to bed, she didn't argue.

Scotty emerged from sleep the next morning as though he was stuck in glue. Kim opened her eyes, sat bolt upright, and hugged me.

I cooked pancakes for breakfast. I tried to make smiling faces on them with raisins, but when I flipped them over the raisins sank into the batter.

"I think I found his smile," Kim announced, picking at her pancake with a fork.

Scotty looked over at Kim's plate. "That's her eye," he said. I heard my own laughter. It reminded me of spring water bubbling from the earth.

"Are you married?" Kim asked me.

I looked at the gold band on my finger. My throat tightened. "Not any more."

Scotty nodded. "My mommy and daddy are diborced."

"Di-vorced," Kim corrected him. "Who were you married to?"

If I spoke openly with the kids would Gloria forbid me to see them? I took a deep breath. "Her name is Theresa."

Kim weighed the information. "Was she pretty?"

I smiled. "Very pretty."

Kim frowned. "Wait a minute, girls can't get married to girls."

Syrup dripped slowly down Scotty's chin. "Yes they can," he said. I wiped his chin with my thumb.

"No they can't, stupid." Kim told him. She looked back at me. "My teacher says boys and girls get married when they grow up."

I checked my watch. It was almost time to drive them to school. "Well, Kim, teachers know a lot of things, but they don't know everything. Finish your breakfast." Kim stabbed her pancake, angry because I hadn't really answered her.

I sighed. "You know, anyone can fall in love with anyone," I told her. "If a boy and a girl fall in love, everybody's real nice to them. But when a girl falls in love with a girl or a boy falls in love with a boy, some people make fun of them or try to beat them up. And you're right, Kim. They're not allowed to get married the same way a man and a woman can. But they really love each other. "

Kim's forehead furrowed. I could see her mind working as she chewed. "Did you ever kiss her?"

Warning lights flashed behind my eyes. "Um, sure," I said, as casually as I could.

"Ewww!" Kim dropped her fork. "With your tongue? I saw Daddy stick his tongue in Mommy's mouth once. Yuck, it was disgusting."

I laughed. "You don't ever have to kiss somebody that way if you don't want to."

"I'll never do that," Kim declared.

"Me either," Scotty added.

Kim ate in silence. When she looked up I could feel the question before she asked it. "Did you love her?"

My chin trembled. "Yes, I do."

"Then why did you get divorced?"

That question hung in the air. "I don't know," I told her honestly. "I can't explain it."

On the ride to school Scotty called out the name of every brand of car that passed. Kim watched me as I drove. "Was she nice?" Kim pressed. I nodded. "Do you think she misses you?"

I smiled. "I hope so."

It was a relief to pull up in front of their school and kiss and hug them goodbye. As soon as I was sure they were safely inside, I pressed my forehead against the steering wheel and cried.

I had a car and the whole day to kill.

Scotty's pet rock! I wanted to see if the Science Museum had a souvenir shop that sold rocks and crystals. I'd never been to the Museum before. A giant stuffed buffalo stared at me as I walked in. The space felt still and quiet inside the building. I found exactly what I was looking for at the gift counter. I picked out a fist-sized rock for Scotty. It was cut in half. Inside was a small cave studded with purple and milky white crystals. It was a rock you could get lost in if you wanted to. I figured he would.

Kim's gift wasn't hard to choose: a flat green polished stone the size of my hand, swirled with white, like currents in a fast-moving river.

"Do you know what these are?" I asked the young woman behind the counter.

She shrugged. "I just work here."

I wanted to spend the day there. Each room off the huge center hall was devoted to a different branch of science. One was named the Hall of Man—it turned out to include women, too. There were rooms that revealed the secrets of atoms, of universes.

I wished I could stay and devour all that knowledge. I hoped somehow it would make sense of the world to me. But I could feel my bladder begin to ache, and the two bathrooms were in plain sight of the woman behind the souvenir counter. I just couldn't deal with it. I left the secrets of the universe behind, got back in the car, and drove to Gloria's house to use the bathroom in privacy.

Grant and I sat in the car outside the doctor's office. "I'm scared," she admitted.

"Me too. When I was a kid," I told her, "I felt like there was no place in the world for me to fit. That's how I feel now."

Grant nodded and exhaled cigarette smoke through her teeth. "I tell you, kid, I don't know what's worse. Never knowing what it's like to be accepted or having what little bit you had taken away, you know?"

I sure did. "C'mon, let's go," I urged her.

The doctor's name was stenciled on the translucent glass door. It looked dark inside. "Maybe he's not here," Grant said.

I grabbed her arm. "I'm not pushing you," I told her, "but I've run out of options."

Grant sucked in her breath. I tried the door—it was open. The doctor was in. Dr. Monroe led us to his inner office and gestured for us to sit down. I declined. I looked around his office walls. "Where are all your diplomas?" Grant glared at me.

She addressed Dr. Monroe. "You remember I called you."

He looked me up and down. God, he hates us, I thought to myself. He licked his lips. "I believe it was concerning a hormone imbalance you both share." What did this guy think, that we had tape recorders wired to our bodies? "Did you bring the money?" he asked. As we pulled out our wallets, Monroe pulled out his prescription pad. "I assume you've given this a great deal of thought," he said, like he was really concerned. We both nodded.

He showed us how to draw one cc of male hormones into a syringe and stick it into the thigh muscle. "You give yourself one shot every two weeks. Any questions?"

"I've got some questions," I said. Grant and the doctor both looked startled. "Like how long before it works and are there any side effects?"

"Well," the doctor rolled a pencil between his index finger and his thumb, "that's hard to say."

"Why is that?" I wanted to know.

"Because this is rather," he hesitated, "experimental. You may experience side effects: hair loss, weight gain, acne." Great, I thought, just great.

"Is it dangerous?" I asked. Grant leaned forward to hear his answer.

Dr. Monroe ripped the script off the pad. "It's just hormones. Your body produces hormones naturally. Do you want this or not?" he asked, as he waved it back and forth. I nodded and took it. He ripped off a second and handed it to Grant. She looked unsure, but she put it in her pocket. Dr. Monroe counted our money, slipped it into his desk drawer, and bid us adieu.

"One more thing," I said. The doctor sighed heavily. "I need a referral for breast surgery."

He scribbled on a piece of paper. "Two thousand dollars," he told me, handing me a name and phone number.

It was over and we were back on the street.

"C'mon." I slapped Grant on the shoulder. "We'll go to the pharmacy, then I'll buy you a beer." She reluctantly agreed.

We sat at the bar in the middle of the day. The bartender seemed to barely tolerate us. We each put our big brown paper bag filled with boxes of syringes and vials of hormones on the bar in front of us.

"We'll have two beers and two shots," I told the bartender. "No pun intended," I added as an aside to Grant, but she wasn't listening. "What's up, Grant?"

"My whole fucking life is turning upside down," she said. I could sure relate to that.

"It's a big deal, what we're doing," I agreed. She nodded, but there was something else on her mind.

We ordered another round, and then another. Grant started to open up a little. "How's it going to be with women? I mean, who would ever go out with us?" I wished she hadn't said that out loud.

"I'm forty-one years old," she told me. "My life is so fucked up. There's no place left for us. I just don't know what to do." Her tears plopped on the bar. We both looked around to see if any of the guys noticed she was crying. We picked up our packages and quickly moved over to a booth. Grant broke into silent sobs. It scared me to see her cry that way.

I leaned across the table and stroked Grant's hair. "It's gonna be OK," I reassured her.

"Oh yeah?" she said angrily. "Bullshit. It's different for you."

"Are you kidding? Why's it any different for me?"

Grant blew her nose on a bar napkin. "There's things about me you don't know. Things I can't tell anybody."

I tossed back a shot of whiskey. It burned my throat and warmed me all over. "Grant," my voice sounded gentle, "there's nothing you can't tell me."

She studied my face. "I'm not a real butch," she said.

I looked at her blankly. "What?"

"I'm not really butch."

I laughed incredulously. "Well, you could have fooled me."

She shook her head. "You don't really know me."

The booze hit my brain like a ton of bricks. I wished I hadn't had so many drinks. The bartender came over and began wiping the table we were sitting at. "Time to go," he said. We recognized the hatred on the faces of men who were blocking the door we would have gone out of. The bartender nodded toward the back door. "Time to go."

We grabbed our bags and raced out the back door and into Grant's car. I locked the doors as she started the engine. Several of the men fanned out across the parking lot. One of them had a tire iron. Grant peeled rubber. She drove right over the curb and in front of a oncoming car that swerved and hit a parked car. Grant took off at full speed until we were safely away.

We stopped in front of my house. Each of us lit a cigarette. My hands trembled. "Jeez, Grant. You got a shot at the Indy 500." She didn't smile. I knew she was too drunk to be behind the wheel. "C'mon upstairs with me," I told her. "You can drive home later."

Grant shook her head. "Where you going?" I asked her.

She shook her head. "I don't know."

"C'mon upstairs with me," I urged again, but I knew it was no use. Grant flicked her cigarette out the car window and started up the engine.

Before I closed the car door I told her, "Hey, Grant. Try telling those guys back there you're not butch."

Grant looked at me. It was hard not to turn away from the sadness in her eyes. I pointed to the rearview mirror. "You look at yourself and tell me you're not butch. You are what you are, Grant. You don't need to prove it."

Grant handed me her package of hormones. "Are you sure?" I asked her.

She shrugged. "I'm not sure of anything right now."

When I got upstairs I called Edwin's house and let the phone ring a long, long time. I drank a beer before I took out the syringes and looked at them. Needles scared me so much I couldn't believe I was about to stab myself with one. I examined the vials of hormones as though their mysteries would reveal themselves to me right there at the kitchen table. They didn't.

I went into the bathroom, took off my chinos, and hung them on the bathroom door. I sat down the toilet seat and prepared the syringe. Was I really going to do this?

I thought about one of Grant's questions that hit too close to home. Would I ever lie in a woman's arms again? For just a moment I remembered the sheer pleasure of Theresa's arms around me. It made me feel even more alone. I flashed with anger at Theresa. She didn't love me enough to stay when it was hard.

My life ran through my head like a movie I didn't want to see again. I remembered how it felt to grow up different. I thought about the time my parents caught me dressed in my father's clothes.

Warm memories flooded over me: butch friends, drag queen confidants, femme lovers. I couldn't find them now. I was alone at this crossroads.

I couldn't bring myself to sink the needle into my thigh. Then I pictured my Norton, all smashed to smithereens in the pizzeria parking lot. I stabbed my thigh with the needle and injected the hormone. It wasn't as hard as I thought it would be.

I felt a wave of excitement—the possibility that something was going to change, that an enormous weight might be lifted from me. Maybe now I could finally be myself and just live. I closed my eyes and leaned my head against the tile wall.

After a while I stood up and put my chinos back on. I looked at my reflection in the bathroom mirror. Still me, looking back at me.

Nothing happened for the first two months. My voice hadn't deepened. I knew that for a fact because every day I called telephone information and the operators still called me ma'am. The only changes I could notice were not what I'd hoped for. My skin broke out. My body plumpened. My moods swung. Whatever was going to emerge wasn't here yet, but it was coming.

I'd have to say goodbye to Kim and Scotty soon. Gloria would never let me see the kids once I started to change.

On a wintry Saturday I arranged to take them to the zoo. It was snowing so hard that the bus ride to Gloria's house seemed to take forever.

"I'm going away," I told Gloria.

"You want more coffee?" she asked. I covered my cup with one hand and shook my head.

Gloria sat down next to me. "You tell the kids yet?" I shook my head. "Those kids think the sun rises and sets with you—I don't get it."

Her words wounded me. "I'm loveable, Gloria, what can I tell you?"

She shook her head. "Be careful when you tell them, OK? They're still shook up about their father and me." I nodded.

Scotty and Kim practically knocked each other over running into the kitchen to greet me. They were both so bundled up I could only see their eyes between their hats and their scarves.

Gloria tossed me the keys to her car. She looked upset. "Be careful, driving in the snow." I didn't think that's what she was concerned about.

"Don't worry about us," I told her.

By the time we got to the zoo the snow was deep and fat flakes continued to fall. There weren't many people out, just a few parents with their kids.

"Let's make snow angels," Kim suggested.

"Not yet," I told her. "Let's not get wet till we're ready to leave."

I could see the profile of a golden eagle on her perch. When we got closer, I realized there were two eagles—a male and female sitting next to each other. The female hopped down into the snow and unfolded her powerful wings. She leaped and twirled in the snow. I remembered the newspaper reported her egg had hatched last week, but the eaglet had died. I wondered if she danced in bitter grief.

"What's he doing?" Kim asked me.

"She's playing in the snow." I figured it was as good an answer as any. "That's the girl eagle."

"How do you know?" she asked.

"Because the girls are bigger than the boys."

Both kids spotted the polar bears before I did and ran ahead. The mother bear was out with her cub. According to the newspaper, the cub was born three months ago and hadn't been seen outside of the cave yet.

"Aw," the kids cooed as the cub toppled over into a snow bank. The mother bear sat back on her haunches. The little bear rooted for her breast and suckled. "I'm hungry," Scotty announced.

The concession stand was almost deserted inside: two zoo maintenance men sipped hot coffee in the corner. I ordered hot dogs and hot chocolates.

"We need peanuts," Kim reminded me, "for the animals."

"I don't think we're supposed to feed them," I told her.

"Then we need peanuts for us," she said.

"And three bags of peanuts," I added to the man behind the counter. He glared at me in open disgust. *Oh, please,* I thought, *not in front of the kids.* I got my money ready—the faster the transaction the better.

He came back with the food and drinks in a cardboard container. "That'll be $9.80, sir," he smirked.

I threw a ten dollar bill on the counter and picked up the container. "Keep the change, ma'am," I told him.

"C'mon kids. Want to eat outside on a park bench?" It was OK with Scotty; Kim didn't seem so sure.

I brushed the snow off a bench. "Why did you call him ma'am?" Kim asked.

I shrugged. "He was being mean to me."

She wouldn't let it go. "He didn't like you?" I shook my head. "Why not? How does he know he doesn't like you?"

"I don't know," I told her. "Don't you ever meet bullies at school who are mean to you for no reason?"

She nodded. "Why did he call you sir? Doesn't he know you're a girl?"

I sighed and put my hot dog back in the cardboard container. The last bite I'd chewed was stuck like a knot in my throat. I sipped some hot chocolate before I answered. "He knew I was a girl. He was picking on me cause I'm different." I anticipated her next question. "I don't look like your mom. I look different from a lot of other girls. Some people don't like that, they don't think it's right."

Kim knitted her eyebrows. "Then why don't you wear dresses and let your hair grow long, like other girls?"

I smiled. "Don't you like me the way I am?"

Scotty looked up at me and beamed. I wiped the ketchup off his nose with my glove. "I don't want to change," I told her. "I think girls and boys should be able to be any way they want to be without getting picked on."

Kim knelt on the bench, facing me. She took off her gloves and stroked my cheeks. I wondered if she could see beard growth already. "What do you see?" I asked her. She shrugged and put her gloves back on.

"You know what we're getting you for Christmas? A radio!" Scotty told me excitedly.

"Scotty!" Kim's voice rose in anger. "You're weren't supposed to tell. You ruined it." Scotty's eyes filled with tears.

"It's OK," I hugged him. "It's OK. Listen you guys—you kids—I have to tell you something." Kim sat down heavily, as though she had been expecting this. I put my arm around both of them. "I have to go away before Christmas. I have to find a job."

There was a long silence. Scotty wrapped his arms around me and cried. "No! Don't go away," he pleaded. "Please? I'll be good. Please don't go away."

I kissed the top of his snowsuit hood. "Oh, Scotty, you're not bad. Both of you are very, very good. It's not your fault I'm going away. I love you both so much. I've just got to get a job."

Kim sat with her hands on her lap, looking straight ahead. "I love you a lot," I told them again. "I'm really gonna miss the two of you."

"Then why are you going away?" Kim's voice pounded with rage. "Why can't you get a job here?"

She needed more of an explanation. "Kim, it's not safe for me here, because I'm different." Her face softened, which allowed the tears to well up. "I'm going somewhere I'll be safe."

"Can I come too?" she asked. I pulled Scotty closer to me and extended my arm to Kim. She didn't move closer, but I could tell she wanted to.

"It's not really a place I'm going to." I wondered how much the unwritten laws allowed me to tell a child. "Imagine that you're looking for me in a room. You look everywhere—in the closet, under the bed, behind the door—but I'm not there."

Scotty looked up. "Where are you?" he asked.

"I'm somewhere safe where no one would look. I'm up near the ceiling. Imagine you're looking for me here—behind the trees, under the benches, behind the elephant house. Where would I be that's safe?"

Both kids looked at each other and shook their heads. "Up in the sky, where the wind blows," I told them. "I'd be safe in the sky, where no one would look for me. But I'm still around. I'll still be watching over you."

Scotty wiped the tears from his eyes with his mittens. "When I'm the wind I could be in the sky with you."

I nodded and pulled him closer. Tears dripped down Kim's chin, but her face appeared calm. "Can you come back and visit us?"

I thought before I answered. "You'll see me again, but not for a while. Not till it's safe for me to come back."

I pointed to the golden eagles nearby. "You know there's not many eagles left. The food they eat got all poisoned with chemicals, and sometimes people shot at them. You know what the eagles did?" They both shook their heads. "They flew high up into the mountains, way up above the clouds and they're going to stay up there and fly around in the wind until it's safe to come visit."

Kim knelt on the bench and put her gloves on my cheeks. They were cold and wet with snow. "Please take me with you," she whispered.

My eyes burned with tears. "I have to hide alone, Kim. And your mommy loves you a lot. She needs you, too. Grow up the best way you can, Kim. I'll come back to you, I promise."

The snow was falling so heavily that it nearly covered us on the bench. I got up and brushed us off. I kissed Scotty's cold nose before I retied his scarf across his face. I waited on one knee for Kim to come to me. She fell into my arms so hard we both almost tumbled over.

As we approached the eagles, Kim ran ahead. She stopped and watched them. "Are they happy in there?" she asked me.

I shook my head. "They'd be happier up there." I looked at the sky. Snowflakes fell on my eyelashes and cheeks.

"Can we make snow angels now?" Scotty demanded.

I nodded. Scotty and Kim flopped backward in the snow and thrashed their arms and legs. "Look at me, look at me," they each shouted.

I made a snowball and rolled it until it was as big as a boulder. "What are you making?" Kim asked. They both came close.

"I'm making a snowwoman," I told her.

Kim made a face. "It's not a snowwoman, it's a snowman," she sulked.

"How do you know?" I asked her. "You haven't seen her yet."

Scotty started rolling a tiny lump of snow. "Can I help make her?" he asked. I nodded and started a good-sized snowball for him.

Kim stamped her foot. "There's no such thing as a snowwoman. It's a snowman."

I put Scotty's smaller snow boulder on top of the first. "Help me make her head," I told them both.

Kim flew into a rage and sobbed. I touched her shoulders. "Are you really that upset?" She nodded and cried. I wiped her runny nose.

"It's OK," Scotty said gently. "She could be a snowman, right?"

I nodded. "Help us make his head, OK?" Kim sniffled and nodded. We rolled the head, and I put it in place. I scrounged for stones under the snow, and we used them to make a mouth and nose and eyes.

"He needs a scarf, right?" I asked. They both nodded. I pulled off my scarf and put it around his neck.

I took out my pack of cigarettes. "No," they both shouted in unison, "don't smoke!"

"Well, I don't have a pipe for the snowman. Should I put a cigarette in his mouth?"

"No!" they shouted. "He doesn't smoke! He's smart."

I laughed. "OK, OK. But that's a pretty good-looking snowman we made, isn't it?"

Scotty nodded and fell on the ground. "Watch me make a snow angel!" He wildly flailed his arms and legs.

"Are you OK?" I asked Kim.

She nodded. I pulled her scarf snug around her neck. "I'm sorry I upset you," I told her. "I was just teasing."

She shrugged. "It's OK."

"I'm sorry anyway," I said.

"No," she told me. "I mean it's OK about it being a snowwoman."

I smiled. "How about if we decide that this is a snowperson and we like him or her just the way she is?" Kim nodded without smiling.

She silently stared out the car window during the long ride home.

"Did they eat?" Gloria wanted to know. I nodded. "Time for your bath," she told them.

"Aw, Mom, we're too pooped," Scotty said.

Gloria laughed. "Alright, smart aleck. But tomorrow night you both take a bath, and I don't want to hear any whining."

Scotty beamed in triumph. "Can Jess put us to bed?" Gloria glanced at me. I nodded.

Scotty and Kim changed into their pajamas and kissed Gloria good night. I tucked each one under their covers.

"You have to read us the story about when we were little kids," Scotty instructed me. I picked up the book from the nightstand.

Kim pointed to a bookmark. "That's where Mom left off," she said. I began to read, my voice quiet and low:

Where am I going? I don't quite know.
Down to the stream where the king-cups grow—
Up on the hill where the pine-trees blow—
Anywhere, anywhere, I don't know.

Scotty yawned. I kissed his sweaty hair. A mobile turned slowly over our heads, casting the shadows of moving ships against the walls.

If you were a bird, and lived on high,
You'd lean on the wind when the wind came by,
You'd say to the wind as it took you away:
'That's where I wanted to go today!'

My voice cracked like a teenage boy's and then dropped a bit deeper as I read. The hormones were beginning to work. Kim stared at me. Her face was still and sad. "I'm never going to see you again, am I?" she asked.

I came over to her bed and kissed her forehead. "I'll come back to you when it's safe. You'll see me again, I promise. I love you, Kim. Go to sleep now." She sighed and pulled the covers up to her chin. I continued to read until her breathing became heavy and rhythmic.

Where am I going? I don't quite know.
What does it matter where people go?
Down to the wood where the blue-bells grow—
Anywhere, anywhere. I don't know.

CHAPTER 15

It was a morning in April that everything seemed to change at once. The birds chirped loudly outside my window at dawn. I rolled around lazily in bed. The sheets felt cool, the air smelled sweet.

I reached for a cigarette, but the thought revolted me. I decided to take a long shower instead. As I brushed my teeth, I glanced in the mirror and had to look a second time. Beard stubble roughed my cheeks. My face looked slimmer and more angular. I stripped off my T-shirt and BVD's. My body was lean and hard. My hips had melted away. I could actually see muscles in my thighs and arms I never knew I had. Were the hormones stimulating muscles or just revealing them?

This was almost the body I'd expected before puberty confounded me. Almost.

I remembered the girls in high school who moaned because their breasts were small. I envied them for being flat-chested. That was within my reach now. I had saved sixteen hundred dollars over the winter toward breast reduction surgery.

I took a hot, soapy shower, enjoying the feel of my hands on my skin. It had been so long since I'd been at home in my body. Soon that was going to change.

As I combed my hair in front of the mirror, it occurred to me that I might be able to go to a barbershop. Our perfect DA's—one-inch long all over—were maintained in the kitchens of hairdresser friends.

I'd bought an old Triumph motorcycle during the winter from a guy at work. I took it out of the garage, put a fresh quart of oil in it, and drove it crosstown to a barbershop in a neighborhood I'd never have to come back to if it turned out badly.

The barber smiled at me. "I'll be with you in just a minute, sir." I tried to hide my excitement as I leafed through a copy of *Popular Mechanics*. I'd never dared enter men's turf like this before.

The barber snapped a huge red cloth in the air. "Sir?" he beckoned for me to sit in the chair. He covered me with the red material and pulled it snug around my neck. "A trim?"

I looked at myself in the mirror. "Well, maybe something different. Maybe it's time for a change."

The barber smiled. "That's up to you."

"I don't know. Something neat."

The barber smoothed back my hair and pursed his lips. "What about a flat top?"

"Yeah! That would be a change."

The electric razor buzzed across the top of my DA from back to front. Clumps of hair fell on my nose. The barber brushed them off with the soft hairs of a brush. He clipped and trimmed my hair until it formed a perfectly symmetrical flat top. He brushed me off thoroughly. I started to get up. "Not yet," he said. He lathered my sideburns and the back of my hairline with shaving cream and scraped a clean line with a straight razor. He toweled the last bits of lather from my neck. Just when I thought he must be finished he splashed a little bay rum on his palms and rubbed it on my cheeks. He shook powder on the brush and swept it across the back of my neck. With a flourish he pulled away the red cloth that covered me and gave me a hand mirror so I could see the back of my hair. "What do you think, my friend?"

This time I didn't try to hide my excitement. I was passing.

It was time for the most important test of all: the men's room. I walked around a department store until I couldn't stand it any longer. I paced outside the men's room. What would happen if I walked in? I'd have to find out sooner or later. I pushed open the door. Two men stood in front of urinals. They glanced at me and looked away. Nothing happened. I found an empty stall and locked the door.

They could still see my feet if they looked. Did men ever sit down to urinate? I flushed the toilet to cover the sound. I immediately felt something wet and cold against my ass and thighs. The toilet was overflowing. I jumped up but it was too late, my Levis were soaked. I rebuttoned my jeans and hurried out of the men's room. I pushed my way through the crowds of shoppers and made my way back to my Triumph.

All I wanted was to drive home, strip off my jeans, and shower off the feeling of stupidity. I sat down on my bike and thought about it. It hadn't been so bad, really. Now I knew better than to flush the toilet without paying attention to the water level as it rose. But I thought back to the moment I'd walked into the men's room. They hardly noticed me.

I could go to the bathroom whenever and wherever I needed to without pressure or shame. What an enormous relief.

At first, everything was fun. The world stopped feeling like a gauntlet I had to run through. But very quickly I discovered that passing didn't just mean slipping below the surface, it meant being buried alive. I was still me on the inside, trapped in there with all my wounds and fears. But I was no longer me on the outside.

I remember the morning I left work at the macaroni plant just before dawn. I was walking up Elmwood toward my bike. A woman on the sidewalk ahead of me looked over her shoulder nervously. I slowed my pace as she crossed the street and hurried away. She was afraid of me. That's when I began to understand that passing changed almost everything.

Two things didn't change: I still had to work for a living, and I still lived in fear, only now it was the constant terror of discovery. I never realized what a small town Buffalo could be.

"Where'd you go to high school, Jesse?" Eddy asked me after we finished unloading cartons from a truck.

Should I lie or tell the truth? "Bennett," I answered honestly.

"No kidding? When did you graduate?"

I fumbled for an answer. I had lied on my job application for this truck delivery position. I said I'd graduated from high school. "Uh, I transferred in my junior year."

"Yeah? When?"

"Oh, I don't know. Around '65, I guess."

"No kidding? My brother-in-law went to Bennett around the same time. His name's Bobby—played football. You know him?" Bobby the rapist. My fists clenched and I ground my teeth. "Naw, I don't think so."

Eddie nodded. "No loss. He could really be an asshole, if you ask me. You alright?"

"Yeah, just a little sick, that's all."

"Well, sit down a minute," Eddie said.

"Listen Eddie, I'm gonna run to the store for something." And then I walked away. I just kept walking, faster and faster. I was running from my own past.

I guess I could have left the city, but it felt as though I'd fall off the edge of the earth. So I stayed. But I always had to be looking over my shoulder in public, afraid I'd run into someone who knew me as a woman. Sometimes I didn't see them until they saw me, like the time Gloria and the kids were shopping downtown. I was an aisle away in the men's department. Gloria recognized me just a moment before I saw her. Her jaw dropped. She grabbed Kim and Scotty by their hands and tried to drag them away. Scotty got scared and cried. Kim called my name. "Jess! It's Jess!"

I came up to Gloria and put my hand on her shoulder. She pulled away in horror and wrapped her arms around Scotty and Kim as though she was protecting them from

Count Dracula. "Gloria, for Christsakes, I'm just trying to survive, you know? It's not such a big deal."

"Get away from me. What have you done?" she asked me in a strange, low voice. "What are you doing?"

"Trying to live, Gloria. Give me a break, will ya?"

Kim reached out to me, but Gloria grabbed her hand and squeezed it. "Come on Kim, Scotty," Gloria said, pulling them toward the door. "You are really sick, you know that? You really need help."

I turned up my palms in a gesture of exasperation. "Gloria." People nearby stopped to watch.

Kim broke loose and ran toward me at full speed. I lifted her into my arms and hugged her tightly. "Do you still love me?" she whispered.

I kissed her nose. "More than ever." I put her down and she ran back to Gloria.

"Ex?" a salesman asked me.

"Huh?"

"Ex-girlfriend?" he nodded with his chin toward the door.

"She's an ex, alright," I answered.

I got a steady gig at a bindery as a mechanic's apprentice. The guy who interviewed me looked me up and down real hard. I felt color rise in my face. "You look like a clean-cut young man," he concluded. Only a short time before I had been a monster.

Having a job was the good news. But there wasn't much else to do or anyone to do it with. That was the bad news. My greatest recreation was riding my motorcycle. I decided to buy a really nice bike. Early one Saturday afternoon I rode to the West Side to take a look at a Harley Sportster I saw advertised in the newspaper. "Ask for Mike," the ad read.

"You know about bikes?" Mike asked me. We squatted next to the bike in his driveway.

I said yes, but I felt like I was lying. It's funny, a guy gets a Honda 50 mini-bike and he talks like he's an expert on bikes. A woman could ride a full-dress Harley all her life and she still feels like she's faking her end of the conversation. He told me he loved that bike, and I could tell by the way he touched it that he meant every word. He hated to sell it, he told me, but he fell in love with a woman who made him choose between her or the bike. He made the right decision.

I handed Mike a wad of bills and revved the engine. "Take her up to Canada," he suggested. "You'll be across the Peace Bridge in ten minutes and you can really open her up on those roads." I put on my helmet, waved, and drove away.

I stopped at Ted's for a foot-long hot dog. I sat on top of a picnic table outside, surrounded by gulls impatiently waiting for the end of my bun.

I could see the line of cars at the Peace Bridge. How many hundreds of times had I gone to Canada this way? But passing as a man meant I hadn't been able to cross the

Peace Bridge because I didn't have a draft card.

The Vietnam War had just officially ended. It seemed amazing to me that the people of that tiny country had won against such monstrous odds. Maybe all those rallies Theresa had attended helped. President Ford was expected to pardon the draft resisters so they could finally come home.

But I still couldn't cross the border. I had no valid ID in case I was pulled over at customs. I opened my wallet and looked at my ID. Birth certificate, drivers license. They were all clearly marked female. How could I get ID as a male? Getting identification required identification. I couldn't even open a checking account without some sort of ID. A credit card was out of the question. I felt like a nonperson. Even outlaws probably had more ID than me.

I turned my license over and looked at the expiration date: *July 1976.* It was valid for fourteen more months. How could I get a license marked *Female* renewed as *Male?* What would happen to me if I got stopped by state troopers on a lonely road in the dead of night and handed them this license? But what if I was caught driving without a license? Either option sounded like a nightmare. Yet it was impossible to work or live in Buffalo without some form of transportation.

I stared across the Niagara River, longing to open up my Harley on those roads I knew so well. A feeling of claustrophobia choked me. Even as my world was expanding, it was shrinking.

My beard grew in full of color: blond streaked with red and brown and white. In the open fields of life, my beard was a bush to hide behind. Almost no one seemed to recognize me anymore when I was out in public.

I hated my breasts more than ever. Binding them every day had flattened the muscles, and they hurt. But I had finally saved up two thousand dollars. I called the surgeon Dr. Monroe had referred me to. I told him I wanted to be flat-chested. "Yes, yes," he said. "Breast reduction."

"Is it going to be very painful? Will I be out of work a long time?"

"No," he told me. "It's not a radical mastectomy. We make an incision and remove some of the fatty tissue. Although you'll be uncomfortable, you should be back at work within a week or two." I felt a little queasy, but all surgical descriptions made me feel that way.

"Do you have the money?" he asked.

I did. I was ready. I scheduled the surgery and left work Tuesday pretending to be ill.

Tuesday night I lay in bed and stared at the ceiling. I felt anxious, but not scared. I was excited at the thought of feeling good in my body once again. I wished Theresa could have come this far with me. Why couldn't I have had one night to make love with her while I felt comfortable in my body? Theresa. Once I'd thought of her it was too late to put her memory away. I tossed and turned.

Wherever I was going, I knew I was headed there alone.

The next morning I arrived at the hospital before my scheduled appointment to fill out the necessary forms. "Who are you here to see?" the admissions nurse smiled.

"Dr. Costanza."

Her expression cooled. "Just a moment, please." She returned five minutes later. The doctor wasn't in. No arrangements seemed to have been made. But she told me to go to the nurses' desk on the sixth floor.

There were three nurses at the sixth floor desk. "I have an appointment for surgery with Dr. Costanza." The nurses glanced at each other.

One sighed. "There's no room ready for you right now. You'll have to prep yourself in the bathroom."

I hesitated. "I don't know what you mean."

"Just a minute," she said. She came back with a hospital gown, razor, and Betadine. "Shave your underarms, chest hair, and pubic hair with this and then put on the gown."

"Pubic hair?"

She frowned. "That's the procedure." I hoped they didn't do the wrong surgery on me. I figured I'd have time to consult with someone before the operation began.

"Don't go in there," one of the nurses cried out as I neared the men's room. I turned toward the women's bathroom. "No, not there either," another called out. I stood stock-still. They found a room for me. I washed myself with Betadine and shaved my armpits for the first time in many years. When my underarm hair had first grown my mother insisted I shave regularly. This would be the last time.

As I shaved my beard I promised to take good care of myself. And I swore that no matter what happened I would never allow madness to consume me.

I sat down on a chair in the room to await surgery. Two nurses talked loudly at the desk outside the room. They said there would be hell to pay when healthy tissue was sent down to the pathology lab. They said sooner or later this would blow up and there'd be trouble.

A nurse came in the room, smiled, and dipped her head shyly. She pointed to a gurney in the hall. "Can't I walk?" I asked her. She shook her head.

I lay on the gurney as she rolled it down the hall. All I could see were ceilings. Huge lights appeared over me. I was in surgery. Masked faces above me. I hoped they weren't too hostile. "Which one of you is Dr. Costanza?" I asked.

One of them answered, "He's on vacation. Don't worry." I started to protest but a needle pierced my arm and the room started to dissolve.

When I awoke the world seemed fuzzy. I couldn't focus. The man in the bed across from mine stared at me. Nurses peered in at me from the doorway. I fought for consciousness.

A priest came into the room. "Where is she?" he looked around.

"Who?" I asked. The room spun.

The priest came close to my bed. "There's a lost soul who needs my help," he whispered.

"They just wheeled her down the hall, father," I said, pointing. "If you hurry, you can catch her."

I tried to sit up. A dull pain pounded in my chest. I called out to the nurses standing in the doorway. "Can I get something for the pain?" They walked away.

One of the nurses came back. "Look," she said, "I don't understand any of this. But I can tell you this hospital is for sick people. You people make some arrangement with Costanza on the side, that's your business. But this bed and our time is for sick people."

How much time would they give me to recuperate? An hour? Two? I didn't want to be there another minute. I wanted to be safe in my own home. I swung my legs over the bed and tested standing on them. Once I felt steady, I carefully dressed.

It took forever for the elevator to arrive. I stepped inside and pushed the button for the lobby. The young nurse who had brought me down for surgery held the elevator door open and pressed something into my hand. It was four Darvon wrapped in a paper towel. "I'm sorry," she whispered.

I had to walk a long way from the bus to my house. When I finally got home I put my key in the door, but I remembered the door needed to be pulled inward as the key was turned. When I finally pulled hard enough to turn the key, I knew I had hurt myself a little. But I was home.

I lay down on my bed. The last thing I remember is wondering what day it was.

When I woke up I couldn't figure out where I was. A dull pain throbbed in my chest. I stood up carefully. When I opened the closet door, I saw myself reflected in the full-length mirror mounted inside. I could tell from my beard growth I had slept for days. My chest was bandaged. There it was—the body I'd wanted. I wondered why it had to have been so hard.

I stumbled into the kitchen and chugged a Pepsi. I found a slice of cold pepperoni pizza and a piece of chocolate cake in the refrigerator. My childhood dream breakfast.

I called Edwin's house. *We're sorry,* I listened to the recording in shock, *but the number you dialed has been disconnected.* I rang her sister's house. In a quavering voice Edwin's sister said, "She shot herself—weeks ago."

I put the receiver down gently, trying not to disturb Ed's memory. "Edwin, Ed," I whispered as though she was asleep in my arms and I could wake her.

I went back to the bedroom and lost consciousness. When I woke, I hoped Edwin's death was just a dream. I called my foreman. "Where the hell you been, boy?" he shouted.

"I've been sick. Real sick."

"Can you get a doctor's note?"

I stopped and thought for a moment. "No," I said.

"You're fired," he growled and hung up.

I slept on and off for several days. A nagging pain woke me up, but it was emotional, not a result of the surgery. I changed my bandages in the bathroom. Just two surgical lines crossed my chest. Together with the stitches they looked like railroad tracks. After a little more than a week it looked like it was healing pretty well. I pulled on a clean white T-shirt.

Something propelled me into the kitchen to get a beer. As I snapped off the cap I located the source of the pain: Edwin's suicide. It couldn't be true that Ed no longer existed in the world. How could she be gone? Hadn't I known she was seething inside? I remembered she said she'd marked a page in the book she gave me that summed up what she was struggling with. I tore through the books on my shelf, but I couldn't find the slim volume she'd given me. I finally discovered it in an unpacked box in my hall closet and sat down on the floor to leaf through the book. She'd marked the page in blue ink:

> *It is a peculiar sensation, this double-consciousness, this sense of always looking at one's self through the eyes of others, of measuring one's soul by the tape of a world that looks on in amused contempt and pity. One ever feels his twoness—an American, a Negro; two souls, two thoughts, two unreconciled strivings; two warring ideals in one dark body, whose dogged strength alone keeps it from being torn asunder.*

I looked at the inscription, the way she'd dotted the *i* in her name with an inky heart. Pain roared through my body like a fire whipped by the wind. "Ed," I cried out loud. "Please come back. Give me another chance to understand. I'll be a better friend if you'll just come back."

Silence.

One beer followed another; I got pretty drunk. And then I broke down and cried for the loss of Edwin and for all the tears I'd suppressed since I'd lost Theresa.

I went for a walk and ended up on a bus headed to the amusement park. I wanted to win one of those big stuffed bears that Theresa always loved. First I thought I needed more beer. The two young women behind the concession counter whispered and giggled as I approached. "Can I help you, sir?" The dark-haired woman asked me.

"A beer." I pulled out my wallet.

The red-haired woman nudged her and giggled. "Tell him."

"Tell me what?" I asked.

"She thinks you're cute."

The dark-haired woman pushed her. "I do not. She's just a jerk."

My face flushed. I walked away from the counter without the beer. A powerful rage rose inside me. Why was I so angry? This was what I wanted, wasn't it? To be able to be myself and yet live without fear? It just didn't seem fair. All my life I'd been told everything about me was really twisted and sick. But if I was a man, I was "cute." Acceptance of me as a he felt like an ongoing indictment of me as a he-she.

I obsessed about winning the bear for Theresa. As I threw the baseballs at those dolls on the shelf I could feel a few stitches on my chest tear, but I didn't care. I pitched in a frenzy. I kept putting money down on the counter, and the man kept taking it. A small crowd formed. The prizes I won got a little bigger each time, but I couldn't seem to knock down a couple of those dolls.

"Sorry pal," the guy behind the counter told me. His teeth were clenched on a cigar.

I handed him five dollars. "Here," I said real loud. "You take my money and I'll show the people here which dolls are weighted."

He swung around and handed me a giant pink bear. "I want the blue one," I told him.

"Fuck you," he muttered, but he exchanged it.

As I bolted up Theresa's stairs that night I felt excited. By the time I knocked, I was scared. A young woman with a soft butch exterior answered the door. I stood there with a big blue bear in my arms. She called Theresa.

Theresa stood outside her door to talk to me, but she left it ajar.

"How are you?" I asked her. She shrugged. I beckoned with my chin toward the door. "Housekeeping butch?" It was a mean-spirited thing to say. I was glad she didn't respond. There was a long silence, then Theresa turned to go.

I whispered Edwin's name out loud as tears ran down my cheeks. Theresa wheeled around and threw her arms around me. She knew. She understood. She held me while I choked on my tears. I sniffled and looked at my boots. She watched my face. There were tears in her eyes, too. She touched the stubble on my cheek with her fingertips. I couldn't read her thoughts; I never could. It was time to leave. "You working?" I asked her.

"Some," she said.

She touched my cheek again and turned to go. "Theresa," I called her name. She looked at me. "Does she sit between the rows in your garden?"

Theresa shook her head. "No, Jess. You're the only one."

I picked up the big blue bear and extended it to her. She smiled sadly and shook her head. Then the door shut and she was gone.

I walked a couple of blocks to the supermarket and stood outside the automatic doors. After a while this little kid came by, holding onto his mother's hand. He stared at the bear as he approached and then turned to watch it as he walked by. His mother sort of dragged him along before she turned to see what he was looking at.

"Is it OK?" I asked her, nodding toward the bear. She looked surprised, but she nodded. I handed the bear to the boy. "Take good care of her, promise?"

He nodded. His arms could hardly get around the stuffed animal.

His mother nudged his shoulder. "Say thank you to the nice man."

CHAPTER 16

The sun was just peeking over the horizon. My breath froze on my beard. I wearily boarded the temp labor bus.

"Hey, Jesse." Ben sat down next to me and reached out his huge, calloused hand, as he did every morning. He could have crushed my hand in his, but it was in his firm handshake that I always rediscovered his gentleness. I looked at this great bear of a man and smiled, genuinely glad to see him.

The bitter cold didn't seem to affect him. I remembered why when he pulled a silver hip flask from his coat pocket. He offered it to me first. I took a long swig and coughed as I handed it back to him. "Wild Turkey," he smiled. "I like a little nip in the morning to get me going." Actually Ben liked little nips throughout the day to keep him going.

We were parked next to a diner. From where I sat I could see through the restaurant window. Annie, the waitress who had my complete attention, was pouring coffee and joking with the men at the counter. A powerful longing pulled on me, almost drawing tears.

"How'd you like a piece of her?" a guy in the seat in front of us asked his friend.

Ben watched me cringe. "Hey, shut up," Ben told him.

The man looked over the top of his seat at us. "What's it to you?"

"That's my sister you're talking about," Ben glared.

"Oh, sorry," the guy said. He looked at me and squinted. "Don't I know you from somewhere?"

"You ever work in Texas?" I asked him. He shook his head. "Then you don't know me," I told him.

The bus lurched into motion. We were headed out to a plant in Tonawanda. The agency promised us a steady gig with the possibility of permanent hire. Ben and I rode in comfortable silence. When the noise level on the bus became boisterous I whispered to him, "Is Annie really your sister?" He smiled and winked.

"Did you really work in Texas?" he asked me. I smiled and winked back.

As we approached the plant I saw picket lines barricading the entrance. Then I understood—we were hired to break a strike. "Scabs!" the shout went up the moment we got off the bus. It was hard to catch my breath in the frigid air.

Ben stood at my side. "I don't want any part of this," he said.

I heard a woman's voice shouting through a bullhorn, "We're gonna hold this line. We're not going to let a single scab through. I'm ready to do whatever I have to do to defend our jobs and our union! Are you?" The union women and men roared their agreement.

The cops flipped the visors down on their riot helmets and held their clubs horizontally across their chest. Those billy clubs were almost as thick and long as baseball bats. The cops were ready to attack in order to bring us in as scabs.

Another temp bus arrived. The men who got off that bus gravitated toward us. We formed a group of sixty men. I looked around at the guys I rode in with. The oldest of the men announced loudly, "The Devil can't buy my soul!"

"Well, I need a job, goddamn it. I got a family to feed," someone behind me yelled.

"I'm no scab," Ben shouted. "I never crossed a picket line in my life and I never will. And I've got no respect for any man who does." He took his UAW card out of his wallet and held it aloft so the picketers could see. Several of the other men pulled out their union cards and held them up proudly, too. I clenched my fist and pumped the air. The strikers cheered us.

Less than a dozen of the temp laborers agreed to be escorted by police into the plant. Most of the guys got on the bus again and asked the driver to take us back to the agency. I listened to the men talk to each other as we rode. This bicentennial year was supposed to be filled with patriotism, but the guys were sounding more and more like Theresa used to talk.

"There's more hard times coming, mark my words."

"Yeah, but you can bet the rich are still gettin' richer."

"It wasn't just Nixon—they're all a bunch of crooks. This new peanut man in the White House isn't going to change anything."

They talked about the layoffs that had abruptly altered their lives. Harrison, Chevrolet, Anaconda. Fifteen years seniority, twenty years, thirty years.

"I gave Chevy my whole life," Ben told me. "When I got laid off I figured it was a vacation. But to tell you the truth, I'm scared shitless that I'm never going back. My whole life's in that plant, you know what I mean?" I nodded. Ben nudged me. "We'll still get paid today for last week. Let's go cash our checks at the bar and have a drink."

I shook my head. "Naw, I better get home."

"Jesus, Jesse. You always have something you gotta do. You're gonna have a drink with me and that's that. Unless you think you're too good for me."

I sighed. "Just one drink." Ben smiled and thumped my thigh with his gloved hand.

Someone played "Stand By Your Man" on the bar jukebox. I was lost in my own past as Ben talked to me about growing up without his father. "How about you, Jesse?" he asked. "Did you grow up with your dad around?" I nodded. "Were you close to him?"

I shook my head. "No."

"Why not?"

I shrugged. "Oh, it's a long story. I don't really like to talk about it."

"Where'd you grow up?" he asked, signaling the waitress for another round.

"Different places." I worried that I couldn't keep up this evasion for a third round.

The waitress brought two shots and two beers. Ben smiled warmly at her. "Thank you, darlin'." Ben turned his attention back to me. "You know, I'm curious about you." I tensed. "I told my wife about you. I told her there's this guy I really like." Ben stopped and held up one hand. "Don't get me wrong."

I waved away his momentary fear that I might think he was sexually attracted to me. His speech was a little slurred. "I told her that every time I try to get to know this guy, he clams up. You know what my wife said? She says I'm the same way with her. She says that's what she's always complaining about."

Ben leaned forward. "Are you in trouble, Jesse? Cause if you are, you can tell me. I'm not much in life. But I'm a good mechanic and a good friend. All my buddies worked at Chevy with me. I miss those guys." I nodded, thinking about my old friends.

"Are you running from the law?" he asked me. "Cause if you are, I understand." His voice dropped. "I was in jail. Two years."

Suddenly something changed in Ben. His whole body settled into a stillness that frightened me, like the smooth surface of a lake before a storm. I felt the turbulence churning beneath his surface. Ben's hurt was presenting itself. I waited. Pain emerges at its own pace. I sat in silence, my heart pounding. Maybe this was just my imagination or the drama that Wild Turkey ushers in. But when I looked at Ben I knew I wasn't wrong. The storm was closing in, and it was too late to run.

Ben opened his wallet and pulled out two pictures. "Did I ever show you my wife and daughter?" I saw an exquisitely warm Down's Syndrome smile on his daughter's face. "I love that child," his eyes filled with tears. "She's taught me a lot." I wanted to ask him what he'd learned but I was still emotionally barricading myself from Ben. He wanted so much to know me, and I couldn't let him. What if I trusted him and I was wrong?

Ben flipped a small old photo on the table in front of me. I studied it and laughed. "Is that you?" He nodded, without smiling. I looked at the young Ben, a skinny kid with huge hands, slicked-back hair, and a beat-up leather jacket. "You were a greaser?" He nodded again.

"Nice bike," I pointed to the Harley in the photo. He smiled.

I could feel the pressure building. "When I was young," Ben said, "I thought I was a tough guy." Funny how much men express in a few flat words. It was a butch's way, too, of revealing heart.

"Then I got busted for stealing a car. You ever been arrested, Jesse?" I took a deep breath and shook my head no. Ben nodded. "I'd been in reform school a couple of times. I was a wild kid, I broke my poor mother's heart." Ben tossed back another shot. The waitress caught my eye. *Another round?* I shook my head slightly. "I was a tough guy. You think jail's nothing, those guards can't break me." I leaned toward him. I already knew.

And then suddenly it was there, in his eyes, all of his shame. His eyes filled with water. I waited for the tears to drip down his cheeks, but they didn't. I wanted to touch him, to lay my hand on his arm. But I looked around at the guys we worked with every day and I knew I couldn't. I leaned closer to Ben. He looked me in the eyes.

In silence, without words, his eyes told me what had happened to him in prison. I didn't look away. Instead, I let him see himself in my own mirror. He saw his reflection in a woman's eyes.

"I never told anyone," Ben said, as though our conversation had been out loud.

In his own way he had done what I had never been able to do—reveal the humiliation. And I wanted to trust him, to tell him everything. But I was afraid. Yet I couldn't leave him alone inside himself. "You know why I like you so much, Ben?" His eyes were eager as a child's for the answer. "I like you because you're as gentle as you are strong." Ben blushed and dropped his eyes. "There's something about you, Ben, that's good and that I trust. And I'm wondering: how did you turn out this way? How did you get from all your hurt to the man you are now? What changed for you? What decisions did you make?"

The great bear smiled shyly. This was the intimacy he'd wanted, the attention he needed. He leaned closer. "When I got out on parole, I went to work at a gas station. The mechanic there, Frank. That guy changed my life." Ben's voice dropped low. "Frank cared about me. He taught me to be a mechanic. He taught me about a lot of things. But there's one thing he told me I'll never forget. One day I was gonna run away. There was this guy who was always fucking with me at the garage and I couldn't fight him cause I'd go back to the joint if I did. It was making me crazy. I was all upset inside, you know?" I nodded.

"I wanted to kill that guy and then take off. Frank knew. He pushed me up against the garage wall and he was yelling at me, trying to get through." Ben laughed. "You'd have to know what a quiet guy he was to appreciate him yelling at me like that. I told him I had to prove I was a man." He took a swig of beer.

I smiled at the butchness in his story. "What happened?"

"I'll never forget what Frank told me. He said, 'You're already a man, you don't have to prove that. You just have to prove what kind of man you want to be.' " My eyes filled with tears.

Ben's voice was as intimate as his smile. "What about you, Jesse? What made you the way you are? What's your life been about?"

In a world with any justice I would have poured out my life story to him. I would have given him back in kind the trust he'd shown to me. But I was afraid and so I betrayed him. "There's not much to tell," I said.

He blinked in disbelief. I wanted him to let it go, but he wouldn't. He was brave enough to bloody his head against my brick wall again. "Jesse," he whispered, "tell me something about you."

I was frozen with fear, unable to collect my thoughts enough to invent a story that even appeared to reveal something about me. "There's nothing to tell," I told him. I was closed and protected. He was left naked.

The warmth drained from his face and anger rose to replace it. He was too gentle a man to lash out at me. Like a butch, he kept it inside.

I stood up. "I'd better be going," I said. He nodded and stared at his beer bottle. I let my hand rest for a moment on his shoulder. He would not accept the comfort or look at me. I wanted to say, *Ben, I'm so sorry I hurt you. I only did it because I was scared. I didn't know men could hurt the way I do. Please let me back inside.*

But of course, I didn't. Instead I said, "See you Monday."

The loneliness became more and more unbearable. I ached to be touched. I feared I was disappearing and I'd cease to exist if someone didn't touch me.

One woman in particular turned my head every morning: Annie, the waitress at the coffee shop near my job. When she brought me coffee, it seemed she didn't notice me. But then she'd catch my eye and turn away from me, wrapping my attention around her like a shawl. She was as tough as a gangster. God, I liked Annie. She treated every customer like a trick. She worked them for a tip and didn't let them drop till they left it.

I sat at the counter and watched Annie relax with her coworker, Frances. The men in the restaurant seemed to think the women's attention only existed for them. If they had seen how intimate the women were with each other, the men might have been jealous. But they didn't notice. I did.

Annie saw me at the counter. "Hey, sweetheart, what's shaking this morning?"

I laughed. "How are you, Annie?"

"Finer than a frog's hair quartered, darlin'. Whatcha havin'?"

"Coffee and eggs over easy."

"You got it," she said over her shoulder as she swung away from me. Her body demanded I pay attention.

Frances and Annie showed each other their kids' school photos while they waited for their orders from the grill.

"Can I see?" I asked Annie as she brought me my eggs.

She eyed me warily as she handed me the photo. "Don't see why not."

Four rows of sweet childrens' faces looked back at me. "Which one?" I asked. Annie wiped her hands on her apron and pointed out her daughter.

"God, she's great," I told her. "She's got your eyes—smart and angry at the same time."

"Where do you see that?" Annie demanded as she snatched the photo from my hand. She stormed off. A moment later she brought my coffee and slammed it down so hard it sloshed over the rim of the cup. Then she lifted it up, wiped the counter, and spilled it again. "Next time you want to read a book, go to the goddamn library." She spun on her heel. I put down a tip, paid the cashier, and left.

The next day I brought her a single flower. "I'm sorry I got personal," I told her.

"Aw, well, I don't mind you gettin' personal, darlin'. Just take your damn sweet time about it, OK?"

"Agreed," I agreed.

"What kinda flower is this anyway?"

I smiled, "A mum for a mum."

She frowned. "Oh, I get it."

Annie's body language was very reserved with me. But as soon as Annie and Francis got together, she loosened up. They whispered. Francis smelled the flower and put her hand over her heart. Annie smacked Francis on the shoulder.

I wanted to spend time with Annie when she wasn't working. It was no secret now.

Annie brought me a white paper bag. "What's this?" I asked.

She shrugged. "Coffee and a cherry Danish."

I was confused. "I didn't ask for it."

"I didn't ask for no flower either. It's on the house," she shot back. "It's fresh. The Danish is fresh."

I smiled, left a tip, and paid the cashier for my breakfast. Then I came back to the counter and tried to get Annie's attention. She made me wait.

"Whatdya forget?" she asked.

"I wanted to know if you. . ." I hesitated. It could be a big mistake to go out with someone who knew my coworkers. She could make real trouble for me if she found out; I'd have to quit my job. But I was deperately lonely.

"If I'd what?" she sounded suspicious.

"If you'd want to go out with me sometime?"

Annie put both her hands on her hips and looked me up and down several times. "Ask me again sometime." Somehow I thought that was a good sign.

Our serious flirtation began the next morning. It was fun. It felt good. It reminded me of the old days between femmes and butches. But this was not between women. At least that's not how the world around us saw it. And, I reminded myself over and over again, that's not how Annie saw it.

The amazing part was that this courtship dance could take place in public and everyone—coworkers and strangers alike—encouraged and approved. Meanwhile, Anita Bryant was thumping the Bible in a well-publicized campaign to overturn a simple gay rights ordinance. I wondered how human affection could be judged so differently.

When I finally got up the nerve to ask Annie out again, she wiped her hands on her apron and answered, "Sure, I guess. Why not?"

Friday night I knocked on her door. It took a long time for her to answer. I heard her yelling something. I got a funny feeling in the pit of my stomach. Annie only opened the door partway. "Uh. . . ," she started. I could see a child wrapped around her legs.

"It's OK," I interrupted. She wanted to cancel. I tried to conceal my disappointment. "Maybe another time."

"Wait, she opened the door all the way. "I mean if you want to come in I could make you some coffee or something." I did want to come in.

The three of us stood awkwardly in her living room. "My babysitter, well it's my sister's kid actually, she got sick, so I have Kathy home tonight and she's running a little fever."

I raised my hand to stop her. "It's OK. I can see you've got your hands full. Relax!"

Annie unwound a notch. "Sit down. Would you like something to eat? I could make us something."

"Aren't you sick of serving food?"

She laughed. "It's OK. I don't mind."

"Want me to sit in the kitchen so you can function in one room?" She smiled and nodded.

I set the small canvas bag I'd brought on the floor near the couch, out of sight. Maybe bringing a dildo had been too optimistic. Then again, being caught without one could present its own crisis. I tried to breathe past my anxiety as I followed Annie and Kathy into the kitchen.

"Can I help?" I offered.

She looked surprised, "Naw, that's OK."

Kathy clung to Annie's leg with one arm and clutched a stuffed rabbit with the other. I smiled at Kathy. "Does your rabbit have a fever, too?" Kathy looked at the rabbit and then at me without answering.

"Later," I told Kathy, "if you think your rabbit has a fever, I'll take it's temperature. Is it a girl rabbit or a boy?" Kathy held the rabbit up in the air as though I could determine its sex.

"Ah, it's a girl," I surmised. Kathy looked up at her mother.

"Go show him your rabbit," Annie urged. Kathy shook her head violently and clung to her mother for protection.

"You like macaroni and cheese?" Annie asked. I hate macaroni and cheese.

"That would be great," I answered.

Annie served up three plates of sliced ham, macaroni and cheese, corn and white bread. The first plate had small portions with pictures of the Flintstones still visible underneath. "Is that mine?" I asked Kathy. She shook her head and squeezed her bunny tighter.

Annie set my plate in front of me and sat down. Kathy held up an empty glass. Annie jumped up to fill it with milk. "Want a beer?" she asked me while the refrigerator door was open.

"Sure," I said.

"Need a glass?" I shook my head. She smiled.

Annie brought two beer bottles to the table and sat back down. We lifted our beers in a toast. Kathy tried to do the same thing. Her glass tipped over, pouring milk all over the table. Annie immediately tried to mop the milk off my plate with her napkin. I jumped up and came back from the sink with a sponge. We got most of it.

Annie looked tense. "Your meal's all spoiled."

"Naw," I said, "milk's good for you."

Kathy seemed ready to cry. She hugged her bunny tighter. I smiled at her. "Sometimes when I drop something I think everybody is gonna be mad at me," I told her. "I'm not mad at you." Kathy narrowed her eyes as she checked me out, just the way her mother did.

"Would it make you feel better if I spilled my beer?" I asked her. Kathy smiled and nodded emphatically.

"Don't you dare," Annie warned me with a hidden smile.

The rest of the dinner went much smoother. After dessert Kathy thrust her bunny at me. "Take her temperature?" I asked. She nodded.

"This wabbit needs to go to bed soon," I told her. "I think she's got a cold." Kathy weighed the information and nodded. "Does your wabbit need a bath first?" I asked. Kathy shook her head from side to side.

"Oh yes she does," Annie laughed and scooped up Kathy in her arms.

"I'll clean up," I told Annie. "Take your time." Annie eyed me suspiciously.

I was washing the last of the dishes when Annie came up behind me. She grabbed a dishtowel off the refrigerator door. I washed the pots while she dried the dishes. It felt good. But the longer Annie dried dishes, the angrier she seemed to become. "What's up?" I asked her.

She threw down the towel and glared at me. "I'm not an easy lay, you know. You guys know a woman with a kid's been fucked before so you figure you can get whatever you want, right?"

I rinsed a sponge under the faucet and walked over to the kitchen table to wipe it off. "I got what I wanted at dinner," I told her.

She looked stunned. "What, macaroni and cheese in milk gravy?" We both laughed.

"I just wanted to spend some time with you when we're both off-duty, you know."

"Why?" she measured me with those keen eyes again.

"I like you. I guess I really like tough cookies, and god knows, you are one."

She shook her head. "I can't figure you out."

"So what?"

"So a man you can't figure out is a dangerous man," she told me. She came closer. My body turned toward hers. It was happening.

"I'm not dangerous," I promised. "I'm complicated, but I'm not dangerous."

"Whatchya lookin for darlin'?" Annie ran her fingers lightly through my hair. Oh, god, it felt so good.

I sighed deeply. "I've been hurt. I'm not looking to get married, I'm not looking to disrespect anyone. I guess I just need some comfort."

"That's it?" she probed. "Like a one-nighter?"

I shrugged my shoulders. "I don't know," I told her honestly.

Annie weighed my words carefully in the scales of her own need. She turned away from me, but I knew after a moment it was alright to touch her. I kissed the closest cheek. My lips brushed her ear and traveled down her neck. I could hear her breathing change. She turned and looked at me for a long moment before offering me her mouth. We kissed deeply, but still carefully. Slowly we began to move against each other. I could feel how she offered her body to a man as a test. I was gentle. I was slow. Gradually her body became aware that my tempo was slightly behind hers. Her face flushed with heat. She pressed her pelvis against mine and looked at me quizzically. We both knew I didn't have a hard-on.

"Mommy!" Kathy called from upstairs. Annie looked apologetic. I nodded toward the sound of Kathy's voice. Annie was gone for a few minutes. She came back into the kitchen and filled a plastic Cinderella glass with water. "I'll be right back," she said hoarsely.

I remembered the bag I'd left in the other room. Now was definitely the right time to get it. I grabbed the bag and raced into the bathroom. I locked the door and took off my pants and BVD'S.

The harness and rubber cock fit nicely in my briefs. I pulled my pants back on and checked my wallet for a condom. I heard Annie call my name from the kitchen. I flushed the toilet, ran the tap water for a moment, and came out to meet her. I was out of breath.

"What were you doing in there, running?" she laughed.

It would take time to get back the feeling. I ran my fingers through her hair.

She closed her eyes and parted her lips. The phone rang. We both laughed. "Forget it," she said. It kept ringing. I pulled her close to me. She pressed her pelvis against mine. This time she smiled.

She pulled back and searched my face with her eyes. I leaned against the sink and waited for her to come back to me. Then she took my hand and led me to her bedroom.

Annie was afraid. I knew that was true. What she couldn't know was that I was too. I wanted so much to be in her arms that I was willing to risk exposure and humiliation.

She turned on the light in her bedroom as we walked in. A Harley-Davidson gas tank hung from the ceiling. "You like bikes?" she asked me. I nodded. I walked over to the light switch and snapped it off. She stood awkwardly near her bed. I came up behind her and rested my hands on her shoulders. I lifted her hair with one hand and nipped the nape of her neck with my lips. I pressed my pelvis gently against her ass as I pulled her shoulders back so that my mouth could take more of her neck.

Annie turned and gently pulled me down on the bed. She trembled. "Are you afraid?" I asked.

"Fuck you," she answered with a twisted smile.

"You've been hurt before," I said to myself out loud.

"What woman hasn't?" she snapped.

I rolled over on my back and pulled her against my body. "I'd really like to make you feel good," I whispered. "If you'd trust me enough to show me what you want."

"What's your trip, mister?" she snorted. "You want to fuck or not?"

"We can if you want to," I said. "Or we can do other things. It's up to you."

Annie did a double take. "Whatdya mean it's up to me?"

"It's your body. What do you want? I mean, you can show me how you really want to be touched. Or you can act excited and hope I come—not too quick, but don't take too long—right?"

Annie shook her head and sat bolt upright. "You're scaring me," she said.

"Because I want you to really be there when I touch you?"

She nodded, "Yeah, exactly." I lay quietly.

"I don't know if I can," she said.

I sat up and took her in my arms. "Try," I whispered and pulled her down on top of me. I rolled Annie over on her back as I kissed her, deep and long. I unbuttoned her blouse with slow steady fingers and teased her breasts for a long time before I came near them with my fingertips. Then I brushed them, lightly, and felt her body shudder. I took each nipple in my mouth and played with it ever so gently. Somehow she told me with her body where to touch, how to touch, when to touch. As I rubbed the front of her jeans I could feel her passion building, but she deserved the luxury of wanting it real bad.

Then she said something to me I knew took a lot of courage. "I've always wanted to come before I fuck." She turned her head away in shame.

I kissed the part of her throat she left exposed. "Anything you want," I told her.

She turned her head to look at me. She had tears in her eyes. "Anything?" she asked.

Together we began to undress her—my need, her urgency. I pulled off my chinos and my dress shirt. I was wearing only a white T-shirt and BVD'S.

My hands ran up her thighs and down the inside crevices. I could feel her heat and wetness through her underwear. I began to work my body down her, using my lips and tongue to create new erogenous zones all over her rib cage and stomach. My fingers took hold of the elastic on her underwear and began to slide it down her thighs as her hands grabbed my ears firmly and stopped me.

I looked at her with a question on my face. "I'm just gettin' over my period," she said.

I shrugged. "So?"

Emotions played across Annie's face: disbelief, anger, relief, pleasure. Pleasure was the unmistakable emotion still on her face as I began to tease her thighs with my mouth. She gave in to her own desire and, in doing so, reached her orgasm with an almost relaxed trust.

I held her close to me as her breathing slowed. She ran her fingers through my hair, stroked my back. Her touch felt so good that tears welled up in my eyes and spilled down my cheeks. "What's wrong, darlin'?" she asked with concern. I shook my head and buried my face in her shoulder. For the moment her arms protected me from my own life.

My mouth was near her nipple. I felt Annie's breath quicken. She tugged at my T-shirt. "Take it off," she insisted. I hesitated. It was dark in the room. I was on top of her, so she couldn't see the two lines across my chest that revealed it had been reshaped.

I took off my T-shirt. Annie ran her nails across my shoulders, down my back. I shivered with pleasure. Her nails pressed deeper into my flesh as she moved her pelvis against mine. She was relaxed with me, until the moment I was above her, ready to enter her. I stroked her thighs until she looked up at me. "It's for you, or not at all," I told her.

"I want you so bad," she whispered hoarsely. We both moaned softly as she said that. I pulled my dildo carefully out of my briefs in the dark, afraid of being discovered. What made me think this could work?

I rolled a condom onto my dildo. "I don't think I can have any more kids," she told me.

"I don't want to take any chances, and it's up to me, after all," I said.

"Well, ain't that a switch," she laughed.

I pushed the head of my cock gently inside of her. She tensed her body; I waited. Then Annie relaxed and her hips began to move, pulling me into her. When I was deep inside of her I lay still on top of her. Our bodies relaxed, fitting into each other. I didn't move until she did. I stroked her just a little slower than her motion demanded; her body demanded more.

I felt her orgasm building long before she came. As she began to come her hands clawed at my back. Once she pulled my hair so hard I cried out with her. As her orgasm began to ebb I followed it gently—circles in the broken surface of a pool of water. I searched with her for the next orgasm before the last one had subsided. Together we found it, and later a smaller one.

"Oh, Jesse." It sounded so pretty the way she sighed my name. Her fingertips slid down my back like warm raindrops.

I was still rock hard inside of her. We both realized it at once. "What's the matter, darlin', you stuck?"

"I can't come with a rubber on," I said. "Let me take it off and I'll pull out just before I come, I promise."

She turned her head away. "I've heard that one before."

"I promise. Trust me."

"Lord have mercy, those are the four most dangerous words out of a man's mouth. OK, sweetheart, you're lucky I don't think I can get pregnant again."

It's true I faked an ejaculation, but not my pleasure. Annie's body felt so good. She kissed me deep and slow, moved for me, gave me everything a woman can give to a lover, and I was excited. At the moment when it became unbearable for me to go on any longer I pulled out gently, ground my pelvis against the sheets, and cried out.

I lay face down on the bed with my head resting on her belly. Her hands played with my hair. Her fingertips ran across my shoulders, arousing the surface of my skin. I wished I could just stay in that moment in time.

We lay together without speaking for a while. "I have to go to the bathroom," I said.

"Me too," she laughed.

"Me first." Still face down I tucked my dildo into my briefs. I turned away from her, slipped on my T-shirt, and headed to the bathroom in the darkness. I locked the door, pulled my bag out from behind the tub, and replaced my dildo with a sock in my briefs. I looked in the mirror as I splashed cold water on my face. Still me looking back at me.

There was a knock at the bathroom door. I unlocked it. Annie came into my arms and kissed me deeply. She put her hand gently between my thighs and squeezed the sock. "I got a lot of pleasure out of this tonight," she said. "It was like magic." My body tensed, and she withdrew her hand.

I stroked her hair. "All magic is illusion," I admitted.

The light was on when I returned to the bedroom. I clicked it off. Annie came back and sat down on the edge of the bed. "Hungry?" she asked me.

"Mmm," I pulled her back on top of me and kissed her until I realized I was making promises I couldn't keep. "I'm tired," I said, "but I want to hold you."

Annie came into my arms and nestled against my shoulder. "You are one strange man."

"Whatdya mean?"

"First of all, I never met a guy who wasn't afraid of a little bit of woman's blood. But you know what's the weirdest about you?"

Every muscle in my body got hard, except the sock. Annie laughed. "Relax, baby. I'm not complaining. What really blew me away is that you knew I had to take care of my kid and you didn't demand my attention till she went to bed. That, and the fact that even my ex-husband never did the dishes, and he's the one that dirtied most of them."

Annie shook her head. "You don't fuck like some other guys, either." I rolled over on my stomach protectively. She massaged my shoulders. "I mean, you take your time, you know. It's like you got a brain in your dick instead of a dick for a brain, you know?" We both laughed and rolled around the bed together.

I fell asleep, safe in her arms.

The first voice I awoke to was Kathy's. "Can I turn on the cartoons?"

Annie mumbled, "go ahead." Shortly afterward she kissed me on the ear and got up to make breakfast. While Annie cooked pancakes, Kathy sat on my lap and told me everything she could think of about the Road Runner and Wily Coyote. Annie tried to hide her pleasure at watching us together. "She's usually scared of men," Annie said when Kathy left the room. "You're real good with her."

I noticed Annie's body language as she cooked. "Something on your mind?" I asked.

She turned and wiped her hands on her apron. "I know this is crazy to ask you."

"Go ahead," I said.

"Well, my sister's getting married tomorrow, and, well, it's crazy, I mean it's too short notice and you didn't commit to nothing last night—"

"Yeah, sure," I said.

Annie sat down in a kitchen chair next to mine. "You really don't mind?"

"I really don't mind, as long as you understand."

She pressed her fingertips against my lips. "My heart asks for more sometimes," she said, "but my head wants the same thing you do." I nodded.

Annie got up and walked to the stove. "There's one catch," I added. She didn't turn around, but her entire body clenched like a fist. "What?" she said over her shoulder.

"We have to go on my Harley. It's the only wheels I got."

Annie took off her apron, threw it in the sink and came over and sat in my lap. She kissed my mouth so sweetly. "Nine o'clock," she said, "not a minute later."

I got near her place at 8:30 actually. I turned off the engine a block away and rolled it in front of her house so I wouldn't wake the whole neighborhood. I sat on her porch, smoking a cigarette, until I heard her door open and Annie said, "You comin' in or not?"

She looked me up and down appreciatively. "You look real handsome, darlin'." My blush visibly delighted her. "I gotta finish gettin' dressed. I made coffee," she called out from her bedroom.

"I'll get it," I yelled back, "you want some?"

She came to the door of her bedroom, holding the back of her dress together. "Yeah." She smiled. "Help me zip my dress up first." She looked back at me over her shoulder as I did. I kissed the side of her face. Her hair was swept up and held in place with bobby pins. I kissed the base of her neck. "You keep that up and I'll never get ready, darlin'," she pulled away from me.

I made two cups of coffee and brought them to her bedroom door. The door was ajar, but I knocked on the doorframe. "Your coffee's out here."

When she came out moments later I sucked in my breath and let it out slowly. She smoothed her dress. "How do I look?"

I sighed. "Like I died and went to heaven." She made a face and lifted her arms to wrap them around my neck, but I pulled back and handed her an orchid corsage I bought the night before.

She blinked back tears. Then she sounded angry. "Whatdya go and do that for?" she scolded. I smiled at the powerful woman who stood before me. Her face softened and she smiled back.

"Where's Kathy?" I asked her.

She scowled, "With Frances, from the restaurant. My ex-husband might be skulking around the wedding." I didn't understand, but I let it drop.

The wedding was a formal church affair. I'd never been to a wedding before. Everyone in the audience looked so teary-eyed and melted by the ceremony. Annie's sister honestly had to promise to obey this guy for the rest of her life before the priest would proclaim the two married. I thought it was kind of feudal.

The reception was held outdoors. There were tables and chairs set up all over the lawn. Drinks and food were served under a huge striped tent.

Annie introduced me to all her people who'd traveled up to Buffalo for the wedding. She stayed on my arm the whole time. I met Cousin Wilma. She flashed an evil smile. "How wonderful it was of you to agree to come with Annie today." Annie squeezed my arm like a tourniquet.

"It's my pleasure," I put my hand on Annie's hand, which was cutting off the circulation in my arm. Without taking my eyes off Annie's I told Wilma, "It isn't everyday that a woman as strong and beautiful as Annie will give me the time of day." Wilma turned on her heel, and Annie chuckled into my shoulder.

"Get us a bottle of champagne," she said.

I did. "How many glasses, sir?" the bartender asked me.

"One." I picked up a small bottle of club soda. "Can I have this?" The bartender nodded.

"What's that for?" Annie wanted to know.

"Hell, somebody's got to drive us home." She kissed me so tenderly right then and there under the tent that not a man or a woman within eyesight didn't stare wistfully.

Annie and I found a shady place under a tree where we could watch all the goings-on. She kicked off her shoes. I put my suit jacket down for her to sit on. Annie shook her head. "Your momma sure taught her little boy some manners."

She gave me the lowdown on all her folks: who was a closet drunk, who beat or cheated on their wife and who was giving it to the milkman.

"That fag," she said contemptuously. I was stunned at the hatred in her eyes. She was glaring at a man in his early fifties. His arm was around the shoulder of one of the many aunts who roamed this reception. "Who let that queer in here?" Annie hissed.

"Is he really gay?" I asked her.

"You bet. Probably fuckin' all the children in the family."

"Jeez, Annie." My blood ran cold. "How can you hate somebody just because of who they love?"

She looked at me with shock. "You like faggots?"

I shrugged. "We aren't all the same, Annie. So what?"

She shook her head and spat on the ground. "I wouldn't let a faggot near my daughter."

I thought before I spoke. "Annie, if anybody was gonna fuck with Kathy it would probably be a straight guy, not a gay man."

"Yeah?" she yelled. Annie stood up and gripped the champagne bottle tightly at her side. "Well, I ain't lettin' no funny men around my daughter. I left my own husband cause I caught him molesting Kathy. I tried to kill the man with my bare hands. No fucking fags are coming near my girl, you understand?"

I did understand that this conversation could go no further. Annie kicked up some dirt and grass with her pumps and then sat down again. "Aw, shit, what're we wasting our time talkin' about queers for anyway?"

I couldn't wait till we left the reception. Annie rode with her arms around my neck and her face against my back. By the time we got to her home both her shoes were gone and the exhaust pipe had burned a hole in the hem of her dress. "Pay it no mind," Annie said. She was drunk.

When we got to the porch she threw her arms around me. "You comin' in, darlin'?"

"Naw," I said. "I gotta get ready for work in the morning."

She looked down at her stocking feet and back up to my face. "I ain't gonna see you again, am I?" she asked.

I looked down at my shoes. "I don't think so."

She nodded. "Why not?" It hurt my heart the way she asked it.

"I'm afraid I'd fall in love with you," I said. It was partly true, but it sure didn't tell the whole story. It's one thing for the magician to reveal the art of illusion. It's another thing to tell a straight woman that the man she slept with is a woman. That's not what Annie agreed to get into. Sooner or later it was going to blow up. And after this afternoon, I had even more reason to fear the explosion.

"What's wrong with falling in love? What's the matter with you guys, anyway?" she slurred.

"I've been hurt, Annie. I need time."

"Shit, I thought you were different. You ain't any different from any other guy who stands up to pee."

"Well," I shrugged, "maybe just a little different."

"You tell that woman who hurt you I'm gonna come after her and rip her to shreds. She spoiled it for the rest of us." Annie's smile faded. "Ain't no use us standing out here talkin', is it? You best be goin'."

I nodded. We looked at each other for a long moment. I took the keys from her hand and unlocked the front door. I kissed her lightly on the mouth.

"Hey, thanks for what you said to Wilma back there."

"I meant every word of it."

She looked me straight in the eye. "Thanks for everything, darlin'." I smiled and turned to go. She stood on the porch and watched me kick-start my bike. "Hey," she yelled over the roar of the engine.

"What?" I cupped my hand near my ear to hear.

"The wabbit."

"What?"

"Kathy's wabbit."

I nodded and strained to hear what she was repeating.

"Kathy's wabbit isn't a girl, it's a boy!"

CHAPTER 17

I felt light-headed and dizzy. My stomach clenched. I was about to heave my guts up. The worst part of it was I knew I couldn't leave the injection-mold machine I was working on. If I switched it off, the plastic would harden throughout the machine. The machines ran continuously—the repetitive sounds were the music we worked to in the molding department.

I looked around for the foreman, but I didn't see him on the shop floor. I tried to concentrate on my work. I checked the barrel filled with plastic pellets on the skid to my left and pushed the suction hose in a little deeper. Puffs of steam shot from the machine as it cooked the pellets and popped out little plastic parts. It stunk as bad as a burning rubber dish drain.

Mind over matter. I willed myself not to think about the stench, my stomach, and the hot, stagnant air in the factory. Matter won out. I vomited all over the side of the machine and the greasy concrete floor.

Bolt ran to me. He was lead man on the set-up crew. He put his hand on my shoulder while I threw up my breakfast. "It's OK, you'll be OK," he reassured. I was more embarrassed than anything. I wiped my mouth with the back of my hand. Bolt pulled an oily rag out of the back pocket of his blue work chinos and handed it to me. "You're the third guy on this shift to puke."

"How hot you think it is in here today, Bolt?"

"Hundred and ten degrees."

I whistled. "That's probably right on the nose. How do you do that?"

Bolt laughed. "The thermometer on the wall in assembly. You alright?"

"Yeah," I smiled sheepishly. Throwing up had only made the smell worse.

Bolt patted my shoulder. "No shame in puking. I do it myself about every Saturday night. I'll send one of the guys from maintenance over to clean this up."

"Hey, Bolt, what are these parts we're making?"

Bolt shrugged. "Something for computers."

I shook my head. "It's weird to spend half my waking day making something and I don't even know what the hell it is."

Bolt laughed. "Be glad it has something to do with computers. That means we'll probably both have a job down the line." He started to walk away and then hesitated. Bolt turned around and put his hand on my shoulder. "Listen," he said, "if you're interested, there may be a job opening up soon in shipping and receiving. At least you can breathe in there. How long you been working here?"

I thought about it. "Almost a year. But the first three months I was a temp, I don't know if that counts."

Bolt nodded. "I get around the plant. I'll keep my ear to the ground for you." He slapped me on the shoulder and walked away.

A few minutes later Jimmy came over to clean up my vomit. Jimmy was Mohawk. All the other guys on the maintenance and set-up gangs were white.

"Can I help you clean it up?" I asked him. "It *is* my mess, after all."

Jimmy shook his head. "Just a job."

"Does Bolt let you work fixing the machines much, or mostly clean up?"

Jimmy eyed me suspiciously, then he shrugged. "Bolt's not a bad guy. He tries to throw some decent work my way."

The lunch whistle blew. "I better not eat lunch," I told Jimmy. "I'm sure you got enough work to do this afternoon."

He laughed. "The air in here doesn't move. You should get outside and breathe."

I punched out for lunch and started to walk to the shipping and receiving end of the plant. The factory was the size of a large supermarket. I didn't know the guys on this end; I'd never even been back here. It was another world, and besides, I was afraid to leave the safety of working alone on a machine. When I got to shipping and receiving, all the guys had already gone to lunch. I walked out on the open loading dock. The temperature was thirty degrees cooler. The summer air smelled fresh.

I wanted to stay at this plant. No one knew me out here in Tonawanda, on the outskirts of Buffalo. But working that machine was making me sick. Maybe it was worth taking a risk and bidding for this job.

Scotty was at least thirty years my senior, but I could never have gotten that last box hoisted up and into place in the truck's trailer without him. My arms felt like jelly after loading this one. Scotty wasn't even winded.

"So how do you like working in shipping and receiving, young fella?" Scotty asked me.

"Can I breathe first?"

"Sure. You'll get the rhythm of this job down. You work real hard, then you take it easy. It's almost lunchtime. Come on, let's go wash up."

I took a deep breath as we walked into the men's room together. It looked just like the one on the other end of the plant. There was a huge concrete circular sink in the center of the room. Scotty and I each slapped the powdered soap dispenser in the middle of the sink and stepped on the foot pedals that sent sprays of water our way.

"You got a locker yet?" Scotty asked me. I shook my head. "C'mon," he said, "follow me."

Scotty silenced the banter in the locker room. "Some of you guys met Jesse this morning. He just got transferred from operator."

Except for Scotty and Walter, most of the guys were in their late twenties or early thirties. Walter shook my hand. "Hey, son. You worked here long?"

I shook my head. "A year."

He laughed. "Where'd you work before?"

I shrugged. "Around." Walter and Scotty glanced at each other.

I was relieved when another one of the guys interrupted us. "I'm Ernie. This here's my sidekick, Skids. I used to be an operator. I quit when I started coughing up blood."

Skids threw a towel at him. "You coughed up blood because you smoke, asshole." Ernie grabbed Skids in a headlock and ran his knuckles back and forth across Skids' scalp.

A young man with a ponytail shook my hand. "I'm Pat."

Ernie laughed. "You haven't met Patty yet?"

Pat made a face at Ernie. "Shut up. I'll tell you before they do: I was a conscientious objector. If you got a problem with that, keep it to yourself."

Skids thrust his chest out. "I was in Nam. Hey, Jesse. Did you get drafted or did you join up?"

All the blood rushed to my head. I wished I was back in the molding department where the noise level protected me from idle questions. "I didn't go," I mumbled.

Ernie groaned. "Another one. What'd you do, tell them a fairy tale?"

I thought hard. "I was exempt. Medical."

Walter interrupted. "Leave the kid alone. You got a locker? Here, use this one."

"Hey," Ernie said. "You need to spice up that locker a little." I knew what he meant. All the other guys had pin-up posters on their locker doors. "Get yourself a calendar from the restaurant on the corner. We all go there together on payday. Miss August will cook your balls. Hey, Walter, you better get one, too."

Walter shook his head slowly. "Some guys need pictures, some guys get the real thing. Right, Jesse?"

I smiled. "I brought my pin up over from my old locker." Ernie handed me two bandaids from the first-aid kit on the wall. I used them to tape up a color magazine ad of my old Norton.

Pat whistled. "I'd rather ride Jesse's than yours, Ernie."

The lunch whistle blew. I looked around for Scotty, but he was gone. "Hey, Walter, where's Scotty?"

Walter shrugged and pantomimed lifting a bottle to his lips. "He's having a rough go of it. His wife's dying of cancer. He don't stick around when the guys start talking about pussy."

By the end of the summer I was considered one of the guys. I actually looked forward to coming to work most mornings because it was my only human contact.

Friday at lunchtime we were headed to the Italian restaurant on the corner when Bolt stopped me. "You know somebody named Frankie?"

I felt the blood rush up into my face. "What's he look like?"

Bolt shook his head. "It's not a he. It's a bulldagger. She used to work with you at a bindery—said you two were on strike together. She told me you did a lot of work with the union."

Frankie told Bolt about me. She must have. I wondered if I should quit now. Just walk out on the dock, hop down onto the driveway, and keep on walking to my bike. "Where did you meet Frankie?" I asked Bolt.

"She was on second shift. Starting Monday she's moving onto day side. She's an operator. She said you're a good guy."

I blinked in disbelief. "She said that?"

Bolt nodded. "She said you're a good union man."

I laughed in relief. "How did she know I worked here?"

"She saw you leaving the parking lot. She a friend of yours?" Bolt asked me.

"Naw," I distanced myself. "Just somebody I used to work with." My own disloyalty sickened me.

Bolt headed for the dock. "You coming to lunch?"

I shook my head. "I'll be along, go ahead." It was a relief to be alone. I wandered into the warehouse and sat down on a stack of skids to think about Bolt's bombshell.

Frankie was coming onto the day shift. It scared me to realize she might have exposed me. But apparently she didn't. Frankie was sharp. She must have figured out the score right away.

A feeling of excitement flooded me. Working with another butch! Maybe we could hang out sometimes. Maybe she knew where some of the old crowd was. Maybe she could introduce me to a femme.

"Hey, young fella," Scotty interrupted my thoughts. He was sitting on the floor, leaning up against the skids. Scotty unscrewed a bottle of Jack Daniels and offered it to me.

"Thanks," I said, taking a swig.

Scotty tipped the bottle to his lips and swallowed three times. We sat in silence. "You married?" he asked me. I shook my head.

He dropped his head to his chest. "My wife's real sick." He rubbed his eyes with his hands. His face brightened. "Did I ever show you a picture of my wife?"

I shook my head. He pulled out a leather wallet, thin and smooth from wear. "Here she is. That's my girl."

I laughed and whistled. "That's you?"

He smiled. "Yep. You think I was born this age? I was once a young fella just like you. Had my whole life ahead of me."

We both laughed. But when I looked at him again, his eyes were filled with tears. His voice sounded hoarse. "I wish I could go before she does. I know that sounds terrible. I mean, who would take care of her, you know? But sometimes I don't think I can stand letting go of her when the time comes."

His head dropped down again. I reached out and lay my hand gently on his back, ready to remove it quickly if my touch offended him. It didn't.

"You're young," Scotty said, abruptly. "Don't get stuck in a job like this."

I shrugged. "This job seems pretty good to me."

Scotty shook his head. "I mean a real job. I had twenty years in the Chevy plant. I got my UAW card, you want to see it? Twenty years of my life in that plant and they laid me off. Can you believe it?"

"Chevy? Did you work with Bolt?"

Scotty nodded. "Yeah. But he wasn't there as long as I was. He worked at Harrison for a while. Got laid off there, too."

Bolt interested me. "Was he in the same union?"

"All us old-timers are UAW," he said. "I'll be a union man on the day they lower my casket into the ground. You gotta have a union, young fella. If you don't have a union, you better fight to get one."

I laughed. "Not too likely we'll get one here any time soon."

Scotty shrugged. "Well, you never can tell. There's been talk. We need a union here. I'm too old to do it. You young ones, you're gonna have to do it."

I sighed. "I wish we had a union, too. But I just want to keep my job, Scotty. By the way, what do you think about Bolt? He seems like a good guy."

Scotty wagged his finger near my nose. "Watch out for Bolt. He's not really one of us anymore. He's part gang foreman, part set-up man. Mark my words: When push comes to shove he won't know which side he's on. Don't trust him."

His warning disappointed me because I liked Bolt. But lucky for me, I didn't really trust anyone.

I felt a hand on my shoulder as I punched out Monday afternoon. "Hey," Frankie spun me around.

"Hey, Frankie. Listen, we got to talk."

She put her index finger to her lips. "It's OK, I know."

I followed her out to the parking lot. "I'm really glad to see you and everything, Frankie. It's just I'm scared. I've got a good thing going here. And the newspapers are talking about another recession."

Frankie stopped walking. "I understand, Jess. Don't you think I get it?"

"How did you survive this long?" I asked her.

She shrugged. "I'm living out here in Tonawanda with my parents till I can save up for my own place. It's not too bad. I stay at my girlfriend's on the weekend."

I whistled. "You got a girlfriend? Lucky you."

Frankie pursed her lips. A car horn blared. "You know my girlfriend, Jess. Me and Johnny been together a year," she smiled. "Just like the song."

I stopped dead in my tracks. "Who's Johnny?"

Frankie sighed. "You know Johnny. We worked together before the strike. We all played softball together."

I shook my head. "The only Johnny I remember was butch and I know you don't mean her," I laughed.

Frankie widened her stance. "Yeah, that's exactly who I mean. She's waiting for me in our car over there."

"Hey, Jess!" I heard Johnny yell from the car. "C'mere."

"You must be kidding," I whispered to Frankie.

She put her hands on her hips. "She's my lover, Jess. Do I look like I'm kidding?"

My mouth hung open. I shook my head from side to side. "Honest, Frankie, I just don't get it. I don't understand."

Frankie smoldered. "You don't have to understand it, Jess. But you gotta accept it. If you can't, then just keep walking."

That's exactly what I did. I couldn't deal with it, so I just walked away.

It wasn't hard to avoid Frankie after that—we worked at opposite ends of the plant. I hung back in the afternoons. I didn't want to run into either of them at the time clock.

The more I thought about the two of them being lovers, the more it upset me. I couldn't stop thinking about them kissing each other. It was like two guys. Well, two gay guys would be alright. But two butches? How could they be attracted to each other? Who was the femme in bed?

I found myself obsessing about Frankie and Johnny. I was so deep in thought on Wednesday morning that I didn't notice Scotty and I were the only guys in the department. Scotty motioned toward the men's room. "You better go in there," he said.

"What?" He just nodded toward the men's room.

I didn't know what to expect when I opened the door. The men's room was filled with guys—some from my department, some I didn't recognize. Bolt spoke first. "We've been waiting for you," he said.

My fists clenched at my sides. Frankie must have told the guys about me out of spite. I should have known better than to trust her. Whatever misunderstanding we had should have been between us. I'd deal with her later. Right now I was badly outnumbered.

Bolt reached out his hand and moved toward me. I backed up against the wall. My temples pounded with blood. Bolt grabbed me by the shoulder; I pushed his hand off. I was cornered. "Leave me alone," I growled.

Walter moved toward me. "Take it easy, son. We just want to talk to you."

"Yeah? About what?" Bolt and Walter looked at each other and backed away from me.

"About the union," Walter said. I shook my head in confusion. "Ernie's wife works at a factory that the textile workers' union organized. She put us in contact with a really good guy who helped them. We need to know where you stand."

I had trouble regaining my composure. "You mean this is an organizing drive?"

Bolt shrugged. "We been talking up till now. We need to get a union organizer out here and call a general interest meeting. This shit can't go on much longer without blowing up."

This job didn't seem that bad to me. "What kind of grievances?" I asked.

"Like we make shit wages and they make us work overtime practically every weekend," Ernie said.

I nodded. "Yeah, but then we get other days off."

Skids answered me. "Sure, because they don't want to pay us time and a half."

Walter nodded. "Two people can be working the same machine and get paid different. It's all based on whether you suck up to the foremen."

"The fumes are terrible," Ernie added. "None of us know what we're breathing. And it's so fucking hot you can hardly breathe some days."

Bolt touched my arm. I jumped back; he looked hurt. "There's big safety problems here, too. We see a lot of stuff in maintenance and set-up that you don't see. People have accidents—fingers caught in molds, stuff like that. The company tries to intimidate them out of filing for compensation. We write up equipment problems, and management just files them in the wastepaper basket."

I listened and nodded. Bolt shrugged. "So we gotta know, Jesse. Where do you stand?"

I sighed. This was a good job for me. I wished it would stay that way. But everything was always changing. "Look," I told the guys. "You want to bring a union in here, that's fine with me."

Bolt moved closer to me. "That's not good enough. We need you on the organizing committee."

I didn't want to make waves. Why couldn't I just sign a union card like everybody else and do my job? "I don't want to get involved," I told him.

"Listen," he said as he leaned toward me. I backed up a bit. "I'm sticking my neck out on this thing and I don't even know if I'll be eligible for the union because the labor board might consider me a gang boss."

"You can count on me in an election," I told him, "but I'm not an organizer."

Bolt shook his head. "That's not what Frankie told me. She said you helped win that strike."

"Look, Bolt, I don't want to get involved. I'll support you all and do my job. Just leave me alone."

Bolt shook his head. "I thought you were different."

I sighed. "I don't want to be different."

We heard the shouting all the way from the other end of the plant. We ran the length of the factory. By the time we got there, all that was left was blood on the concrete floor.

"Who got hurt?" I whispered to Bolt.

His calloused hands formed tight fists. "George."

I looked at the lake of blood on the floor. "Is he dead?"

Bolt shrugged. "We don't know yet." He pounded his fist on the forklift next to us. "I wrote up this tow motor myself last month. The brakes were shot."

The plant superintendent waved his arms. "Let's everybody get back to work. It does no good to stand around."

I was surprised when everyone went back to their jobs. I was half expecting an insurrection. That came two weeks later.

The accident was all we talked about. The company was experimenting with bigger molds that could stamp out plastic garbage cans. George was assigned to use the forklift to carry the mold over to the injection machine. While he was standing in front of the forklift attaching the mold, the brakes gave out. One of the arms of the forklift pierced George's back just below the lung.

Anger still simmered a week later. Walter rushed into our department on Wednesday afternoon. "Have you heard? Management wrote up George for the accident! They're blaming him."

Bolt was right behind him. "Listen up, guys. We're calling a meeting Friday at the VFW post down the road. An organizer from the textile workers is gonna meet with us. They've pushed us too far this time."

He was right.

We all punched out at 3:00 Friday afternoon. I didn't rush out right away; I didn't want to run into Frankie. I wondered if she'd be at the meeting.

When I got to the VFW post at 3:45 there were twenty-five workers there. Every department was represented. Excitement buzzed in the air, with people waving their arms and talking a mile a minute. Bolt caught my eye from across the room. I nodded and smiled. Frankie was standing next to him. I avoided looking at her. I was still unnerved about finding out that she and Johnny were lovers, though I couldn't explain why.

I noticed Frankie whisper in some guy's ear. When he turned around, I recognized

Duffy. The smile on Duffy's face when he saw me made me feel warm inside. Frankie grabbed his arm and whispered something else to him. I wondered if she was explaining my situation.

Duffy made a beeline for me. "Jess," he grasped my hand. His grip felt familiar in mine. "I've thought about you so many times. How long you worked here?"

"More than a year."

He smiled. "We're gonna need your help."

I started to protest, but Duffy noticed Ernie and Scotty bringing drinks from the bar into the meeting room. He waved to them. "Get the booze out of here. We're serious in here."

I tugged his sleeve. "Go easy on the older guy. Booze is his Achilles' heel, but he's a good guy. He's an old UAW man. So's Bolt."

Duffy nodded. "Tell me about Bolt."

Two Black women I didn't recognize tapped Duffy. "Excuse me," one of the women said. "I'm Dottie. I work in the assembly department. This is my friend Gladys. She's worked there longer than me."

Duffy shook their hands. "How many here from your department?"

"Six," Dottie said, "out of twenty on day side. There's another fifteen or so on second shift."

Someone yelled from across the room. "Let's get this meeting started." A cheer went up.

Duffy excused himself and moved to the front of the room. "I've heard a lot of the grievances this afternoon."

"Yeah!" Discipline broke down. Everyone shouted about conditions at the plant.

Duffy held up his hands. "Every single one of your grievances will be addressed. I promise you that. There's not a single one that's not important. But let's focus first on the grievances that affect everyone."

Bolt patted me on the shoulder. "C'mon out here a minute. I want to talk to you." I started to protest. "C'mon, this meeting will still be going on." I followed Bolt out to the bar.

He ordered two beers and paid for them. He lifted his bottle. "To the union," he said.

I nodded. "I'll drink to that."

"Listen, Jesse. How well you know this guy Duffy?"

I shrugged. "He's alright in my book. I trust him."

"Some of the guys heard something about him. Somebody said he's a communist."

I laughed. "He's no communist. He's a good guy."

Bolt smiled and nodded. "Alright. As long as somebody knows the guy."

"Hey, Bolt. Did you ask Duffy about whether or not you'd be eligible to join the union?"

Bolt shook his head. "I'll ask him later. After the meeting."

We both heard a roar from the other room. "C'mon," I said, "let's get back." I was starting to feel a little excited.

"Let's sign the cards now!" Ernie shouted.

Duffy raised both hands. "You got 120 people in your shop. It'll take 30 percent plus one as a bare minimum to file for an election. This is a great turnout, but we need more."

"Where the hell is everybody?" someone yelled.

Duffy shook his head. "This really is a great turnout for a first meeting. But we've got to get more workers from every department lined up."

Bolt yelled out, "Maintenance and set-up are solid."

"What about assembly?" Ernie shouted. "Those girls aren't going to be with us. They've got husbands to take care of them. Shit, I heard two of them still live with their parents."

Dottie stood up. "And I'm one of them. Yeah, I live with my parents. I'm trying to raise two kids without a husband. And Gladys is living with her parents because she's supporting them and she can't afford her own place. But we're both here. You don't know jack squat about our department."

Gladys stood up beside her. "That's right. Our fingers and wrists are killing us from trimming flash all day. We're making lousy money and we have to work weekends. A lot of the girls have husbands who also bring home a paycheck, it's true. But a lot of them are fed up and they'll sign—you'll see."

Duffy smiled at them. "The sisters are speaking up, guys. You better listen."

We all agreed to end the meeting and hold another one the following week. But nobody was eager to leave. We milled around talking.

"Hey, Duffy," Bolt called him over. "Am I gonna be able to get into the union? I'm lead set-up man."

I wished I could tip off Duffy about Bolt's worth, but I could see Duffy already recognized it. "Management knows you're a leader," he told Bolt. I saw Bolt stand a little taller. "But do you hire and fire? Do you review the guys or discipline them?"

Bolt shrugged. "It's kind of hazy. I'm really just the most experienced guy in set-up, but they sort of treat me like gang boss, too."

Duffy nodded. "The company will argue about which side you're on in order to delay the elections and use the time to intimidate people. I think you already know which side you're on, but you have to make it real clear. If you work hard to bring the union in, it'll make our argument easier that you should be in."

Bolt shook Duffy's hand. "Do you think we're gonna win?"

Duffy smiled and nodded. "Yeah. But it'll take a fight. We got strong people in each department. If we had more like Jess, we'd win it hands down. I trust Jess. She's proved she's for the union 100 percent."

Everything happened in slow motion. When I heard Duffy say *she* I turned in horror, my jaw dropped. Frankie slapped her forehead with her palm and shook her head. The guys looked from Duffy to me and back again. I stormed out of the VFW post and headed for my motorcycle.

"Jess, wait!" I heard Duffy shouting. He caught up to me and grabbed my arm.

I yanked it away. "Thanks a lot, Duffy." Seeing tears in his eyes made it worse.

"I'm so sorry, Jess. It just jumped out. I didn't mean it."

I shrugged. "It doesn't matter what you meant to do. I'm out of this job now."

He shook his head. "We'll work it out, Jess. You could stay. I'll talk to the guys."

I laughed bitterly. "You don't get it, do you? Which bathroom you think I'm going to use on Monday, Duffy?"

Duffy put his hand on my arm. I glared at him. "Jess, I'd never do anything to hurt you. You know that."

I pushed his hand off my arm. "Well, you did." I turned and walked away.

"Jess, wait up!" It was Frankie. "Jess, I know you're mad. That was really fucked up. But it was a mistake. He's really upset."

"Leave me alone, Frankie. You don't understand, either."

Frankie looked stunned. "What's your fuckin' problem with me? Are you really gonna cut another butch loose just because you can't deal with who turns me on?"

I wished someone had muzzled me because I was so worked up I couldn't control my mouth. "What makes you think you're still a butch?" I asked her sarcastically.

Her smile was cruel and defensive. "What makes you think you're still a butch?" she countered.

I spun around and stormed off. Part of me was hoping that Frankie or Duffy wouldn't let me go. But they did.

CHAPTER 18

The leaf was big and wet and glowed with the oranges and reds of autumn. I found it stuck to the seat of my Harley on Saturday morning. It made me sad when the leaves began to fall. I wanted another beginning, another chance.

I hated the thought of putting my Harley away for the winter. It was dangerous for me to ride—I'd been driving without a license for three years—but I lived to cruise on that bike. It was my joy and my freedom.

There were only two things I looked forward to every day: pumping iron at the nearby YMCA and whipping into the wind astride my motorcycle.

When my alarm jangled in the morning, I awoke feeling small and terrified. I couldn't find myself in my own life—there was no memory of me that I could grasp. There was no place outside of me where I belonged. So every morning I willed myself back into existence. I went to the gym already dressed in sweatclothes. That's where I brought my tension and frustration, my rage and my fear. I put it all into my workout.

I thought about my body a lot as I pressed against the resistance of cold iron. I enjoyed getting leaner and harder. Was that a goal the world had taught me? Probably. I thought of my femme lovers who cursed each thickness and fold in their bodies—the beautiful flesh I loved. But as I watched myself clench my muscles while I pumped, I found the weight and shape of my own body that pleased me. I concentrated on my discipline and endurance. I tried, in the best way I knew how, to love myself.

I learned that strength, like height, is measured by who you're standing next to. I was considered a scrawny guy in the gym. That opinion was written on the faces of men whose muscles were bigger than mine. And all the while the lifetime of cruel judgments about my body and my self throbbed like unhealed wounds.

Yet sometimes when I stood in front of my own mirror at home, I saw a powerful me. I couldn't hold onto the image, though. It slipped like a globule of mercury from under my index finger.

Maybe that was the lesson I tried to teach myself with each repetition—that power is something qualitatively more than strength. And that the world was wrong about me. I had a right to live.

Every day the men around me came to exercise their bodies; I came to exorcise my demons.

Euphoria was my reward for the tenacious workout that autumn morning. It was Saturday. There was nowhere to go, there was nothing to do. I turned up the collar on my leather jacket. Fall was here and winter was just behind it. The sky was overcast. The clouds were low, flat-bottomed, and dark as a bruise.

I revved my bike without knowing where I was headed. I had money in my wallet and a whole weekend to ride as far as gasoline would take me.

When the first raindrops plopped on my gas tank, I pulled over and put on my gear. Bolts of lightning illuminated the sky over the park. I loved dramatic weather. It was the excitement that made one day different from another.

The women in the zoo entrance booth were enjoying a lazy day. They waved me in without paying.

The condor's head was tilted back into the wind, and her wings were spread wider than my height. I opened my own arms and turned my face toward the sky and laughed.

The snowy owl's neck puffed up as I came near, and he huffed as though he was out of breath. I hurried past.

Raindrops dripped from the beak of the red-tailed hawk whose left wing had been sheared by a shotgun blast. She looked miserable.

The male eagle was balanced on a branch—his feathers slicked back by rain and wind. He moved with the wind on extended wings as though in flight. His eyes focused on the distance. There was no border between his frustration and his madness. For just a moment he dropped his gaze and held me in the intensity of his golden stare. He looked up again, wildness flashing in his eyes as he flew through his past on widespread wings.

After the storm let up, I rode my motorcycle through the rain-soaked streets longing for so much I couldn't name. Sometimes mundane tasks stuffed that feeling back down—I decided to go food shopping.

The supermarket was packed with women. The conveyor belt at the checkout line wasn't working, so I pushed the food forward as the woman at the cash register rang it up. "That'll be $22.80," she said. I held out a twenty and a ten; she reached for the bills. We caught each other's eyes.

I whispered her name out loud: "Edna." Funny how, even years later, I still thought of her as Butch Jan's ex-lover and myself as a baby butch in her eyes.

She searched my eyes. Her face softened. "Jess."

The woman behind me in line sighed heavily. "Honey, can we speed this up?"

The last time I'd seen Edna I had told her I was too young to be the kind of lover I'd wanted to be for her. Now life was giving me another chance.

I helped her bag my groceries. Neither of us spoke. I pressed my lips together to keep from asking, "Are you with someone?" I thought of a neutral question. "Can we talk?"

The woman behind me banged a box of laundry detergent on the conveyor belt and asked Edna, "Honey, do you go on break soon?" Edna looked at her blankly and nodded. "Then could you please continue your reunion then?"

We both laughed. Edna blushed. "I get off at 3:30." It was only 2:00.

I paced the pavement near my Harley, rode figure eights around the parking lot, looked in store windows, stopped for coffee—it was still only 3:00.

At 3:30 I pulled my bike up in front of the supermarket. I wished I had a second helmet. Edna looked my Harley up and down and smiled, as though she liked what she saw. Then she looked at me the same way. "It's good to see you, Jess. How long has it been?"

I could have asked her when she broke up with Jan, but I thought better of it. "Well, my hand was in that contraption and we were on strike. I think it was '67, so it's been twelve years. I'm almost thirty, can you believe it?"

Edna nodded. "That means you're just about the age I was when you thought I was such an old woman."

I shook my head. "That's not fair, Edna. The problem was I was so young. I never thought you were old."

Edna took my face in her hands. I felt my cheeks flush. "I'm sorry," she said, "that was my fear."

I offered her my helmet. She swung her leg over the bike and settled behind me. Her body felt so damn good against mine. "Where are we going?" she asked.

"I don't know." I gently popped the clutch.

We ended up at the zoo. The air smelled fresh there, washed by the rain. We walked on a bed of wet leaves, under a latticework of branches. I ached to hold her hand. We tried to make small talk, but there wasn't anything either of us said that seemed insignificant. I tried to wait before I asked the question clenched in my throat, but I couldn't put it off any longer.

I turned to her. "I can't take another step till I ask you a question."

She shook her head shyly. "No."

"No, I can't ask you a question?"

She smiled. "No I'm not with anyone."

A grin spread across my face, then I checked it. "I was just wondering."

We stood and faced each other under a maple tree. "How about you? Are you with anyone?" she asked. I shook my head.

The maple seeds whirled around us. I caught one on my palm. "We used to call these helicopters," I said, as I let it twirl to the ground.

Edna ran her fingertips across the beard stubble on my cheek. I wished I had shaved before I'd gone to the gym. She touched my lips, my hair, my neck—as though she was searching for me with her hands.

"Have I changed so much?" I asked her, afraid to hear her answer.

She smiled and shook her head. "No. In a way I don't know how anyone in the world could think you're a man, especially if they looked into your eyes."

With a light touch she turned my face to hers. Then her hands settled on my chest like a bird's wings at rest. Our faces were very close. It felt to me as though my whole life was held in the balance of that moment. If Edna had turned away from me, I don't know where I would have gone or how I would have found the strength to go on. But she didn't. She brought her lips near mine, allowed me to celebrate the moment before it began, and then gave me her mouth. All I had to offer was in that kiss. Edna's hands cupped the back of my head and pulled me toward her.

The kiss lasted until I stopped fearing it would end and enjoyed it as a journey we'd just begun. Our lips didn't part until the wind splattered cold rain down on us from the branches above. She pulled away from me and began to walk. I caught up to her and took her hand. Our hands fit so comfortably that I sloughed off the first layer of my loneliness.

"Are you hungry?" I asked her.

She stopped and turned toward me again. "I have to get home soon." My disappointment showed. "I'm sorry," she said.

"Can I see you?" All my hopes rested on her reply.

She hesitated and nodded. "Next Friday night."

Friday! Today was Saturday and I had trouble just killing an hour and a half until she'd gotten out of work. Edna tugged on a branch overhead. A shower of raindrops fell on us.

As I drove her home, her hands rested on my shoulders, the side of her face pressed against my back. "This is it," she pointed. I slowed and parked.

"You sure you want to see me Friday?" I needed reassurance. Edna stroked my cheeks. I couldn't really feel the touch of her fingertips on my skin—my stubble was too rough. For the first time since I'd grown a beard I wished it would vanish.

Edna nibbled at my mouth, pulled away when I moved forward, then drew me back hungrily. "I'm so happy to see you, Jess." She sounded like she meant it. My feelings rose in my throat. I swallowed and nodded. "Meet me here, at 9:00 on Friday?" she asked.

I nodded again and watched her walk up the sidewalk to her porch. She looked back and waved. Even after her front door closed and the lights came on behind her curtains I didn't leave. A light rain fell on me. The wind carried autumn and the scent of fallen leaves.

When the waiter walked away from our table Edna leaned forward. "What's it like, passing?" I could tell she'd wanted to ask me that all evening.

"All my life I've been told there's something really wrong with me because of the way I am as a woman. But if I'm a man, then I'm a nice young man. The way I am is just fine." Edna waited for more.

"Some of it is fun. I was tied up so tight all the time as a he-she. It feels good to be free to do little things, like go to a public bathroom in peace or to be touched by a barber. It's nice to be smiled at by strangers or flirted with at a lunch counter."

Edna studied my face. "Then why are your eyes even sadder than I remember?"

"Oh, I think. . ." I sighed.

Edna interrupted me. "I'm interested in what you think, Jess. But tell me how you feel." I had forgotten how much I loved femmes. Another butch would have nodded when I sighed, content that the whole story had been articulated in the rush of air. But Edna pressed for words.

"I feel like a ghost, Edna. Like I've been buried alive. As far as the world's concerned, I was born the day I began to pass. I have no past, no loved ones, no memories, no me. No one really sees me or speaks to me or touches me."

Edna's eyes filled with tears. She reached forward and took my hand in hers. The waiter interrupted us. "More coffee, sir?" I shook my head.

When he'd walked out of earshot, Edna told me, "I feel like a ghost, too, Jess. Should I still call you Jess?"

My smile felt shy. "Sometimes people call me Jesse and I don't correct them. You can call me whatever you want, just try to remember the right pronoun in a public place. It could get real ugly." Edna sighed and nodded. I'd forgotten she was Rocco's lover, too.

"Did you know, Edna," I asked her, "did you know I would make the same decision Rocco made?"

Edna shook her head. "I only knew your options were as few as hers. But when you were young I recognized something in you that I'd seen in Rocco."

I chewed my lower lip, waiting for the words of a woman who knew me.

"I don't know how to say this. I'm afraid I'll make a mistake," she hesitated.

"Try," I urged her. "Please. I need to hear it."

"I don't think femmes ever see butches as one big group. After a while you see how many different ways there are for butches to be. You see them young and defiant, you see them change, you watch them harden up or be destroyed. Soft ones and bitter ones and troubled ones. You and Rocco were granite butches who couldn't soften your edges. It just wasn't in your nature."

Edna took a bite of food. I wished she'd hurry chewing and continue. "I love all the different ways butches can be. I love butches' hearts. But the ones I worry most about are the ones who aren't tough inside."

I frowned and dropped my eyes. Edna leaned forward. "You see, I hurt you. I'm sorry. You and Rocco both had beautiful hearts that were so easily hurt, and I loved you for it. But I didn't know how long you could survive."

"I think about her a lot," I told Edna.

She stared at her plate and nodded. "Me too."

"I'd give anything to talk to Rocco," I said, wishing Edna knew how to reach her.

Edna smiled. "I'll bet."

I sat back in my chair and scuffed the rug with my shoe. "I wish I could ask her a million questions."

Edna leaned forward. "What don't you know?"

I shrugged and played with my fork. "I'm not sure. How to survive this, I guess."

Edna smiled gently. "What makes you think Rocco knows?" Her answer surprised me.

"I'm not like Rocco," I said. "She's like a legend or something. She's so strong, so sure of herself. I don't feel that way at all. If I could just get to know her."

Edna gently took the fork from my hand and put it down on the tablecloth. She rested her fingertips on my forearm. "People get buried under legends. Rocco doesn't have all the answers. She's got questions, just like you do. She's trying to get through it the best way she can, just the way you are. That's what makes you both so strong. There's only one thing Rocco had that you don't have," Edna told me.

I leaned forward. "What?"

She smiled and said, "I'll show you later."

Was she always going to make me wait?

"Edna, where have you been all these years?" I asked her.

She smiled and picked at her lasagna. "After the bar scene changed I stopped going. The butches I loved weren't there anymore. It was mostly university women. I started to feel embarrassed about showing up in a dress, with makeup on. It seemed like everyone in the bar was wearing flannel shirts, jeans, and boots. That's not me. But there was no other place to go. A few of us went to a dance on campus," she said. "But we were dressed different, we danced different." She clenched her fist in anger. "One of the women at the dance made fun of the butch I was with because she helped me off with my coat. I was so upset that we left right away."

I nodded. "My ex-lover Theresa worked up at UB. I remember getting mad and telling her how much I hated those women for rejecting us. She used to say: 'They're right about needing a revolution, but they're wrong to think they can do it without all of us.'"

Edna shrugged. "I know I'm not a straight woman, and lesbians won't accept me as one of them. I don't know where to go to find the butches I love or the other femmes. I feel completely misunderstood. I feel like a ghost too, Jess."

For a long moment we held a conversation without words. Our eyes welcomed each other home. The waiter brought the check to me, an automatic gesture.

I chuckled. Edna frowned. "What's so funny?"

"Until I talked to you tonight, part of me really believed that everyone I knew was sitting in a bar somewhere together having a good time without me."

We rode back to her home in silence. I wanted to touch her. I wanted to matter to her. And I ached to sleep, safe, with her body close to mine.

I pulled up in front of her house. She took off the helmet and beckoned for me to follow her. I stood in her living room trying to know her through her home. She rummaged through her hall closet. "I found it!" She came back into the room smiling. "There's only one thing Rocco had that you don't have. Armor!" Edna handed me a heavy black motorcycle jacket gleaming with silver zippers. I took it in my hands. It was soft with wear. The right elbow was badly scuffed. "That's where she skidded when she dumped her Harley on the way back from Niagara Falls." Edna fingered the sleeve. "This was the jacket she loved almost as much as her bike. She called this her second skin."

Edna's eyes glazed. "She left it to protect me. That's what she said. It was so much a part of her that I could never bear to wear it." I couldn't speak. "Try it on," Edna urged, holding the jacket for me to slip into. It was heavy; the weight felt reassuring. "It fits you perfectly." She pressed her knuckles to her lips.

I opened my arms. She shook her head. "I need to be alone. I'm sorry, I'm just not ready. I hope you understand." I didn't. But I was so afraid to lose her that I forced myself to smile and nod.

I walked back out to my Harley and swung my leg over it. I heard my own power in the engine's roar.

I drove away wearing Rocco's armor.

"Be careful!" Edna shouted as the ladder tipped. I grabbed the metal tray before the paint inside of it could spill. "Get down from there!" Edna ordered. I climbed down and wiped my forearm across my forehead. Edna laughed. "You just smeared paint on your face, c'mere."

She held my arm as she gently rubbed my forehead with a cloth. I clenched my biceps. "I've been working out," I boasted.

Edna suppressed a smile and said, "I noticed." I didn't suppress mine.

She kissed my lips. "Thank you for helping me paint my living room."

I smiled and shrugged. "What are butches for?" Contained in those four words were all my hurt and confusion over why, a month after we'd been reunited, Edna still wouldn't let me make love to her.

"Oh no," Edna said, shaking her head slowly. "Butches are wonderful about lending a hand. But that's not all you're good for. Butches have moved my world. They've made me feel beautiful when the world took that away from me. It's butch love that's sustained me."

My eyes filled with tears of gratitude and with the frustration of restraining myself from touching her.

She stroked my face with fingertips that wanted me, and yet I couldn't be sure that her whole body wanted the same. "You are so beautiful," she whispered. "Handsome, I should have said you are so handsome."

I laughed. "Oh, I'll take either right about now."

All I saw was her mouth, so close to mine I felt the warmth of her breath. Still I didn't move toward her. Edna hesitated. I held my breath as I waited for her to come to me—hoping she would, fearing she wouldn't. She came into my arms afraid, but trusting me. I welcomed her with my embrace.

Edna fumbled with the buttons on my paint-splattered shirt. We left it on the living room floor. In her bedroom she unzipped my jeans. Only then did I allow my passion to meet hers.

Once it began, all of our needs were unleashed. She knew exactly what she wanted and she took me there, demanding everything from me that I could give. And I gave gladly, without restraint. Even as I touched her body with my mouth, with my hands, with my thighs—I knew it was not only pleasure I was trying to give her, it was all my love. And as she alternately caressed me with her hands and dug her nails into my back, I could feel all of hers.

I lay in her arms, dressed only in a T-shirt and briefs. Her fingernails drifted down my neck, across my shoulders. She smiled seductively. I'd forgotten the sheer pleasure of a high femme tease.

Edna moved against me, tormenting me with her nails and her lips until I felt crazy with wanting more. Fear gripped my throat. I couldn't remember how to submit, but I wanted her to guide me there. Her nails trailed up the inside of one of my thighs. "I'm scared," I admitted out loud.

She stopped touching me and lay still in my arms. Even after she'd fallen asleep in my embrace I stared at the ceiling, longing for her to take me past my own fear and not knowing how to ask.

Edna gasped with pleasure at the flowers I brought her. "Oh, irises. They're so beautiful."

I kissed her on the cheek. "They remind me of you." Edna found the card I'd tucked inside.

"Wait," I restrained her hand.

Edna laughed. "What's wrong? Did you write something you shouldn't have?"

I shifted my weight from foot to foot. "I wrote you a poem. I never did that before. Maybe you'll think it's stupid."

Edna pulled my face against her neck and wrapped her arms around me. "Oh, honey, you wrote a poem for me? Oh, thank you. That means so much to me. I don't even have to read it if you don't want me too."

Femmes can be so smart about these things. Of course I wanted her to read it, especially since she was giving me a choice. "Oh, alright, go ahead and read it," I told her, and braced myself for her reaction.

I blushed because it surprised me when she read it out loud. But I liked the way her voice elevated my words:

As yellow leaves give way
to the gentle insistence of the green
you touched my loneliness
and my crisp, brown husks
yielded to a tender newness.

Edna burst into tears. She kissed my face all over till my embarrassment subsided. "Oh, Jess. Did you really write that just for me? It's beautiful."

"Edna," I whispered in her ear, "was that expressing a feeling?"

Edna pulled back and held my face in her hands. Her lower lip trembled. "Oh yes, honey. That's exactly what it was."

We held each other and swayed to a music only we could hear. She took my hand and led me to her bedroom. I tried to make good love to her. But I couldn't read her body's signals—all I got was static. I couldn't figure out what I was doing wrong.

Edna's nipple tightened like a bud and then blossomed in my mouth. I heard her gasp. One sob followed another. I brought my face near hers, and she grabbed my T-shirt in both her fists. Her body shook violently. She buried her face against my neck and cried so hard it frightened me. I held her tight. "I can't," she said.

"Shh. It's alright."

"Don't be mad at me," she pleaded.

"I'm not," I whispered. "I'm not mad at you."

Edna didn't say what was going on inside of her, and I was afraid to ask. If I was undesirable it was something I was in no hurry to find out. Besides, I'd been so unbearably lonely for so long that the sex didn't matter to me as much as this intimacy. I continued holding her and settled into the simple comfort that her closeness offered.

We lay without speaking for a long, long time. I finally broke the silence with a question. "Do you think I'm a woman?"

Edna got up on one elbow and looked at me. "What do you think?" she asked gently.

I sighed. "I don't know. There's never been many other women in the world I could identify with. But I sure as hell don't feel like a guy, either. I don't know what I am. It makes me feel crazy."

Edna nestled against my shoulder. "I know, honey, I really do. I don't think I've ever had a butch lover who hasn't felt torn up in the same way."

"Yeah," I shrugged, "but it's different for me because I'm living as a man. I don't even know if I'm still butch any more."

She nodded. "It's true that you and Rocco have a tough time figuring out how to be yourselves and still live. But believe me, honey, you're not alone in the feeling that you're not a man or a woman."

I sighed. "I don't like being neither."

Edna moved her face close to mine. "You're more than just neither, honey. There's other ways to be than either-or. It's not so simple. Otherwise there wouldn't be so many people who don't fit. You're beautiful, Jess, but I don't have words to help people see that."

"I wish everything could go back to the way it was," I told her.

Edna looked off into the distance. "I don't," she said. "I don't want to go back to the bars and the fights. I just want a place to be with the people I love. I want to be accepted for who I am, and not just in the gay world."

I felt left out of the fantasy. "What about me? Can I be accepted too?"

Edna lifted my hand to her mouth and kissed my fingers. "I'm not accepted till you are."

I smiled. "It's a nice dream. How do we make it happen?"

"I don't know," she said. "That's the problem."

Edna stretched her thigh across my hip. Her lips rested on my T-shirt. "I wish I could save you," she whispered. "I wish I could be everything that's been taken from you."

I laughed. "Just be my lover."

Edna leaned on one elbow and looked me in the eye. "You wish I could save you, don't you?"

"No," I lied, afraid of losing her.

She sat up. "I don't know how you couldn't. It terrifies me when I think how little you have, how much you must need. I don't have that much to give you."

I rolled over and wrapped my arms around her waist. "Then I'll try to need less."

She grabbed a handful of my hair and pulled my head back until I looked her in the eyes. "Oh, Jess. I'm so sorry I'm hurting you. Don't you think I know how much it's hurt you when I couldn't let you touch me after that first time? And I don't know how to tell you that it has nothing to do with you."

"Thanks a lot," I laughed bitterly. "I'm the one you don't want, so it has plenty to do with me. All that means to me is that there's nothing I can do about it."

Edna put her fingertips against my lips to silence me. "Something's tearing me up inside, Jess, and I can't explain it."

I sat up eagerly. "Then talk to me, Edna. I could help."

She shook her head. "You can't fix it, sweetheart. Butches always want to fix the places that hurt."

I sighed. "If I can't make love to you, and I can't fix what hurts you, then where's my butch magic? What can I give you?"

Edna smiled and settled back into my arms. "Give me time," she said, "and a little space."

Edna noticed the buds on the trees at the zoo before I did. She rarely touched me anymore. I envied the way she touched them.

We bought some peanuts and walked around aimlessly. I watched a caged tiger pace back and forth across his tiny cell. He dipped his head and roared. Edna watched my face. "Sometimes I get the feeling that when no one's here you talk to these animals and they answer you."

I smiled. "I'd walk into these cages without fear."

Edna frowned. "They could maul you, without meaning to."

I nodded. "But I'm not afraid of them."

We walked in silence till we came to the still pond where the ducks drifted and dunked. As we sat by the pool I realized something was going to happen. And nothing could delay that moment from arriving.

"You know," Edna began, "I've always waited for a butch to ride up on a horse and save me. I've always leaned on my butch when I felt weak."

I cracked open peanuts, one after another, and tossed them to eager ducks. I knew better than to utter a word. Edna stared at the ducks for a long time without speaking. She pressed against my body. As she turned her face toward me I could see the streaks of tears.

I think I knew right then, but sometimes knowing comes in layers. I whispered her name out loud. "We can work things out," I told her.

She shook her head. "I just can't be with anyone right now, Jess. I don't even know why. It doesn't make sense. If there was ever a hero, you could surely be mine. You're everything I ever wanted in a butch. You're strong and gentle and you listen and you try so hard. I love you so much, Jess."

As Edna cried, she turned her face away from me. I didn't touch her. I longed to, but I knew I shouldn't. "You know," I told her, "the moments I remember most in my life are the ones where something happened that I didn't want to have happen and I couldn't control it."

Edna sniffled and nodded. "I'm in deep freeze, Jess. And somehow I have to save myself. You can't do it for me. And I don't know how. I'm so scared." I reached for her out of instinct. She held me at an arm's length with a light touch.

Tears filled my eyes, but I reined myself in, knowing I had many nights ahead of me to grieve. "Why?" I asked her. "I just don't understand why you can't try."

She bit her lower lip. "I am trying, Jess. I have tried. I just don't know what's happening. I'm just as lonely as you are. I need so much. That's what scares me, that and how much you need me."

"Oh, Edna. Isn't there something I can do to keep you from leaving me? Isn't there anything I can do to change your mind?"

Edna shook her head. Tears streamed down her face. "Oh, Jess. I love you so much. Please believe me."

I was relieved when she came into my arms to cry, until I realized she was letting me hold her for the last time. A wave of panic almost drowned me. I could feel in my gut what my life was like before Edna came back into it. "Edna," I whispered.

She covered my lips with her fingertips. "I can't," she said.

Edna held my face in both her hands and looked into my eyes. "What will you do, Jess? Oh god, I wish was strong enough to save us both."

I looked away from her. "I'll be fine," I heard myself say. We both laughed out loud. "That was a very butch thing to say, wasn't it?" I admitted.

"Oh, very," Edna laughed.

We slipped back over the boundary of our laughter to our tears.

I wondered if she would have left me if there had been more inside of me to love, or if I just could have needed less.

Edna kissed me on the mouth. If I had moved toward her she would have pulled away. And so I held very still and her kiss lingered a moment longer.

She stood up. "I'm so sorry, Jess."

If pleading would have kept her in my life I would have dropped to my knees, but I knew she wouldn't stay.

"Can I drive you home?" I asked, hoping for time to try to change her mind. She shook her head.

I stood up and let my lips memorize her forehead, her cheeks, her chin. I loved the way age had softened her face. "Can't I see you sometime? Talk to you?"

She put her hand on my chest. "Maybe at some point. Not now." Her lips were close to mine. I kissed her hesitantly. She didn't draw away from me. For a moment I felt her need, then she pulled back. I watched Edna walk away from me.

One at a time I broke the shells of the peanuts. I threw some of them to the ducks and ate the others myself. I felt more alone and afraid than ever before.

CHAPTER 19

It seemed to be a Saturday morning like any other. One day had become so much like the next. Each hour dragged so slowly that I didn't pay attention as months turned into years.

As I made myself coffee, I watched a blue jay fight with a starling over the crumbs in the bird feeder. Neither noticed the orange-marmalade cat crouched below them, ready to spring.

I took my time in the shower, trying to scrub away the grime of isolation with hot, soapy water. Loneliness had become an environment—the air I breathed, the spatial dimension in which I was trapped. I sat in a boat on a deathly calm sea, waiting for a breeze to fill my sails.

And so it never occurred to me my life might change again dramatically that day. It was quite simple, really. I drew one cc of hormones into a syringe, lifted it above my naked thigh—and then paused. My arm felt restrained by an unseen hand. No matter how I tried I could not sink that needle into my quadriceps as I'd done hundreds of times before.

I stood up and looked in the bathroom mirror. The depth of sadness in my eyes frightened me. I lathered my morning beard stubble, scraped it clean with a razor, and splashed cold water on my face. The stubble still felt rough. As much as I loved my beard as part of my body, I felt trapped behind it. What I saw reflected in the mirror was not a man, but I couldn't recognize the he-she. My face no longer revealed the contrasts of my gender. I could see my passing self, but even I could no longer see the more complicated me beneath my surface.

I stared far back into my past and remembered the child who couldn't be catalogued by Sears. I saw her standing in front of her own mirror, in her father's suit, asking me if I was the person she would grow up and become. Yes, I answered her. And I thought how brave she was to have begun this journey, to have withstood the towering judgments.

But who was I now—woman or man? I fought long and hard to be included as woman among women, but I always felt so excluded by my differences. I hadn't just believed that passing would hide me. I hoped that it would allow me to express the part of myself that didn't seem to be woman. I didn't get to explore being a he-she, though. I simply became a he—a man without a past.

Who was I now—woman or man? That question could never be answered as long as those were the only choices; it could never be answered if it had to be asked.

I thought about the long road I'd traveled. I had never stopped looking out at the world through my own eyes. I'd never stopped feeling like me on the inside. What *if* the real me could emerge, changed by the journey. Who would I be? Suddenly, I needed to know. What would my life be worth if I stopped short of finding out? Fingers of excitement and fear tightened around my throat. Where was I going now? Who was I becoming? I couldn't answer those questions, but even asking them was a sign to me that tumultuous change had been boiling just below the surface of my consciousness.

I searched the apartment for a cigarette, but as I picked up the pack I watched my hand crush it.

That night I dreamt I was struggling in deep murky water. I flailed my arms and legs against its molasses resistance. My lungs ached from holding my breath. I desperately needed to inhale. I began to slowly swim toward the surface. The pressure eased on my body. I felt liquid velvet against my hands as they sliced through the water. I could see the sky, facets of light shimmering above me. My lungs were ready to explode. I broke through the skin of the water. I felt the sun and breeze against my face, warm and cool at the same time. I heard the sound of my own laughter.

I think I really believed that when the hormones wore off I would discover I'd traveled full circle and returned home to my own past. But the journey wasn't over yet. I realized that the day I saw Theresa shopping in K-Mart.

I held my breath the moment I recognized her. She had hardly changed a bit. Would she say the same about me? I hid behind the men's underwear display and watched her. What would she do if I called out her name? I wanted her to embrace me and take me home. After all, she'd left me because I'd begun hormones; now I'd stopped. Could she love me again?

I saw someone put her arm around Theresa. I angled around the aisles to get a better look at the woman. It was the same soft butch who had opened Theresa's door almost ten years ago—the same lover. What could Theresa possibly see in that Saturday-night butch? It was so much harder to be me; I needed Theresa's love a lot more than she did. I hated to admit that she must be special if Theresa loved her.

I heard Theresa laugh, warm and relaxed. Her face crinkled with love. And then I knew I wasn't going home, I wasn't traveling backward. I was hurtling forward toward a destination I couldn't see. And if I was ever going to lie in Theresa's arms again, it would be in some distant future, not now.

I hurried out of the store before they could see me and raced home on my bike, just ahead of the tears. I lay on my bed for hours, until the steamy afternoon shifted to evening. Oak leaves rustled in the breeze outside my bedroom window; the streetlight projected their shadows on my wall. The whine of cicadas rose and fell.

Theresa had asked me to send her a letter someday. I wanted to write it now. I longed to deliver a bundle of sentences wrapped like a gift to her doorstep—words that would light up the night sky, words that would soothe and heal. But the words still wouldn't come.

During the long night I realized that if love had been enough, I might never have lost Theresa. But I did. I could say we came to a fork in the road. That was the truth, but it wasn't the whole truth. I knew I had lost Theresa in little ways long before we parted. I had been at the center of her world; she had become my whole world. As my universe shrank, I needed her to be everything for me, and in return I longed to be everything she needed. Neither of us could live up to the expectations.

And yet, how could it be otherwise? How could I not sink to my knees at the end of the day and ask her for sanctuary? How could she refuse, loving me the way she did? The moments she pulled my head onto her lap and stroked my face were all I knew of refuge and acceptance. For her, my admission of need was what she'd asked of me in infinite ways. I don't know where else I could have gone for safety in an unsafe world. And I don't think she could have possibly sustained her love for me if I had remained a fortress. Maybe the problem was that I'd begun to believe her love could protect me, begun to expect it, to demand it. Maybe she believed if she just tried harder she could keep me safe. When she wiped the blood from my face did it mock her power? Would it be any different if we were in each other's arms again?

Someday I would tell her the little things I was beginning to understand. But for now, I could only write seven lines for her—a short poem squeezed from the clenched heart of a he-she:

Especially in the cool night
when leafy boughs make patterns on the walls
and consciousness gently ebbs
making way for sleep to lap my shores
in that long moment of no control

coals of remembering glow softly
lending the darkness a different hue.

Nothing happened when I stopped taking hormones. For months I got up every morning and raced to the mirror, breathless with anticipation. Nothing changed. It was sort of anticlimactic. It took many of hours of electrolysis before I began to feel the softness of my cheeks again. One morning I got up and found menstrual blood on my BVD's. I threw them out rather than risk anyone at the laundry seeing the apparent contradiction. But the real motion was taking place inside of me. I had to be honest with myself, it was as urgent as breathing. When I sat alone and asked what it was I really wanted, the answer was *change.*

I didn't regret the decision to take hormones. I wouldn't have survived much longer without passing. And the surgery was a gift to myself, a coming home to my body. But I wanted more than to just barely exist, a stranger always trying not to get involved. I wanted to find out who I was, to define myself. Whoever I was, I wanted to deal with it, I wanted to live it again. I wanted to be able to explain my life, how the world looked from behind my eyes.

Yet I was so afraid to come out and face the world again. I wondered why I had to choose the opening years of the Reagan administration and the rise of the Moral Majority to demand the right to be myself. Would they arm villagers with torches and stakes and stalk me through the countryside? Would I stand alone, handcuffed in a precinct cell, with no one to turn to if I survived the nightmare? But then I acknowledged that no matter who had been in the White House, it had always been hard to be me. Between a rock and a hard place—something told me this lifetime wasn't going to get any easier. I'd already been through a lot though, and it didn't seem to me it could get much worse.

Once again I couldn't see the road ahead. I was still steering my own course through uncharted waters, relying on constellations that were not fixed. I wished there was someone, somewhere I could ask: *What should I do?* But no such person existed in my world. I was the only expert on living my own life, the only person I could turn to for answers.

I knew I was changing when people began to gawk at me again. It had taken a year. My hips strained the seams of men's pants. My beard grew wispy and fine from electrolysis. My face looked softer. Once my voice was hormone-lowered, however, it stayed there. And my chest was still flat. My body was blending gender characteristics, and I wasn't the only one who noticed.

I remembered what it was like to walk a gauntlet of strangers who stare—their eyes angry, confused, intrigued. Woman or man: they are outraged that I confuse them. The punishment will follow. The only recognition I can find in their eyes is that I am "other." I am different. I will always be different. I will never be able to nestle my skin against the comfort of sameness.

"How the hell should I know what it is?" the man behind the counter remarked to a customer as I walked away. The pronoun echoed in my ears. I had gone back to being an *it.*

Before, strangers had raged at me for being a woman who crossed a forbidden boundary. Now they really didn't know what my sex was, and that was unimaginable, terrifying to them. Woman or man—the bedrock crumbled beneath their feet as I passed by. *How the hell should I know what it is?* I had forgotten how hard this was to endure. But I knew I was emerging into the next phase of my life. Fear and excitement gnawed at me.

There was not much keeping me in Buffalo any longer. Yet I was still afraid to leave. I wanted to believe that whatever home I was looking for, I'd find it here. But the time had come to accept that my home might be waiting for me somewhere else. Or maybe I had to travel in order to find that home inside myself. In any case, there were jobs in New York City. The dispatcher at the temp agency told me I could get work in Manhattan. And he said the twenty-four-hour movie theaters in Times Square were the cheapest hotels in the city. While I told myself I couldn't move because I didn't have enough money, deep down I feared New York would chew me up and spit me out.

It wasn't just the hope of steady work that drew me there, however; it was partly the anonymity that attracted me. Somehow it seemed easier to be a stranger in a city of strangers. And I hoped I might find others like me there. Only fear kept me in Buffalo.

One morning I came down stairs and found an oil slick where my Harley had been parked. I couldn't believe it had been stolen. I walked around the block for an hour trying to convince myself I'd simply forgotten where I'd parked it. When I finally sat down on the curb and faced that my bike was gone, I knew it was time to leave Buffalo.

As the Amtrak train pulled out of the Buffalo station I felt as though I'd left myself behind. I didn't know what lay ahead, but the train was hurtling through the darkness toward that destination.

The winter sky was as blue as a childhood dream, and the clouds formed shapes waiting to be named. New scenery shot past my window. The earth emerged—wooded, bleak, and bare. A long ride lay ahead of me.

"Is anyone sitting here?" a woman asked me. I shook my head. She put her luggage in the rack overhead. A little girl peeked around the woman's legs at me. "I'm Joan, and this is my daughter Amy."

Amy stared at me. I nodded and smiled. "I'm Jess." I turned and looked out the window. I wanted to be left alone to think and to wonder.

Amy curled up on her mother's lap. "Tell me a story." Joan smiled and leaned her head back against the seat.

"Once upon a time. . . ." She wove a story about a little girl who traveled out into the world to find the sorcerer who would tell her what she was supposed to do with her life. But on the way the girl was confronted by a fire-breathing dragon who blocked her path. She was very frightened by the dragon. "What shall I do?" the girl cried out. Suddenly she noticed a huge boulder balanced on the cliff above. If she could push the rock, it would fall and kill the dragon. But how could she get up there? The girl called out to an eagle, "Brother Eagle, please help me slay the dragon!" And the eagle swooped down and lifted the girl up to the cliff. The dragon saw the boulder falling, but it was too late. When the rock crushed the dragon, it disappeared in a cloud of smoke. The girl was very happy, but she was afraid the whole mess had made her late on her journey and now she'd never find the sorcerer. That evening she stopped and camped under a weeping willow beside a river. She started a small fire to cook her hot dogs and went into the forest to find more wood. When she returned, she found the sorcerer sitting by her fire, toasting marshmallows. She knew it was the sorcerer because he was wearing a tall pointed cap with stars and moons on it. So she sat down and asked him, "Mr. Sorcerer, please tell me what I'm supposed to do with my life." And the sorcerer smiled and told her, "You are supposed to slay a dragon."

Amy smiled at her mother and curled against her breast. "Mommy, is that a girl or a man?" she asked, looking up at Joan.

Joan flashed me an apologetic expression and turned back to Amy. "That's Jess," she said.

"Can I get you anything from the cafe car?" I asked Joan as I stood up and inched past them both. She shook her head.

I bought a bottle of pop and a deck of cards and sat in the cafe car and played solitaire. When I came back to my seat, Joan and Amy were gone. They must have gotten off at Rochester. I relished the privacy.

The world rushed past my window: streaks of vermilion, magenta, burnt umber. Silver birch and patches of snow. Crispy ocher leaves still glued to branches. Golden waves of graceful weeds reigning over marshland. Brown ducks bobbing in still ponds. The sky filled with crows and hawks and turkey vultures. Weather-beaten houses tucked away on hills between evergreens. Fallow fields and gleaming silos.

Sleepy rural towns turned their shabby backs toward the railroad tracks. Block-long main drags: five and dime, hardware, auto parts, gasoline, home-cooking. Lime, lemon, peach pastel homes. Sagging porches. Pick-up trucks and children's swings rusting in the backyards. Trailer parks—yesterday's dreams of mobility stripped of wheels. Abandoned factories, familiar as a lover's sigh. Ribbons of roads, trestle, and track tied all of our lives together like a gift.

I began to feel the pleasure of the weightless state between here and there.

But hours later the earth began to recede under the weight of acres and acres of factories and high-rise apartment buildings. We were approaching New York City. The buildings loomed larger till they blocked the sky. I descended deeper into a forest of tenements. Some lived in, some abandoned—the differences were slight: boards or cloth tacked up over windows. Laundry snapping in the air, strung from fire escapes. Every inch of wall space seemed to be spray-painted with names.

I could taste the poverty—familiar grit between my teeth.

"That's Harlem," I heard a man say to his traveling companion. Harlem! I felt breathless with excitement.

CHAPTER 20

I stood stock-still outside Grand Central Station looking up. I felt like a child again, standing at the bottom of a concrete canyon with sky-high walls. Crowds of people rushed like rapids. Strangers slammed me as they passed. *Move it, asshole.* I remembered how it felt to grow up in the adults' world, as though everyone had met together and figured out a plan of action, and I didn't have a clue.

I worked my way to the curb and asked the guy at the newsstand, "Where's 42nd Street?"

"You're standing on it," he snapped.

"How do you find an apartment in this city?" I asked.

"You want an apartment? Go find someone who's got a rent-controlled apartment and kill them." He wasn't smiling as he handed me a copy of the *Village Voice* and took my money.

I pressed my back against the facade of a building and watched the crowd flow past me. I realized this city required a strategy and I didn't have one. I had six hundred dollars. It had to get me an apartment with enough left for food and tokens till my first paycheck.

It turned out to be true that 42nd Street was filled with all-night theaters. Admission was three dollars for kung fu movies endlessly strung together. I chose a theater and entered an all-male world. The theater smelled like stale cigarettes and reefer. Many of the seats were broken, something I didn't discover until I sat down and landed on the sticky floor. The men nearest me checked me out and went back to staring at the screen.

I loved the movies. They seemed to share a theme. A young man is faced with a powerful enemy. He's forced to find a teacher who can train him in monkey style, praying mantis, tiger, eagle claw, scorpion. The twist is that the teacher is not powerful enough on his own or dies before the young man is ready. It always takes some special combination of skills and insights to defeat the foe. The hero was honorable—marked by humility and discipline and was very respectful, if not chaste, with his girlfriend.

But every time a woman appeared on the screen, the men around me shouted, "Eat that pussy! Fuck that bitch!" At first it scared me. Then I realized, with the exception of me, this was an all-male audience. Who were they talking to if not each other? Was each man who shouted from his stoned stupor trying to convince the men nearby that a woman could still make his dick hard? That no matter how the weight of the streets had crushed him he was still a real man?

I kept putting off going to the bathroom, but after a while I just had to. The stench hit me as I opened the men's room door. An older man was sitting on one toilet, a needle stuck in his arm, nodding. The tile was gummy with crud. There were no doors on the stalls. Most of the toilets were overflowing with shit and toilet paper.

I snuck into the women's bathroom. It was musty from lack of use. Just as I was zipping my pants back up, the door opened. "What are you doing in here?" a man in a red blazer asked me.

I let my voice settle into rough. "Taking a shit. Do ya mind?" I pushed past him and went back to my seat. By the time I'd seen each film twice I began to doze.

The next morning I walked, asking directions of nearly everyone I passed, till I was on the doorstep of the first rental agency I'd found in the *Voice.*

"Do you have anything cheaper?" I asked the woman agent.

"You want an apartment or a dump? Two hundred fifty—that's a bargain."

I thought about it. "When can I move in?"

"Here's the keys," she said.

I reached for the keys, she pulled them back. "That's one month rent, one month security, and a finder's fee: $750, payable now."

"I only have $500," I told her, hoping the extra $100 would last me till I found a job and got paid.

She looked me up and down and held out an open palm. "Give me the $500 now. You'll owe me the finder's fee. You have till Friday. You don't come up with the money by then, you're out." I thanked her as I signed the lease.

She needn't have given me keys. The apartment had no locks. It also had no stove, refrigerator, running water, or floor boards. I stepped carefully between the two-by-fours underfoot.

I raced back down five flights of stairs and called the agency. "It's unliveable," I told the woman.

"That's not my problem," she said.

"I want my money back!"

She laughed, almost gently. "You signed a lease, honey. It's yours for thirty days."

"I want my money back! There's gotta be laws. You can't do that," I sputtered into the dead receiver.

It was dusk and I was cold. The man in the corner liquor store gave me a couple of cardboard cartons. I climbed back up the five flights of stairs. I wedged a piece of cardboard in the door to keep it shut, flattened the rest of the boxes and used them for a bed. I lay there feeling like a damn fool. Now most of my money was gone and I had no income.

I heard footsteps on the hall stairs. I wondered who it could be since the building appeared to be deserted. The footsteps grew closer, paused on my flight, and approached my door. I lay still, trying not to breathe. One push on my door and this stranger would know I had wedged it from the inside. I was quiet for a long time as someone stood silently outside my door. Then I heard the footsteps recede back down the stairs. I jumped to my feet and grabbed my duffel bag, eager to get out of this dangerous dump. What had made me think I could survive this city?

I didn't know any other place to spend the night except the kung fu theaters. They felt a whole lot safer than an abandoned building. I stopped a Chinese man on the street and asked him where I was. "Mott Street," he answered. "Where you wanna go?"

I sighed. "Times Square—42nd Street."

He indicated the distance with a wave of his arm. "A-train."

Where were the damn trains? How did people find the subways in this city? I asked and asked until someone pointed to a staircase leading down under the street. I bought a token and entered the world of New York City subways. Nothing in life had prepared me for this.

In Buffalo I always had my own vehicle. Even when I had to take a bus, we all sat day-dreaming in the same direction. On the subway, we faced each other.

The subway car was crowded. I had never had the opportunity to observe people this way. Most of the riders looked asleep on their feet, their eyes glazed over. Others buried their noses in newspapers and books. I suddenly realized that at least a few people were doing exactly what I was doing. They were looking at people; they were looking at me.

The woman sitting across from me stared as though I was from another planet. She nudged her boyfriend. "Is that a guy or a girl?"

He looked at me from head to toe. "How should I know?" I hoped we would arrive at 42nd Street soon.

"Hey," he demanded, "are you a guy or what?" I stared back at him with my flat face on. "Hey, I asked you a fucking question. Are you deaf?" I didn't answer.

He got up and stood over me, holding the straps for support. He leaned near my face. I could smell beer. "I'm asking you one more time, you motherfucker. What the fuck are you?" The train stopped at 42nd Street and the doors opened. He was blocking my escape.

"C'mon, hon," his girlfriend tugged at him. I stood up. We both squared off nose-to-nose. I clenched my fists at my side. "C'mon, hon," she cajoled. "You promised me you wouldn't get in a fight again today."

They both turned to get off the train. I decided to stay on. "You fucking faggot," he shouted at me.

"Fuck you," I yelled back at him.

"It's a guy," he told his girlfriend.

I got off at the next station and walked back down 8th Avenue to 42nd Street. If I made enough money, maybe I'd go back to Buffalo. At that moment I believed it.

"Looking for fun, honey?" A woman stepped out in front of me on the sidewalk and opened her fake leopard coat to show me her black bustier. "Let me take good care of you," she pursed her lips and hooked her arm through mine. I remembered coming out as a baby butch and being nurtured by the strength of pros like her. Once I had been on their side in the world. Now I was seen as a trick. I pulled away from her in horror. "Fuck you," she spat on the sidewalk in front of me.

I noticed a squad car parked diagonally across the intersection. I heard sirens racing up behind me.

I neared a small throng of cops. One of them pushed a Black drag queen in fishnet stockings up against a squad car and cuffed her hands behind her back. She turned her face toward me. *Help me,* she asked wordlessly.

I don't know how, my eyes answered.

Two cops were hovering over another drag queen who was sprawled on the asphalt. The blood bubbled out of a wide crack in her forehead. One of the cops knelt down beside her. He never took his eyes off me as he reached forward and took one of her hormone-swollen breasts in his hand. "Honk, honk," he laughed as he squeezed it.

I stopped dead in my tracks, chilled and filled with hatred. I couldn't think of a way to intervene except to stand there and witness. The cop standing nearest me walked over. He brought his face up close to mine. "What's your fucking problem?" he asked me. He'd eaten garlic recently. I didn't move or speak. He jabbed me in the rib with the end of his nightstick. "How'd you like me to run you in?" he asked. The thought of getting busted alone in New York City terrified me. "Answer me, huh? Yes or no?" I paused. He grabbed his nightstick with both hands and held it horizontally across my chest. "Yes or no, asshole?"

I exhaled. "No."

"You mean *No sir,*" he taunted me.

I pressed my lips together. He stared into my eyes. "Get the fuck out of here," he ordered.

I ran down 46th Street until I couldn't hear their laughter any more. My breath came in short gasps. An icy wind blew off the river.

A young child was standing near the driver's side of a car, talking to the man behind the steering wheel. If she hadn't been wearing high heels, she wouldn't have been tall enough to meet the driver's eyes. She wore a thin, short jacket and seamed stockings. She must have been freezing. I saw her walk around to the passenger side of the car and get in.

I couldn't run or walk any further. I leaned my forehead against the cold brick face of a building. The physical pain began in my chest and worked its way up to my throat. I opened my mouth to scream, but no sound would come.

The next morning I was waiting in front of the 42nd Street temporary labor office when it opened. A man in a plaid sports coat read over my application. "What kind of discharge?" he asked me.

"Huh?"

"The service. What kind of discharge you got?"

I shrugged. I hadn't filled out that section of the application. "I wasn't in the service."

He leaned back in his chair. "Why not?"

I leaned forward. "Mister, you got a job for me or not?"

He slammed his pen down. "You got a driver's license?" I shook my head. "Get one," he said.

"No," I told him. "I don't want to drive in this city. Too crazy."

He wrote something down on a piece of paper. "Know how to drive a forklift?" I nodded. "Sewing machine factory," he said. "Skid work." He was a man of few words.

"What's it pay?"

He smiled. "$80 a week. We take $40 out this week and next."

I leaned forward in anger. "What for?"

"For finding you the job. You want it or not?"

I exhaled through clenched teeth. "Yeah, I'll take it."

His spirits seemed brighter. "Good, here's the directions. Listen kid, nothing in life comes free."

During the week I lived on peanut butter sandwiches. On payday I treated myself to the cafeteria across from the factory.

"Brisket," I pointed to it. The man behind the cafeteria counter nodded and began to carve it.

"*Lo mismo,*" the older woman on my left told him.

My stomach growled. The woman smiled knowingly at me. We both hungrily eyed the meat being carved.

The stack of meat on my plate continued to grow, and still the man piled on more. The woman nodded at me. I raised both eyebrows.

She sighed. "A man needs more food," she said.

After work I bought two strong hasps and two locks at the hardware store and went back to the abandoned building on Mott Street. I installed them so I could lock the door from the inside or the outside. Then I bought a piece of plywood to cover a patch of floorboards and a cheap air mattress for a bed. On my first night in New York City I'd been scared to death in this building at night. Now, a week later, I thought I'd die if I didn't get a few nights of privacy.

There was no running water in the building. But when one of the guys at the movie theater had found me rinsing a T-shirt in the men's room sink, he told me Grand Central was a much better place to clean up.

During the day I worked temp assignments washing dishes and loading trucks. After work I waited till the rush hour thinned, washed out a T-shirt in the men's room in Grand Central Station, and took it home to dry. At dawn I went back to Grand Central Station to wash up. At that hour the men's room belonged to homeless men who, like myself, struggled to hang onto the last shred of self-worth. On two occasions I suspected that a homeless man, bundled up in coats, was really a woman.

Through a second agency I got a job as a night watchman. At least I could use the bathroom in private. I had to make rounds every sixty minutes. With the help of an alarm clock I could sleep forty-two minutes each hour.

Double shifts were killing me, but I was driven to earn enough money to get a real apartment.

As the weather got colder, I developed a cough I couldn't quiet with lozenges and syrups. My throat was raw. I hoped it would go away. "Go home, for Christsakes," one of the guys on the loading platform said earlier in the week.

"Can't afford to," I told him.

Fever consumed me. Sidewalks rolled under my feet. Buildings curved over me and blocked the sky. Wind tore at my clothing. I made it to my apartment by leaning against the flimsy banister and resting on each landing.

My sleeping bag and pillow looked inviting. The room was dark. For the first time in weeks I was warm enough. Too warm, really. As I lay down to sleep I thought I saw a batlike demon flying back and forth above me, filling the room with the hum of beating wings. I fell asleep to escape my terror. When I awoke I saw Theresa sitting next to me. My pillow was soaking wet. Her hand felt cool on my cheek. I'd almost forgotten her smile was a gift.

"Theresa," I whispered, "I love you so much. I miss you, honey. Please take me back."

She silenced me with her hand. *Jess, you have to go to the hospital.*

I shook my head. "I can't. I'm too sick to protect myself."

She soothed me with her fingertips. *It's time now, sweetheart. You can do it. I know you can.*

"Theresa, I'm so scared."

She nodded as she ran her fingers through my hair. *I know, Jess. I know.*

I shook my head. "I don't just mean the hospital. I don't know how to live my life anymore. I'm afraid."

She nodded. *You're doing it, Jess. Just hang on.*

I tried to get up on one elbow, but I sank back down. "I'm so alone, Theresa. I don't belong anywhere. I don't even know if I still exist." Theresa wiped the tears from my eyes. I took her hand in mine. "Please, Theresa, stay with me. Please don't go. I'm so scared."

I'm right here, baby, she reassured me. *I've always been here with you.*

I rolled down a hill toward unconsciousness. "But you're fading," I whispered.

I strained to walk against a bitter wind. I couldn't make it to the hospital. My legs wouldn't carry me much further, and I felt too weak to submit to an examination. Theresa had overestimated my strength—physically and emotionally.

I coughed so violently I was afraid my ribs might crack. The sound of a distant siren seemed to bend like taffy. City lights shimmered. I walked aimlessly through the streets of the Lower East Side, unsure how to get back to my apartment. "C&D," a young man whispered as I passed. "What you looking for?"

I shook my head. "I don't know."

His eyes lit up. "What you need?" I coughed and coughed, until the street lights spun around me. "Man," he said, "you're sick, huh?"

"It was just a sore throat, but now I can't stop coughing."

"How much money you got?" he asked. I shrugged. "You got twenty dollars?" I nodded. "Wait here," he told me.

I stood on the corner so long I forgot what I was waiting for. He came back with an amber vial. As I reached for it he pulled it back. I handed him a twenty dollar bill.

"You take them four times a day. You gotta take all of them, you know? That's what the man said."

I frowned. "What is it?"

He shrugged. "Medicine. I told him what you told me. You got another ten dollars?"

"Why?" I answered. That meant yes.

"I got four codeine here. That oughta make you stop coughin', or at least stop carin'."

I smiled and handed him another ten dollars. "Thanks," I said, and meant it.

He shook my hand. "You take care of yourself now, hear?"

I bought two quarts of juice and went back to the abandoned space I called home. Every few hours when the coughing woke me, I'd pop a pill and a codeine tablet and go back to sleep. When I woke up Sunday morning my bedroll was soaked. I sat up and rubbed my eyes. I felt stronger. The illness was breaking up and leaving me.

The rent on this place was due at the end of the week. I'd found a cheap hotel near the temp agencies where I could rent by the week until I could save up for a decent apartment—a real home. I looked around. I couldn't believe I'd lived in this dump for a whole month.

"How much?" I asked the super.

"Three twenty-five a month with heat and hot water. The toilet's in the hall. Three twenty-five security deposit."

I nodded. It had a small bedroom, kitchen, and living room, all in one straight line. I gave him the cash; he handed me the lease. "Wait," I said as he turned to leave. "There's no bathtub?"

"There," he pointed to a corner of the kitchen. It was a tub covered with a sheet of metal. Strange city.

I locked the door of my apartment and turned to look around. It needed paint: yellow for the kitchen, sky blue for the bedroom, creamy ivory for the living room. I needed rugs. And dishes, silverware, pots and pans. Cleanser for the sink.

I opened my duffel bag to look for a pad and pen to make a list. There was the china kitten that Milli had left me. I placed it gingerly on the mantle in the living room. I put the amber glass, from the home Theresa and I once had, on the windowsill in the kitchen and made a mental note to buy some flowers. I left the wedding ring Theresa had bought me on the mantle.

I decided to buy yellow calico curtains for the living room windows, like the kind Betty had made for my garage apartment. I glanced at the door once more to make sure it was locked.

I pried open the window that led to the fire escape. From there I could see the East River. Competing sounds of Latin music from cars and apartment windows filled my ears. Children played in the street. Their mothers yelled at them from the windows. In any language their warnings meant *Be careful.*

New buds were popping from the skinny trees that lined the street. It was spring. I noticed wiry weeds, almost as big as saplings, growing between the buildings and in vacant lots. They pushed through cracks in the cement, growing with scarcely any soil or light. The sight was strangely reassuring. I figured if they could survive here, so could I.

A woman in the supermarket turned and stared at me as I clawed at my crotch. The itching and burning had become unbearable over the months. It wasn't going away by itself. I had a vaginal infection. I'd put off doing anything about it, refusing to admit I needed to see a doctor. Why did the infection have to be there of all places? Why couldn't it be an ear infection?

I had a flyer on my refrigerator door that I'd lifted off a lamp post advertising a women's health clinic in my neighborhood. On Wednesday night I mustered my courage and went. "This clinic is for women," the receptionist smiled.

I nodded. "I know. I have a vaginal infection," I whispered.

"A what?" she asked.

I took a deep breath and spoke in a stronger voice. "A vaginal infection."

Stillness fell over the crowded waiting room. The silence punished me. The receptionist looked me up and down. "Are you kidding?"

I shook my head. "I have a vaginal infection. I came here for help."

The receptionist nodded. "Have a seat, sir."

I debated leaving, but the itching and burning were getting worse every day. I watched the receptionist greet the woman who arrived after me. "Just pull your own chart and have a seat," she said. "The doctor will be with you shortly. Help yourself to herbal tea."

Everyone in the waiting room was staring at me. I looked at the bulletin board: women's dances and rituals; therapists, masseuses, and accountants. New symbols: a two-edged hatchet, a circle with a cross on the bottom. New names: Goodwomyn, Silverwomyn.

I could hear myself being discussed in loud voices. "He's crazy."

"Well, why can't they be crazy in their own space?"

I found an empty chair and sat down. I noticed a book on the rack next to me called *Our Bodies, Ourselves* and made a mental note to buy it in a bookstore.

A shadow fell across me—a woman with a clipboard. Her nameplate read *Roz*. Once inside the examining room Roz threw down her clipboard on the desk and nodded toward a chair. "What's this all about?" All my words tumbled out. I tried to tell her everything—who I was, why I'd come.

Roz sat back in her chair and nodded as though she really understood. Then she said, "I don't know what your problem is, but this is a clinic for women who are sick and you're using up that resource right now."

"What?"

"You may think you're a woman," Roz continued, "but that doesn't mean you are one."

My anger ignited. "Fuck you," I shouted.

She leaned back in her chair and smirked. "What a very male thing to say."

I felt my face grow purple with rage. "Fuck all of you!" I got up to leave.

A doctor blocked my exit. "What's going on in here?" she asked. Roz must have made a gesture I couldn't see. The doctor nodded. "Come with me," the doctor said. I followed her into the hall.

"What's going on?" she asked me.

I sighed. "I have a vaginal infection."

She searched my face with her eyes. "Have you taken any antibiotics recently?"

I brightened. "Maybe. I took something a couple of months ago for a bad cough."

She nodded. "How long have you had the vaginal infection?"

I shrugged. "A couple of months.

Her eyes widened. "You've had this for a couple of months and you didn't do anything about it?"

"Well, I was hoping it would go away."

She smiled slightly. "Let's take a look. Come with me."

I stiffened with fear. Too much had already happened to me here. I couldn't let her touch me there. "I can't," I told her. "Please. It's been hard to do this. I just can't."

She watched the emotions I couldn't hide. "This is a prescription for Monostat," she scribbled on a pad. "It should stop the itching and burning sensation. Next time you take antibiotics, eat a cup of yogurt each day."

I wondered if she was pulling my leg about the yogurt. "You believe me, don't you?" I asked her.

She shrugged. "You might be a man. But if you are a woman, I don't want to send you away. It doesn't cost me anything to write you out a prescription. When's the last time you had a pap smear?"

I froze. She pressed. "Within the last three years?" I dropped my eyes, but she wouldn't let go of the question. "Within the last five, six?"

I shook my head. "I don't know what that is," I admitted.

When I looked up she had tears in her eyes. "Now I believe you," she said.

"Why?" I asked her. "Plenty of men don't know this stuff either, do they?"

She nodded. "Yes, but they don't feel ashamed. Who's your regular doctor?"

"I don't have one."

She continued to watch my face in a way that unnerved me. "I'd like you to come back for an examination and a pap smear."

"Sure," I lied. I doubted I'd be able to get up the emotional energy to face the scene in the reception area again unless I was in real bad shape. And besides, the thought of a doctor opening my legs and examining me chilled me to the bone.

"Thanks for listening," I told her. "Almost nobody hears me anymore."

She squeezed my arm. "You can make an appointment at the front desk on your way out. Don't put it off too long."

I could still feel her hand on my arm after she'd walked away. I suddenly realized I didn't know her name. I might need to come back someday. I started down the hall after her. Roz came out of the examining room and blocked my way.

"What's her name?" I asked Roz. "I forgot to ask."

Roz's voice was cold. "You got what you wanted, now leave."

"You're wrong, Roz," I corrected her. "I got what I needed. You have no idea how much I want."

Every time I got a paycheck I used part of it on my apartment. I spent one whole weekend spackling the cracks in my walls and ceilings. As I applied paint to each room with broad strokes my spirits lifted.

On my most ambitious weekend I sanded all the wood floors. Then I started from the furthest corner of the apartment and polyurethaned myself out the door. That night I slept at a 42nd Street theater again—just for one more night!

The floors were dazzling. It added a new dimension underfoot, as though the ceilings were raised, or the apartment had grown in size.

I found a black Guatemalan rug at a flea market. It had tiny flecks of white in it. I unrolled it in my living room and stood back to look. It reminded me of the night sky filled with stars.

Gradually I bought furniture—a sturdy couch and reading chair, a mahogany kitchen table and chairs. At the Salvation Army I found a bed—the head and footboards were ovals carved out of cherry. I went crazy buying sheets at Macy's.

As my house came together, I suddenly wanted things that made my body feel good. I threw out my old jeans and bought new chinos, underwear, shirts, and two pair of sneakers, so that I didn't have to pound the pavement in the same pair every day.

I bought thick, soft towels and fragrances for my bath that pleased me.

And then one day I looked around at my apartment and realized I'd made a home.

CHAPTER 21

Living in New York City wasn't easy—sometimes my nerves felt like grated cheese—but it was never boring. I liked that. Something was always happening in Manhattan, good or bad. There were things to do almost any hour of the day or night.

There's a bookstore on practically every corner in New York City. I read the books furtively until I realized nobody cared if I hung out for hours. I only read the poetry and fiction. I didn't want to discover I wasn't smart enough to understand nonfiction. But the Women's Studies section tempted me. By leafing through the books I could eavesdrop on the discussions going on between women without being seen. It turned out to be true that I couldn't understand a lot of the theory. But I felt as though I was rushing into a burning building to rescue the ideas I needed in my own life.

At first I skimmed past all the words and pages about reproductive rights. I had no relationship to my own uterus. But I remembered how upset Theresa had been after I got busted in Rochester because she couldn't remember when she had her last period. I never kept track of my menstrual cycle. But Theresa always knew when my period was in relation to hers. It suddenly made sense to me: she was afraid I might have gotten pregnant. The idea had never occurred to me. What would I have done if

I'd gotten pregnant after a rape?

I stopped skipping over the sections in books about women controlling their own bodies. Maybe all of these things that were so important to other women would prove to have meaning for me, too. No matter how much I read at the bookstores, I always ended up spending a lot of my paychecks on books.

I also discovered classical music. On my way to work one morning I stood and listened to a man playing the cello in the subway station. The music grabbed me by the collar and wouldn't let me go. I crouched down next to the pillar nearest him as he played. The music articulated emotions for me, the way poetry did. When the rush hour crowd thinned I realized I was late for work.

The musician put down his bow and wiped his brow. "What were you playing?" I asked him.

He smiled. "Mozart."

I began to haunt music stores as well. I scraped together enough money for a stereo. I also explored reggae and merengue, charanga and guaguancó, jazz and blues. One spring afternoon I found myself scrubbing my apartment. I had turned up Pachelbel's *Canon in D Major* full blast.

I realized I was changing on the inside as much as I was on the outside.

"If you're an organizer for Local 6," the owner leaned across his desk, "you can punch in, but you may not punch out." Ironic. He was afraid the union had sent me to organize his typesetters. I was afraid he'd find out I'd only recently learned to type.

The foreman led me to a machine. "Here's the manual. I don't have time to train you now. Start typing this text. When it's done, run it out and give it to the proofreaders in there. I'll show you the format codes later, or look them up. Got it?"

I nodded. "Wait," I stopped him, "how do I run it out?"

He shook his head disgustedly. "That's what you got a manual for."

From where I typeset I could see four women working inside the proofreaders' room. I could hear their laughter, easy and relaxed. The foreman poked his head in and said something I couldn't hear. They broke off their conversation. One women nodded. He left. Their laughter rose again.

I wondered if men know that women talk differently among themselves. I guessed the same must be true for the Black and Latino workers too, when no whites were around.

The women huddled to share a secret.

I typed up the text and looked up the codes to run it out. I actually looked forward to being inside the proofreaders' space for a moment—women's space. The women stopped talking as I walked in. I held up the repros. "Put them over there," one of the women said. She didn't look at me as she spoke. I sighed, dropped them in the basket, and left. As I walked away, I heard their conversation resume and their voices rise in laughter once again.

I only lasted one shift in that shop. But New York City was chock full of typesetting shops that ran round the clock. They were always hiring on third shift—lobster shift. After faking my way into enough shops and learning a bit at each, I soon realized I wasn't bluffing any longer. I had become a typesetter.

It wasn't a bad rhythm of life. For six or eight months out of the year I earned top dollar.

I loved the leisurely predawn ride home, traveling in the opposite direction of packed rush hour trains and crowded streets. But it was dark when I got up, and I began to feel like a mole. Just when I thought I'd lose my sanity, it was summertime—layoffs. I became eligible for the maximum unemployment benefits.

During the summer I explored the city. My biggest problem was loneliness. I didn't have anyone to talk to all summer long. By fall I longed for casual conversation between coworkers.

Bill pounded the lunchroom table for emphasis. I read the newspaper. "Isn't that the truth?" Bill asked me. He leaned forward. "It's too fucking weird working nights in a plant with no windows. You could come out in the morning and find out there's been a nuclear meltdown and you never even knew it."

Jim laughed. "Well, if you see the sun rising in the west, come back and tell the rest of us, OK?" Jim sighed. "I know what you mean, though. I remember one time I came out of work at dawn and there was two feet of snow on the ground. I didn't even know it was going to snow. I felt like I missed something the whole rest of the world saw and I was somewhere else."

"It's like working in a fucking submarine," Bill agreed.

"You know what I hate the most?" Jim continued. "I get so disoriented about which is today and when is tomorrow. When I get up at night to go to work, my girlfriend says she'll see me tomorrow. But for me, I'm going to see her later today."

I nodded. "I know exactly what you mean. I feel like I'm living between the cracks of today and tomorrow."

"Ooh," Bill said, "I like that. Can I quote you?" We all laughed.

"You know what I really hate about shift work?" I said. "The way the whole world is geared to first shift. When I get off work I don't want bacon and eggs. I want steak and baked potato. I want dinner!"

Yeah," Jim chimed in. "And I want to see a movie."

"And go dancing with my old lady at a club so wild it stays open past noon," Bill said.

"And when I turn on TV," I added, "I don't want to see game shows and soap operas—it's depressing."

"Hey, guy," Bill said. "Why don't you come to the gym with us in the morning? We go swimming right after work. They got a steam room, too. We can get you in on a pass."

It sounded like heaven, but I fumbled for an excuse. "I don't have a swimsuit or towel or anything. Maybe another time."

Jim cut me off. "They got towels there. Hell, they wouldn't care if you swim naked."

I shook my head. "I knew I shouldn't have worn my Fred Flintstones boxer shorts today." The guys laughed. "Another time. But thanks for the offer."

Bill shrugged. "Suit yourself."

During the summer I made a list of things I'd like to accomplish: join a gym, find out more about my aunt who had been a union organizer, and have my picture taken in front of the Stonewall bar where the rebellion took place in 1969.

After visiting a lot of gyms I found one in Chelsea that felt comfortable. It was mostly gay men, some lesbians, different nationalities. It was expensive, but the nice thing about having a decent-paying job most of the year is it meant I could join.

Next I set out to learn about my aunt who died in New York City around 1929. She became an organizer for the International Ladies Garment Workers after her husband died. My father was always so proud that she merited an obituary in the *New York Times*. I remembered seeing it in the family scrapbook.

I spent two weeks searching obituaries at the library, with no luck. I came close to giving up, but decided to try 1930. "There's a half-hour limit today because we're busy," the woman behind the research counter said as she handed me the spool.

I threaded the film and quickly fell into my routine of scanning headlines. I almost passed this one without registering its meaning: *Male Butler Discovered After Death To Be Woman.*

My breathing slowed. I popped a quarter in the machine and printed out the article. I read each word carefully. The obituary reported the death of a servant in 1930. Her body was found in a rooming house. Her name was never mentioned. Nothing more: no diary, no clues. All I had were these few words on a page to know her by. I closed my eyes. I would never have the details of her life and yet I could feel its texture with my fingertips.

Now I knew there was another woman in the world who had made the same complicated decision Rocco and I made. Time separated me from this anonymous servant. Space separated me from Rocco.

The headline chilled me—her life reduced to eight flat words. I wondered if my life would be recorded in eight words or less. I stared at a spot high up on the wall, feeling empty and small.

"Sir," the librarian's voice broke my thoughts, "your time is up."

The last task I'd set for myself was finding the Stonewall bar. I remembered the impact when we heard about the battle with the cops in 1969. I wanted to ask a passerby to take my picture in front of it. I thought someday, after I'd died, someone might find the photo and understand me a little better.

"Do you know where the Stonewall bar is?" I asked two gay men who were leaning up against a lamppost in Sheridan Square.

"That used to be the bar." One of the men pointed to a bagel shop.

I sat down wearily on a park bench. A homeless man picked through the garbage can nearby. I'd seen him before. His bright African print fabric skirt brushed the sidewalk. Gauzy material wrapped his upper body, slung across one shoulder like an East Indian sari. He glided with grace and dignity. For a moment he looked up to argue with someone only he could see. The guttural words he spoke were strangely beautiful. No one else on this planet understood his language. His hands fluttered near his face as he talked, like dark birds winging on warm currents of air.

I closed my eyes. The sun was hot and high. I tried to recall what my life had been like back in Buffalo. My past already felt like a dream that receded in the moment of waking. Life in New York City shot past me every day, hurtling by like clattering subway cars. I couldn't remember a time when the world was slower and I was part of it.

Screeching tires woke me from my reverie. A woman's scream raised goosebumps on my arms. I raced to the corner. "Call an ambulance," she shouted. "Hurry! For god's sake, hurry!" The ambulance needn't have rushed.

I knelt down beside his lifeless body. His hands were finally still. I wiped the trickle of blood running from his lip with my thumb. A gurgling sound came from his mouth and blood bubbled over his lips and down his cheek. A pool of blood spread under his head.

A nightstick poked me in the shoulder. "On the sidewalk, buddy," the cop nudged me. His squad car was parked in the middle of 7th Avenue.

The man from the newsstand came over to look at the body. "What's he wearing, a skirt?" he asked the cop.

"Beats me," the cop shrugged.

The woman sobbed. "They hit him on purpose, officer. There were four of them: two men and two women. The light was red. They stepped on the gas and ran him over. They were laughing." The words tumbled out, punctuated with sobs.

She dropped to her knees and keened. "Oh my god," she sobbed, louder and louder. "Oh my god!"

An older man put down his briefcase and moved toward her. "Are you alright?" he asked.

"Oh god!" her voice rose.

"Lady, are you hurt?" He sounded panicky. "Are you OK?"

She shook her head and rocked back and forth on her knees. "Oh god," she repeated, "they were laughing."

He patted her on the shoulder. "Calm down, lady," he soothed her. "It was only a bum."

It was one of those muggy New York City summer nights when the temperature sticks at one hundred damn degrees. I stripped down to light sweatpants and a tenement T-shirt and headed for the gym.

I didn't usually go to the gym in the evening. I hated the after-work crowd lined up for the weights. But I guessed right that night. The city's population wilted in the intense heat and headed for the coolest spots in town. The gym was practically all mine. I worked my body till it felt like coiled steel and groaned when the trainer announced it was past 11:00 P.M. closing time.

I bounded home like a panther, feeling fine as could be. As I turned from Avenue A onto 4th Street I could see red lights revolving, illuminating the buildings, the crowd. The whole neighborhood looked up in the same direction, riveted. I walked a little slower. The street was slick and glistening. There had been no rain for weeks. I walked slower still.

I heard the fire before I saw it. The hellfire roared from the windows of my building straight up into the sky. Sparks shot up like a volcanic eruption and floated down on nearby roofs. My yellow calico curtains blew between broken shards of glass as though a storm was raging inside my apartment. A small spot of flame appeared on each curtain, and they dissolved in a poof, the way cotton candy melted on my tongue.

The wedding band Theresa had given me! In an irrational moment I thought maybe I could find the cooled pool of metal on the mantle and get it recast. I imagined the pop of Milli's ceramic kitten. I pictured the water in the amber glass on the kitchen windowsill boiling furiously in the furnace of heat. I saw a small flame licking the stem of each narcissus in the glass, until they curled in on themselves and exploded in brighter yellows and oranges than ever before. I envisioned Edwin's slim volume of W.E.B. Du Bois burning down to the single page she had marked.

Why couldn't the landlord have just told us he was going to have the building torched? Everyone knew he was having trouble selling it. Most of the other buildings in the area had been burned during the decade of gentrification. Why couldn't he have slipped a note under each of our kitchen doors this morning warning us to take the things we loved most with us? He sure notified us promptly before each rent increase.

My wallet! I left it home when I went to the gym. The rest of my paycheck was in it. More important, the only picture I had of Theresa was inside that billfold. I'd lost everything. Everything except Rocco's leather jacket. I'd brought it to the cleaners to get a zipper fixed.

"*Abuela! Abuela!*" A woman broke free from the arms of loved ones and pushed her way through the crowd toward the burning building. Friends restrained her. She fought to break free.

"What's she saying?" I asked the super.

He lifted his eyes to the top floor. "Her grandmother."

I shivered. Did he mean the old woman who could never leave her house because she lived on the sixth floor? Occasionally she asked me in Spanish to bring her bread, coffee, milk, or sugar—showed me the wrappers when I didn't understand.

"Mrs. Rodriguez?" I asked incredulously. The super nodded. The young woman stopped screaming when she heard me say her grandmother's name. Our eyes and our lives connected in one timeless moment. She began to sob uncontrollably. Friends led her away.

I turned and looked at the waves of flame sweeping each floor and I wondered, *Where do my tears go? Why is it that I can't cry now when I need to?* Yet I knew that later my tears would be unexpectedly triggered by the scent of lilacs, or the low hum of a cello.

Eventually the black sky lightened over the East River. I sat on the curb, my back to the smoldering building. A fine mist fell on me from the tiny punctures in the firehoses, still pumping water into our homes. I sat very still, not knowing quite where to go from this spot.

I was starting all over. I sat on a bench in Washington Square Park and inventoried my possessions: a pair of sweatpants, a T-shirt, and twenty dollars in my pocket. All my money had been hidden in the apartment. Back to double shifts. Back to sleeping in the 42nd Street movie theaters on weekends. I had no energy; I had no choice.

My mind couldn't fully accept the loss. I bought a hot dog and soda pop for one dollar and walked around the park, hungry for diversion. I was drawn toward a large crowd watching a young man in a top hat and tails juggling fiery torches. This was the silly part of the life of this city that I grudgingly loved, no matter how excruciatingly hard it was to survive here.

"Who would ever want to be a juggler?" the woman next to me asked her companion. "I mean, what's the point?" They both shook their heads and walked away.

The joy I'd felt watching the juggler drained from my face. At the moment she'd spoken, I was thinking how wonderful it would be to learn a skill that could be practiced alone, simply for the pleasure of self-amazement.

The man standing near my right elbow looked me in the eyes and cocked his head. His gaze made me uncomfortable. I wanted to turn away from him. It was as though he could see the play of emotions I was feeling. But somehow he drew me to look at him more closely. I saw a gentle man whose own feelings rippled across his face. It was as though we were carrying on an emotional dialogue without words.

He raised his eyebrows in question. I shrugged. "Cynics." I smiled.

He shook his head and executed graceful motions with his hands—Deaf. He saw on my face that I understood. I smiled. He smiled. Then I was stuck. I looked at my hands, inarticulate at my sides. Once again I was bereft of words, left longing for language that could speak from heart to heart.

I turned up my palms and shrugged helplessly. He held up an index finger. One? No. Wait, he indicated.

He examined the ground. He pointed to something behind a tree and nodded with a smile. Then he picked up an imaginary thing with three fingers. What was it? It was round. I could tell by the way he lifted it with both hands to his face. Still holding it with three fingers, he drew it back as though he was—bowling! A bowling ball.

I nodded emphatically. He found a second bowling ball on a branch over my head. This one he placed carefully on his right foot. He searched with his eyes for a third and found it. With a bowling ball in his right hand and another balanced on his foot, he slowly bent down to lift a third ball with his free hand. He wobbled. Could he keep the ball from falling off his foot? He did it!

I held my breath as he began to juggle. I could see the heavy weight of the bowling balls, the strength required to send each one higher. His skill increased: the balls passed under one leg, behind his back, and over his shoulder. All three balls were sent high into the air. . .they didn't come back down. He paused and looked up at the sky, scratching his head in bewilderment. Suddenly he lurched forward and caught one in his left hand, then staggered to the right and caught another. The third one landed on his toe, sending him hopping behind a tree in mock agony. He peeked out from behind the tree and winked.

It felt like such a relief to laugh—not in spite of my grief, but because of it. We laughed together. It was deep, belly laughter. The kind that brings you to tears. The kind that releases emotions thick as mud.

Two men approached him from either side. He smiled at them and their arms turned in windmills of exchange. He indicated my presence. We all shook hands.

Before he turned to go, he reached forward very slowly with his hand and touched a tear on my cheek. He touched his own eye with my tear. And then he walked away.

CHAPTER 22

I felt like the fire left me no choice. How could I give up? Surrender was unimaginably more dangerous than struggling for survival.

The typesetting industry didn't pick up till early fall, but I found work catch as catch can.

By September I signed a lease on a tenement apartment just above Canal Street. It was a pretty big one-bedroom railroad flat, but it was filthy. I didn't have the energy to clean it when I moved in. I figured I'd do it a little at a time. I bought an air mattress, a blanket, and a pillow. That's what I really needed in the apartment. It was a safe place to sleep, that's all.

My first night there I crawled out onto the fire escape. I could see a few green trees lining a tiny strip of something people in this city call a park. The traffic backed up for the bridge to Brooklyn had thinned. The music of mariachi and mandarin melded in the night. Three little girls sat on a fire escape across the street, combing each other's hair as they sang pop tunes from Hong Kong. A man and a woman fought bitterly in an apartment below me. I tensed at the sound of a crash. It was followed by an even more ominous silence. From the open living room window of my next-door neighbor's apartment I could hear the steady hum of a sewing machine.

The faint glow of the city softened the darkness of night. If there were still stars in the sky, they weren't within my sight.

I saw my next-door neighbor a month later. As I unlocked my apartment, she opened hers. I said hello before I even looked up. She didn't answer.

Her face startled me. It was badly bruised on one side like a rainbow—yellow, red, blue. Her hair was outrageously crimson. I could tell that womanhood had not come easily to her. It wasn't just her large Adam's apple or her broad, big-boned hands. It was the way she dropped her eyes and rushed away when I spoke to her.

Every day I saw others like me in this city—enough of us to populate our own town. But we only acknowledged each other with a furtive glance, fearful of calling attention to ourselves. Being alone in public was painful enough; two could find themselves smack in the center of an unbearable sideshow. We didn't seem to have any of our own places to gather in community, to immerse ourselves in our own ways and our own languages.

But now I had a neighbor who was different like me. As weeks passed I became intrigued by the sounds and smells coming from her apartment. She sewed endlessly. She loved Miles Davis. And whenever she opened her oven, the hall outside her door filled with the most tantalizing aromas.

One Saturday afternoon I found her clutching two huge bags of groceries and fumbling with the downstairs front-door lock. I pulled out my key. "Here, let me." She didn't say thank you. She hurried ahead of me on the stairs. "Can I help you carry those?" I offered.

"Do I look weak to you?" she asked.

I stopped on the stairs. "No. Where I come from it's just a sign of respect, that's all."

She continued up the stairs. "Well, where I come from," she called out, "men don't reward women for pretending to be helpless." Once I heard her apartment door close I kicked the stair in anger and frustration.

All day long I sat in my apartment rehearsing how I would introduce myself to her. I stood outside her door and listened to the Motown music blaring on her stereo before I finally got up the courage to knock. Someone turned the music down as she cracked open the door. I lifted my hand to silence her before she could speak. "I'm sorry to bother you," I said, "but I didn't make a very good impression before. I know you think I'm a man, but I'm not. I'm a woman."

She sighed and unhooked the chain. "Listen," she opened her door a little wider, "I don't need a gender identity crisis on my doorstep. This is my home and I'm with friends. Please understand, I really don't want to be bothered."

I heard a drag queen's voice from inside her apartment. "Who's that, Ruth? Ooh, he's cute! Let him in."

"Tanya, please." Ruth silenced the drag queen with a glare. I could see someone else peering at me from the living room.

Ruth was visibly annoyed at the curious way her friends and I were checking each other out. "I'm not trying to be rude," she told me, "but let me make myself clear: This is my home. I do not want to be annoyed."

I rested my hand on her doorframe. "But I need to talk to you." She glared at my hand. I removed it.

"But I don't need to talk to you. Excuse me," she closed her door.

I had no choice but to give Ruth the wide berth she demanded.

I shivered in a blanket on my fire escape, unwilling to let go of the day. The temperature had risen to seventy-five degrees, unusual in late October. The chilly evening breeze still smelled fresh by Manhattan standards.

Ruth poked her head out of her living room window. "Oh," she sounded startled. "I didn't know you were out here. I'm going to close my window because it's cold." I sighed and looked up at the sky.

She spoke more softly. "It's a beautiful night, isn't it?" The shades of gender in her voice were intricate, like mine.

I smiled. "That's a harvest moon up there tonight."

Ruth laughed. "What's a city slicker like you know about harvests?"

Her words and tone angered me. I was sick of being everybody's "other." But part of me still needed Ruth's friendship so damn much. So I took a moment before I answered and spoke without anger.

"I know how it feels to stand in a field in the pitch dark under a billion stars, with no sound except the music of crickets and cicadas." Ruth nodded as she stared at the moon. I leaned my head back against the brick. "And I know how a white-capped river looks when it's racing toward the falls—how it's translucent and green at the place where it bends over the edge, like bottle glass when it washes up in the surf."

I smiled at Ruth. "And I know your hair is as red as wild sumac in early autumn."

Ruth looked at me wide-eyed. "What a lovely thing to say. You're from upstate. I can tell by your accent. Me, too."

I nodded. "I know."

Ruth's whole demeanor toward me changed. She seemed ready to open her door partway for me. That's when I discovered I was still hurt and angry at her earlier rejections. Before she could say another word I told her "Good night" and climbed back inside my living room.

I leaned my head against the windowsill and watched the moon continue to rise over Manhattan. I never would have known Ruth was doing the same thing only a few feet away from me if I hadn't heard the scratch of a match and smelled the smoke from her cigarette.

I didn't see her again for a couple of months. I think she went away for a few weeks over the holidays because I didn't hear music or sewing, and the hallway went back to smelling like a urinal.

I got tired of sleeping on an air mattress and I bought a bed from the Salvation Army. I also got a used record and tape player that was so beat-up I wouldn't care if someone stole it.

One Saturday afternoon, after weeks of working overtime I woke up late. My apartment looked so filthy it disgusted me. The daylight had thinned to gray by the time I bundled up to go out for cleaning supplies.

Ruth and I opened our doors at the same moment and looked away in embarrassment. I held back to let her go ahead of me. From the landing she called up to me, "I hope this doesn't sound rude, but what was the music you were playing yesterday? Do you remember?"

"Why?" I called down to her. "Is this an indirect way of saying it was too loud?"

There was a long silence. "No," she said. "I liked it, that's all. Do you mind me asking?"

"If it sounded African it was King Sunny Ade."

"Thank you," she said curtly. I heard the front door shut.

Now I knew that she listened to my music just as I listened to hers. So I began to play tapes for both of us, wondering as I did which ones she enjoyed most. I imagined our lives connected in spite of the thin walls and closed doors physically separating us. That's when I realized just how lonely I was.

On the morning of the spring equinox, I wearily climbed my stairs at dawn, eager for a hot shower and a long sleep. The pungent aroma of simmering rhubarb pulled me up the steps two at a time. The irresistible smell was coming from Ruth's kitchen. I was a child the last time I'd smelled rhubarb cooking. I rested my head against her door. My mouth filled with saliva and my glands ached from the aroma.

Just as I got out my keys, Ruth opened her door. "I'm sorry," I said. "I'm not skulking—honestly. It's just been a long time since I smelled rhubarb cooking. It takes me back."

Ruth nodded. "I'm making pies. Would you like some coffee?"

I hesitated. We both faced each other stiffly. But I was so weary of our caution and defensiveness. "Thank you," I smiled. "Oh," I groaned as I walked into her kitchen. "It smells so good."

Ruth smiled. "Well, I wish I could send you home with a small pie, but these are for friends in the hospital."

I nodded. "When I was a kid I used to eat it plain in a bowl with brown sugar."

Ruth stirred the pot. "I'm sure there's enough for that." She stopped puttering and buried her hands in the pockets of her old-fashioned floral apron.

I pointed to one of the small watercolor paintings on her kitchen wall. "I recognize the Queen Anne's Lace, but what are these purple flowers?"

"Asters," she said. "And that's goldenrod."

I didn't usually like pictures of flowers, but these reminded me of the way flowers looked the first time I saw them. "These are really nice," I said.

"Thank you."

"Did you paint them?" I asked. She nodded. "This is beautiful." I pointed to a framed handkerchief, embroidered with colorful pansies. "I always loved pansies, but they embarrassed me, too, because that's what kids used to call me when I was a little girl."

Ruth looked me in the eye and then went back to stirring the pot. "It's almost ready," she said. "Sit down. Would you like decaf so you can still sleep? You work nights, don't you?"

I smiled and nodded. She had directed at least a little attention toward her neighbor, just as I had. "Some regular coffee would be great. I'm trying to stay up and clean on the weekends, but all I get is one layer deeper into the crud." Ruth's immaculate home inspired me.

"Where are you from?" she asked me.

"Buffalo."

She smiled. "We are neighbors. You know where Canandaigua Lake is?" I nodded. It was about two hours outside of Buffalo. "I'm from Vine Valley."

I frowned. "I never heard of Vine Valley. Is it farm country?"

Ruth nodded. "Oh, yes—vineyards." As she poured the coffee I could smell cinnamon in it.

"I miss Buffalo," I sighed. "Well, at least I miss the way it used to be. It was such a blue-collar town when I grew up. I never could have imagined that the plants would close and the people from the suburbs would move in and buy our houses dirt-cheap."

Ruth nodded and stirred her coffee. "I know. I saw life in the country change, too. When the big wineries took over the flat land, it got harder to keep the little family vineyards on the hills alive. The call of the cities lured people to work and shop."

I smiled. "I always thought country life didn't change much."

Ruth laughed gently. "That's the view from the city."

"I know how it felt to grow up in Buffalo. But it must have been hard growing up in such a small place." I wondered if what I'd said sounded too personal.

Ruth sighed and leaned back in her chair. "I don't know if it was hard. I just know it wasn't easy. I'd be surprised if the population of the whole valley is more than two hundred. But in a way, I think that's why I survived. We didn't have outside help for the vineyards—we all had to rely on each other. So those old bonds of cooperation weren't completely broken. I had a place there. But if I hadn't left I would never have discovered Miles Davis, and my hair might always have been brown as dirt."

Ruth got up and spooned soft rhubarb into a dish, then crumbled brown sugar over it. I slipped a spoonful into my mouth and sighed. "I had forgotten about taste."

She frowned. "What do you mean?"

"Oh, I eat just because I'm hungry. Fast food, take-out. I don't really taste it. But this tastes so good it makes me want to cry."

Ruth nodded without smiling. "I cook for my own pleasure. I enjoy the preparing as much as the eating."

I shrugged. "I'm not really set up to cook."

She leaned forward. "This is very personal. You don't have to answer, but why don't you have curtains?"

"Well, my apartment is just where I sleep."

Ruth shook her head. "That's strange to me. I really live here."

"It's different working nights." I made excuses. "I just crash when I get home. Besides, I lost everything in a fire last summer. I had really cared about fixing that place up and making a home out of it. Now I don't want to care."

Ruth pursed her lips. "You mean if you don't have anything you care about, then you won't have anything to lose?"

I nodded. "Yeah, something like that."

Ruth looked at me wistfully. "Then I guess everything's already been taken from you. You've nothing left to lose, have you?"

I didn't know why she had finally decided to invite me in, but suddenly I felt stripped and vulnerable. So I took a last swig of coffee, and the last tart mouthful of rhubarb, and stood up to go. "Thank you," I told her. "That was a treat."

Ruth saw me to the door. "I go to the farmer's market at Union Square today. Can I get you anything?"

I unlocked my front door and shook my head. "No, but thank you." Once inside, I threw open the windows and began a serious cleaning frenzy.

Hours later I furiously scrubbed the gunk under my sink while my music blasted. The knock at the door startled me, and I hit my skull on the pipes. I rubbed my head angrily as I opened the door. Ruth extended an armful of orange gladiolas. "I thought you might like these. I heard you cleaning and I hoped they would brighten up the place after all that hard work."

I opened the door a little further. "Thanks. I don't think I have anything to put these in."

Ruth returned a moment later with a cut-glass vase. She couldn't conceal her horror at my barren apartment. I shifted my weight uncomfortably. "I haven't had time to shop for furniture or anything."

I put the flowers in water and set them in the middle of the empty living room. "They're really pretty, Ruth. I've brought women flowers, but no woman ever gave me flowers before. It's a beautiful thing to do."

Ruth blushed. "People need flowers." She turned to go and stopped. "You know, I don't even know your name."

"Jess."

She smiled. "I had an uncle named Jesse. Is it short for Jesse?"

I shook my head. "Just Jess."

"I'll leave you to your cleaning, Jess."

I nodded. "Thanks for the flowers."

When she left I went back to scrubbing. Hours later, I sat down wearily on the living room floor next to the flowers. Maybe Ruth had been right: being afraid to lose anything I cared about meant I'd already lost it all. I heard another knock on my door, the second time in one day. It was Ruth. She extended a bundle of unbleached muslin. "These are the curtains I used to have in my living room. My windows are the same size as yours so I thought I'd offer them. It's up to you."

I stood and looked at Ruth and at the gift in her large hands, and I said yes to both.

A week later I brought Ruth's vase back to her, filled with irises. Her smile was my reward. "Do you have a vase?" she asked me. I shook my head. "Come in. Here, do you like this?" She handed me a cobalt blue glass vase.

I sighed. "Oh! The color is so intense it pulls me in. I can almost taste the color."

Ruth rested her fingertips on my cheek. "You're hungry, Jess. Your senses are starved." I stared into the depth of the deep blue. "If I made you dinner tonight, what would you eat? Fish?"

I laughed. "Is fish food?"

Ruth shook her head. "Oh no, you're not a meat and potatoes kind of guy, are you?"

I dropped my eyes. "I'm not a guy, Ruth."

She nodded. "Well, then it has a little twist when I say that, doesn't it? Alright, I'll make you red meat. But I warn you, I'm going to expand your appetite."

What a wonderful offer! But why was she being nice to me now?

I shopped that afternoon for new chinos and a dress shirt. I stopped at the farmer's market and bought Queen Anne's Lace jelly, just because I loved the way it sounded. I found fat blueberries at Balducci's and a Miles Davis tape at Tower Records that I was sure she didn't have.

Ruth laughed with pleasure at the small shower of gifts. "These blueberries are going to be our dessert. And I think I'll use a spoonful of this jelly for our tea. But how did you know I wanted this concert tape?"

I smiled shyly. "I'm your neighbor."

Ruth laughed. "That you are. Sit down."

Her kitchen was layered with smells. Ruth set a huge salad in front of me. There were yellow-and-orange blossoms in the bowl along with greens I'd never seen before. My eyes filled with tears. "Ruth, there's flowers in my salad."

Ruth smiled. "Those are nasturtium. They're beautiful, aren't they?"

"Can I eat them?" She nodded. I shook my head. "I hate to eat this. It's like a work of art."

Ruth sat down next to me. "That's part of how starved you've been. I think you're afraid this is the last beautiful thing that's going to happen to you, and you want to hold onto it."

"How did you know that?"

Ruth smiled. "I'm your neighbor. It's a wonderful salad, Jess. I made it just for you to enjoy. But the next one will be luscious, too."

I blushed and put down my fork. "You know when your leg falls asleep how it hurts when the circulation starts again? I'm not sure I want to hope. I don't want to get disappointed again."

Ruth patted my arm. "We both already know all about disappointment. Let's not anticipate it." She got up and put on the music I'd brought her.

As I ate the salad, tears ran down my cheeks for no apparent reason. Ruth smiled. "It's balsamic vinegar. Isn't it wonderful?"

How could I explain why the tastes of nasturtium and balsamic vinegar on my tongue made me cry? "I'm sorry," I wiped my eyes. "This is just why you didn't want to let me in, isn't it? Why are you being so nice to me now?"

Ruth put down her fork and covered my hand with hers. "I'm sorry I was so cold. I misunderstood you. I thought you were frightened and confused and I was afraid you'd sap my strength. After you backed off I realized I couldn't figure you out—that's a very attractive quality in my book. You seemed to be much stronger and calmer than I'd first given you credit for. So I changed my mind." Ruth smiled, "It's a woman's prerogative."

"What finally made you decide to let me in?"

Ruth squeezed my hand. "The color of my hair is my declaration to the world that I'm not hiding. It's a hard color to stand behind, but I do it to celebrate my life and my decisions. Most people are embarrassed by the color of my hair. It took a very special person to compare it to the color of sumac."

I laughed and picked at my salad. "Do you know if I'm a man or a woman?"

"No," Ruth said. "That's why I know so much about you."

I sighed. "Did you think I was a man when you first met me?"

She nodded. "Yes. At first I thought you were a straight man. Then I thought you were gay. It's been a shock for me to realize that even I make assumptions about sex and gender that aren't true. I thought I was liberated from all of that."

I smiled. "I didn't want you to think I was a man. I wanted you to see how much more complicated I am. I wanted you to like what you saw."

Ruth brushed my cheek with her fingertips. I shivered. "Well, I didn't understand right away, but I thought you were awfully cute and handsome and interesting-looking." Even Ruth's words were gifts.

I dropped my eyes so she couldn't see my hunger for her attention. "Oh, Ruth. I wish we had our own words to describe ourselves, to connect us."

Ruth stood up and opened the broiler. "I don't need another label," she sighed. "I just am what I am. I call myself Ruth. My mother is Ruth Anne; my grandmother was Anne. That's who I am. That's where I come from."

I shrugged. "I don't want another label either. I just wish we had words so pretty we'd go out of our way to say them out loud."

As Ruth set the plate down I stared at the steak. "What are these little sprigs of things on top?" I asked.

"Sage." She spooned tiny carrots and miniature squash onto my plate. She opened the oven door and served me steaming bread and sweet butter. Every bite tasted like music in my mouth.

"Now we'll have the wonderful dessert you brought," Ruth said. She filled two earthen bowls with blueberries, drizzled them with heavy cream, and sprinkled them with sugar.

I blinked away tears and squeezed her arm. "Ruth. . . ." The words got stuck in my throat.

She covered my hand with hers. "I know all about hunger, Jess." She lifted her mug. "To friendship?"

I clinked my mug against hers. "Yes," I answered, "to our friendship."

I shopped for used furniture, the first sign of my own spring thaw. Ruth seemed more excited than I did as the steady stream of deliveries arrived. Gradually my rooms began to assume shapes. Ruth hung her framed handkerchief embroidered with pansies on my kitchen wall and gave me the tie quilt she'd made with her grandmother for my bed.

But I really knew Ruth and I were becoming close when she admitted how much she wanted help repainting her apartment. It was an absolute pleasure to see the joy on her face as I covered her walls with fresh colors. She excitedly cut shelf paper while the cupboards were still tacky with white enamel.

I enjoyed the complex layers of life in the city and longed to explore those nooks and crannies with Ruth. But we never left our apartment building together because of what she called her geometric theory: two people like us in public are more than double the trouble.

Instead we brought each other little gifts from our daily travels. I gave her Villa-Lobos, she gave me Keith Jarrett; I brought her forsythia, she brought me impatiens. And after a while we exchanged our tears and our frustrations, as well.

"Why, Ruth?" I stormed around her kitchen. "Why do heads turn when we walk down the street? Why are we so hated?"

Ruth stopped scrubbing the inside walls of her stove. "Oh, honey. We've been taught to hate people who are different. It's been pumped into our brains. It keeps everybody fighting each other."

I slumped in a chair. "I used to want to change the world. Now I just want to survive it."

Ruth laughed. Her rubber gloves snapped as she pulled them off. "Well, don't give up just yet, honey. Sometimes things don't change for a long time and then they catch up so fast it makes your head spin."

I sighed. "When I was growing up, I believed I was gonna do something really important with my life, like explore the universe or cure diseases. I never thought I'd spend so much of my life fighting over which bathroom I could use."

Ruth nodded. "Well, I've seen people risk their lives for the right to sit at a lunch counter. If you and I aren't going to fight for the right to live, then the kids coming up will have to do it."

I leaned my head back against the back of the kitchen chair and laughed. "You are my pleasure, Ruth. You're the last ice-cold Coca-Cola in the desert." I flashed her a smile that clearly charmed her. I had forgotten I could do that.

That evening we crawled out onto the fire escape and sat close to each other as the afternoon shifted to evening. I'd never held a body larger than mine before. The street below us was blocked off for a festival—tiny lanterns strung up between booths of food, couples dancing in the intersection to a live mariachi band.

"Ruth, if we lived in a world where we could be anything we wanted to be, what would you do with your life?"

Ruth smiled wistfully. "Oh, I'd still sew. I'd dress people in their dreams so they could walk proudly down the street. And I'd cook for all the people who had ever been hungry. I wouldn't be afraid to leave my house. Oh, I'd love to explore this world. What about you, Jess?"

I leaned my head back against the brick. "I think I'd be a gardener in a woods just for children, and when they came by I'd sit and listen to their wonderings. And the ocean would be nearby. I'd live in a little house on the shore. At dawn I'd strip off all my clothes and swim. At night I'd sing a song about the way life used to be. It would be such a sad song it would make the grownups nod and the children cry. But I'd sing it every night so that no one would ever confuse nostalgia with wanting to return."

Ruth began to cry. "Oh, Jess. Even in your dreams I can hear how much you hurt." I kissed her very red hair. "Jess, I had grown so comfortable with being alone, I forgot how lonely I am underneath. I have friends I love, like Tanya and Esperanza and the showgirls I sew for. But I feel so close to you . . . I can't explain it."

I rocked her gently. "Ruth, if your life was set to music, what kind of instrument would be playing?"

She snuggled against me. "A soprano saxophone."

I smiled. "Because it's so sad?"

She shook her head. "No, because it's so evocative. What kind of instrument would play your music, Jess?"

I sighed. "I think a cello."

Ruth held me tight. "Because it's so sad?"

I shook my head and looked out over the city. "No, because it's so complicated."

CHAPTER 23

I clutched the quarts of elderberries against my leather jacket and grinned, knowing how excited Ruth would be that I'd found them in the wintertime. They'd taste like home to her, like her life's seasons. I could already smell hot elderberry pie. I leaned forward on the subway track and looked down as far as I could see. I was anxious to get home. The sun would be up within hours. Ruth's sewing machine would be humming. Wait till she saw the elderberries. Her smile would be my dawn.

I heard the three teenage boys before I saw them. They shouted in boisterous camaraderie as they jumped the turnstile. White boys pumped up on chemicals. Their first target was an old man asleep on a bench. They rousted him, kicked him, passed him from one set of brutal hands to another. They laughed as he pushed through the turnstile and ran.

That's when I made a mistake. I moved further back into the station, away from them. In doing so, I moved further from the exit or any possibility of help. Some mistakes in life are not punishable, others teach you a lesson you never forget.

When I heard their footsteps growing closer, I knew better than to hide behind the pillar. It's far worse to be caught cowering. I reached inside the bag and pulled out a small handful of elderberries. Their tart taste heightened my senses. They stained my hands with the color of battles won and lost. I set the rest of the berries down on the platform, wishing Ruth could have known I had found her elderberries in the winter in this paved city. I wanted more time with Ruth. I wished I had thanked her for breathing a little life back into me.

I positioned my house keys between my fingers so that my fist bristled with coppery spikes. I was trapped between the end of the station and the three faces getting closer. They are the hunters; I am the prey. For just a moment, before it began, I cursed Ruth for making me hope again. Then I let go of everything except the moment confronting me.

The leader of the pack emerged. He reached for my face. "What have we here?" he asked, almost gently. I blocked his hand with my own. He smiled. Now it had begun. My spiked fist was out of their sight. I didn't reveal my readiness. His buddies leered and sneered. But his smile was harder to stand up to. It reminded of a cop's smirk, meant to force me to admit powerlessness.

"What the fuck are you?" he asked quietly. "I can't tell what you are. Maybe we should just find out, huh, guys?" His taunts and threats rolled off me, not because I was impervious to them, but because I was filled to overflowing.

I tried not to listen. It didn't matter what he said. It didn't matter what I answered. All that was important was the action, the positioning of their bodies and mine, the juxtaposition of matter and space, open throats and unguarded kneecaps. At the instant the action exploded I would have a moment to strike, to change the relationship of forces. When one their punches connected with my body, when blood filled my eyes, when I could no longer catch a breath—I would be theirs. I braced myself against the leftover grit of elderberries between my teeth. Any moment it would erupt. Any moment.

I looked the leader in his eyes, refusing to show him my fear. Of course we both knew I was afraid. I wasn't ready to die. Oh, I was scared alright. But what I hadn't shown him yet was my rage. I might never get my hands on the powers that twisted and unleashed these bullies on me, but if I was going to die, I was sure as hell going to try to take them with me. I could feel a breeze on my face—a train was approaching. Would it come in time to save me?

The attack began at that moment. His body betrayed him. He telegraphed his intention to move. I swung my spiked fist in an uppercut to his chin. At the moment of impact he bit off the end of his tongue. His blood sprayed my face. More of his blood ran down my wrist as I yanked out my fist. The train roared into the station.

Another open throat. I thrust my clenched fist into it as hard as I could. Even over the racket of the train I could heard the gurgling sound as I pulled out my keys.

A fist as hard as an anvil smashed the side of my jaw. The opposite side of my skull slammed into the metal column. I staggered down the platform, rubbing someone else's blood from my eyes.

The train doors opened. The early morning rush hour crowd moved away from me in horror. When the doors closed I looked around. They hadn't followed me onto the train. I looked at my hands, stained with elderberries and blood. I wondered how much of the blood was my own. My head throbbed more and more insistently. A steel rod of pain pierced my jaw—fiery hot, icy cold. My vision doubled, focused and blurred again. I couldn't hear the sounds of the train over the roar in my ears.

I got off the train at 14th Street. It was Ruth I wanted to see. If I was going to die, I wanted it to be in the arms of someone who understood me. But I knew we risked a hideous scene if we went to the hospital together. Maybe if I went alone and they didn't make me take off my T-shirt they might help me.

No one noticed me at first as I staggered through the double doors of St. Vincent's Hospital. Then hands reached out for me, guided me. A nurse peered in my face as she pushed forms toward me. I invented someone who had insurance and no fear of being traced. How long it would take them to check out my lies?

Another nurse lay me down gently. A gale wind blew behind my eyes. Doctors and nurses bent over the table and peered at me. I wondered what they saw. The ceiling began to move. I was being wheeled somewhere. I remember opening my eyes and watching a doctor sewing my mouth. I wanted to struggle but I lay still. My head ached.

When I opened my eyes again there was only a nurse in the room, writing on a clipboard. I tried to sit up. She came over and steadied me. "Take it easy," she whispered. She read the fear in my eyes. "Do you know where you are?" she asked. I nodded. "You've been in and out since you got here. Your jaw is broken. You're going to be drinking a lot of milkshakes for the next couple of months. We're going to bandage your head wound. You have a concussion. The doctor's waiting for the x-rays to come down. He may want you to stay overnight for observation." My face and head felt huge and bloated.

There was kindness in her smile. "One of the police officers will help you fill out a crime report." My eyes widened in fear. "It's required by law," she said. "You just lie there, now. Don't try to get up. I'll be back in a while." I stood up as soon as she left. The room rotated around the axis of my feet. I had trouble focusing my eyes. My head wasn't working right.

Soon they would find out I didn't have insurance. Momentarily a cop would arrive. Every bit of information I gave him would be a lie. I was still a gender outlaw—any encounter with the police might end up with me in their custody. I panicked. It was time to escape. I checked my wallet. I had more than enough for a cab ride home.

The emergency room was so chaotic no one noticed me leave. The icy blast of wind outside felt good against my swollen face, but it made my scalp ache. I stumbled to the corner of 14th Street and hailed a cab. The driver turned around in his seat. "Where to, pal?" I couldn't answer. He frowned. "Where to, mister?" My hands moved in frustration. "You drunk or something?"

Ruth. I wanted to get to Ruth. I grimaced so he could see my gums were wired. "Holy shit," he said. I mimed writing. He handed me a pad and I wrote down my address. He watched me in the rearview mirror as he drove. "What happened?" I shrugged.

"Oh, yeah. You can't talk. I forgot." He pulled up in front of my building. "That'll be $3.40," he told me. I gave him a five and waved for him to keep it.

All I could think of was Ruth's arms. But by the time I got to her door I hesitated. Even though I could hear her in her apartment, I didn't knock. I quietly took out my own house keys. They were clotted with blood. I calmed my breathing, fearing I'd choke to death if I vomited. A moment after I'd closed my door I heard a knock. I knew it must be Ruth. I held still and didn't move until she walked away and closed her door.

Why? Why was I suddenly so afraid to see her? Because I feared bringing so much need to her? What if I asked for too much? What if she turned away from me? What if I lost her?

I wanted to go to her, though. I wanted to kneel in front of her and ask her to hide me, to keep me safe. And I wanted her love to protect me from harm's way. More than anything I just wanted to be held. But I was so afraid to ask.

My head hurt and hurt and hurt. I couldn't open my jaws. Panic burned like acid in my throat. I felt claustrophobic, trapped inside my head. My skull throbbed, and the room tilted like the fun house at Crystal Beach. For just a moment I was more terrified not to ask for what I needed than I was to be rejected. I fumbled trying to open the lock on my door. I slammed it behind me and hurled myself against Ruth's door, pounding it with my fist. If she didn't answer fast I'd lose my nerve.

Ruth opened her door, wearing that old-fashioned apron. She pushed her very red hair out of her frightened eyes. My chin ached and trembled. I struggled to speak. She saw my gums, laced with wire. Ruth reached out one hand to me, led me into her kitchen, sat me down. I tried to repeat two words over and over again but she couldn't understand me.

She brought me a pad and pencil. I couldn't hold the pencil in my swollen right hand. She pulled an old baking sheet from the dish drain and opened a can of Crisco, then Ruth smoothed a thick layer of lard over the aluminum and set it on the table in front of me. With my left index finger I wrote the two words I'd been repeating: *Help me?*

Ruth knelt in front of me and buried her face in my lap. She cried so bitterly I tried to comfort *her,* stroking her hair and smoothing the floral material covering her wide shoulders. "This is why I didn't want to let you in my life," she sobbed. "Because I knew I'd have to look. When it's me I don't have to see it. But when I care about you I have to look. I see it and I don't want to."

Her words confirmed what I'd feared most—I'd asked for too much. I stood up slowly and staggered to the door. Ruth put her hand on the door. "Jess, sit down. Where are you going?" She wiped her eyes with the back of her hand. I looked at her calmly, hiding the crisis of rejection.

"Honey," she stroked my cheek. "I'm so sorry. I just don't want it to be you. C'mon, honey. Please. Come." Ruth guided me to her bedroom. I covered my eyes against the sunlight streaming in her window. She pulled the shades.

Ruth laid me down on her bed. I could feel the embroidered edges of her pillowcases against my cheek. My head hurt even worse when I lay down. I sat up, unable to explain why. Ruth touched the back of my head. I winced in pain. She stared at her hand in horror. It was covered with blood. "Jess," she whispered, "I'm afraid."

My eyes narrowed in anticipation of another rejection. Ruth lifted my hand in both of hers and kissed each bruised knuckle. I wasn't afraid to die in her bed with my hand in hers.

She gently pressed my head against her body. It hurt, but I needed her closeness. Her voice dropped low, like a whisper: "I once read in an old drag magazine about a time, long, long ago, when people like us were honored. If I had the power, Jess, I'd take you back and leave you there with people who would care for you as much as I do. I'd know you were safe, and you'd be loved."

I tried to sit up. "Lean against me, Jess. You need to rest." I moaned as I tried to lay my head against her breastbone. Ruth propped me up with pillows. She curled up between my thighs and stroked my chest with her wide hand. "Shh," she whispered. "I know you're frightened, too, but it's gonna be alright. It's always the worst when they hurt my head. I'm always afraid I'll lose my thoughts, my memories. I'm scared I'll lose me. Is that how you're feeling?" She wiped the tears from my cheeks.

I closed my eyes. "Try to stay awake, honey," she pleaded. "Please. I'm afraid for you to fall asleep right now." I wanted to go away. "I'll tell you stories," she smiled. "I'll tell you about where I grew up. Would you like that?"

I blinked back to consciousness and nodded. Ruth rested her cheek against my chest and squeezed me tight. "Oh, Jess. I wish I could show you the vineyards. I wish you could smell the grapes in the fall air." Ruth looked up at me and smiled. "Someday I'm going to make you grape pie. After my grandma Anne's and my mama's, I make the best grape pie in the valley." Grape pie didn't sound very good to me, but it didn't matter much at the moment.

Ruth mesmerized me with her voice. "I wish I could show it all to you—how the hills change with the seasons. In the winter, my Uncle Dale could name every tree for me just by the shape of its silhouette outlined against the sky. But it was the vines that brought us out to discover spring. We might not have noticed the smell of the earth thawing if it hadn't been for the work that needed doing. The men trimmed the vines, and we tied them to the locust posts.

"The women all working together in the vineyards were the best times of my life, Jess. I know it was hard work lugging those heavy grape trays. But all I remember is talking and laughing together. All the stories seemed to begin with the same sentence: 'Remember the time that. . . .' "

Ruth glanced up to make sure I was awake. "When I was eight or nine, my Uncle Dale tried to take me out with the men to prune the vines. But my mother said no. She and my aunt and my grandma took me to work with them. They already knew my nature."

I stiffened as the pain grew inside my head. Ruth rubbed my chest until the hurt subsided. "I remember my Uncle Dale told my mother I needed a man around. My dad died when I was so young. Dale used to come by to take me hunting. Mostly we just walked in the woods. He taught me to respect Bare Hill—that's the birthplace of the Seneca nation. The government cut a road right through the burial grounds there.

"Anyway, Dale seemed to get more and more upset about the way I was growing up. There certainly wasn't anything manly about me, and I think he felt it was his fault. One spring day we were walking on Bare Hill. The clouds were moving fast, throwing shadows over the valley and the lake as they passed. Uncle Dale seemed so disgusted with me I thought he'd stop taking me on those walks.

"At the top of the hill I saw a man whose hair was long and chocolate brown, like muck. Someday I'll show you the land we call muck—it's very fertile and very beautiful. They stood there talking. Then Dale nodded toward me and said, 'I'm trying to teach the boy to be a man.' His voice sounded like he'd already failed. I felt so ashamed standing there, this stranger hearing the disappointment in my uncle's voice at the same moment I did.

"But the man put his hand on my uncle's shoulder and he said, 'Let the child be.' After a minute Dale hung his head and nodded. He looked at me different after that, like he was seeing me for the first time."

Ruth cried softly against my stomach. I ran my fingers through her hair. "I wanted him to love me so much. And after that he did. I knew he cared about me before, but I didn't think he'd be able to accept that I wasn't growing up to be a man. But after that day we didn't pretend to hunt anymore. We just went for walks. He loved those hills more than any human being. I was so proud he'd take me up there with him."

She reached for a Kleenex and blew her nose. "Want to hear something funny?" she smiled. "Years later I reminded him about the man we met on the hill and Uncle Dale told me it never happened like that. He said it must have been one of the spirits of the Senecas who walk those hills. I didn't know if it really happened or not. I do know that something changed between me and Dale that day, and I know it was real hard for him to admit."

I rolled my head gently against the pillows until I found a place on my skull that didn't hurt. My eyelids fluttered. "Jess, fight to stay awake, honey. Please. Wake up, Jess." That's the last thing I heard her say before I lost consciousness.

In the days that followed I drifted in and out of awareness. A woman came into the bedroom with Ruth. Their hands felt reassuring on my body. Ruth propped me up while the woman cleaned a spot on my scalp that hurt real bad. When she was done she wrapped my whole head in gauze. Ruth helped me sit up and urged me to drink through a straw. I saw my blood was everywhere: sponge-print circles on the wall behind the bed, soaked stains in Ruth's beautiful embroidered pillow cases.

As the days passed I could hear the sound of Ruth's weeping replace the steady hum of her sewing machine. Even in a state of semiconsciousness I knew I asked too much of Ruth this time. My blood was all over her life, and the stains weren't going to scrub out.

One morning I felt her lips on my forehead and opened my eyes. I forgot about my jaw and tried to speak. When I couldn't, I grabbed my face. She put her hands over mine. "It's OK, honey. You're getting better. Look at me. Let me see your eyes." She held my head between her hands as though it was a crystal ball. When I saw her expression I wondered what had made me think I had to ask for her love.

She dropped her eyes. "I've done something terrible. Jess, I was just trying to help. I let myself in next door and found the name of the company where you work on the check stubs you keep on the kitchen table. I thought if I called you in sick, you might be able to keep your job. I told them you got mugged and you'd be out for a week or two. Jess, I referred to you as *she.* I wasn't thinking. They heard it. I'm so sorry. I know it means I lost that job for you."

Ruth touched my face. "I know you must be really mad at me." I shook my head. It was a mistake, that's all. I thought about Duffy, the union organizer who'd done the same thing, and I forgave him in retrospect.

I fluttered my hand to ask for something to write with. Ruth came back with a pen and paper. My right hand was stiff and sore, but the words I wrote were legible—the message life had given me another chance to deliver. Ruth read the words out loud: *Thank you for your love.* And then we cried together.

I visited the graphic arts employment agency in person and wrote down that I was looking for work. I started a new job the same night. That's when I realized I'd become a valuable typesetter. Christmas was a month and a half away and the third shift could hardly handle the volume of work the ad agencies were sending over. I took all the overtime they offered. I wanted a chunk of money, fast.

At night I lived inside the coding strings, my face illuminated by the ghostly light of the terminal. The code phrases became my poetry. The curves of type against space sang to me: the melody meant everything, the words meant very little.

At dawn I worked out at the gym, pausing only when the throbbing in my head frightened me. I moved my will to live down deeper into my body. Since my rage and frustration couldn't escape through my clamped jaws, I screamed through my muscles. I thought I might explode with rage. At first working out at the gym reduced the pressure, but after a while the frenzied workouts became part of it. I was a time bomb, ticking, ticking, moments away from detonation.

I didn't sleep very much, just a few hours in the morning and late afternoon. I feared losing consciousness, afraid I'd never find my way back.

Ruth seemed worried about how much time I spent away from the apartment. I could tell by the relief on her face every day when I knocked on her door to check in with her. "Where do you go?" she'd sigh as she poured me a protein shake. I could tell she didn't expect an answer.

Restlessness drew me to Far Rockaway beach on a cold December morning. As

I walked along the shore I thought about how fear and silence had welded my jaw shut for more of my life than I'd realized. I wondered if silence had killed Rocco, and the anonymous butler, a little bit at a time, too. What would I say when I finally snipped the wires that held my jaws clamped?

The lobster-shift foreman handed me the last check I needed two days before the Christmas weekend. In the morning I'd go to the check-cashing office, flash my company card, and walk out with all the money I needed to buy the gift for Ruth.

I snuck into the lunchroom without punching out and slipped between the two vending machines in the corner that formed my favorite hiding place at work, carefully leaning my head against the wall. The headaches were milder, but they still frightened me.

I heard Marija and Karen, both typesetters, come into the lunchroom, laughing. "You got change?" Marija asked. I sat very still, afraid of being discovered.

Marija's hands always captured my attention. Some people drag their hands through life like heavy weights; others speak with their hands. But Marija's hands were different. Although they communicated, they seemed to be carrying on an entirely separate conversation than the one she was verbally engaged in. When she talked with other typesetters, she laughed nervously and chewed her lip. But her hands were calm. While her words cut cruelly to the quick, her hands found the sore places on a coworker's shoulder or neck. I imagined feeling those remarkable hands stroking my head, caressing my neck.

"I tell you it's creepy," Marija said, "the way he looks at me."

"Who?" Karen asked.

Marija sighed. "That guy who never talks–Jesse. I'm telling you the way he stares at me creeps me out."

Karen laughed. "Maybe he's got the hots for you."

"Yecch!" Marija said. "He looks at me like I'm a piece of meat or something."

"He's harmless," Karen chuckled.

"You don't know that," Marija countered. "He could be a psycho."

Karen interrupted. "He's so effeminate. He's gotta be gay."

I heard them leaving. "I'm telling you," Marija concluded, "he's the kind you gotta watch out for." I could see Marija's hand gently rest on the small of Karen's back. I closed my eyes and waited until I was sure they were gone. Then I walked out of the shop knowing I would never return.

When I got home I leaned the bathroom mirror up against the couch and found a pair of scissors and tweezers. I took a couple of long pulls of whiskey through a straw before I cut each wire that laced my gums shut. I pulled each segment out with a sure stroke, the way I pulled off old bandaids—not fast, not slow, just steady. After I was sure I'd gotten the last piece of wire out of my gums, I rinsed my mouth with whiskey and then drank the rest of it so I could sleep without remembering how Marija's words had stripped me of my humanity.

When I awoke I walked up to 34th Street, maneuvering in the throng of shoppers like a warrior. I knew exactly what I was looking for. *The best sewing machine you have,* I wrote on a piece of paper and handed it to the saleswoman. And then I realized my jaw wasn't wired shut anymore. Silence had become a habit.

She led me to the display models. They all looked pretty much the same—except for one. I didn't sew, but I knew it was the right machine when she pointed to it. It glinted in the light like a motorcycle. The saleswoman talked to me about attachments and the endless things it could do. I smiled, not understanding a word. I could already see Ruth hunched over this magnificent machine, stitching her magic into fabric. As I paid for it in cash I felt excitement, something I hadn't felt in a long time.

A light snow fell as I lugged the machine back through the crowded streets and hailed a cab.

As soon as I got home I cleaned my apartment with a vengeance. When the house sparkled I realized that I was filthy. I took a long, hot shower, letting the water soften my jaw so it didn't click each time I opened my mouth. I dried off and put on a clean white T-shirt and khaki chinos. While I combed my hair, I caught sight of myself in the kitchen mirror. My eyes looked so sad I couldn't meet my own gaze. My face seemed much older than I'd remembered it. I ran my fingertips over the muscles that rippled across my shoulders and chest and arms. Suddenly all those long hours at the gym seemed to be proof of my will to live. I'd sent myself a gift—a memory of body, of self.

I shopped on Grand Street for handmade Chinese wrapping paper. I pointed to what I needed. I still didn't speak.

The first words I spoke were to Ruth. I knocked on her door on Christmas Eve. "Jess, where were you? I was scared silly. Come on in. Tanya and Esperanza are here." I didn't move. "Are you OK?" She looked worried.

I moved my jaw slightly. "Ruth." Tears welled up in her eyes when she heard my voice. "Thank you," I told her. "Thank you for everything you've done for me." We pressed our foreheads together.

"I'm sorry," I said. "I know it was an awful lot to ask."

"Hush," she whispered.

"Ruth, I love you."

"Shh, I know." She held my face in her cupped hands. "I love you too, honey." Ruth pulled me close against her body. We hugged as though we'd never let go.

"Ooh, let me have some of that," Tanya said. "Come in here, boy."

Ruth smiled and shook her head. "Jess is a B-girl," she told Tanya. I hadn't heard that word in many years. *B-girl*—the old code word femmes used in public to refer to butches when they were afraid of being overheard. There was so much about Ruth I still didn't know.

"Ooh, honey," Tanya looked me up and down appreciatively. "I could swing for you, girl."

Ruth introduced me to Esperanza. "*Mucho gusto,*" Esperanza whispered in a voice as complicated as Ruth's and mine. Esperanza blushed as I kissed her hand. "We're trimming the tree. You want to help us?" She handed me tinsel.

I smiled shyly. "I never did this before."

Esperanza frowned. "You never decorated a Christmas tree before?" I shook my head. "You didn't have Christmas when you were a child?" I shook my head again. "Too poor?"

I laughed. My jaw clicked as I answered. "Too Jewish."

Ruth offered me a cookie she'd just decorated. "It's still warm so it's soft. It's gingerbread. Try it. Just a bite." I rediscovered taste. "We're making cookies to take to friends who are stuck in the hospital with AIDS."

Up until that moment I had felt as though the epidemic was taking place a million miles away from me. "Can I go with?" I asked.

Ruth sighed heavily. "Yes, if you want to."

Tanya offered me a mug. "This is Tanya's killer eggnog. If this don't give you the holiday spirit nothing will."

Ruth wiped her hands on her apron. "Take it easy with that stuff."

Tanya made a face at her. "Don't listen to her. Just cause she's a friend of Bill W's doesn't mean we all have to hang out with him."

"We're going out to a drag club later tonight. You want to come?" Esperanza asked. I looked at Ruth. She smiled and shrugged.

"I'll teach you to bump and grind on the dance floor, honey," Tanya said.

I laughed. "I'll show you a thing or two on the dance floor."

"Lord have mercy," Tanya fanned herself with her large hand. "Kill me now."

Esperanza smiled. "I'll teach you an old slave dance, the merengue."

I remembered Ruth's present. "I'll be right back," I said. When I lugged the heavy rectangular present into her living room Ruth sat down heavily on the couch as though she'd been hit with bad news. "It's for you," I smiled.

"Open it, girl," Tanya urged.

Ruth chewed her lip. "You shouldn't have."

All my love was in my smile. "Oh, hush."

She sighed, opened the paper carefully, folded it, and put it aside. When Ruth took the cover off the sewing machine she gasped. I could tell by the way her fingers trailed across the machine how happy it made her. "I'll make you a suit," she whispered.

I beamed. "Really?" Ruth nodded and bit her knuckles. She stood up and walked over to the half-decorated evergreen. "These are for you," she handed me two flat packages.

The first was a book called *Gay American History.* My hands trembled as I leafed through the pages.

"Look," Ruth took the book from my hands and turned to the index. "Remember I told you about what I read in a drag magazine about how people like us used to be honored? Look at this whole section about Native societies. But, wait, look at this." She flipped the pages. "This whole part is about women like you who lived as men."

Tears clouded my vision.

Esperanza looked at the title and shook her head. "I wish we weren't always lumped into gay."

"Hush," Ruth shook her head. She handed me a package wrapped in red tissue paper. "Open this." Inside was a watercolor of a face filled with emotion, looking up at a host of stars. It was a beautiful face, a face I'd never seen before. It was my face.

"Let me see that, honey," Tanya reached for it. "Ooh, Ruth. That's nice. That looks just like him."

"Ruth," I chewed my lip. "Do I really look like this?"

She nodded and smiled through her tears. "When I thought you might die, I started to sketch your face. I wanted something more than my memories of you to remain. Your eyes were closed, but I could shut my own and remember the way the color of your eyes changes in the light."

Ruth sat down next to me on the couch. We put our arms around each other and rocked. Esperanza and Tanya sat on the floor near us.

My chin ached and trembled. "You know," I told them, "I've been searching for you all for such a long time. I can't believe I've finally found you." I squeezed Ruth tightly in my arms as we both cried.

Esperanza rested her hand on my thigh. "Do you know what my name means?"

I shook my head. "No, but it sure is pretty."

She smiled and looked me at me with a sure, unwavering expression. "*Esperanza*," she explained—"it means hope."

CHAPTER 24

It was the first day of spring, when everyone who lives in this city agrees to feel good at the same time—a day when it seems as though every woman, man, and child is flirting with my difference. I browsed at the farmer's market in Union Square, killing time. The sun dipped behind the buildings to the west of the island. Ruth made me promise not to come home until late afternoon. It was time to discover my surprise.

I knocked on my own door and waited for Ruth to answer it. She wiped her hands on a cloth and led me into my bedroom. "Close your eyes," she urged. "Remember you told me I could do anything I wanted to to it?" I smiled and nodded. "OK, open your eyes." I looked around and then up at the ceiling—there it was.

I sat down on my bed and fell back to look at the ceiling. Ruth had painted it velvety black with pinpoints of constellations I recognized. The darkness softened to light around the edges. I could see the outline of trees against the sky.

Ruth lay down next to me. "Do you like it?"

"It's just incredible. I can't believe you've given me the sky to sleep under. But I can't tell if it's dawn or dusk you've painted."

She smiled up at the ceiling. "It's neither. It's both. Does that unnerve you?"

I nodded slowly. "Yeah, in a funny way it does."

"I figured that," she said. "It's the place inside of me I have to accept. I thought it might be what you need to deal with, too."

I sighed. "I really do have trouble not being able to figure out if what you've painted is about to be day or about to be night."

Ruth rolled toward me and rested her hand on my chest. "It's not going to be day or night, Jess. It's always going to be that moment of infinite possibility that connects them."

Ruth's face was very close to mine. We became aware of the symmetry of our breathing. She slid her hand slowly along my body from my chest to my stomach. She dropped her eyes. I chewed my lip. "I'm afraid," I answered the question she hadn't asked out loud.

"Why?" she asked. "Because I'm neither night nor day?" I squeezed my eyes shut. I knew I would lose her if I wasn't honest; I knew I might lose her if I was.

"Yes," I told her. "That's part of it. Remember your geometric theory? More than double the trouble?"

Ruth rolled onto her back. "I'm not suggesting we do it in the road."

I stared up at my sky. "You know what I mean. But that's only part of it. If I really have to be honest, it's because I'm afraid not to be with someone who is night or day. I guess I felt like the femmes I was with anchored me. It was the closest to normal I've ever felt."

Ruth curled up into my arm. "Were you her dawn or her dusk?"

I smiled sadly. "In the beginning I was her dawn. By the end I was her twilight." We both sighed.

"You want more truth, Ruth? There's a place somewhere inside of me where I've never been touched before. I'm afraid you'll touch me there. And I'm afraid you won't. My femme lovers knew me well, but they never crossed those boundaries inside of me. They tried to coax me across the borders into their arms, but they never came after me. You're right there with me. There's no place for me to hide. It scares me."

Ruth smiled sadly. "Isn't it funny? That's exactly why I would like to make love with you."

We lay quietly. I kissed her hair. "Oh, Ruth, I haven't had to navigate sex in a long time, with anyone. I don't even know who I am as a lover anymore. But I'm scared you'll leave me now. Can't we figure it out as we go along? Please stay in my life. I need you so much."

Ruth got up on one elbow and kissed my lips. "I need you, too." I held one of her hands, marveling at how small mine looked in hers. She dropped her eyes while I kissed each one of her knuckles.

"I've been thinking a lot about my life since my jaw got broken," I told her. "I once read about warriors who resolve before they go into battle that 'Today is a good day to die.' "

Ruth smiled. "It's a brave thought, but I don't want to die."

I nodded. "At first I thought it meant resigning myself to death. But now I think it means facing my own life at the moment I'm facing my enemy. Maybe that's the key to fighting fearlessly, to surviving. I've left a lot of things unfinished in my life. It makes me more afraid to die. It holds me back in a fight."

Ruth frowned. "Like what?"

"I always wanted to leave something important behind. Remember the history book you gave me for Christmas?" Ruth nodded. "I've been going to the library, looking up our history. There's a ton of it in anthropology books, a ton of it, Ruth. We haven't always been hated. Why didn't we grow up knowing that?"

Ruth propped herself up on her elbow and watched my face as I spoke. "It's changed the way I think. I grew up believing the way things are now is the way they've always been, so why even bother trying to change the world? But just finding out that it was ever different, even if it was long ago, made me feel things could change again. Whether or not I live to see it.

"At work, when everyone else is at lunch, I've been typesetting all the history I've found, trying to make it look as important as it feels to me. That's what I want to leave behind, Ruth—the history of this ancient path we're walking. I want it to help us restore our dignity." Ruth pressed my hand to her lips.

"But I want more, Ruth. There's things I've been afraid to face in my life. They may sound small, but they hold me back from pride. Remember when I told you about Butch Al? I want to find out what really happened to her.

"And there's a butch I once put down because I couldn't deal with the fact that she got turned on by other butches. I thought being butch automatically meant being attracted to femmes, just like I assumed transvestism meant gay."

Ruth smiled. "It's an easy misunderstanding. You were hanging out in gay bars."

I nodded. "Yeah, but I always wanted all of us who were different to be the same. I can't believe I rejected a butch friend because she took a butch lover. I want to tell Frankie I'm sorry."

Ruth kissed my cheek. "Anything else?"

I nodded. "Yeah. There were two little kids—Kim and Scotty. I promised I'd come back and find them someday. Oh, and there's one more thing I need to do."

Ruth ran her fingers through my hair. "What?"

I lay back and stared into the universe on the ceiling. "I want to write a letter to Theresa, a woman I still carry around in my heart. We parted in a real rough way. I want to finally find the words, even if she never reads them."

My eyelids felt heavy. Ruth curled up against me as I yawned. "You'll find the words," she reassured me.

I sighed. "First I have to let my own memories come back. I put them away somewhere because they hurt. Now I have to remember where I put them."

The breeze from the window chilled me. I pulled the tie quilt over both of us and snuggled up against Ruth. She felt warm and comforting beside me. "Sleepy?" she asked me.

I nodded. "Stay with me for a while, Ruth. Please?" She nodded. I buried my face in her neck.

She stroked my hair and kissed my forehead. "Sleep now, my sweet drag king."

I almost hung up when I heard Frankie's voice on the other end of the phone. "It's me—Jess. Do you remember me, Frankie?" That's all I could think of to say.

There was a long silence. "Jess? Jesus, is that really you? It's been a long time."

I cleared my throat. "Yeah, it has been. Listen, Frankie, I really want to talk to you. If you don't want to, I'll understand. But I owe you an apology, and it's long overdue. I'd like to offer it to you in person, if you'll see me. I'm living in New York City now, but I could come to Buffalo."

Another long silence. "You know something, Jess? I'm still mad at you, but not as mad as you're afraid I am. And I'll tell you something else. It matters to me that you called to say that. I'll be in Manhattan on the 15th, at the labor college. I could meet you at the Duchess for a drink around 11:00."

I paused. "Is that the lesbian bar in Sheridan Square?"

"Yeah."

"Well, I don't know if they'll let me in. Can I meet you outside the bar?"

"Sure," Frankie said. "I'll see you then."

When the night finally arrived I paced under a streetlamp outside the bar chewing my thumbnail. I saw Frankie approach from across the street. We stood awkwardly. Neither of us knew where to begin. I reached out my hand; she shook it. I found our shared past in her grasp.

I'd forgotten how much I love butches until I looked at her standing there—the defensive defiance of her stance, one hand jammed in her trouser pocket, her head cocked to the side.

I don't know which shocked me more, the ways Frankie had changed or how much she looked exactly the way I remembered her. Strange to see soft wrinkles in that freckled teenage face, silver hairs among the wiry red ones. "It's good to see you, Frankie."

She scuffed her shoe against the pavement. "It's good to see you, too."

I tried to keep my lower lip from trembling. "I don't just mean it's nice to see you, Frankie. Just looking at you is bringing back a whole part of my life I really need right now. It's really good to see you."

I opened my arms and we hugged each other tight, then we wrestled playfully. I scuffed her hair, she punched my shoulder. "Jess, no matter what went down in the past, we're still from the old days. You still matter to me," Frankie said.

I thought that was such a generous thing to say. "You ever see anyone from the old crowd?" I asked.

She nodded. "I see Grant a lot."

"What about Theresa?" I held my breath.

Frankie shook her head. "You remember Butch Jan? She and her lover got a flower shop on Elmwood Avenue—Blue Violets. I can't think of anybody else, except for Duffy. You remember Duffy, the union organizer?"

I smiled. "Yeah, I remember Duffy."

Frankie leaned forward. "You don't know how sorry he was that he fucked up that job for you. He really didn't mean it, Jess."

I nodded. "Yeah, I know he didn't. I want his phone number, if you've got it. I'd like to talk to him, too." Frankie nodded.

We stood in shy silence. "Frankie, I'm sorry. I always thought I was so open-minded. But when I came up against my own fears, I tried to separate myself from you. I've done some growing up since then. I can't take it back, but I'm real sorry."

Frankie gestured with her thumb toward the Duchess. "You don't know if they'll let you in there? Well in our day I was afraid if I showed who turned me on my own people would shut the door in my face. That's a terrible way to feel. I'm sorry that's happening to you now. Shit, Jess, what hurt the most is I respected you. I wanted you to respect me."

I rubbed the sadness out of my eyes. "Well, you deserved it. C'mon," I took her by the shoulder. "Let's go to the piers." We walked slowly down Christopher Street toward the Hudson River. "You know, Frankie, when we were younger, I thought I had it figured out: I'm a butch because I love femmes. That was something beautiful. Nobody ever honored our love. You scared me. I felt like you were taking that away from me."

Frankie shook her head. "I wasn't taking anything from you. But how do you think I felt when you told me I wasn't a real butch because I sleep with other butches? You were taking away who I am. Jesus, Jess, when I walk down the street guys fuck with me. I don't have to prove I'm butch to them. How come I got to prove it to you?"

I shook my head. "You don't." I put my arm around her shoulder. We crossed the West Side highway and walked to the end of the pier. The full moon illuminated the clouds. Light shimmered on the dark water.

Frankie's voice dropped low. "Jess, which old bull really brought you out?"

I smiled at her memory. "Butch Al, from Niagara Falls."

"For me it was Grant," Frankie said.

"Grant?" I remembered Grant as a mean drunk who could offend everyone.

Frankie watched my face. "Grant meant the world to me. She taught me that I am what I am, that I got nothing to prove. It was a very liberating concept for a baby butch."

I smiled gently. "I never thought of Grant as very liberated—not that any of us were."

Frankie nodded. "Grant never took her own wisdom to heart. She's a prisoner of her shame, but she didn't want us young ones to end up like her. She only seduced baby butches when she got real drunk. But I never felt like we made her happy. I think she has some secret passion that scares the shit out of her."

I frowned. "Like what?"

Frankie shrugged. "I think she's horrified by something inside of her she thinks is twisted, like maybe she fantasizes about being with strong old bulls, or men or something. Poor Grant. I wish she'd let me in. I love that old bulldagger so much."

We sat in silence, listening to the waves lapping against the pilings beneath us. Frankie sighed. "You know, Jess, I never learned to love myself until I gave in to loving other butches."

I laughed. "I don't know why, but I have this image of you sleeping with a different femme every week."

Frankie nodded without smiling. "I thought that was what I was supposed to do. Inside my head I was asking each one: *Could you love me? Do you love me? Am I loveable?* Of course, the minute they did care about me I knew I couldn't respect their judgment so I moved on to the next. God, I was a shit to femmes."

Frankie looked out over the water. "It was only when I finally admitted it was butch hands I wanted on my body that everything changed for me. The more I saw what I loved about other butches, the more I began to accept myself. You know who gets it for me, Jess?" I smiled and shook my head. "An old bull with graying hair, a cocky smile, and sad eyes. You know the kind of butch with arms as big as your thigh? Those are the arms I want to hold me."

I ran my fingertips over the dark wood near my thigh. "I love them so much, too. But what gets it for me is high femme. It's funny—it doesn't matter whether it's women or men—it's always high femme that pulls me by the waist and makes me sweat."

Frankie rested her hand on my arm. "You and I have to hammer out a definition of butch that doesn't leave me out. I'm sick of hearing *butch* used to mean sexual aggression or courage. If that's what butch means, what does it mean in reverse for femmes?"

I shook my head. "I never thought about it like that. But I have to admit that when you told me about you and Johnny, the first thing I wondered was, who's the femme in bed?"

Frankie leaned forward. "Neither of us were. What you meant was who does the fucking and who gets fucked? Who ran the fuck? That's not the same as being butch or femme, Jess."

Frankie moved closer to me and touched my shoulder. I tensed. "Relax," she whispered, "I'm not coming on to you, Jess."

"I'm sorry. I'm not so used to getting touched."

Frankie's hands kneaded the soreness from my shoulders. "You know, I have a confession to make. I used to have a crush on you in the old days."

I laughed nervously. "Oh shit. I was just starting to relax with you."

She patted me on the back. "You'll get over it." Frankie rubbed my neck. "You were like a fucking legend when you started to pass. What's it like, Jess?"

I shrugged. "I don't know. Just trying to survive has pulled me through, but it hasn't left much leisure to think about it."

"Am I so different from you?" She whispered her thought out loud.

"You have to decide that. To me we're still kin."

A cruise ship passed; laughter from the people on deck floated across the water. I sat, facing New Jersey, with Frankie's hands on my shoulders. "Are you still with Johnny?"

I felt her body sink against mine. "It's hard for two butches, Jess. It's very hard."

I sighed and nodded. "Hey, Frankie. When two butches are together—like lovers I mean—do they talk about their feelings?"

"Feelings?" Frankie asked. "What are those?" We both chuckled, warm and relaxed. We laughed harder and harder, until tears streamed down our cheeks. For the first time since she touched me, I relaxed my body against Frankie's. I allowed myself to enjoy the strength of her arms around me.

"You know, Frankie," I whispered. "There's things that happened to me because I'm a he-she that I've never talked about to a femme. I've never had the words."

Frankie nodded. "You don't need words with me, Jess. I know."

I shook my head. "I do need words, Frankie. Sometimes I feel like I'm choking to death on what I'm feeling. I need to talk and I don't even know how. Femmes always tried to teach me to talk about my feelings, but it was their words they used for their feelings. I needed my own words—butch words to talk about butch feelings."

Frankie pulled me tighter. Tears welled up in my eyes. "I feel like I'm clogged up with all this toxic goo, Frankie. But I can't hear my own voice say the words out loud. I've got no language."

Frankie opened her arms wider, took more of me in. I leaned my face against her arm. She offered me refuge, the way I held Butch Al years ago in a jail cell. "Frankie, I've got no words for feelings that are tearing me apart. What would our words sound like?" I looked up at the sky. "Like thunder, maybe."

Frankie pressed her lips against my hair. "Yeah, like thunder. And yearning."

I smiled and kissed the hard muscle of her biceps. "Yearning," I repeated softly. "What a beautiful word to hear a butch say out loud."

CHAPTER 25

"You make your own trip to Buffalo, and I'll make my own trip home," Ruth insisted.

"But why?" I couldn't understand why she refused Esperanza's offer to lend us her car. "You said you haven't been home since your grandma died. You've been saying you should visit. I could see where you're from. I want to see the lake and the hills and the vineyards you talk so much about."

Ruth sighed. "To you it's pretty. But I escaped to save my life. It's not easy for me to go back there. I want to do it alone."

I shook my head. "I'll just drop you off and get back on the Thruway to Buffalo. Where we're going is only two hours apart, and I can't drive without a license. We could pass as a nice married couple."

Ruth made a face. "Jess, you don't understand. You can't just drive up to someone's house and let them off and drive away. I've got to introduce you. They'll offer you coffee."

I grew sullen. "Oh, now I understand."

Ruth's anger flared. "No you don't. I'm not ashamed of you." Her voice dropped. "I'm ashamed of them sometimes." I started to protest but she held up one hand to stop me. "It's a no-win situation. If you like them a lot, I'll be angry with you for not understanding why it was so hard for me to grow up with them. And if you don't like them, I'll despise you for not recognizing their worth."

I shrugged. "OK, I get that it's complicated. I'll drop the subject. But I'm going to Buffalo to visit. I've got to face some things and find my memories."

Although I didn't discuss it further, we both knew the subject wasn't dropped. I kept putting off my trip, partly because I knew it could be painful, but mostly because I still hoped Ruth would come with me.

In early September I asked Esperanza if I could borrow her car to make the trip. Ruth puttered around the kitchen pretending not to hear us.

Days before I left I brought Ruth a half-gallon of mulled cider. She sat down in a kitchen chair next to me and stared at her mug. "When I get beat up," she began in a quiet voice, "it's always worse when it's visible. It means other people can see I've been hurt. That's humiliating to me."

I waited for her to continue. "My people aren't bad," she said. "I love them more since I left. They love me the best way they know how. I'm family. But it's hard, and I don't want anyone who's not family to see it. I think they'd make you feel welcome as a guest, but I'm not sure. If they were unkind to you, I'd hate them for it. They're not cruel. But it's a big risk for me because I could never forgive them if they hurt you."

I stirred my cider with a cinnamon stick. "When are we leaving, Ruth?"

She looked surprised. "I didn't say we were going."

I smiled and nodded. "Yes you did, honey. Neither of us wrestle that hard with things we're not ready to take on."

Ruth sighed and patted my hand. "Thursday."

The world is our restroom! That was our motto on the trip upstate. We brought plenty of toilet paper so we wouldn't need to risk a rest stop. We left the city well before dawn on our six-hour trek. By the time the sun shone, I was so happy we'd made this difficult trip together.

Ruth packed muenster cheese sandwiches with sun-dried tomatoes and arugula on freshly baked bread. We drank quarts of ice tea. *The world is our restroom!* We laughed.

Ruth's face softened as I drove. She called out the names of all the beautiful wild weeds. The anxiety of Manhattan melted into the distance behind us. The upcoming tension was hundreds of miles ahead. Somewhere between here and there Ruth and I really met each other all over again.

As we finally turned off the Thruway and headed toward Canandaigua Lake, Ruth grew visibly excited. "See?" she pointed to a condominium development. "That used to be Roseland Amusement Park. Pull over. Let me drive now." Ruth knew those roads like the veins on her hands.

We passed fields of sunflowers. "That's a new crop since I grew up here." I recognized the goldenrod and purple asters that Ruth captured as memories in her watercolors.

She pulled over near the lake and parked in a space no wider than three car widths. "I could never figure out if this lake mirrored my mood swings or if my moods reflected the changes in the lake. Every square inch around the lake is private now except for two little spaces like this one and the patch behind the country store. They're even posting the hills now."

She turned the key in the ignition and backed the car out. "The summer people killed my daddy." Her voice was flat and cold. "A couple in a car stopped on a hairpin curve to watch the deer. My daddy swerved to avoid them. Went off the road right over there." We drove past in silence. "I hate the summer people. Only problem is, my mama's one of them." I didn't speak. Ruth knew what she was and wasn't willing to say. "Of course, my mama was a renter. Her people weren't yuppies. She fell in love with my daddy before the summer passed. But if you loved that man, you knew he'd never leave this valley. He and my Uncle Dale hear the hills calling them like lovers."

Ruth smiled. "Funny thing. My mama's a city girl, but after my daddy died she stayed here in these hills he loved. I'm like him. My heart's in these hills, but I left for the city."

We pulled up in front of a small home at the edge of a woods. A golden Labrador retriever barked and clawed at the screen door as Ruth turned off the ignition. "This is Dale's place." She handed me a piece of paper. "Here are directions to pick me up at my mama's house."

I nodded. We sat in the car until our arrival was acknowledged. "Robbie!" I heard Dale call out to Ruth. "Robbie, you're home!"

Ruth sighed. We both got out of the car. I watched how their bodies fit as they hugged, how their hands knew each other's back and shoulders. Ruth pulled away. "Dale, this is my friend, Jess. She lives in Manhattan, too."

The dog jumped up and licked my face. Dale pulled his collar. "Bone, get off of him. Where's your manners?" Dale shook my hand. His hand was hard and calloused within his gentle grip. "You all want some coffee? I just made some fresh."

My eyes lit up. Ruth shook her head. "You best be going," she told me. "You think you can find your way back to the Thruway?"

I laughed. "Yeah, follow the lake and make a left at the sunflowers."

"You sure you don't want to come in and rest up a little while?" Dale asked. I looked at Ruth. Her face was resolutely impassive.

"Thank you, Dale. But I still got a chunk of driving to do. I'm headed to Buffalo. Maybe I'll see you when I drive back to pick up Ruth." I froze. Did I make a mistake by calling her Ruth?

Dale nodded. "Well, you be sure to stop in around suppertime if you do. I'll make Dale's famous fried zucchini for you. Robbie'll tell you I make it real good. I got some killer zucchini out of my garden this year."

Ruth sighed. I took it as my cue to leave. I got back in the car and started it up.

Dale still held onto Bone's collar and waved with his other hand. Ruth looked at me with soulful eyes.

The streets of Buffalo were as familiar as my own reflection in the mirror.

I pulled up in front of the apartment building where Theresa and I had lived. Her name wasn't on the mailbox anymore. I walked around back, half expecting to find my young self still sitting on a milk crate staring up at the sky, straining for a glimpse of her own future. Here I was, back searching for her.

A memory suddenly gripped me: the look of pain in Theresa's eyes the night I was arrested in Rochester. I covered my face with my hands so I wouldn't see it, but the image was behind my eyes. Let it come, I thought to myself. It's all in there anyway. Let it come up.

I walked to a pay phone on the corner and called information. I wanted to keep the promise I had made to Kim and Scotty to come back and visit. I remembered how my coming had shaken Kim, root and branch, and my leaving had hurt her most. Would she remember me? Would Scotty? Did he become the wind? I couldn't find their names in the phone book. Maybe they still lived at home with Gloria. Her number was listed.

Gloria couldn't figure out who I was. "Jess Goldberg," I repeated. "We worked together at the print shop. You let me stay at your house. I'm back in town for a day or two, and I wanted to see Kim and Scotty."

There was a long, long silence. Gloria's voice dropped to a hoarse whisper. "You leave my children alone. Do you hear me?" The phone went dead in my hand. I stared at the receiver, stunned. Slowly I began to realize that Gloria held the power to keep me from finding the kids. I called back. She hung up on me again. I slapped the glass wall of the phone booth with my open hand over and over until it stung and burned. Then I kicked the glass as hard as I could. A police cruiser pulled over to the curb. "What's going on?" a cop called out to me.

I took a deep breath. "Sorry. I just lost some money in it."

"Let's take it easy, son. It's just a quarter." He waved and drove off. When he was out of sight I kicked the glass over and over again. I told myself I'd find Kim and Scotty, even if I couldn't figure out how at the moment.

The operator gave me the address and phone number for Butch Jan's store on Elmwood Avenue. Brass bells tinkled as I opened the door to her flower shop. I could smell the perfume of roses and lilies.

"Can I help you?" A familiar face looked up at me. We both stood transfixed. "Edna." I whispered her name out loud. Her face froze. I couldn't figure out what she was doing there, working behind the counter. And then I remembered she was Butch Jan's ex-lover. They must be together again.

It wasn't fair! I could understand if Edna left me because she couldn't be with anyone. But then how could she be with Jan? Questions made my face burn: Does she touch Jan? Was it just me she didn't want? How come everybody else is getting a happily-ever-after?

It hurt so much to see her standing there I wanted to run outside and get back in the car and go. But I discovered an important piece of my dignity in the way I held my body and in the soft strength in my voice as I whispered, "Hello, Edna."

She came out from behind the counter and started toward me. I stiffened my body involuntarily. She paused. "Jess. I've thought about you so many times."

I felt my anger rise up to block her words from penetrating my defenses. "I came to see Jan. Is she here?"

Edna chewed her lower lip. "She's in the greenhouse out back." The phone rang. I took the opportunity to leave while Edna answered it. I leaned against the cool brick outside the door. I'd thought the pain might splatter me all over the walls of the shop, but it hadn't. It just hurt, a lot.

Did Jan know Edna and I had been lovers? I'd soon find out.

The greenhouse looked like a grownup's playhouse—a self-contained world. Humidity fogged the glass inside. I opened the door and stepped over the threshold. My boots sank into the wet straw strewn on the floor. I took a deep breath and inhaled the good smell of damp earth.

Jan bent over a crate of violets. I recognized her strong, broad shoulders. Her hair had turned to silver. She rose and looked at me. Her glasses rested on top of her head. She slid them down to her nose. "Am I getting so old I can't trust my own eyes?" she asked. "Is that really you, Jess?" She wiped her hands on a towel and welcomed me into her arms. Jan stroked my hair and kissed my head as I cried. "I've thought about you so many times," she whispered.

My lip quivered. "I didn't really believe I lived in anyone's memory except my own."

Jan patted my cheek. "I could never forget you. You were one of those baby butches I knew I'd grow old with. How long you here for? Where are you living? How'd you find this place?"

"Manhattan," I answered. "Frankie told me about your shop. There's something I need to find out while I'm here, if I can. I want to find out whatever happened to Butch Al. I want to find out if she's still alive."

Jan rubbed her face and sucked in her breath. "Well, if anyone could find out, it's Edna. Did you see Edna?" I watched Jan's face as I nodded. "Edna's still in touch with Lydia, whose butch worked at the auto plant with Al for a long time."

My voice rose. "Do you think Lydia knows?"

Jan shrugged. "She might. And Edna knows how to find Lydia."

I took a deep breath. "Would you ask Edna if she'd find out?"

I watched Jan's face as she said, "Sure, I'd be happy to." That's when I knew for sure Jan didn't know Edna and I had been lovers. "Tell you what," Jan smiled, "what say we all get together tonight for a drink?"

It sounded excruciatingly painful, and unavoidable. I nodded. "Maybe Frankie would want to come too?"

Jan slapped me on the shoulder. "Good idea." She wrote down the address of the bar.

When Jan opened the greenhouse door, the chilly air startled me. Her pick-up truck was parked in the garage behind the store. Next to it was an old Triumph motorcycle. Jan followed my eyes to the bike. "I haven't ridden it for a long time but I keep it running. You want to use it while you're here?" I smiled and nodded emphatically. It had been years since I straddled a motorcycle. Jan grinned as the bike sputtered to life. She squeezed my shoulder. "You are a sight for sore eyes. It's good to see you, kid." I waited till she was back inside the flower shop before I whispered out loud, "I'm not a kid anymore."

We met that night in a working-class bar on the outskirts of Buffalo. It had been a long time since I'd been in a bar with lesbians. It was still early in the evening, so the place wasn't packed yet. There were about twenty or thirty women in the front room. I figured they'd move into the backroom to dance soon. Was it my imagination or were a few of the young women butch, a few femme?

Everybody looked at me, and then each other, when I walked in, but nobody stopped me. I peeked in the backroom, hoping that Edna wouldn't be there with Jan. She was. They were sitting at a table with Frankie and Grant. Jan rose as I approached the table. "Jess!" I guessed she still didn't know. Edna dropped her eyes as I formally kissed her cheek. Frankie and I hugged. Grant shook my hand. "Well, I'll be damned. Look who's here!" She signaled the waitress. "What's everybody drinking?" Grant asked.

"Just a ginger ale for me," I said. I wanted to be clear-headed, especially with Edna at the table.

"You too good to have a drink with us anymore?" Grant challenged.

"A whiskey," Frankie interrupted. "Straight up, so to speak."

"Two beers, here," Jan said. "Right, honey?" Edna stared at her lap and nodded.

We all sat in the uncomfortable silence.

Jan filled me in. "We're talking about what happened to all the old butches and femmes."

"I think we're sort of underground," I said quietly. My heart was in the conversation Edna and I weren't having. "Waiting for a time when it's safer to come out."

Grant sighed bitterly. "But some of these young kids you can't even tell what they are—goddamn green hair and safety pins in their faces." We all sighed collectively.

"Grant," I shrugged, "who cares?"

"It just isn't right," Grant slapped the tabletop.

I laughed, which made her angrier. "Grant, that's what they said about us!"

"Well, that's different," Grant said with a wave of her hand.

I leaned toward her. "There's a lot of things I couldn't accept when I was younger, Grant, like the fact that there's lots of different ways for butches to be." I watched her expression change. Frankie audibly sucked in her breath. "But now I'm trying to accept people as they are."

Jan tried to change the subject. She leaned over and stroked the arm of my leather jacket. "Nice," she said.

Edna shot me an alarmed look. I fingered the soft, worn leather of Rocco's armor. "Thank you." I closed the subject. Edna exhaled in relief.

"I'm sure glad I didn't do those hormones," Grant announced.

I bit down hard on the plastic bar straw in my mouth. "Why's that, Grant?" I braced myself.

"Well you're sort of stuck now, aren't you? I mean you're not a butch or a guy. You look like a guy."

Everyone at the table stiffened, but no one answered her. I bent the straw into a circle. "Be careful, Grant," I warned her. "You're looking at your own reflection."

Grant laughed. "I ain't like you. I didn't do the change."

My anger was greater than the situation called for. I could taste it, bitter on my tongue. I leaned forward. Everyone held their breath. My voice was low and menacing. "How far are you willing to go, Grant? How much of yourself are you willing to give up in order to distance yourself from me?"

Grant's face betrayed her. She had felt my power for a moment and it aroused her. I knew it had, I could see it in her eyes. I knew a secret about Grant's desire and I wanted to wield it like a weapon. I wanted butchness to be a quantity, not a quality, so I could out-butch her.

Grant stirred her drink with her finger. Her face flushed. Edna and Jan stared at their laps. I could feel Frankie silently pleading with me to let Grant off the hook.

I refocused on Grant and saw a beaten butch, preserved in alcohol. I could smell her humiliation. I remembered how she forced the men in the factories to show her some respect. Slowly her belief that she deserved it had eroded. And suddenly my own words echoed in my ears: *How much of myself was I willing to give up to distance myself from her?*

"You know what I remember, Grant?" Everyone looked up at me. "I remember when we unloaded frozen food on the docks near the lake." I glanced at Edna. The faint smile on her lips was a gift for me.

Grant nodded. "Yeah, those were the good old days, weren't they?"

I shook my head. "Some of it was a nightmare. I sure wouldn't want to go back to the bar raids and the drunken fights. They're only good old days cause I don't have to live them anymore."

Grant leaned forward. "You wouldn't want to go back to those days?"

I laughed. "Not even at gunpoint. The only things I miss are the ways we stood up for each other, how we tried to make a home for each other. And we could do that right here."

It was time to change the subject. I glanced over at Edna. "Did Jan tell you I'm trying to find out what happened to Al?"

Edna looked up at Jan, not at me. Jan dropped her eyes. "Maybe it wasn't such a good idea, kid." Edna watched the anger flare in my eyes.

"Is she still alive?" I asked. Silence. I took a deep breath and addressed Jan with words meant for Edna to hear. "You know Al meant the world to me. If I'd known I might never see her again, there's a lot of things I would've told her. When I was young, I thought I had all the time in the world. I don't feel that way anymore. If she's still living, I want to see her."

Edna stared at her beer bottle, apparently unmoved. I was so afraid I'd explode in anger that I got up and stormed into the women's bathroom without realizing how long it had been since I'd been inside of one. I splashed cold water on my face.

I was surprised when Edna came in. "I'm sorry," she said in a gentle voice. "I know you're real mad at me."

We both knew she was talking about more than Al, but I refused to admit it. "Goddamn it, Edna! I don't care if Al is on Death Row or married with kids and wearing high heels. I love her and I want to see her." My teeth clenched. "I just want to say goodbye. Is that so hard to understand?"

Edna shook her head. "No. It's just hard to do." She put out her hand as though I were a dog that might bite. "Please, Jess. Please don't be mad at me. It's just that some things are better left alone."

"I have a right to learn my own lessons." I tried to soften my voice. "Look, Edna. There's some things that eat me up more than pain—like always feeling so damn powerless. I wanted to find Theresa, but nobody can tell me where she went. I promised a little girl years ago I'd come back, and her mother just refused to tell me where she is. Now you're telling me Al is alive and I can't see her."

Edna turned away from me as I continued. "I'll tell you what I'm already discovering on this visit, Edna. I can deal with a lot more pain than I realized. But I don't know where to go with this frustration. I want to find Butch Al."

"It's not a good idea." Edna said it so simply, like the subject was closed.

"How dare you?" I raged at her. "You have no right to keep that information from me."

Jan opened the bathroom door. Frankie and Grant came in behind her. Jan frowned. "Is everything OK in here?" Edna and I were locked in a glare.

Grant rose to the occasion. "Let's leave them alone in here," she tugged Jan's sleeve.

Jan yanked her arm away. "What's going on in here?" She was getting the picture.

I never took my eyes off Edna's. My voice was wintry with irony. "Now you're gonna protect me, Edna? Now you're gonna save me?"

"Damn you, Jess," Edna whispered. "Damn you. Al's in the asylum."

I opened my eyes wider. "On Elmwood Avenue? She's that close?"

"Damn you," Edna repeated as she stormed out of the bathroom.

Frankie and Grant left Jan and I alone, facing each other. "Kid, I think you'd better leave right now," Jan muttered through clenched teeth.

"I'm not a kid anymore," I told her as I pushed my way out the door.

I felt connected to the Triumph as I turned sharply into the curves of the expressway. An old power flowed through me. That exhilaration drained the moment I cut the engine in the parking lot of the asylum. I took off my helmet and looked up at the medieval building. Every window was latticed with iron bars. A cold shiver ran through me. But I wanted to see Al more than I wanted to run away.

I'd spent a long, sleepless night in the back seat of Esperanza's car, parked on the street across from Jan and Edna's shop. All night long I thought about what I wanted to tell Al. But while I was going through visitor intake I panicked because I couldn't remember what I'd wanted to say. I kept coming back to two simple things I'd never said out loud to her: *Thank you* and *I love you.*

As an elevator door opened, I tried to recall what floor the guard told me. *Sixth Floor*—it was printed in bold letters on the big plastic visitors ID I'd been given at some point in this process.

"Are you related?" I blinked. A nurse addressed the question to me. I was standing at the nurse's station. It was time to pay attention.

"Her nephew," I answered. She looked at charts I couldn't see. "Hmm," she said.

"I haven't seen my aunt for a long time," I made small talk nervously. "Is she well?" The nurse looked at me over her spectacles.

"I mean. . ." I quit talking.

"I'm afraid she's in therapy," the nurse concluded. "I don't know who arranged your visit, but it won't be possible today."

All the color rose in my face. "I have to see her today."

The nurse took off her spectacles and put one end near her lips. "Why is that?"

For a moment I was afraid if I showed them how upset I really was they might have the power to keep me here too. "I flew here just for this visit. It was arranged with her family, my family. I have to fly back to be at my job. I haven't seen my aunt for a long time. I'm afraid she might die without me ever having seen her again. You see, it's very important to me." The nurse was taken aback. She looked around.

"Can't I wait while she's in therapy? How long could it be? An hour? Fifty minutes?"

"She's in physical therapy, Mr. . .umm." She was looking at Al's chart and questioning my relationship to her, I was sure of it. "Wait over there, please," she said, beckoning to some chairs.

I sat and fidgeted. What if she knew I wasn't a nephew, or called the family? Was cross-dressing still a punishable crime? Could they use force to keep me here? I felt their power over me. Most of all they had the power to keep me from seeing Al. An hour passed. I noticed the nurse whispering to a doctor. I wanted out of here, but I didn't want to leave without Al.

"Mr. . .umm," the nurse was standing over me. I jumped to my feet. Without a word she turned on her heels and walked off. I raced to catch up with her. As we got to a dayroom she stopped and pointed toward a bank of windows.

I looked in that direction. "Ah, you said physical therapy? Is that why Al. . .auntie is here?"

"She suffered a stroke while she was here. She has lost the use of one of her arms and leg."

"Can she walk?"

The nurse pushed her spectacles further up the bridge of her nose, signaling that the conversation was nearing an end. "She does nothing. She sits and stares. I doubt she'll recognize you," she said over her shoulder as she walked away. She left me standing, filled with dread.

The rays of light between the bars illuminated a snowstorm of dust particles. A dozen patients were in the dayroom. A few spoke to themselves.

"Young man, you shouldn't have come," an old woman chastised me. Her gnarled finger pointed at my nose in emphasis. "No good will come of it! I've told you that before, over and over again. I told you, I told you." She was old and very beautiful, not in spite of her age but because of it. I smiled and eased past her, hoping she was not an Oracle.

It wasn't hard to recognize Butch Al. She sat in front of the windows. She was slumped in the chair, staring either through the windows, or at them. I couldn't tell which. She was wearing a hospital gown and slippers. The arm furthest from me was in a plastic brace. As I got closer I saw that she was tied to the chair with a strip of a bed sheet.

"She doesn't talk to mortals," the Oracle said behind me. "She listens to voices you can't hear. She can't hear you."

I smiled over my shoulder. "It's OK," I reassured her, "I'm a ghost."

The old woman came around and peered into my face. "Why blessed be," she exclaimed, crossing herself. "That's a real live ghost," she announced to patients who did not seem to hear.

I pulled up a chair beside Al. In a way she had changed dramatically. Her hair was almost entirely white and longer than I had ever seen it. If this were the old days I'd tease her about looking like Prince Valiant. Of course, if this were the old days she'd get a haircut.

I sat down next to her. Al's face reminded me of a dried riverbed, etched by the currents of waters that no longer flow. Her cheek looked so soft I had to restrain myself to keep from stroking it. It felt intrusive to be peering at her so closely, so I sat back in the chair. From another point of view Al had hardly changed a bit. Everything about her seemed familiar and comforting.

I looked out the window. I wanted to see what she was seeing and give her time to feel my presence. The windows were half obscured by a brick wall with barred windows. Part of the view looked out over the parking lot. If I leaned forward I could see my motorcycle. I thought for a moment Al might have seen me pull up and knew, somehow, that it was me. Of course, this was my fantasy.

Beyond the parking lot was a strip of grass and a few trees. Seagulls wheeled and turned in the distant sky. I took everything in as though I had been looking out at this view for years and had no hope of seeing any other landscapes on the horizon. That's when I knew I was seeing exactly what Al saw. "Not much to look at, is it?" I said out loud, almost to myself.

Al glanced at me for a moment. Her eyes were glazed over as though she suffered from emotional cataracts. Then she looked back at the windows.

I put my feet up on the windowsill and leaned back. "Young man, please don't do that," a nurse admonished me. I sat up, chagrined. Al glanced at me again and looked away. For a moment I thought I saw her smile, but I was wrong.

Al was locked up in a fortress. I didn't know how to scale its walls. I remembered a fairy tale about a prince who had to climb a mountain of glass to free the woman he loved. I couldn't remember how he accomplished it.

Somewhere I read that people in comas can hear you. I knew she wasn't in a coma, but I didn't think it could hurt to talk to her.

I almost felt as if no time had passed. If I could find the right words, we would just pick up the conversation we'd ended a quarter of a century ago. "Al," I said softly. I looked around, but no one was paying any attention to us, except the Oracle. "Al, it's me, Jess. Maybe you don't recognize me, but maybe if you looked at me you would."

Al didn't move, but I pretended that her presence was closer, that she was listening, in order to focus what I was trying to say to her. "There's things I would have told you, Al, but I always thought I'd see you again. You know, that's how kids are, they think things are never gonna end."

I thought Al nodded. Maybe it was my imagination. I put my hand ever so gently on Al's arm and looked long and hard at her profile. Minutes later she turned and looked at me, then looked away. In that brief moment I saw her peeking from behind a wall.

"Al," I tried to say, but I choked on the words. I put my forehead down on her arm and cried. I just couldn't hold my body up anymore. I pushed the tears back down and wiped my eyes. I fished around in my pockets for a Kleenex. One appeared before my eyes, thrust forward by the Oracle. I nodded in thanks.

"Butch Al," I said quietly, "if you can hear me, please just nod, blink, do anything."

She turned and looked at me.

"Al," I smiled.

Her hand clamped on my arm like a claw, her face contorted with anger. "Don't bring me back," she growled.

"Run away, now!" the Oracle warned me.

"No," I said. I could hear the fear in my voice. I wouldn't run from Al, I was willing to face anything. This moment was all I had with her and it would be my last.

"Don't bring me back," Al repeated. Her nails cut into the flesh of my arms. I tried to calm down.

Suddenly I understood what she was saying and I felt ashamed. How had Al survived? By forgetting, going to sleep, going away! She went underground, hid for safety just as I'd done.

I faced her gaze. Her eyes were steely but filling with tears. So were mine. I put my free hand gently over her fingers, and they began to relax.

"I'm sorry," I said, "forgive me, Al. This was selfish. I didn't realize until just now that I did this for me. I wasn't thinking about how it would be for you. People tried to tell me, and I didn't listen." I covered my face with my hand. "Go back to wherever you go to be safe, I won't bother you anymore. I'm sorry."

"It's OK, kid," a familiar old friend's voice said. "It's alright." I looked up and saw Butch Al smiling at me. The tears streamed down my face. She wiped them with one hand. I could feel the effort it took to lift her arm.

"You look nice," she said. "Can anybody else see you, or just me?"

"I'm real, but only you can see me."

Al looked over my head and then her eyes lowered to mine. "You look young," she told me.

I smiled. "I'm gonna be forty in a couple of years, if I play my cards right."

Al nodded and turned back to the window. "We're from the old days." She did remember!

An emotional storm cloud passed over her face. She turned to me angrily. "Leave the old days alone. Don't bring me back, I'm dead."

I pulled away from her and then forced myself to lean forward again. "You're not dead, Al. You just got hurt real bad. You fought long and hard, but they hurt you bad. You did real good."

She turned her head toward me and let it droop. Her hand grasped for my arm, "I just couldn't, I just. . .I. . . ."

My voice dropped low, like a lover's. "It's OK now, it's alright. You did so good that now you get to rest. It's alright, Al."

She rested one hand on my head. The weight of her hand made me feel like a child. "Did Jackie give you that haircut?" I missed a beat, then I smiled and nodded.

Al squeezed my arm. "Kid, tell her I'm sorry."

I put my hand over hers. "Jackie told me she's not mad, Al." She searched my face for confirmation it was true. "It's true," I lied, "she said don't worry. She loves you, Al. There isn't a day goes by she doesn't think about you, and so do I." Al smiled and patted my cheek.

"Al," I said, but her spirit had left like wind slamming a door shut. "Al?" She was staring out the window. Her body temperature dropped several degrees.

"She's gone," said the Oracle.

"Al," I said, jiggling her arm. "Al, please, don't go. Not yet, please, just give me another minute."

I hated myself for doing that. Only moments before I had sworn I would let her go back to her peace and now I was trying to drag her back again. My lip started to quiver and then my whole chin. My jaw ached. I had a second chance in life to tell her I loved her and then I blew it, just like I did as a teenager. And, like a kid, I didn't want to leave until she reassured me that she loved me too. I leaned forward and put both my arms around her neck. "I'm sorry," I said. "I'll leave you, Al." The tears wouldn't stop. "It's just that I came all this way, across all these years, to tell you how much I love you, and now it's too late.

"I wanted to thank you. If it wasn't for you, I'd never have known I had a right to be me. You taught me enough to keep me alive all these years. There isn't a day goes by that I'm not grateful for everything you gave me. You've meant so much in my life, Al. I always wanted to grow up in a way that would make you proud of me. Al, I loved you then and I love you now."

I wiped tears off my arm twice before I realized they weren't coming from my eyes.

"I told you, you shouldn't have come," the Oracle whispered over my shoulder.

"No, it was important to come," I said. I stood up and put my arms around Al again. I kissed her gently on top of her head, and let my lips linger on her hair.

"I love you, Butch Al," I whispered.

The nurse watched me from the doorway. I straightened up to go.

The Oracle crossed herself. "Blessed be," she said, looking at me and shaking her head. Moving very slowly, I took her hand in mine and kissed it lightly. She dropped her eyes and blushed.

"Goodbye, Grandmother," I told her, "thank you for letting me come."

I pulled the Triumph into the driveway behind Blue Violets. I found Jan and Edna inside the shop. They both looked grim. Edna wouldn't meet my eyes; Jan smoldered. I walked outside behind the greenhouse and waited for Jan to follow. She stood three feet away from me. Her fists were balled up at her sides. "Why the fuck didn't you tell me?" she demanded.

"It wasn't my place," I shrugged. "I didn't want to come between you two."

Jan came closer. "Well, you couldn't if you tried."

I inhaled through clenched teeth. "Actually, I know that. I couldn't hold onto Edna. But am I gonna lose you too? I didn't do anything to you. It's not fair."

"Fair?" Jan shook her head. "It doesn't have to be fair. I've got a right to be pissed."

"No, you don't," I shouted at her. "You're the one that got her. You two have each other. I'm the one who has a right to be hurt."

"You went behind my back and fucked my girl!" Jan yelled.

"What?" I slapped my thigh. "You must be kidding! You and Edna hadn't been lovers for twelve years!"

Jan obviously missed the logic. I smiled. "What's so fucking funny?" she demanded.

I shrugged. "You're mad at me for dating Edna a dozen years after you broke up. I'm mad at Edna for getting back together with you almost a decade after she and I stopped seeing each other. You know what I think?"

Jan kicked the cement. "I don't really give a fuck what you think."

I shrugged. "I'm gonna tell you anyway. I think there's not enough love to go around. I'll tell you what else I think. We all go back a long way. We really need each other, even if we're real upset right now." My voice softened. "I'll speak for myself. I really need you, Jan. I didn't betray you. I've always been a friend to you."

Jan shook her head. "Just let it be for now. Don't tell me I don't have a right to feel what I'm feeling."

I shrugged. "I'm just scared about losing you. What if I gave it a little time and I tried to be brave and called you. Would you speak to me?"

Jan sighed. "Give it time." I tossed her the bike's ignition key and turned to go. "You see her?" Jan called after me.

"Yeah."

"She recognize you?" I nodded. "Was it hard?"

I could feel the sadness in my smile. "It would have been hard either way. I almost couldn't stand thinking about strangers touching her, controlling her body. I got real scared. When I was a kid I looked at Al and I saw my future in her. I looked at her today and thought maybe that's my future, too."

Jan shrugged. "You don't know what's coming down the road."

My voice dropped low. "I was thinking about Edwin's suicide, too. I took it for granted that Ed would always be around. Then she shot herself. Suddenly I wanted another chance and it was too late, she was gone. So I buried her in my memory because it hurt too much. Maybe I was afraid her suicide was my future, too." I rubbed my face. "I've gotta go, Jan." She nodded and turned to walk back inside.

"Jan. Say goodbye to Edna for me, will ya?"

Jan answered me over her shoulder. "Don't push your luck, kid."

I pulled onto the gravel in front of Ruth's mother's house and waited in the car until someone came to the door. Mist draped the hills. The surface of Canandaigua Lake mirrored bright blue. I heard the front door open. Patsy Cline was singing, *Crazy for thinking that my love could hold you.*

Ruth called out to me. "C'mon on in, honey." She looked happier and more relaxed than when I'd last seen her.

Ruth introduced me to her mother—Ruth Anne—and her Aunt Hazel. They had just finished canning tomatoes. All three were wearing the same style floral-print aprons. They had been laughing uproariously as I entered the room. Hazel wiped tears from her eyes. "We were just telling stories about the old days."

"Come sit in the kitchen, child. Have you eaten? Can I make you a little something?" Ruth's mother asked me. I glanced at Ruth. She smiled and nodded.

"Yes, ma'am. That'd be real nice."

"Call me Anne. Everybody calls me by my mother's name. How about a big piece of elderberry pie?"

"Oh, yes. Please!" Anne set down a huge wedge of pie in front of me. "Eat it all, now. You're a growing boy."

Ruth looked at me nervously. I told her with my eyes it didn't matter. "Mama, Jess is my friend from New York I told you about. She used to live in Buffalo."

Hazel rolled her eyes. "I don't know how you girls could live in that city with all them—"

"Aunt Hazel," Ruth's tone cut her off mid-sentence.

"I didn't mean anything by it," Hazel said. "I just think—"

Anne cut in. "Hazel, eat your pie."

I rolled my eyes with pleasure. "Did you make this pie?"

Hazel smiled. "Anne makes the best elderberry pie in the Valley. You could ask anybody. You ever taste a pie that good?"

Ruth dropped her eyes. "Well," I said, "I've eaten Ruth's elderberry pie." I looked around nervously to see if I'd upset anyone by using the name I knew my friend by. Ruth shrugged. "I must say, ma'am, I can taste the family inspiration in your child's pie."

"Well, that was some fancy footwork." Anne smiled as I devoured the pie.

Hazel rocked with laughter. "Anne, do you remember the time you shot your first deer?" Hazel began the story. "She was a city girl when she married my brother Cody. First winter she was here, she was hardly good for nothing. I'm going back fifty years now. So over breakfast one morning, my brother tells her he's gonna go hunting. He told her that deer meat would help see them through the winter and sooner or later she'd have to learn to prepare it. I had told her I'd show her how. But she was willful. She told Cody: 'I'll shoot the damn deer. That's the easy part. You clean the damn thing!' Well, my brother just laughed and went upstairs to shave."

Anne picked up the story. "So I was washing dishes, right over there," she pointed. "I was wondering what the hell I'd gotten myself into marrying this man in the first place. Anyhoo, I look out the kitchen window and I see this buck standing in the clearing outside. I didn't even stop to think. I got one of Cody's guns and I shot that deer. I ran outside and started dragging it by the antlers. It was heavy, but I was so damn mad at Cody I had the strength of a bull. Cody comes downstairs a few minutes later and there's a buck on the kitchen floor. I told him, 'Now you clean the damn thing.' "

I knew laughter had rolled around the kitchen this way all weekend long.

"Oh, I wish I'd a camera to show you Cody's face. I can see it now." Anne hooted. Her smile trembled. "I wish you could have met him," she told me. "I think you would have liked him a lot. He was a real good man." She sighed. "You want some more pie?"

I nodded emphatically. Ruth shook her head. "You're gonna be puking purple all over the car."

Anne put her hands on her hips. "This boy's not leaving this valley without tasting my grape pie."

I held up my hands in surrender. "Yes, ma'am."

"That's better," she said, putting an even larger slab of pie in front of me.

Anne, Hazel, and Ruth hovered as I tasted the first bite. I slapped my chest. "I have died and gone to heaven. This is the best pie I have ever eaten in my whole life."

Anne beamed. "Robbie, you take a couple of my pies home with you."

Ruth shrugged. "I'll make her my own pie, Mama. I'm going upstairs to pack. Then we gotta go."

Anne called up the stairs after her. "Honey, look in my cedar chest. Your grandma's apron is in there. You might want to take it with you."

Hazel went out back for wood. Anne struggled to get up from her kitchen chair. "It's not easy getting old," she told me.

I stood up when she did. "I've actually been thinking about that. To tell you the truth, I never expected to live this long."

Anne came close to me. "It'll come soon enough. But you got the whole rest of your life ahead of you. You can't waste time worrying about it." Her smile faded. "You're a gleaner too, aren't you? Just like my Robbie. You know what a gleaner is?" I shook my head.

"When the farmer's done with the harvest, he lets the gleaners come pick through whatever's left. I wanted more for my child than that. I expect you deserve more, too."

I shrugged. "Well, we're doing it with all the dignity we can. And Robbie—Ruth—she's real loved in New York City by her friends."

Anne nodded without smiling. "She's real loved here, too. Folks may not understand her, and they may not always know what to say, but they know she's one of us."

Ruth came downstairs. "Ready, Jess?" Hazel and Anne hugged and kissed and fussed all over Ruth.

Anne called me. "Jess, you get over here now." She put her arms around me. Touch is something I could never take for granted. "You come back here anytime, you hear? And I'll make you another grape pie that'll knock your socks off."

I blushed. "Thank you."

"Take good care of my child," she whispered.

I squeezed her shoulders. "Yes, ma'am."

Ruth and I rode in silence through the vine-covered hills. I could smell grapes, the aroma of home for Ruth. "You need help driving, Jess?" she asked sleepily.

I nodded. "Soon, I think."

"Then I'm gonna need some coffee. We should have filled up the thermos before we left."

I looked at her nervously. "You think we should risk stopping at a restaurant?"

She sat up and sighed. "We need coffee. Pull over to that diner. Let's live dangerously."

I laughed. "Yeah. Like we don't already."

No one paid any attention to us inside the diner. Men dressed in flannel and truckers' caps shared their own stories at booths and tables. The waitress looked weary. We stood in front of the cashier, waiting to pay, anxious to leave before there was trouble. A man appeared from the kitchen. He couldn't have been more than three feet tall. He climbed up onto a stool in front of the register and rang up our purchase. He looked at Ruth's face and then at mine. His expression softened. Ruth and I looked at each other shyly, then smiled at him. He beamed at us. "How's your trip going, gals?"

Ruth and I looked at each other wide-eyed and chuckled. I leaned closer. "It's been an amazing journey. And somehow we've survived it. So far, anyway. How about yours?"

His smile was a series of expressions. "It's not what I thought it was gonna be, but it's made me into somebody I can live with."

Ruth shook his hand. "Are you from around here too?"

He nodded. "Born and bred here. My name's Carlin."

Ruth smiled. "I'm from Vine Valley. I'm Ruth. Jess is from Buffalo. We're headed back to New York City."

His eyes brightened. "I want to get out of here. I want to go to a big city where there's never a dull moment."

Ruth laughed. "Then Manhattan's just the place for you."

"Come with us," I told him. "Come on! Let's all get in the car and go."

Carlin shook his head sadly. "Part of me wishes I was the kind of person who could do that. But I've got people here. I'd have to disengage slower than that."

Ruth scribbled her name and phone number on the back of a napkin. "Call us. Come visit. We'll show you why we love New York."

I nodded. "We'll show you why we hate it, too."

He leaned closer. "Are you gals really serious?"

I leaned forward till my forehead was almost touching his. "We don't have the time to waste on being insincere."

Carlin patted my cheek. "How about a nice fresh peach pie for the road? Helen, bring me that pie, please."

As Carlin and Ruth shook hands, I saw how beautiful his very small hand looked as it clasped her very large hand. We all said our goodbyes.

Ruth and I got back in the car. I poured us each a cup of coffee. "You think we'll hear from Carlin?"

She nodded. "Oh, I'd bet on it." Ruth rested her hand on my arm. "How was Buffalo? Did you find what you were looking for?"

I sighed. "I don't know. Every time I go looking for something, I find something else. I'll tell you about the trip later. I'm just too tired to sort it out now. How about you?"

Ruth sighed. "It was a patchwork quilt." She leaned over and kissed my cheek. I felt my color rise. "It's nice to remember where you come from. But now I'm ready to go home," she said. Ruth squeezed my hand. "C'mon, Jess. Let's go home."

CHAPTER 26

The moment I climbed the subway stairs at Christopher Street I heard an amplified voice say the words lesbian and gay. When I emerged to street level, I found myself in the midst of a crowd of hundreds of people listening to speakers at a rally.

I'd seen gay demonstrations in the streets before. I had always paused to watch from across the street, proud this young movement was not beaten back into the closets. But I always walked away feeling outside of that movement and alone. This time one voice stopped me in my tracks. It was a young man who took the mike and in a strong voice, trembling with emotion, described being restrained and forced to watch his lover being beaten to death with baseball bats by a gang. "I watched him die there on the sidewalk," he cried, "and I couldn't save him. We have to do something. This can't keep going on."

He handed the microphone to a woman whose hair was wrapped in bright African fabric. She urged others to come up and speak.

A young woman from the crowd climbed up on the stage. "There were these guys in my neighborhood in Queens." Her voice could hardly be heard, even with the microphone. "They used to yell things at me and my lover. One night, I heard them behind me. I was alone. They pulled me into the parking lot behind the hardware store and raped me. I couldn't stop them."

Tears streamed down my face. The man next to me put his hand on my shoulder. His eyes were filled with tears, too.

"I never told my lover what happened," she whispered into the microphone. "I felt like we'd have both been raped if I told her."

As she climbed down from the stage I thought: This is what courage is. It's not just living through the nightmare, it's doing something with it afterward. It's being brave enough to talk about it to other people. It's trying to organize to change things.

And suddenly I felt so sick to death of my own silence that I needed to speak too. It wasn't that there was something in particular I was burning to say. I didn't even know what it would be. I just needed to open my throat for once and hear my own voice. And I was afraid if I let this moment pass, I might never be brave enough to try again.

I moved closer to the stage, nearer to finding my voice. The woman who was chairing looked at me. "Did you want to speak?" I nodded, dizzy with anxiety. "C'mon up, brother," she urged me.

My legs could hardly get me up on stage. I looked at the hundreds of faces staring at me. "I'm not a gay man." My own amplified voice startled me. "I'm a butch, a he-she. I don't know if the people who hate our guts call us that anymore. But that single epithet shaped my teenage years." Everyone got very quiet as I spoke, and I knew they were listening; I knew they had heard me. I spotted a femme woman, about my age, who stood near the back of the crowd. She nodded as I spoke, as though she recognized me. Her eyes were warm with memories.

"I know about getting hurt," I said. "But I don't have much experience talking about it. And I know about fighting back, but I mostly know how to do it alone. That's a tough way to fight, cause I'm usually outnumbered and I usually lose." An older drag queen on the edges of the protest slowly waved her hand back and forth over her head in silent testimony.

"I watch protests and rallies from across the street. And part of me feels so connected to you all, but I don't know if I'm welcome to join. There's lots of us who are on the outside and we don't want to be. We're getting busted and beaten up. We're dying out here. We need you—but you need us, too.

"I don't know what it would take to really change the world. But couldn't we get together and try to figure it out? Couldn't the *we* be bigger? Isn't there a way we could help fight each other's battles so that we're not always alone?"

I got the same thunderous applause that those gathered gave each person who found the courage to speak. To me, the applause was an answer: yes, it was possible to still hope. This rally didn't change night into day, but I saw people speaking and listening to each other.

When I handed the mike to the woman who was chairing, she put her arm around me. "Good for you, sister," she whispered in my ear. No one had ever called me that before.

I stepped down and made my way through the crowd. Hands reached out and shook mine or patted me on the shoulder. A young gay man who was passing out leaflets smiled and nodded at me. "That was really brave to get up there and say that."

I laughed. "You don't know the half of it." He handed me a leaflet calling for a protest against the government's neglect of the AIDS epidemic.

"Hold up," I heard someone say. A young butch extended her hand to me. She reminded me so much of my old friend Edwin that for just a split second I thought Ed had come back to life to give me another shot at friendship.

"My name's Bernice. I really liked what you said." I shook her hand and found her power in the sureness of her grip. "You been out a long time, huh?" she asked me.

I didn't know if she meant how long I'd been gay or how long I'd stood and watched the gay movement from the outside. Both were true.

"There's lesbian dances at the Community Center on the third Saturday of each month. I could introduce you to some of my friends. Maybe we could talk."

I shrugged. "I don't know if I can deal with arguing my way into a women's dance."

Bernice shrugged. "We could meet you outside. We could all go in together. My friend's on the door. Nobody'll hassle you if we're all together. That's part of what you were talking about, isn't it?"

I laughed. "I didn't quite expect to see it right away."

Bernice shifted from foot to foot. "So what do you say? You wanna come?"

"Yeah," I nodded. "I'm scared, but I do want to go."

"Cool," she said. "Here's my number. Give me a call."

I climbed up on the rim of a garbage can and looked around the edges of the crowd for the femme woman whose eyes had recognized me.

She was gone.

I hurried home and ran up the stairs two at a time. "Ruth," I knocked on her door. "Open up."

She looked alarmed. "Jess, what is it?"

"I spoke, Ruth. There was this rally in Sheridan Square and they let people get up and talk and I did. I spoke, Ruth. In front of hundreds of people. I wish you could have been there. I wish you could have heard me."

Ruth wrapped her arms around me and sighed. "I have been hearing you, honey," she whispered in my ear. "Once you break the silence, it's just the beginning."

"Can I use your phone?"

She shrugged. "Sure."

I knew exactly who I wanted to see. I called the union office on 17th Street and asked for Duffy. I recognized his voice right away. Its familiarity warmed me. "Duffy, it's me—Jess. Jess Goldberg."

"Jess?" He spoke my name in a rush of air. "Oh, Jess. I've had an apology in my mouth for a long time. Can you forgive me for exposing you on the job the way I did?"

I smiled. "Oh, I forgave you a while ago. But I'm all excited today. I want to talk to you. I want to see you right this minute."

Duffy laughed. "Where are you? How did you know where to find me?"

"I'm living here. Frankie told me where you worked."

"How long would it take you to get here?" he asked.

I checked my watch. "Fifteen minutes, tops."

"There's a restaurant on 16th, on the west side of Union Square. I'll meet you there."

I had wondered if Duffy and I would still recognize each other. Of course we did. He spotted me the moment he walked into the restaurant. I stood up as he approached the booth. "Jess." He shook my hand. His eyes immediately filled with tears. "Jess, I've waited years to tell you how sorry I am."

"It's alright, Duffy. I know you didn't do it on purpose. It was just a mistake."

Duffy dipped his head. "Can I have another chance?"

I laughed. "You haven't used up your chances yet."

Duffy dropped his eyes. "I think in all the years I've organized it might have been the biggest mistake I've ever made. And all I could think about was what I'd cost you. I would have done anything to make your life easier, Jess. And I screwed up so bad. I'm sorry."

I smiled. "You know, Duffy, there's this person I love named Ruth. She's different like I am. One time I got beat up and she called me in sick to work and she did the same damn thing. I know I was real mad at you at the time. But even then I knew you were always on my side. There weren't that many people I could count on to stand with me, but I always knew you were one of them. Hey, how about the mistakes I made that you let slide?"

Duffy smiled and chewed his lip. "Thanks, Jess. You let me off real easy."

I laughed. "Well, you've always been a good friend." He blushed. "Sit down, Duffy."

We caught up quick by painting our lives in broad strokes.

"Got red-baited out of the bindery where we used to work," Duffy explained. "I got kind of burned out, drank too much. Then I quit drinking and got that job organizing, and I'm still working for the same union."

I told him I'd stopped taking hormones and moved to New York City and now I was a typesetter.

"Nonunion?" he asked.

I nodded. "Yeah. When the computers came on the scene, the owners could see first how it was going to transform the old hot-lead industry. So they hired all the people the old craft union didn't realize were important to organize. That's how they broke the back of Local 6."

He looked right at me in a way that made me uncomfortable. "It's been real hard for you, Jess, hasn't it?" I shrugged and nodded.

"It shows in your face," he said. "You look less scared but more hurt." Strange, him knowing me like that.

I changed the subject. "Something incredible happened to me today, Duffy. I got up in front of a rally and talked over a microphone. I wanted to tell them how it was in the plants, how when a contract's almost up management works overtime trying to divide everybody. I didn't know if they'd get what I meant if I said it took the whole membership to win the strike."

Duffy smiled. "Yeah, and nowadays it takes more than just one union to win."

I sighed. "I came to ask you if you think it's possible to change the world? Or do you it's always gonna be a defensive battle?"

Duffy nodded very slowly. "Yeah, Jess. I really do believe we can change the world. It's changing all the time, only a lot of the time it's getting worse. I'm not just an optimist. I think conditions are gonna make it impossible for us not to fight to change things."

Duffy smiled as I pounded my fist on the table. "I want to understand about change—I don't just want to be at the mercy of it. I feel like I'm waking up inside. I want to know about history. I have all this new information about people like me down through the ages, but I don't know anything about the ages."

Duffy leaned forward in the booth. "That's the Jess I remember—the hungry one, the one who's ready to do battle." I laughed. "So, Jess, why don't you consider working with me as an organizer."

"What?" I shouted.

Duffy held up both hands like shields. "Just think about it. You were always an organizer. I know it would be complicated, but your life has always been that way. I know it would hard for you to organize openly as a woman. But maybe you could. I'd back you up all the way. There's some others I think also would. And if that's too hard, then you could tell me how you wanted to do it and I promise I won't mess it up."

Duffy pounded the table with the heel of his hand. "You've got a power you've hardly used yet. But you can't do it alone. I really think there's people who are ready to stand with you now. I think we can make them understand."

I exhaled slowly. "I don't know, Duffy. This hope thing is kind of new for me. I'm a little afraid to get my hopes up too much all at once."

Duffy shook his head. "I'm not saying we'll live to see some sort of paradise. But just fighting for change makes you stronger. Not hoping for anything will kill you for sure. Take a chance, Jess. You're already wondering if the world could change. Try imagining a world worth living in, and then ask yourself if that isn't worth fighting for. You've come too far to give up on hope, Jess."

"Wow," was all I could say. "I got to think about all of this."

He smiled. "Take your time. Just think about it. I've got to go back to work," he said. "If you're free tomorrow night, I'll buy you supper. Let's talk some more."

"Let me check my schedule." I squeezed my eyes shut. "Yup," I opened them. "I'm free. You're on."

Duffy handed me a book titled *Labor's Untold Story.* I opened the cover. Inside he'd written: *To Jess, with great expectations.* "It's a book I always wanted to give you," he explained. "Lucky I had it in my desk drawer when you called.

I thought back to the autobiography of Mother Jones he'd given me years ago and inscribed the same way. "Does this mean I get another chance?" I asked.

He smiled warmly. "You haven't begun to use up your chances, Jess."

We both stood up and shook hands. He turned to go. "Hey, Duffy. I once asked you a question and you never answered it. Are you a communist?"

Duffy turned around slowly. "I don't know what that word means to you, so I don't know what a yes would mean. What do you say we sit down over supper and I'll tell you how I see the world and my place in it?"

I nodded. "Fair enough."

It was hot that night, almost too unbearable to sleep. The air pressure and humidity made it difficult to breath. Thunder rumbled in the distance. I thought about how my life was changing, in little ways and big ways.

And I thought about Theresa. I'd never written that letter she'd asked me for. Could I write it someday soon? What would I say? Where could I send it?

The rain pelted my windows. As I fell asleep thinking about the letter, lightning bolts streaked the sky. During the night I had this dream:

I walked across a vast field. Women and men and children stood on the edges of the field looking at me, smiling and nodding. I headed toward a small round hut near the edge of the woods. I had a feeling I had been in this place before.

There were people who were different like me inside. We could all see our reflections in the faces of those who sat in this circle. I looked around. It was hard to say who was a woman, who was a man. Their faces radiated a different kind of beauty than I'd grown up seeing celebrated on television or in magazines. It's a beauty one isn't born with, but must fight to construct at great sacrifice.

I felt proud to sit among them. I was proud to be one of them.

A fire burned in the center of our gathering. One of the oldest in the circle caught my eyes. I didn't know if she was a man or a woman at birth. She held up an object. I understood I was supposed to accept the realness of this object. I looked more closely. It was the ring that the Dineh women gifted me with as an infant.

I felt an urge to leap to my feet, to plead for the ring to be returned to me. I restrained the impulse.

She pointed to the circle the ring cast on the ground. I nodded, acknowledging that the shadow was as real as the ring. She smiled and waved her hand in the space between the ring and its shadow. Isn't this distance also real? She indicated our circle. I looked at the faces around me. I followed the shadow of her hand against the wall of the hut, seeing for the first time the shadows surrounding us.

She called me to the present. My mind slipped back to the past, forward to the future. Aren't these connected, she asked wordlessly?

I felt my whole life coming full circle. Growing up so different, coming out as a butch, passing as a man, and then back to the same question that had shaped my life: woman or man?

The sound of a street argument, born of frustration, woke me from sleep. I didn't want to come back to this world. I struggled to return to the dream, but I was wide awake. It was near dawn. I unlocked the bedroom window and crawled out on the fire escape. The cool air felt good. I closed my eyes.

I recalled the night Theresa and I broke up, how I stared into the night sky, straining for a glimpse of my own future. If I could send a message back in time to that young butch sitting on a milk crate, it would be this: My neighbor, Ruth, asked me recently if I had my life to live all over again would I make the same decisions? "Yes," I answered unequivocally, "yes."

I'm so sorry it's had to be this hard. But if I hadn't walked this path, who would I be? At the moment I felt at the center of my own life, the dream still braided like sweetgrass in my memory.

I remembered Duffy's challenge. *Imagine a world worth living in, a world worth fighting for.* I closed my eyes and allowed my hopes to soar.

I heard the beating of wings nearby. I opened my eyes. A young man on a nearby rooftop released his pigeons, like dreams, into the dawn.

Afterword

On this, the 10th anniversary of the publication of *Stone Butch Blues,* I've just finished reading the novel for the first time. Does that sound odd to you?

I wrote this narrative from the inside, awash in its depths, towed by its currents. By the time I held the blues in my hands the inked words seemed like faint animal tracks on a smooth landscape, a cold trail I couldn't follow.

Now, a decade later, I am surprised. Astonished to be reintroduced to characters I birthed, who like anyone's grown children developed fictional lives of their own, independent from mine. I discover a journey not identical to my life's path and yet blazed with the intimate familiarity of my own lived experience. I locate theory—the way it is lived in motion and in interconnection. Not hard to understand; hard to live.

And I feel the heat of the inextinguishable fire of resistance to oppression.

Like my own life, this novel defies easy classification. If you found *Stone Butch Blues* in a bookstore or library, which category was it in? Lesbian fiction? Gender studies? Like the germinal novel *The Well of Loneliness* by Radclyffe/John Hall, this book is a lesbian novel and a transgender novel—making "trans" genre a verb as well as an adjective.

"Is it fiction?" I am frequently asked. Is it true? Is it real? Oh, it's real all right. So real it bleeds. And yet it is a remembrance: Never underestimate the power of fiction to tell the truth.

When *Stone Butch Blues* was published, I thought I would keep cartons of copies in my closet to give out to people who were ready to read it. But this book, like the movements for social change it was inextricably connected with, exploded the closet door off its hinges.

Since then I've received the gift of hundreds of thousands of letters, E-mails, and phone calls; heartfelt emotions shared by individuals I've met at rallies, universities, colleges. I've been stopped by strangers—in places from a gas station in rural Iowa to a shopping mall in Jersey City. These people, many of whose life battles do not seem to be related in any way, shape, or form to oppression based on sexuality, gender, or sex, took time and care to explain to me the impact the book had on their thinking, their decisions, their actions.

People who have lived very different lives have generously related to me the similarities they recognized in these pages with their own struggles—the taste of bile, the inferno of rage—transsexual men and women, heterosexual cross-dressers and bearded females, intersexual and androgynous people, bi-gender and tri-gender individuals, and many other exquisitely defined and expressed identities.

Perhaps what resonates most for me are reports that copies of *Stone Butch Blues* are passed around in prison cell blocks until they are worn and tattered.

This book has journeyed to lands that I have not yet seen. Letters and E-mails have traveled to me from the tip of South America to the far reaches of the North, from Africa to Asia. The novel is translated into German and Dutch. The Chinese-language edition, with a preface I wrote for readers there, has been serialized in Taiwan's leading daily newspaper, recommended as reading for teenagers and adults alike. And more translations are in the works.

Has publishing this novel changed my life? Yes. And no. It hasn't altered the trajectory of my life. As I finished writing *Stone Butch Blues,* I had already lived in the vortex of the left-wing LGBT liberation current for 30 years. I'd been a revolutionary activist for more than 20 years and a weekly journalist and editor for *Workers World* newspaper. I had fought against Pentagon wars of aggression. Supported Palestinian self-determination. Worked to defend political prisoners like Mumia Abu-Jamal and Leonard Peltier. Been a leading organizer of the 1974 March Against Racism in Boston. Toured the country in 1984 speaking about the AIDS crisis. I'd mobilized to stop the Nazis and Klan, helped protect women's reproductive rights, and made national rallies and demonstrations more accessible to Deaf and disabled activists.

Stone Butch Blues and the two nonfiction books I've written since—*Transgender Warriors* and *Trans Liberation: Beyond Pink or Blue*—helped to create change, in my life and the lives of others. But these books arose as part of waves of social struggle, contributed to their momentum, were propelled by them, and rode their curl like little surfboards.

I leave it to historians, herstorians, and hirstorians to analyze the changes in the decade since this novel was written and to place the publication of *Stone Butch Blues* within broad and persistent social and political efforts to right societal wrongs.

But with this novel I planted a flag: Here I am—does anyone else want to discuss these important issues? I wrote it not as an expression of individual "high" art but as a working-class organizer mimeographs a leaflet—a call to action. When, at my first public bookstore reading, someone asked me to sign a copy of the book for a friend who was too shy to speak to a published author, it broke my heart. My life's work is about elevating collective organizing, not elevating individuals.

I write this in June 2003—Pride Month—when millions across the United States and around the world are marching in the streets, cheered and applauded by millions more. Rainbow flags snap in the winds of change blowing through the streets of cities and towns, reservations and campuses.

The long-term labors of our movement have wrung a great victory from a Supreme Court dominated by seven Republicans—six of them appointed by Reagan and Bush Sr.—which has just issued a ruling effectively decriminalizing same-sex love. When the narrative of *Stone Butch Blues* begins, the love we made broke the law in all the states. By the time Jess finds her way to the gay drag bars, just one state had been forced to repeal that biblically named edict.

Our inexorable grassroots movement has won so much in the decades this novel spans. It is the struggles of the Jesses and Edwins, Peaches and Teresas, Ruths and Duffys—then and now—that have historically been decisive.

Yet there is still so much activist work to be done.

My partner, Minnie Bruce, and I are packing for a brief vacation to celebrate 11 years of living and loving together. We know we will face gawks and glares; we don't know if they'll be backed up by clenched fists of rage. Those justified fears are weighty luggage to carry on a holiday. We lug them around with us every day. And we feel this Rambo mentality deepening in this epoch of "endless" war, colonial occupation of Iraq, and the racist roundup of Arab, Muslim, and South Asian people in this country.

This is the worst of times; this is the best of times—it will be what we make of it.

If I had written this novel at the dawn of the 21st century, would Jess and her friends be marching for basic LGBT civil rights? Or would they find their way into the widening struggles against capitalism—the dog-eat-dog economic system that excretes inequality and injustice as by-products?

I only know as the author that I have found my way into the forefront of the movement to profoundly transform this economic and social system. And so have a generation of young freedom fighters of all sexualities, genders, sexes, and nationalities. Like the left-wing, gay liberation current of the '60s and '70s, they are on the front lines of every battle for social and economic justice.

From the vantage point of nonfiction and its reflection in the mercury of fiction, Jess and I share this: We both lived long enough to see quantitative resistance transformed into qualitative, collective fight-back. The 1969 Stonewall uprising ignited a massive movement in the streets from coast to coast and around the world. It was the second great international surge demanding sexual and gender liberation in the 20th century. And it was woven with a thousand threads to the historic liberation movements of African-Americans and Latinos, Asian and Native peoples, women, and the upsurge against the Vietnam War.

Stone Butch Blues is a bridge of memory. The immense human toll of the AIDS epidemic—and of oppression as a whole—have created a gaping chasm; virtually generations lost. As a result the history of social movements and their lessons are episodically recalled.

Recovering collective memory is itself an act of struggle. It allows the generational currents of the white-capped river of our movement to flow together—the awesome roar of our many waters. And the course of our movement is not fixed in its banks like the Hudson River—it is ours to determine. From Selma to Stonewall to Seattle, we who believe in freedom will not rest until every battle is won.

I am typing these words as June 2003 surges with pride. What year is it now, as you read them? What has been won? What has been lost? I can't see from here; I can't predict. But I know this: You are experiencing the impact of what we in the movement take a stand on and fight for today. The present and past are the trajectory of the future. But the arc of history does not bend toward justice automatically—as the great abolitionist Frederick Douglass said, without struggle there is no progress.

I can say this with certainty: If your life is being ground up in economic machinery and the burden of oppression is heavy on your back, you hunger for liberation, and so do those around you. Look for our brightly colored banners coming up over the hill of the past and into your present. Listen for our voices—our protest chants drawing nearer. Join us in the front ranks. We are marching toward liberation.

That's what the characters in *Stone Butch Blues* fought for. The last chapter of this saga of struggle has not yet been written.

—Leslie Feinberg

About the Author

Leslie Feinberg is a long-time activist and an award-winning author. Hir works include *Transgender Warriors: Making History from Joan of Arc to Dennis Rodman* and *Trans Liberation: Beyond Pink or Blue*. Feinberg is a political journalist, a managing editor of Workers World newspaper, and a member of the National Writers Union, UAW Local 1981. Ze is a founder of Rainbow Flags for Mumia and a national organizer for the International Action Center, which is a steering committee member of the International ANSWER (Act Now to Stop War & End Racism) coalition. Feinberg's home page in cyberspace is www.transgenderwarrior.org.